I0460599

The twist at the end of Theo & the Ashes took me completely by surprise. In this story, no one can understand why the victim's mouth is stuffed with ashes. I couldn't. I bet you can't either. The reason makes all sorts of sense, but as in Theo's Story, it comes as a complete surprise. Don't read this book for that reason. It's a fast and intriguing tale. The ashes thing is just (forgive the mixed-metaphor) frosting on the cake.

Jason Underwood, author of *A Soldier of the Western Wars*.

The underlying theme in Theo's Story is who gets to decide what is right and what is wrong—and are there consequences. In Theo & the Ashes it's what constitutes justice—and who gets to apply it. This is a dead-run story about a brutal murder, a young reporter trying to make it to the big time by solving it but conflicted by a girl he can't commit to and a place he's not sure he can leave, a Gypsy clan trying to stay clear of the law, and an ambitious Sheriff who wants to jail them. A very, very good story.

Annie Jamerson, Human Resources Manager.

The author's feel for the place he's writing about (his home town) is as strong as his feel for the characters who people this excellent novel. I'd be honored to know Dulin Monroe and to be welcomed into that brotherhood of irrelevant reporters who gathered most night's at King's Bar after the work was done...and maybe a little scared of Emma.

Ryan Immanuel, Staff Writer, The Gunderson Group.

THEO

&
The Mouthful of Ashes

A Novel by Ron Rhody

THEO & The Mouthful of Ashes. Copyright © 2012 by Ron Rhody. All rights reserved. Published in the United States of America by Outer Banks Publishing Group – Outer Banks/Raleigh.

www.outerbankspublishing.com

No part of this book may be reproduced in any manner whatsoever without written permission except in the case of brief quotations embodied in critical articles and reviews.

For information contact Outer Banks Publishing Group at
info@outerbankspublishing.com

All of the characters and events in this book are fictional, and any resemblance to actual events or actual persons living or dead, is unintentional.

Cover design by
Gary Val Tenuta
GVT Grafix
GVTgrafix@aol.com

FIRST EDITION
eISBN 13 - 978-1-4524-0970-2
ISBN 10 - 0-98-2993-161
ISBN 13 - 978-0-9829-9316-3

January 2012

For Ann

Also by Ron Rhody

In October of 1941, the coatless body of a prominent journalist is found lying in the snow beside a lonely road in the mountains of east Kentucky, over one hundred miles from his home. No one knows why he is there, or how he got there. Though the story is the biggest in the state that year, the mystery is never solved.

Theo's Story is available at Amazon.com, the Kindle and bookstores everywhere.

Your son or daughter has just joined the school soccer team and there you are on a pleasant afternoon, standing around a grassy field, watching a lot of kids running back and forth kicking a ball and you are clueless to what they are doing.

Soccer, a Spectator's Guide is for all those who find themselves at soccer games and are not entirely sure of what's going on.

A must read for all parents with soccer players in their family. Available on Amazon and in bookstores everywhere.

At last, a book that explains the how and why of writing for public relations from the perspective of a world class professional and a noted academic. It offers the ideal combination of practice and pedagogy, serving as an advanced text for graduate students and a comprehensive reference for young professionals. A badly need volume written in a conversational style and user-friendly.

Available on Amazon and in bookstores everywhere.

ONE

The place to begin is at the Hockensmith farm.

I was in the fall semester of my senior year at the University, carrying enough hours to make up for the time I'd lost in Korea and holding down a full time job at the *Journal* as a rookie reporter.

I'd never handled a murder.

When I walked in that afternoon, the newsroom was empty. Dulin came rushing in from the back shop the moment he saw me.

"You know the Hockensmith place out on the Leestown Pike?"

Not a hello or a how are you, just that hurried question.

I had no idea where the Hockensmith place was.

"You pass it every day on your way to the University."

I still drew a blank.

"There's a gravel road on the left about a mile after you cross highway sixty. Take it!"

"Take it?"

"Get your raggedy tail out there as fast as you can. I've got a lead on a murder, and I don't want to be beat."

So that's where I was, waiting in the hallway just inside the front door. I was there because Will wasn't.

The house was about a half-mile off the highway down a narrow sunken lane overgrown on either side by hackberry trees and blackberry bushes. It was a large, old, white, two-storied farmhouse sitting on a slight rise overlooking a broad meadow. The meadow must have looked like spun gold in the summer just before haying began. As is true of so many old Southern home places, the house seemed anchored to the land.

The Sheriff's black Ford was sitting in the driveway and behind it was a black and white State Police cruiser. I parked my blue VW on the grass to the side and climbed the steps to the porch. Off across the fields a soft mist blurred the tree line and down by the pond, ground fog was rising.

The door was open so I left it open, assuming it was open for a reason. I pulled my raincoat tighter as little apprehensions lurked unformed in the wind.

After a while the Deputy called to me. "You can come down now."

I was wrong about the door. They had just forgotten to close it. So I eased it shut and started down the hallway to the kitchen. Muddy footprints tracked the hardwood floor.

The door to the cellar was on the far side of the room; the stairwell dimly lit. The deputy stood aside—an overgrown farm boy. I didn't know him.

I started down, counting steps.

She lay at the bottom on the concrete floor. I had to step over her legs to enter.

The cellar was larger than I expected. I knew it was part of the original house, dug as a place for keeping foodstuffs warm in winter and cool in summer. Back then it had been dirt-walled and lighted by the soft bright of kerosene lamps. Now, un-shaded light bulbs hung from ceiling fixtures and threw stark shadows on the whitewashed walls. Pine shelves ran along the walls. Rows of Mason jars with home-canned fruits and vegetables filled them.

There was just the slightest smell of damp.

The Sheriff and two State Troopers were talking by a table against the far wall. The Sheriff looked up.

"Where's Will?"

"Too early in the day for him," I said.

The Sheriff gave a dismissive laugh.

Only a portion of Mrs. Purcell's face was visible. The side of her mouth that I could see was smudged with black. She was dressed in gray slacks and a bulky white sweater. There was a black loafer on her right foot. Her left foot was bare. The naked foot, unprotected in the harsh light, made me think of Chosin, of bare limbs poking out of body bags.

Full dark had come by the time I crested the eastern edge of town on the rolling limestone plane that defines the Bluegrass.

The traffic to my left was steady but thinning as the last of the state workers made their way from the office buildings downtown to the new subdivisions that were nibbling at the farmland along the road to Lexington.

The drizzle had started again. The macadam on the long straight run into the center of town was black and slick, and the lights of the traffic signals reflected off it in shards of green and red.

From the Green Mill to the Negro college the street ran west, dipping slightly, then rising again gently near the Feeble Minded Institute before beginning the steep drop down East Main Hill into the valley where the town lay tucked in the folds of the river.

I stayed straight on Main Street. As I passed the turn to the New Bridge, I could see the dome of the Capitol gleaming in the mist. A few people were in front of the movie theatre next to the police station, but there was no activity there. This was a county matter, so the town police weren't involved.

I crossed the city's principal intersection at Main and St. Clair, passed the fire station, turned left into Workhouse Alley, the narrow cobblestone alley next to the *State Journal*, and found a place to wedge my car behind the courthouse.

Dulin was at his desk. I could see him clearly through the glass that made up the top half of the wall that separated the newsroom from the back shop. He had his jacket off. The back of his vest gave off a satin sheen. He was scanning a paper, holding it out with both arms to let his bifocals work. The only sound was the chatter of the Associated Press and United Press International tickers.

He laid down his paper as I came through the door behind him.

"Was anybody else out there?"

"Just me."

Dulin nodded. "Well?"

"Her head was bashed in and her mouth was full of ashes."

"Ashes!"

Dulin scowled and motioned me to keep going.

"There is an old wood stove in the kitchen. The Sheriff thinks the ashes came from it. There was a flatiron on the floor in the cellar near the body. He thinks that's the murder weapon."

"Does he?" said Dulin. "And who does he think the culprit might be?"

"No candidates so far. The State Police were there. The house wasn't broken into."

"Ashes in her mouth! That's a shabby thing." He slammed his hand down on the desk and stood up. "Go on," he said.

I pulled out my notes and began to recite the facts as I had them.

"Time of death was sometime around mid-day today. Won't know for sure until the coroner finishes his work. Emma found her. You know Emma? Her daughter? Mrs. Purcell was baby-sitting for her.

"The baby was screaming in an upstairs bedroom when Emma returned. The baby's crying caused Emma to start looking for her mother. When she got to the kitchen she saw the open door at the top of the cellar stairs. She looked down, saw her mother sprawled on the floor, saw the blood, panicked, and ran back upstairs to the baby. She called Judge Hockensmith at his office in town, locked the bedroom door and went hysterical.

"The Judge came immediately. Doc Rail and a nurse followed right behind. The doctor gave Emma a sedative, and the nurse put her to bed and took charge of the baby.

"The doctor and the judge went down to the cellar and found the body. The Judge then called the Sheriff, waited for him at the house, told the Sheriff what he had been told by Emma, showed him the body, then left."

"The Judge told the Sheriff what Emma said? Didn't the Sheriff talk with Emma?" Dulin asked.

"No. She was sedated."

"Did you talk with the Judge?"

"He had left by the time I got there. I called from the farm, but he wouldn't talk to me."

"So all we know about what happened is what the Sheriff says the Judge says Emma told him?" Dulin asked.

"So far," I replied.

Dulin shook his head. "Nice of the Sheriff to be so accommodating. What else?"

I looked back at my notes.

"The Sheriff made a fast search of the house. One of Mrs. Purcell's loafers was found in the kitchen. Nothing of any value seemed to be gone. They'll do a more thorough job tomorrow when Emma can help."

"What did the State Police find? Fingerprints? Bloodstains?"

"They wouldn't say. They said any discussion of evidence was up to the Sheriff, and the Sheriff said he'd have nothing to say until he saw the results of the State Police lab work."

"Wonderful," Dulin said. "Is that all?"

"The Sheriff and his deputies were canvassing the nearby farms when I left to see if anything or anyone suspicious had been seen. But since no work had been done in the fields because of the rain, he wasn't hopeful of turning up much. The rain started a little after nine this morning. It was tapering off and not much more than a mist when I got to the farm."

"And nobody was there from the AP or the *Herald*?" Dulin asked again.

"No one," I nodded.

Dulin pulled a gold pocket watch from his vest.

"Seven-thirty," he said. "We have a clean beat."

He sat back down at his desk and looked at his watch again.

"Give me two grafs for the wires right away. Take your time with the story for tomorrow morning's paper. Play up the ashes. Get in all the color you can: her charities, the distillery, the farm, as much as you can manage. Don't speculate. Write it straight. Eleven o'clock deadline. And try the daughter again. You've got her number? See if you can get her version from her rather than secondhand from the Sheriff. And Doc Rail—try him, too. "

I started for my desk, then stopped.

"Dulin?"

"Yes?"

"Where's Will?"

He ignored the question.

The *Journal* newsroom occupied the middle third of a stately building made of glazed white brick, a block west down Main Street from the intersection at Main and St. Clair.

It had been done in Greek revival style and projected a dignity and authority its owners felt consonant with the products that issued therefrom. In this case, the *State Journal*, the Capital City's major and only daily newspaper—plus reams of far more profitable specialty printing done by its job presses for a variety of customers, of which the Commonwealth of Kentucky was the largest and most important.

At work on my story, I was visible to anyone who cared to look in. The newsroom's front wall, the part of it that faced Main Street, was mostly glass— filled with large waist-to-ceiling windows that ran the full length of the newsroom. Dulin's editor's desk, a big horseshoe-shaped affair with four smaller desks for reporters snuggled up against it around the arc, sat in front of the far wall, which separated the editorial section from the back shop and the presses. Associated Press and United Press International tickers were on the wall to its right.

I worked at a small desk across the room, oblivious to the noise and movement around me, partly absorbed in the story, partly overwhelmed with the assignment.

I glanced up at the clock above the ticker—a half-hour to deadline.

There wasn't much to add to what I already had from the afternoon run to the farm.

I'd been unable to get through to Emma, the daughter. She was still sedated, the nurse said.

I got no answer at the Judge's office and a curt "not available" when I identified myself to the male voice that answered the phone at the Judge's home number.

Only the Doctor was reachable. I got him at his home.

"An awful thing, Theo. What an awful thing," Doctor Rail said when I told him why I was calling.

"I'm on a tight deadline, Doc. What can you tell me?"

"You're handling this story?"

"Yes, sir."

"Not Will?"

"He didn't come in tonight."

"And you got stuck with this?"

"Looks like."

He paused. I was afraid he was going to say he didn't have anything to tell me. But he didn't.

"The Judge called me about three o'clock," Doctor Rail said. "He wanted me to get a nurse and meet him at the Purcell place as fast as I could.

"When I got there, the Judge was upstairs with Emma trying to calm her down. I gave her a sedating shot then went with the Judge to the cellar."

The Doctor knew that Adeline Purcell was dead the moment he saw the body. He knelt down and checked for breath, a pulse, but he knew. He was careful not to move or disturb anything. The Judge stood back and away, arms crossed, silent. No questions. Waiting.

The Doctor said it looked as if Mrs. Purcell had been thrown or pushed down the stairs, the way her body lay sprawled on the floor. Her skull was crushed. There were bruises on her throat and hands.

And there were ashes.

Her mouth was full of ashes.

When the Doctor stood up, the Judge turned around and started back up the cellar stairs.

"Did you ask him what happened," I said.

"Of course I asked him," the Doctor said. "It was a brutal death. Adeline was a patient of mine since she was a little girl."

"What did the Judge say?"

The Doctor paused.

"He said Emma had called him at his office, wild and crying. He got out there as rapidly as he could. Emma was locked in a bedroom upstairs with the baby. The Judge calmed her down enough to tell him what was wrong, and they all came downstairs. She wouldn't go with him to the cellar, so he went down alone. He didn't know whether Adeline was dead or not, but he didn't want to touch her. He came back upstairs and called me."

"Mrs. Purcell was his sister?"

"There was just the two of them. She was the oldest."

"How did he seem to be taking it?"

The Doctor considered.

"He was calm."

That seemed to be all there was, so I closed my notebook and started to rise.

Dulin paused and looked off into the distance, as if picturing the scene, then looked back to me.

"Ashes! Ashes in her mouth! Damn, Theo."

TWO

My lede read: "Frankfort, Nov. 15, 1955 - Mrs. Adeline Hockensmith Purcell, 55, owner of the largest tobacco farm in Franklin County and the majority shareholder in Buffalo Springs Distillery, the county's second most important employer next to state government, was found dead in the cellar of the family home off Leestown Pike this afternoon. She died from blows to the head. Ashes had been stuffed down her throat."

Mrs. Purcell was the the sister of the County Judge and the daughter of Col. Ezra Hockensmith, a man who had squeezed a fortune out of tobacco and bourbon. She was a pillar of her church and in her own right a successful businesswoman. Her husband, the late not-so-lamented Lawrence Purcell, was the victim of a collision with the big maple tree on Shady Lane after a night of cards and Ancient Age at the Country Club. He hadn't brought much to the marriage except the Purcell name, which was the equal of any in Bluegrass society. So the folks in Louisville and Lexington would take note.

I finished the story with twenty minutes to spare, got up, walked over to Dulin's desk and handed it to him, then stood there waiting for judgment.

Through the plate glass windows fronting the newsroom, I could see a misty rain falling again. A lone couple hurried by, taking advantage of the roof overhang to stay out of the wet but not looking in.

Motioning me to a chair at an empty desk beside the slot, Dulin read through my story slowly without looking up. When he finished, he glanced at me with an expression I couldn't read, picked up his editing pencil and bent to my copy again. Here it comes, I thought. Dammit, Will should have done this story.

Dulin made a few marks on the copy, slugged a head on it, and sent it back to the composing room. Only then did he lean back in his chair, hook his thumbs in the armholes of his vest, and look at me.

"Not bad. Not a Pulitzer Prize winner, but a workman-like story. Tight. To the point. No hysterics. The known and necessary facts. Readable."

If I hadn't already been sitting down, the relief I felt would have forced me to. He continued to study me.

"I want you to stay on this story."

"Me?"

"And Will. I want the two of you to work this as a team."

"A team?"

"Will is in the middle of something. He won't be able to give this his full attention. He'll need help. He'll take the lead, but you'll have to do most of the legwork and a good bit of the writing. He'll show you the way. You'll share bylines. Are you up for it?"

My god! Work hand in glove with Will Owens! Share bylines with Will Owens! I'd wash windows, take out the garbage and walk the dog for that kind of opportunity. Was I up for it? Jesus, Mary, and Joseph. Yes!

I'm not sure exactly how I replied to Dulin. Something in that vein, because he laughed and then turned serious again.

"Don't think this is a favor. Will's no easy man. There'll be no mistakes, no excuses, no flinching. Whatever it takes in time and effort is what you'll have to come up with."

"I can handle it, Dulin. I will handle it. Let me!"

No laugh this time, but a smile.

"Done, then. Now go home and get some sleep. You'll need to hit the ground running in the morning."

But I didn't. I hung around until the first hard copies of the paper ran off the press to see my byline—my first front-page byline.

THREE

You need to understand about Will.

Why he took up newspapering is still a mystery to me. He came from money. His family was Tidewater aristocracy. He had class and style and the polish that schools like Washington and Lee give the sons of the favored. He could have been a lawyer, a doctor, a politician. Lord, what a natural he would have been with that way he had with people. But something compelled him. What it was I don't know— something in his childhood, something in his character, some genetic memory of outrage and injustice in his Irish blood that wouldn't leave him alone. I don't know. Journalism gave him the sword he needed to slay his dragons. He was relentless. And fearless.

And maybe he drank too much.

A lot of people thought they all drank too much— that whole gang that made up the Capital City press corps in those days. It was part of the ritual, the custom, the canon. Bottled-in-Bond bourbon. One-hundred proof. With just a little water and a couple of cubes of ice. That was the standard. In a pinch, the water and the ice could be done without. There were a few gin drinkers and several who favored scotch, but this was Kentucky. Kentuckians drank bourbon.

The big city papers— the Louisville *Courier-Journal*, the *Cincinnati Post*, the *Lexington Herald*—they had some of their best men here, and the Associated Press and United Press International manned killer bureaus up at the Capitol. I was awed by them. They were first rate. Masterful writers. Tenacious reporters. Hard-nosed and skeptical, deferential to no one, and proud of their craft.

They were intensely competitive, yet there was a strange bond among them, a brotherhood. After their copy was filed and their deadlines past, most of them, sometimes all of them, would gather at the bar at King's Hotel next to the police station downtown, the only one open at that hour of the morning, and stand along an old mahogany bar beneath magnificent Paul Sawyier watercolors, washing the day away and telling their stories.

Yes, maybe they drank too much. Maybe Will foremost among them. And yes, they had flaws and faults just like the rest of us, but Lord, what a grand bunch they were.

Will took me under his wing shortly after I joined the *Journal*.

Rhea Dannan, the *Journal* owner and the mother of my best friend, Michael Dannan, created the job for me when I got back from Korea, so I could pay my way through university and get the journalism degree I wanted.

I was no stranger to the *Journal*. I almost grew up there—as a boy delivering it through the early morning streets with the bag on my bike full of copies still warm from the press, and in and out of the newsroom and the shop with Michael to visit with his father, who was the publisher, before Mr. Dannan's mysterious death when we were nine.

The excitement of newspapering seduced me— the city sleeping, the clock ticking up to deadline, linotypes clacking, phones ringing, irreverent men hunched over typewriters crafting stories that would tell the whole town what it ought to know, the intoxicating smell of wet ink off the page proofs, the rumble of the press from the back shop, exposing bad guys, slaying dragons. How could you resist all that?

My plan was to get my degree and head immediately for the Capital of the World—The Big Apple, The Magic Island—New York City. My ego was big enough that I figured I could land a job. Maybe not the *Times* or the *Herald-Tribune* right away, but surely the *Sun* or the *Telegraph*. But the Korean War came along in the summer of my freshman year, and the Marine Corps Reserve unit I had joined for a little extra cash got called up. I was off to two years of fun and games, most of it on that God forsaken peninsula.

When I got back, Rhea Dannan created the job at the *Journal* for me, and I was running as hard as I could to catch up.

Shortly after that I met Will.

Dulin had already told me about him.

"Will Owens doesn't walk on water. He isn't the second coming, and his copy gets edited just like everybody else's. But he's the best you're going to see, so watch how he does it, listen when he talks to you, and stay out of the way."

Will had made his mark with a series on graft in city hall that forced a mayor's resignation and sent two councilmen to jail. His reportage broke open the Polsgrove murder, and his unmasking of the piratical interest rates local banks were charging blacks resulted in a State Banking Commission investigation and fines to two of the city's most respected institutions. The county's powerful— the businessmen, the managers of the big plants around the county, and most of the landed gentry—had no fondness for him. The politicians had even less. But ordinary people, they loved him.

Will had his own column now, knew everybody it seemed, and could find out almost anything.

I was never sure what Will liked about me that caused him to befriend me. Like him, a restless and irreverent mind perhaps, and I think he respected that I had been a Marine and part of the group that fought its way out of Chosin, but I deserved no accolades for that. I was there. There was nothing else to do.

FOUR

Will was waiting for me when I came into the newsroom that next morning.

Sheriff Peavler had called a one-thirty press conference to announce what his investigation of the Purcell murder had found, and I had come in early to go over my notes and get ready. I expected to have the newsroom to myself. Most of the staff didn't start in until mid-afternoon, and I thought I could make the calls I wanted to make in relative privacy.

But Will was there, sitting at my desk, a copy of the morning's paper with my story in it spread out before him.

He looked up and smiled.

"Nice job, kid."

I didn't know how to accept a compliment. Most of the time I assumed people were just being polite or trying to be nice and that there was no real meaning behind their words, so I usually mumbled something weak— a "you're very kind," or some such inane phrase. In the rare instances a compliment came from someone I respected, I became awkward and tongue-tied.

"Just say thanks." He laughed and stood up. "Come on," he said, starting toward his desk and motioning me to follow.

"Pull a chair up."

I grabbed a beat up old slat-back chair and pushed it up in front of his desk.

He sat back, not saying anything, a quizzical look on his face, measuring me.

"How long have you been working here?"

"Not quite two years."

"You commute up to Lexington each day to school then back here for your shift?"

"Except week-ends."

He considered that, studying me with a faint smile.

Then he said out of nowhere, "What was it like getting out of Chosin?'

"What?"

"Chosin, what was it like?"

I stared at him, dumbfounded.

"Tell me."

I didn't want to go back there.

"What's that got to do with anything?"

"I was wondering how you handled looking death in the face."

He waited.

"It was hell in a deep freeze," I finally said.

"Were you scared?"

His eyes held mine.

Was I scared? I was eighteen; trapped at the end of the earth in mountains so steep they hid the sky. I was cold. I was frozen. The daytime temperatures averaged twenty below zero. And at night? Lord, who knows how low at night? And those damn bugles kept blowing. And the Chinese kept coming.

Was I scared?

We were surrounded. We were cut off.

There was only one way out and that was along a hellish trail slashed out of the side of the Taebaek Mountains just below the Chinese border in North Korea. Nothing but snow and rocks—and Chinese all around.

It was seventy-eight bloody miles from Chosin back down to Hungnam where we could be evacuated by sea. If we could make it. And no cavalry was coming to the rescue.

Was I scared? It took us thirteen days to fight our way back, bringing our dead and our wounded with us.

"Hell yes, I was scared. Everybody was scared."

I shivered at the memory of it all.

"What's this about, Will? What's this have to do with anything?"

He looked away. He straightened up then flashed me a smile.

" Dulin told you what we have in mind for coverage of the ashes murder?"

"Is that what we're going to call it?"

He rubbed his hand over his face and through his hair and smiled again.

"You okay with the arrangement?"

"I couldn't be happier."

He paused, studying me.

"Don't think this will be easy, boy. Consider what we've got. A prominent woman is murdered in her own home. Her brother is the County Judge, one of the most powerful men in town. He finds the body but scurries back to town and leaves his hysterical niece alone on the remote farm where it happened. We have an ambitious Sheriff who seems happy to accept any story he's told. And a body with its mouth stuffed with ashes!"

He sat back in his chair, put his feet up on the side of the desk, put his hands behind his head.

"We're going to open Pandora's box, my boy."

He smiled at that.

"Adeline, the big sister, got the money, you know. Well, most of it. Old Colonel Hockensmith didn't trust the Judge to run the farm or handle the family's business interests in the distillery. So Adeline got the lion's share of the money—and all of the power."

That smile again.

"Emma. Adeline's daughter. She says she was in Lexington shopping when it happened. Maybe. And those Tinkers camped on the backside of the property down by the creek? Tinkers are suspect by definition."

"Tinkers?" I said.

" Gypsies. That's what the people out in the county call them."

"Nobody said anything about Gypsies."

"Well, there were Tinkers on the property. Maybe the Sheriff hasn't caught up with that yet. But he will, and you can bet they'll be the prime suspects."

"Why?"

"Ignorance. Prejudice. A bad name earned over a long history of hostility."

Will took his feet down and looked me square in the face.

Again that smile.

"They'll probably want to lay it on the Tinkers. But we won't be satisfied with what they tell us. We'll have to know for ourselves. The Sheriff will be moving too slow, or be trying too hard to ignore facts that might embarrass someone important. We won't let that happen. We'll have the truth. Not just the facts. The truth. Are you with me on that?"

"I'm with you."

He laughed. As he stood up to leave, he turned to me with just the hint of concern on his face and said, "I don't like it but you're going to have to be on your own at the start. There's something I have to attend to. Find me if you need to. Otherwise, handle it."

FIVE

The Sheriff's office was in the County Courthouse, a classic old building of 1800's vintage that sits on St. Clair Street almost in the center of town.

The town is not large, twenty-thousand or so, but since it is the Capital City it is where the power lies. If you want roads built or taxes eased, favors granted or the state's coffers opened for this purpose or that, this is where it happens.

The Catholic Church shares the south side of the block. The Baptist Church is on the other corner at the foot of the Old Bridge. A long block-and-a-half away to the north, where St. Clair dead ends at Broadway, is the Old State Capitol.

The Courthouse clock tower rises almost as high as the Catholic Church spire and in the early morning dark, when everyone is asleep and the town is quiet, its count of the hours can be heard across the river all the way to Bellepoint, over a mile away. Two men and a small boy were gunned down on its marble steps one spring day in 1867, the former in an argument over a mule. The boy, poor soul, just happened to be standing nearby.

I could have cut through the alley by the side of the press room and gone in the back entrance, but though the day was cold and a misty rain was falling, I decided to make the longer walk up Main Street, around the corner to St. Clair and enter through those dignified front doors. This seemed more appropriate to my mission than slipping in the back way.

Like most small town courthouses, Franklin County's has its war memorial. But unlike most, where the monument honoring the dead is to those who fell in the War Between the States or World War I, ours is to those who died in World War II. That war hit the county hard. I stopped for a moment to scan the names. I have an uncle there and a boy I went to school with.

Sheriff Woodrow Stanley Peavler's office was on the first floor.

Ron Rhody

It took up most of the rear corner of the building. The Sheriff was not only the county's chief law enforcement officer, he was also its tax collector, so he had more clerks than deputies and the need for more room for his staff and his files.

Maise Jones, his secretary, was at the counter window when I arrived. Rotund, gregarious, she knew everybody's business and brooked no smart mouth or disrespect to the Sheriff or to the office which she had served since graduating high school when my mother did.

"Where's Will?" she said when she saw me.

Was everybody going to ask me that question?

"We're working on this together, Maise," I said.

"Humph," she said. "I saw your story this morning. The Sheriff didn't like it."

"What didn't he like?"

"He'll tell you, I imagine. Anyway, they're all up in the Jury Room on the second floor. Nobody expected so many people. You better hurry."

I was surprised, too. I thought a few of us would be standing around in the Sheriff's office, asking questions and taking notes, but the room was almost full when I entered.

Two deputies were sitting up folding chairs into which reporters who hadn't yet found a seat were dropping. The chairs faced an unadorned table with a large freestanding blackboard behind it.

I slipped into a seat near the door and looked around. I recognized most of the print guys, the *Herald-Leader*, the *Courier-Journal*, the *Kentucky Post*, even the *Georgetown* weekly and the wires services—AP and UPI. WLEX and WVLK from Lexington were there and WAVE and WHAS from Louisville. Frankfort's WFKY had a mike with a logo up on the lectern. There were other faces, people I didn't recognize, free-lancers and a few magazine people from the bureaus in Louisville, I supposed, but enough to fill the room.

It must be the ashes, I thought. A prominent woman alone in a secluded home on a remote farm in the heart of the Bluegrass, brutally murdered and her mouth stuffed with ashes. Pass it up? Not a chance.

Later arrivals were still arranging themselves along the walls when the door at the back of the room opened and Sheriff Peavler came in. He was followed by Major Tanner of the State Police and the County Coroner.

The room quieted as the Sheriff took the chair at the center of the big table, and the Major and the Coroner sat down on either side.

He waited until there was absolute quiet. Then he stood up.

Sheriff Peavler had on his formal uniform, the one he wore for swearings-in and the Governors' Inaugurals— black straight leg pants with a knife-sharp crease, black Wellington half-boots with a shine that sparkled, crisply starched grey, military-creased, long sleeve shirt with epaulets and a large silver star over his left breast pocket. Black silk tie knotted in a neat four in hand. He sat his black Troopers hat with its golden braid on the table to his side.

Andy Thomas of the *Herald* nudged me, "Woody knew there'd be TV today," he said and chuckled.

I smiled but didn't fault our Sheriff. Clothes make the man and Woodrow Stanley Peavler, despite his small frame and big ears, was conjuring his best illusion. The next election was a little over two years away, but it makes no sense not to take advantage of every opportunity that presents itself.

The job of Sheriff offers interesting possibilities to enterprising men. Looking the other way when an uncomplicated bootlegging run is being made has certain worth; exercising a little intimidation at polling places has value too. There are other services of value, depending on the imagination of the incumbent.

Woodrow Stanley Peavler won his first four-year term as Sheriff of Franklin County the year I entered kindergarten. His hold on the job hadn't been in doubt since. Between the Updikes and the Fallons, he had enough relatives in the county to keep getting elected on the family vote alone. But Woodrow had more. He had just that right mix of good old boy bonhomie to be appealing to the rural folk and enough unabashed, larcenous appetite to be of value to the business barons, power brokers, political fixers, and social aristocracy that ran the county. If he had his way, the office would still be called "High Sheriff" as it was in olden days when the Sheriff was the right hand man of the ruling nobility. But he didn't quibble.

In twenty years, a smart man with the power to knock heads and overlook transgressions can build a formidable presence. Woodrow Stanley Peavler had done that and was fully aware of it.

"Okay. Here's the rules," Sheriff Peavler began.

"I'm going to layout for you what we know so far about the event that occurred on the Hockensmith farm yesterday. Don't interrupt me. Hold your questions until I finish. Also, I like to know who I'm talking to, so identify yourself and your organization when you ask a question. I know some of you, but identify yourself anyway. Major Tanner, here, can answer questions about what the State Police crime lab found. Coroner will cover the autopsy."

He paused to let this sink in, then turned to the blackboard and flipped the blank side over.

"Some of you know where the Hockensmith farm is. Most of you don't. You need to understand how remote it is so you can understand what we're dealing with."

He picked up a pointer and motioned to the drawing that filled most of the surface of the blackboard.

"The Hockensmith farm is one of the largest in the county. The money crop is tobacco, but they grow a fair amount of corn and lots of hay. There is also a stable and a small thoroughbred operation.

"The farm's northern boundary is South Elkhorn Creek," he said, tracing a squiggly line that snaked along the upper right of the diagram to the point where it intersected with North Elkhorn at the Forks to form the main creek, which flows northwest into the Kentucky River at Stromheier's Camp.

"The western border is Scruggs Lane; the eastern Hickman Hill Road, about six miles from one side to the other. Leestown Pike marks the southern boundary.

"The creek makes a big loop midway between Scruggs Lane and Hickman Hill Road," he said, tracing a wide arc. "The main house sits in the meadow in the loop. It's back of a gravel lane off Leestown Pike after you cross highway sixty to Versailles. The lane runs about half-a-mile and dead-ends just beyond the Main House at a smaller house Mrs. Purcell built for her daughter, Emma, who lives there with her husband, Marko Kane, and their baby.

"There are no other houses around. Farmland and overgrown fields; that's all."

I hadn't appreciated how truly remote the house was until I saw the drawing. There was only one way in and out by road. If you were on foot, there were open fields to negotiate, fences to climb, and a creek to cross.

The Sheriff put the pointer down and turned back to us.

"Now, as for what we know at this point," and he began laying out for us results of his investigation so far.

"Mrs. Purcell was alone in the house. Her daughter, Emma, was in Lexington shopping. Her son-in-law, Marko Heron, Emma's husband, was at a horse sale in Fayette County. The housekeeper and the cook were off for the day."

I had already reported most of it: how and where the body was found after Emma's shopping trip to Lexington, the flatiron and the ashes, Emma's hysteria, and the Judge's call to the Sheriff.

Woodrow Peavler covered all this in dramatic detail, careful to underscore how rapidly he and his team had responded and how thorough their investigation of the site and the surroundings had been.

Major Tanner said blood and human tissue on the flatiron indicated it was the murder weapon, and the Coroner said death was the result of at least two, perhaps three blows from the flatiron that crushed poor Adeline's skull and mashed her brain. He set the time of death at one p.m. or thereabouts, give or take a half-hour. Ashes had been forced down her throat and her mouth packed with them, but she was already dead when the ashes were inserted.

The room was quiet as we all pictured this—no jockeying to get a question in for the moment.

The Sheriff stood up.

"We don't have a theory about the ashes," he said. "We believe they came from an old wood cooking stove in the kitchen. Major Tanner's lab is checking to see if the ashes in the stove and those in Mrs. Purcell's throat are the same."

"This doesn't appear to be connected with a robbery attempt. There was no forced entry and so far as we know at this point, nothing of value is missing. We're waiting until Mrs. Purcell's daughter has recovered enough from the shock of what she went through to conduct an inspection herself."

"What then?" a voice rang out from the back.

"Who said that," the Sheriff demanded. "You know the rules. Stand up and identify yourself."

A few chuckles.

"Jackson," an exasperated voice said. "The *Louisville Times*. What then? If robbery wasn't a motive, then what?"

Woody fixed him with a cold stare.

"I'm not going to guess."

Andy Thomas, sitting next to me, stood up.

"Andy Thomas of the *Herald*, Sheriff," Andy said. "You have no leads of any kind?"

The Sheriff glanced over to Major Tanner, turned his gaze back slowly to Andy. He eased a little. He knew Andy.

"We canvassed every farm in a mile circle. Checked every barn where men were working. Nobody saw anything."

"Where does that leave you then?"

"It leaves us nowhere. But we've got a door or two to look behind."

"Like where?"

The Sheriff paused, seemed to be considering whether he should go forward, looked to Major Tanner again, then said,

"Some Tinkers were camped in the woods back off Scruggs Lane near the creek day before yesterday. They pulled out yesterday, the day of the murder. We're looking for them."

"Tinkers?"

"Gypsies. We get a few through every year. Never been much trouble. But I want to talk to them."

Gypsies? Fortune tellers? Wild music and magic spells? Pockets picked and children stolen? Gypsies!

"That's all," the Sheriff said. "If we have anything else we'll let you know. Don't call here. Everybody is going to be busy."

As the room emptied, he called to me.

"Clark. Hold on a minute. I want to talk to you."

He waited until we were alone, then motioned me up to the desk.

"I didn't appreciate that story of yours this morning. It was disrespectful and provocative. Where do you get off suggesting the County Judge might lie."

It took me by surprise.

"I didn't say that, Sheriff. I wrote what you told me."

"You wrote that I took the Judge's word for what happened without talking to Emma. What's that suggest to you?"

He wasn't exactly shouting, but his voice was rising.

"Nothing. It's what you said happened."

"Why isn't Will here?"

"We're going to be working this story together. He'll be around."

"Well, you better learn a little respect and manners if you expect to get anything out of me."

He turned and left. I stood there feeling I'd just been spanked.

SIX

Of course the Gypsies led every story, even mine. It was pandering, but it was the only bit of real news that came out of the Sheriff's little show.

I was uneasy enough to want to talk it through with Will when I got back to the office.

But he wasn't there.

It's the lede, I told myself. It's the one piece of new information that has some muscle to it. Go with anything else and you've got a blah story. Go with the Gypsies and you've got a headline.

"Gypsies Sought In Ashes Murder" was our banner the next morning.

Most of the others papers played it the same way and so did radio and TV.

The result was the widespread impression by the time noon rolled around that Gypsies were the suspects.

They weren't.

There were no suspects.

Most of the stories tried to make that point. The Sheriff wanted to question the Gypsies about what they might have seen or what they might know. He hadn't tagged them as suspects anymore than he'd tagged anyone talked with so far as a suspect.

Still, unless you were a very careful reader, you got an otherwise impression.

I was uneasy about this. People don't read carefully. What they remember are the headlines. The stereotyping that had been laid on gypsies almost forever made it easy to assume them guilty.

Hell yes, they probably did it. You know the Gypsies!

I hoped the State Police caught up with them quickly and put this matter down. The State Police were doing the searching. The Sheriff's jurisdiction didn't extend past the county lines and the supposition was that the Gypsies were well on their way to wherever they were going, which was well beyond the Franklin County line.

When I finally found Will, he was standing at the bar at King's Hotel with a glass of bourbon in hand.

He gave me no dispensation.

"So everyone's offering the Tinkers up as sacrifices," he said as I moved in beside him.

It was only a little after eight. No one else was in the bar. The lights were dim; the quiet almost complete except for the occasional tinkle of glass as the bartender worked at the other end of the bar, and the muted voice of Johnny Mercer sifted in from the jukebox in the back of the room.

"I looked for you in the office."

"I'm not there," he said smiling.

"You don't look good, Will."

Peering across the bar to the big mirror behind it, he lifted his glass to himself, smiled again, and drank it down.

"I think I look pretty damn good, considering."

"Dulin said you wouldn't be in tonight, but he didn't know where you were?"

"I'm here."

"What's going on, Will?"

I had never seen him look so bad. Not hung-over and dried-out bad, but haunted-and-exhausted bad.

On his good days, Will Owens was a handsome man. He was about five-nine or ten, a bit overweight. He wore Harris Tweed sports jackets in the winter with dark slacks, button-down shirts and rep ties, and Palm Beach or seersucker suits in the summer. He always looked neat and well turned out.

I guess he was in his late thirties. He seemed the youngest of the men he competed against and drank with. I never asked his age. It never made any difference.

His hair was wavy and black, and he wore it medium long because he was a little vain of it, and he took care of it and kept it neatly barbered and combed. He never wore a hat.

Will had bold blue eyes and that smooth, delicate skin the Irish often have. A bright smile. A rich baritone voice. A fine piece of work. On his good days.

This wasn't one of them.

"What do you want, Theo?

He still hadn't turned to see me full face. He kept his gaze on the mirror. "I have places to go, people to see, things to do. What do you need, boy?"

I put my concern for Will away and pulled out my own. "Today's story. I don't feel good about it."

He motioned to the bartender, signaled for another Ancient Age. "You?" he said, still focused on the mirror. I shook my head. No. He turned full face to me then. "Ah, Theo. You've got a conscience." The drink arrived. He picked it up, tipped it in a toast to me and smiled. "I suspected as much," and drank it all down in one swallow. "You're not paid to feel good. You're paid to get the story. You got the story. The Gypsies were the lede."

He turned back to his face in the mirror. "Handle it," he said as I walked away.

SEVEN

Dulin was spooling copy off the AP ticker when I got back to the *Journal*. I'd taken my time trying to digest the interchange with Will and replaying the events of what had not been a fruitful day.

I'd walked down Lewis Street, dark and deserted at that hour, crossed the railroad tracks on Broadway and cut across the big lawn of the Old Capitol to the stone steps in front and sat there in the darkness, thinking.

The night was chilly. It would get down around freezing by daylight.

There was little traffic and no one on the streets. From where I sat I could see all the way up St. Clair to the Old Bridge and the line of fog beginning to rise off the river. The town seemed deserted. Streetlights cast a yellowish glow on empty sidewalks. The Wheel Cafeteria sign blinked red at no one and the marquee at the Grand Theatre blazed unnoticed. Peaceful. Lonely.

Then on the corner across the street, the door to Serafini's Restaurant flashed open, and a man stepped out. He stood silhouetted, looking around, started to walk away, then paused to light a cigarette. The flame from his lighter illuminated his face for just a moment. He looked familiar, someone I felt I should know but whose name I couldn't raise. A little older than me. I should know him.

I don't remember names. That's a weakness. Allie says this is because people aren't important to me. She's wrong about that. Some people are very important to me. I never forget their names. Anyway, I never forget faces.

I remembered the face of the man on the corner. But not his name. He looked around again then shrugged his collar up against the cold and turned down Broadway, lost to me.

I took that as a signal to get on with the night, stood and headed up St. Clair to the *Journal*.

Dulin glanced up as I came through the front door, folding a length of copy off the teletype as he walked over to his desk.

"Well?" he said."

I shook my head, took off my coat and hung it up on the rack by the door.

"Did you get a chance to talk with the daughter?"

"She won't answer the phone, and I couldn't get to the door."

"You went out there?"

"The Sheriff has the main house sealed off and a deputy in a squad car parked in front. The deputy said there'd been a string of reporters coming by since early morning, but he had strict orders no one was to be permitted in the main house or allowed on the lane to Emma's. The nurse and the cook got in, but no one else. Emma's husband came out about nine and went down to the horse barn, walking, then came back about lunchtime. He left again about two o'clock in a car. He told the deputy he was going to town and would be back by dark"

"The Judge?"

"I caught him as he was leaving the Courthouse this afternoon. He said he doesn't want to compromise the investigation, so he'll have no public comment. Said he's told the Sheriff everything he knows and that's sufficient. He said to tell you he knows you won't be happy, but this is the way it has to be."

"He's damn right about that," Dulin said.

He reached for his phone, then thought better of it.

"What's happening with the Tinkers?"

"Nothing. I checked with Major Tanner just after dark. They seemed to have vanished."

"Well, give me something for tomorrow morning's paper."

I stood there, hesitating.

"What?"

"I saw Will tonight."

"So?"

"What's going on? He looks like hell."

Dulin looked up from the copy and fixed me with a long stare. For a moment I thought he was going to speak, but he didn't. He just studied me for a while, then turned back to his work.

I considered the book on Dulin Monroe.

Some of it I got from Will, some from Rhea Dannan, but most from Ken Wynne, my advisor at the University of Kentucky, U of K when he learned I was being given a chance at the *Journal*.

All his peers agreed that Dulin Monroe belonged to that breed of newspapermen who couldn't possibly do anything else. No one knows how it gets in the blood. Maybe there's a vampire that slips around in the middle of the night and bites us.

He'd started out in West Kentucky, down in the Jackson Purchase, that thumb-like protuberance of land that pokes into the ribs of Missouri and Illinois that Andrew Jackson bought from the Chickasaws in 1818 and pasted on to the Commonwealth's southwestern tip.

His family were Episcopalian farmers in Baptist country, not even stopping in the Bluegrass on their way up from Georgia in 1820, drawn by inexpensive land that was perfect for cotton.

His great grandfather built a home outside Murray, just north of the Tennessee border, and prospered.

Large as the Purchase was, covering almost 2,500 square miles and representing six percent of Kentucky's land mass, the area was isolated—three hundred miles by horse or wagon up to the Capitol in Frankfort, over two hundred and fifty miles to St. Louis.

The people who settled there stayed true to the culture and customs of the Deep South where most of them came from. And suffered for it when the Civil War erupted. Murray was burned twice by Yankee troops; sacked twice by Yankee guerillas. Most of its men were off serving with the Confederates.

Dulin's great-grandfather's fields were trampled; his house and barns torched. After the war, with the farm in ruins, his folks gave up on cotton, turned to trade, and in the two decades between the end of the war and his birth, became successful dry goods merchants.

Dulin, of course, had no actual memory of the war, but his father did, and his uncles, and certain memories stay in the blood.

He started on the *Murray Ledger & Times*, the area's oldest and only daily newspaper, as a delivery boy. After high school, his folks sent him to Sewanee, The University of the South, down in Tennessee in hopes its famous Episcopalian seminary would attract him when he graduated.

It didn't.

The vampire found him instead.

He got a solid liberal arts education, came home to the *Ledger*, and signed on as a rookie reporter. He got his real education there. He covered church socials and city council meetings, crop conditions and cattle prices. He covered everything. The *Ledger* had a proud heritage and took its responsibility to serve the people of Calloway County seriously. It kept a close eye on local government, wasn't impressed by titles or station, and put the facts down as completely as it could uncover them, whether some folk liked it or not.

His work caught the eye of the paper in Paducah. He served a short stint there, then made his way upriver to the *Kentucky Post* in Cincinnati where Kenneth Wynne, who was a police reporter himself at the time, met him, and from there to Baltimore.

He was working as City Editor of the *Baltimore Sun* when Paul Isham, the *Journal*'s Managing Editor, recruited him to come home to Kentucky and run the *State Journal* after Benjamin Dannan's mysterious death in 1941.

The point about Dulin Monroe is that he was the pure article. He'd done it all, seen it all, could do it all, and demanded it all be done right.

Whatever was going on with Will, it was between him and Dulin. I decided I should leave it that way.

EIGHT

The weekend came with no trace of the Gypsies and still no leads in the case.

I drove up to Lexington Saturday morning to meet with Professor Wynne. I'd missed a week of classes and knew I'd miss more and wanted to work out a deal to overlook my absences as long as I turned in the work.

It was big game weekend—Kentucky vs. Tennessee, the only football game that mattered. Beat Tennessee and the season is a success. Lose, and—well, losing wasn't even considered.

The Professor had agreed to meet me in his office on campus at mid-morning. All roads leading to Lexington would be heavy with traffic, and parking on campus would be impossible as game time neared. I started early, found a place back down Limestone big enough to squeeze in my car and walked back to the Student Union to have breakfast.

It was a raw morning; light snow falling and cold, but students in small groups were already beginning to appear on the street; excitement already beginning to build.

My first year, that freshman year before Korea, I'd tried out for the team. I wasn't big enough or good enough to grab a scholarship, but I'd been a fair-to-middling high school player, and the coaches agreed to let me see if I had the stuff to make the team. I might have. But I learned that the game they played was monumentally different from the game I'd played back down the road.

What drove that revelation home was the first all out scrimmage in our second week of practice.

A boy from the mountains was in as the linebacker on the scrub team put in to give the varsity something to practice against. He was big enough, around 6'1 and maybe 205, and looked the part. He was fast, tough, and All-Conference.

But he was seventeen and had never been up against guys bigger and tougher than he was, and never up against guys who were just plain mean.

We didn't wear facemasks in those days, and blocking from behind was legal. It was called "deheading."

The kid was backing the left side of the line. I was in at safety. The play was a sweep around right end. He was nowhere near the action and no threat to the runner. The play had passed him. Just as he turned to chase it, a big tackle—Jack Carey, I remember his name still—came up from behind and caught him across the mouth with a forearm that almost, literally, deheaded him.

The play finished. Everyone started back to their positions. The boy lay flat on his back on the ground. I walked over.

He sat up, gagging, reached the back of his hand up to wipe his bleeding mouth and looked at me in disbelief.

His front teeth were gone. He sat there dazed. Coach came over and stared down at him.

"Stand up!" The kid looked up at him, pain in his eyes. "I said, 'stand up.'" The kid struggled to his knees and started to rise. I put my arm under his shoulder to help him up.

Coach studied him. "This is a rough game, son. You gotta suck it up and go. If you want to play this game you gotta suck it up and go. Can you suck it up and go?"

I don't know if the kid heard him or if he understood what he was being asked. Blood was dripping down his chin and he was sagging at the knees. Another player ran up and took his other arm. The kid coughed blood, tried to lift his head but couldn't.

Coach didn't say anything more; he just turned and walked back to the huddle where the offense was gathering for the next play.

With the kid swaying between us, we stood there waiting for Coach to motion to us what to do. But his attention was already on the next play. After a moment, two of the trainers ran up and took charge of our wounded.

I don't know what happened with that boy. He never came back.

I stayed with it through that first season; the coach's question constantly in my mind. I kept hoping the game would turn out to be fun as it was back down the road. It didn't. Anyway, Korea came and I got my answer there.

Why was I replaying that scene, I wondered?

The excitement in the air, I suppose - the anticipation of drums and trumpets and prancing cheerleaders and valiant warriors giving their all for the old Alma

Mater. As much as I knew about what the game was really like, when game time came, I still wanted to be out there playing.

Not today, old buddy. Not any day. Get your breakfast and go see Wynne.

Only a few people were in the cafeteria line. Most already had their coffee and were talking in little groups around the tables in the central room. A game day, a big game day, can work on you like a drug, and I could feel the excitement running through the room.

I took my tray and made my way to a table in the far corner, letting the charge wash over me. Across the room I caught a glimpse of a girl, hair as gold as summer sun, laughing and leaning into a boy who was whispering in her ear. For a moment I thought it was Allie. But of course it wasn't.

Allie didn't do Saturdays anymore.

At one time she had. She'd been the queen of the ball, and both Michael and I were supplicants at her feet. Michael was at Stanford now, getting his Masters. Allie was—I'm not sure where—probably in the little house off the Georgetown Road, doing whatever young divorcees with babies do on November Saturday mornings.

And I was here, on my way to see Professor Kenneth Wynne to talk my way into a little forgiveness for missing classes.

He was waiting for me in his office in the Journalism Building. I entered through the side door, moving down the empty hall to his office with its window looking out on McVey Hall. The building seemed abandoned; classroom doors closed; halls empty; the only light that which the gray morning pushed in.

Professor Wynne's office, though, was a beacon. Light spilled from his open doorway as I made my way down the darkened hall.

He was standing at the window, watching the gaggle of students beginning to make their way across campus to Stoll Field.

He heard me behind him, turned with an enormous smile on his face and said, "Damn, I love big game days!"

Kenneth Wynne was a man of big emotions. He could become adrenalized about a well-crafted lede; apoplectic about a misspelled name. He laughed easily and angered just as easily. He cut slackers no slack, but had no hesitation in standing by his students if he thought they were right, regardless of who might think them wrong. He sometimes sent us after stories that made the University administration uncomfortable. I could imagine him stalking the gambling joints and back alley bars of the wide open river town, Newport, during his days on the *Post*, intimidated by no one. Now he was Associate Dean of the School of Journalism and my faculty advisor— the man I had to satisfy if I expected to get that degree this summer and move out into the big world I knew was waiting eagerly for me.

I needn't have worried. Dulin Monroe had already talked with him.

"Here's my deal," he told me. "I'm freeing you from your class work. I don't care if you make another class this semester. The Ashes Murder is your class. I'm going to grade you on how well you handle this story ... the aggressiveness of your coverage, the quality of your writing, the accuracy of the facts you use, the initiative you show in uncovering information. If you merely follow the pack on this, you might pass, but you'll demonstrate to me that you're only mediocre. If you lead the pack, I'll talk with the people who can get you that New York slot you want."

I started to respond, but he stopped me.

"If you get this done, thank Dulin. If you don't, well ... thank Dulin. Now you can waste the rest of the day if you want, but I'm going to the game."

So saying, he grabbed his coat, put on his hat, slapped me on the back, and headed out the door.

"Go Cats!" he said.

NINE

I'd never been to New York. Never felt its magic or heard its roar. But I knew it was the place where the power and the glory were, where the "there" was.

Ambition is a terrible thing—always nagging, always pushing.

Ambition owned me. I'm embarrassed to admit it. Whether I'm the better for that now I don't know. New York is where the best and the brightest were. That's where I had to be.

A step, I told myself; one step at a time. Slow down. Get this right. Don't do dumb things.

That was Rule # 3 in the Will Owens Playbook: Don't do dumb things.

But I did. I spent my Saturday shivering and cheering in the stands at Stoll Field, watching Kentucky beat Tennessee when I should have been digging at the Purcell story.

That was shamefully obvious Sunday morning when I spread the *Lexington Herald* out in front of my morning coffee and saw the Page One headline "Alibi Doesn't Stand Up In Ashes Murder." The piece carried Andy Thomas' byline.

Andy, bless his heart, had done what I should have been doing. He'd been digging and he'd scored a clean beat on everyone.

I grabbed for my copy of the *Courier-Journal.* It didn't have the story either. I already knew we didn't have it. I'd written my Sunday piece after I got back from the game; focused on the still fruitless search for the missing Gypsies—a lazy piece. All it required was a single phone call to Major Tanner at the State Police. If the *Courier* didn't have the story, then the wire services didn't have it, and that meant nobody had it but the *Herald.*

I could already hear the dressing down I was going to get from Dulin Monroe and imagine the disappointment in Will Owens' eyes when I saw him again.

What Andy had found was that the story Emma Purcell told of where she was the day of the murder didn't check out.

If she'd been on a shopping trip to Lexington, she'd been invisible because no one at any of the shops remembered seeing her. The likelihood of such being the case, since she was well known, ranged from zero to very small.

The Sheriff hadn't discovered the discrepancy. Andy had. Nothing fancy or involved, just straight, slogging, basic reportage, asking questions of people who might know and getting answers—the sort of thing you'd think the Sheriff or his deputies would have done. But apparently Judge Hockensmith's assurance that his niece had been shopping in Lexington was good enough for Sheriff Woodrow Stanley Peavler.

Andy quoted the Sheriff as saying his deputies were presently in the process of checking out the whereabouts of "everyone in any way associated with the case," that the investigation was ongoing, and that he would "review Mrs. Kane's statement with her just as soon as the Doctor says she is ready for such an ordeal."

"I imagine," he quoted the Sheriff as saying, "there is a simple explanation for the confusion. Perhaps she misspoke. She had just found her mother, dead. She was in shock and under sedation. Perhaps her uncle, Judge Hockensmith, misunderstood her. Anyway, we'll clear it up."

I called Andy, caught him at his apartment in Lexington, congratulated him on being smarter and more suspicious than the rest of us.

"What made you check Emma's story? You don't think she did it? Her own mother!"

As soon as I asked the question I realized how dumb it was (I kept adding to the score). If he knew anything more or had reason to suspect anything, he certainly wasn't going to tell me.

"I don't think anything, Theo," he laughed. "I just ask questions."

"How did your good friend Woodrow Stanley Peavler take the news?"

Andy erupted in laughter.

"Damn, I wish you could have heard him. I ran him down by phone at a cocktail party at the Judge's. They'd all been to the game and had come back to his place in South Frankfort to celebrate. I don't know who all was there, but it seemed a fairly big— and wet—party.

"At first the Sheriff wouldn't take my call, but I insisted he'd want to hear what I had to tell him. Finally the maid gave in and went and got him. When I told him what I'd found out, he almost went ballistic. 'Who the hell do you people think you are,' he demanded, 'meddling in police work, stumbling around in places you have no business being. Do you realize you're talking about the niece of the County Judge! What are you trying to suggest!'"

"I'm not trying to suggest anything, Sheriff," I said, "I'm just telling you what I found and asking for your comment."

Andy paused, then said, "If you're going to try a follow-up with him, be careful. He's on the warpath."

I thanked Andy again and hung up. He and I went back a bit. We'd both been in the same freshman class at the University of Kentucky the year Korea broke, and my reserve unit got called up. We'd liked each other, and I made a point of looking him up when I got back. He'd gotten on at the *Lexington Herald* right out of school. He had three years on me now and we were at competing papers, but I knew he'd help me if he could, so long as he didn't lose any advantage.

Andy had set the agenda for tomorrow morning's stories.

Everyone would be trying to get to Emma, or the Judge, or the Sheriff.

Even if it wasn't a Sunday, I knew that would be futile. The Judge would make sure Emma didn't talk with anyone. He had already declared that he wouldn't comment. And all anyone would get from Sheriff Woodrow Stanley Peavler, if they managed to reach him, would be variations on what he'd told Andy Thomas yesterday, and a lecture on knowing their place and showing a little manners.

But I had to have a story and not just a reworking of Andy's information— a real story with new information—something important, something to make up for yesterday.

Will wouldn't have been in this position. He wouldn't have let the obvious slip by. But if he had, he would know what to do. Will had contacts. He knew people who knew people who knew people. He knew people who knew things they weren't supposed to know. People who trusted him. People who owed him. People who would tell him what he wanted to know. I didn't have those kinds of contacts. I hadn't had the time or the opportunity to grow them.

There are two ways to get big stories. One is the way Andy used. Slog it out. Ask questions. Find the people who should know or might know and look them in the eye. Will did that.

Will did it the other way, too.

"People can't keep secrets," he told me. "They need to show they're important and in the know. Or they're mad and want revenge. Or they're ambitious and think their little jewel of information whispered in the right ear will get them an advantage. Or they just can't stand not to share what they know with someone, a friend, a lover, someone they're sure will keep it secret, who of course tells someone else, who tells someone else, etc., etc. Secrets exist only in the mind of the holder. If as many as two people know a thing, you can find it out. Work your contacts!"

For all of that, though, the way he recommended most highly was a third way, the way almost no one admitted to. Get lucky.

As I washed up my breakfast dishes and poured the cold coffee down the drain, I watched the rain dance off the roof of the house across the alley and counted out my ordinance.

Contacts? Contacts of any possible use in this situation?

Doctor Rail. But he had already told me all he knew, hadn't he?

Maise Jones, the Sheriff's secretary, loyal as an oak to the office and the Sheriff. But she was a friend of my mother, had known me since I was a baby, and might take pity on me.

Major Tanner of the State Police. All I'd get from him would be the official line, but I didn't think he'd hold anything back.

Pitifully small pickings.

Who did I know who knew Emma, or her husband, Marko Kane? Odd name, Marko, for a Kentucky boy; what was the story on him?

Could I charm the cook or the housekeeper? I was sudden death on old ladies. But even if I could, what could they tell me? Not likely, but worth a try.

The deputy who was on duty at the farm when I got there; what did he know? Had he overheard the exchanges between the Sheriff and Major Tanner? Did he have an ego that might tempt him to want to show he's in the know? Would he talk to me? Again, not likely, and certainly not if he thought the Sheriff might find out.

Did I have any pull with Lady Luck?

Absolutely not.

Outside, the day was getting worse. The wind had picked up and was blowing rain hard against my windows. My apartment was on the corner of the alley on the river side of Wapping Street, just a short walk from the *Journal*. It was upstairs. A bedroom, a small kitchen, a smaller sitting room that I used as an office, and a big front room facing Wapping with a floor to ceiling window that opened onto a balcony where I could stand and have almost the whole of that stately old street in sight.

On evenings when the mist from the river hangs like lace on the oaks that line the sidewalk, I sometimes feel I could step though time and see the carriages rounding the corner to Liberty Hall, its windows glowing with candlelight while

Senator Brown talks with General LaFayette, and music floats faintly up from the garden on the river. There is a magic in this corner of town.

The afternoon slipped away. I tried to run down people I knew I couldn't find and waited for callbacks I knew wouldn't come.

Major Tanner's duty officer at the State Police reported no new developments in the search for the Gypsies. I ferreted out the name of the Deputy who had been on duty at the murder site when I was there— a country boy who lived with his mother on the family place out near Bridgeport. He wouldn't take my call, so I drove out there. His mother, still burdened with that innate politeness so many of the country women of her generation have, invited me in out of the rain and made me a cup of hot coffee. She explained that the Sheriff had said no one was to talk "about that awful thing at the Hockensmith farm" except himself. "But isn't it dreadful? That poor thing with her mouth full of ashes. And the flatiron and all that blood! Poor Lindsey will have nightmares. He's my youngest. I know he will."

I tried Doc Rail to see if he had heard anything more or remembered something. He hadn't.

The Sheriff's office confirmed what poor Lindsey had told his mother. No one was to speak of the murder except the Sheriff, and no information on what the "continuing investigation" was turning up would be available until the Sheriff decided to make it so.

Sheriff Woodrow Stanley Peavler, of course, wasn't available. It was Sunday. He was in church.

"All day?" I asked.

Most of it, it seems. Sunday School in the morning. Church service at noon. A big Sunday dinner with the Pastor and the deacons. Bible Study in the afternoon. Church service again in the evening. The Sheriff attended eagerly at the table of the Lord.

As the day progressed, the rain began to taper off, and a patch of blue sky could now and then be seen. Though I dreaded it, I knew I was going to have to make my entrance soon into the *Journal* newsroom and acknowledge I'd been beaten. No matter that everyone else had as well, it was my job to stay ahead of the story. I hadn't. Worse, I had no story for tomorrow morning's paper.

And then I thought of Allie. I have no idea why. The thought was just there. Allie knew Emma Purcell. I remembered now that she did. They were both the same age. They went to different high schools; Allie to the one here in town; Emma Purcell to the county high school, but they knew each other.

For a brief moment that thought buoyed me. Emma would talk to Allie. Allie could ask Emma to talk with me. What a story I could build out of that. An exclusive interview with the girl who found the body. That would trump anything anyone had so far produced.

But I knew Allie wouldn't. She wouldn't trade on a friendship. And I shouldn't ask her to. Will would have. If it meant getting the story, he would have. "Use your sources," Rule #5 in the Will Owens' Playbook.

The rain stopped a little before dusk. I put on my coat; it had become colder as night came on; put out the lights and started down the steps to the street and a dispirited walk to the *Journal*.

It was a pretty enough evening. The Catholic Church spire down the street was brightly lit, and the bells of the Methodist Church were ringing reassuringly. A salmon colored sky hung above Butterman's Hill with the spark of the first star of the night twinkling like a beacon.

Oh it was pretty enough, but the knowledge that the best I could do was rehash Andy Thomas' story for our paper tomorrow morning was bitter.

TEN

Nothing of any consequence happened for over a week.

The weather got colder.

Thanksgiving came and went.

The Sheriff's investigation continued, but he shared none of his findings with the public. Those who were covering the murder at the Hockensmith place dug hard but kept coming up with nothing and soon lost interest.

I worked harder than I think at any other time in my career. Dulin Monroe was determined that we weren't going to let this story die. He demanded a story every day— a Page One story. He was going to keep the pressure on the Sheriff. This wasn't going to be another of those murders that just went away because no culprit was ever brought to trial, or worse, that was just forgotten. There were too many on the city's log book.

I dug harder than I had ever imagined digging.

The Upton Septic Tank Company of LaGrange, Kentucky had been finishing an installation at the Anders farm on Scruggs Lane that November 15th. I made the run up there. Talked with all five of the crew, including one of the boys who was on a dove hunt. Caught him on the edge of a cornfield in the late afternoon after the shooting was done and the bottle was being passed. He hadn't seen anything, but offered me a drink so the day wouldn't be a complete loss.

Mrs. Purcell's housekeeper was visiting her daughter all the way down in Somerset. We didn't want to wait for her to get back. I made the drive, dropping down through the outer Bluegrass and climbing up onto the edge of the Cumberland Plateau. Lonely drive in the November gray. Nice lady when I found her. But whatever she might know, she wasn't sharing it.

I even came up on an old boy camped out on the creek on the back of the Hockensmith place as I walked the property line one day. He'd been camping there for almost a month—trying to exorcise with booze and drugs the demons that still rode him. He'd been in Korea. Was wounded there. He'd seen a man coming off the porch at the house, but couldn't remember what day that was, or what the man looked like. Only that he was tall and wore a round, flattish cap made out of black cloth, like something he'd seen in a movie once. We traded war stories. I tried to get him to come back into town with me. He liked the creek better.

Of course I told the Sheriff's office about this— Sheriff Woodrow Stanley Peavler himself wasn't indulging personal contact with the press. By the time they got someone out there, two days had passed, and my camper was gone.

But I kept at it. Anyone who might have the slightest knowledge of the awful event at the Hockensmith farm got a visit from me, wherever they were.

Dulin got his story every day. Sometimes it was real news. When there was no real news, I put my imagination to work.

I did a piece on the State Police Crime lab, then a feature on the Hockensmith farm and Buffalo Springs Distillery and the role they played in the economy of the county. A piece on the flatiron that did Mrs. Purcell in got a lot of interest. It turns out that flatirons can be as varied as keys, depending on the use for which they were intended. This particular flatiron was a collector's item.

I learned things I had absolutely no intention of remembering, but I learned how to weave story out of almost nothing.

Will was proud of me for that.

"One of the things you've got going for you is a child-like innocence, Theo."

He saw me start to bristle.

He laughed. "It's a compliment. You're curious. About everything. I bet you drove your parents crazy asking 'why.' Anybody can make a story out of facts. It takes imagination to make a story out of nothing."

Dulin was listening. There were just the three of us in the newsroom.

A windy, rainy Wednesday night. Almost midnight. Page One was locked up. Tomorrow morning's paper had been put to bed.

I was hanging around because the lights, and the clatter of the teletype, and the rumble of the press starting up in the back shop suited me better than a dark walk home and a cold bed.

Will had just come in. He came in with his usual burst of energy, heading for Dulin, but when he saw me he'd come over and put his arm around my shoulder.

He slid a wink to Dulin.

"We may have a keeper here."

Dulin smiled.

"We'll see."

I could smell the sweet bourbon on Will's breath. He wasn't tight. Or gave no indication of being so, but he seemed wired, excited.

Dulin looked to him, a question in his eyes.

"News?"

Will's mood changed almost immediately. He patted me on the shoulder.

"Go home, Theo. I need to talk with Dulin," he said.

There was something that came into his manner then that drowned the glow I'd been feeling at all the praise. Though he was smiling, there was a cast to Will's eyes that made me feel, for just a moment, that he'd just come from some outrage or injustice or insult that he could not abide.

But then I realized what was really lighting Will Owens's gaze. It was fury— barely contained fury.

About what?

I wanted to stay and find out. Dulin could see that. I knew he could. But what he said, almost gently, was, "Go home, Theo."

Outside, the night was grand.

The rain had stopped. The sky had cleared. There was a full moon that night. I sat on the stone wall at the top of the Louisville Hill overlook with the whole valley at my feet—waiting. For what I didn't know. Enlightenment? Omniscience? A clear conscience?

I watched the stoplight at the intersection of Main and St. Clair playing its game to no audience at all and followed the faint yellow trail of street lights all the way out to Thorn Hill. Nothing stirred in Bellepoint. Below me South Frankfort lay quiet. Across the river the Armory stood bathed in spotlights, on guard.

No car lights cut the scene. No walking figures disturbed the mood. Even the dogs were still. The town was asleep.

Maybe Allie would come to me, as she sometimes had—in the moonlight. Or maybe I was waiting for the full moon to draw me up to Mars as it had John Carter in the Edgar Rice Burroughs story. That would be the thing. Theo Clark of Mars! So long Will Owens and the Gypsies. Goodbye Adeline Purcell's murderer. Out of my way all those things I was going to have to do to make it to The Capital of the World. Give me the monsters of Outer Space! Set me empires to save! So long, Allie.

It was a satisfying moment; then I heard the clock in the Courthouse tower began to strike. Three. It was three o'clock in the morning.

The sky was still clear. The moon was still up. But the wall was cold, and the dew of early morning was already forming.

I put my little fantasies away and went home.

Which is when I met the Gypsy, Thomas Lee.

I'd just turned on the lights in my darkened apartment, taken off my coat, and was walking into the kitchen when I heard a tapping on the French doors that opened to the balcony outside my living room.

It was the dead of morning. There were no outside stairs up to the balcony.

I heard it again.

A tingle of apprehension ran up my back.

I didn't feel danger. I knew the feel of that. Who in hell could be tap, tap, tapping on my balcony door at that hour—and for what reason? And how in hell did he get up there?

I was in full view inside the lighted room. If whoever was out there meant me harm, I doubted he'd give me warning with a polite tap on my door. So whatever bit of caution I might have felt got lost in a surge of curiosity. I turned slowly so as not to show or give alarm and walked to the door.

There, staring at me through the glass was a short, thin man dressed all in black. His features were indistinct in the light from the door, but I noted hair down almost to his shoulders and a black watch cap pulled low on his forehead. His hands were shoved in his jacket pockets and his shoulders scrunched up against the cold. He looked halfway worn-out and wholly miserable.

I opened the door, but before I could say anything he blurted, "Will Owens said to get you."

That was Thomas Lee.

Thomas Lee wasn't his real name, his Gypsy name. Gypsies never give the Gadje, the non-Gypsies, their Gypsy names, their birth names. I never knew his real name. He had been waiting for me on the balcony most of the night. He tried to catch me when I left the *Journal*, but when I went out the back way he missed me. So he came here, scaled the porch column and had been hiding in the cold and the shadows since then.

I took him to be about eighteen, maybe twenty years old, about five-six, maybe one hundred twenty pounds. I made hot coffee, and we sat in the kitchen while he told me what he came for.

He was, he said, the son of Arlo, the Rom Baro, the head of the kumpania, the family group that camped along the creek on the Hockensmith farm.

Arlo knew the police were looking for the Gypsies. He knew it was only a matter of time before he would be found. Nothing wrong had been done. That would make no difference. Gypsies were always the scapegoats. Arlo wanted to try to avoid that this time. He wanted to explain his presence on the Hockensmith farm to someone who would listen fairly, and who could tell the story to the town before anyone had a chance to distort or misrepresent it. Will Owens would do that. Arlo trusted Will Owens. He wanted Will to hear him and to put what Arlo told him in the newspaper so that it couldn't be twisted later by people who wanted to use them or to do them harm.

Will Owens had listened. He seemed eager to help, but finally said he couldn't make the journey. There was no explanation as to why he couldn't. Just that he couldn't. He said to get Theo Clark. Would I come? Will Owens said I would.

"Where do we have to go," I said.

"I'll show you," he said.

The kid was exhausted, almost ready to drop, but his urgency to get to Arlo before the police was so intense I knew the suggestion that we sleep a few hours would get nowhere.

We left as soon as I turned out the lights.

ELEVEN

Thomas Lee called the way as we headed west though the fog and kept our destination to himself. I didn't object. When you are on your way in secret to find a man the police are looking for, a little paranoia is a good thing.

We climbed out of the valley and stayed straight on the Louisville Road, working our way west through the Outer Bluegrass. At Louisville, we turned south. At Elizabethtown we pointed west again. The morning was still dark and inhospitable.

"Much further?"

"Some."

I marveled that Arlo and his troop could have made it this far. Not many choices of roads. The State Police should have been able to sweep them all. Where were they? We crossed the upper edge of the Pennyrile and moved into the Western Coal Fields. Farm land in the Pennyrile. Immense strip-mined areas in the coal fields. Nothing promising in the way of hiding places as far as I could tell. Jesse James began his bank robbing career in the Pennyrile. But he wasn't hiding. He was grabbing and running.

Where would you put a kumpania and keep it hidden in this country—no towns of any size, no heavy forests to nestle in, remote enough that outsiders were sure to be noticed?

We stopped at Beaver Dam, a small crossroads spot of about 3,000, for gas and a little quick energy. The town was just waking up. A cluster of pick-ups and two big-rigs parked in a gravel lot outside Abby's Diner said the place was open, so I pulled in there.

Lee wouldn't leave the car.

"Why?"

"They'll notice."

I couldn't argue.

Olive skin. Shoulder length hair. A black watch cap. Black leather jacket. Black jeans. Didn't belong. They might take him for a biker, but the kerchief around his neck and the earring hanging from his left ear suggested something more exotic.

"Right," I said.

I got us sweet, black coffee to go, had the lady at the counter put a dozen warm yeast donuts in a small cardboard box, nodded pleasantly to the table of locals watching me, and we took off again.

In the old days, Gypsies traveled in horse-drawn wagons—big, chalet-like wheeled homes that were brightly decorated and spacious. They traveled in caravans of family groups—parents and children, married sons and daughters, aunts, uncles, grandparents—tightly knit and buoyant and jaunty. They were nomads, traversing a regular path on an annual route that brought them back to the same places at about the same times each year, camping for a week or two, then moving on.

I remember my mother telling stories of the Gypsies that came and camped each spring on a woodlot beside the creek near her father's farm when she was a child and how mysterious and exotic they seemed. They cast spells and stole children. The men traded horses and repaired pots and pans. The women wore long skirts and gold earrings. They told fortunes and picked pockets. No chicken was safe when the Gypsies were about.

She had to pass the Gypsy camp each morning and afternoon on her way to and from school. It terrified and thrilled her. Despite her parents' warnings, curiosity sometimes drew her close but the Gypsy women would shoo her away. Except one day. A young girl about my mother's age, nine or so—bolder than the rest—called to her. My mother wouldn't go into the camp, but they stood on the side of the road, she and the Gypsy girl, and talked. When it was time to go, they traded tokens. All she had was her Girl Scout pin. In return, the gypsy girl gave her a small, silver pin in the shape of a crescent moon.

Next morning the Gypsies were gone.

My mother lied to her parents that she had lost the Girl Scout pin. The little crescent moon stayed in her jewelry box. She couldn't wear it because she couldn't explain how she got it.

I told that story, hoping it might open him up a bit, but it didn't.

I tried telling him what little I knew about the Gypsies with the same hope in mind. That they had long ago abandoned their wagons. That they made their circuits now in Buicks and Lincolns pulling travel-trailers. I knew this from the research I'd done. I knew they still traveled in family groups, the kumpania, and still followed fairly set routes. They didn't farm. They didn't hold regular jobs. They didn't go to church. They didn't stay in one place.

I knew they were still discriminated against, still considered by many to be charlatans and thieves, and in some minds, sorcerers and threats to decent folk. Thomas Lee would talk of none of it. So we rode in a silence broken only by my fruitless attempts to engage him. I'd sometimes get a *yes* or a *no*, but nothing more.

Arlo told him to be wary, to be closed-mouth—instructions he followed to the letter. Our ride that morning must have been the longest stretch of time he'd ever spent alone with a Gadje. He was uneasy with that, I was sure, and apprehensive for the success of his mission. He didn't want to talk, he just wanted to get me to Arlo and be done with me. So I learned nothing in all those hours except that he had an appetite for yeast doughnuts and sweet coffee.

Well, that's not exactly true. I learned how disciplined a Gypsy can be.

We'd had daylight for almost an hour and were still running west. The coffee was gone. The doughnuts were gone. Dawson Springs came and went. We turned south at Princeton on the road down to Cadiz and turned west again. The road sign read "Golden Pond fourteen miles."

"Not much further," Thomas Lee said, leaning forward to see through the ground fog that was fighting with a weak morning sun.

"Your folks are at Golden Pond?"

He didn't reply, just kept peering ahead.

We were over two hundred miles from Frankfort. I knew about Golden Pond. During Prohibition it had been the moonshine capital of the world. The speakeasies in New York and Chicago and Detroit, all the big cities, sent their trucks down to haul the precious stuff back and fought for the product along the way.

The quality of Golden Pond moonshine was the standard by which all others were measured. And none measured up. This was pure corn liquor—double distilled, fire copper, sour mash whiskey, reinforced with rye, barley malt, and a special yeast—one hundred twenty proof. It had the smoothest taste and the gentlest kick since the Gods made nectar on Mount Olympus. Golden Pond moonshiners took pride in their product. No corner was cut. No batch was rushed. They made only the best and a nation beat a path to their door.

When Prohibition ended, Golden Pond kept right on running. The government wasn't happy about this. A healthy tax was levied on each gallon of distilled spirits made anywhere in the country. The Golden Pond moonshiners ignored it. A bitter little war broke out. Government "revenuers" spread out through the county determined to catch and punish the lawbreaker—to bust up their stills, spill their liquor on the ground, and drag them off to jail.

They might as well have stayed in their offices. The country around Golden Pond is rough and wild, cut by little creeks and studded with thickets and cane breaks and stands of trees that make it one of the best hunting areas in the state, and one of the most difficult to traverse. In many cases, even for the moonshiners, the only way to reach a still, to bring supplies in and transport the product out, was by boat. And you had to know the way. The revenuers didn't. They floundered through the creeks, got lost in the woods, were met by silence and loathing by the locals. They tried bribery, offering big rewards for information on where the stills were, on who was doing the distilling. At first they got some response. Money has a way of tempting people to do things not always in their best interests. The loose-tongued soon learned, though. A drowning. A horsewhipping. A tongue cut out. If moonshine was being made in the Golden Pond area, soon no one knew anything about it.

The revenuers are still around. The people still protect their own. And the product is still Olympian.

If Arlo had found sanctuary in Golden Pond, the police would never roust him.

We eased down the main street through town and out the other side, pointed to Kentucky Lake. I hoped we'd pass the pond for which the town was named. In the afternoon sun, its surface turned a brilliant gold. No one knew why. Not the locals. Not the experts from the University.

Some said an exotic organism in the water reacting to sunlight produced the glow. The old-timers say the light is the reflection of the gold that lines the bottom of the pond. It was jettisoned there by a Confederate detachment trying to spirit away the last of the Confederate treasury at the end of the war. As the detachment neared what is now Golden Pond, it was about to be overtaken by pursuing Union cavalry. Rather than let the gold fall to the Yankees, the Rebel commander sunk the entire shipment of gold ingot and coin in the waters of the large pond, hoping to recover it later but in any case making sure the Yankees wouldn't get it.

There had been a barge at the south end of the pond with two johnboats tied up nearby. The Rebel commander had his men load them with the gold and row out to the middle of the pond. There the ingots and coins were dumped overboard. On the fourth trip, the Yankees came into view on a far hill. Running out of time, the men simply flung the remaining treasure as far out into the water as they could.

A thunderstorm blew up as they were finishing. Under its cover the troop withdrew to the outskirts of the little, nearby village of Fungo. Amid the thunder and the lightening, they made their stand there. None of them survived. When it was over and the skies cleared, all the Union commander found were empty wagons and no trail to follow. The storm had washed out the tracks.

A local farm boy out hunting rabbits was supposed to have seen all this. The story stayed in his family until after the war when his brothers and uncles, who were still alive, made it home. As secretly as they could—on stormy nights and foggy days—they dragged the pond, repeatedly and repeatedly. Nothing.

The story got out, of course, and over the years the pond was dragged and dived and plumbed endlessly. The only result was frustration. If gold was there, it never revealed itself. The locals say it never would, that it is meant to be there always—throwing its reflection in the afternoon sun in testimony to the lost Confederacy and the culture that died with it.

"Do you know the story," I asked.

Thomas Lee nodded, still intent on the road.

"Do you believe it?"

"Yes," he said.

I decided I would believe it, too. We Irish believe such things.

About two miles west of town, still on the main road running to Kentucky Lake, Lee suddenly pointed and said, "There. Turn there."

A hundred yards or so ahead I saw, through patches of ground fog, a gravel lane—unmarked, unnoticeable. We turned right, bumped up the rocky berm, and six miles further along, over potholes and washouts, through dense stands of trees and past winter seared fields, found Arlo Lee.

TWELVE

The Gypsy camp wasn't visible from the lane we'd been on. It was down a barely discernable wagon path overgrown with blackberry and hawthorn. The path ended in a grassy clearing on the banks of a small creek, hidden by a stand of oaks.

Arlo Lee was waiting for us there, standing in the center of a semi-circle formed by an aggregation of cars and travel trailers that made up the camp.

Thomas Lee bolted from the car almost before I stopped, motioning me to stay put, and ran to Arlo.

While they talked, I surveyed the terrain.

The camp was strung out along the creek in a lazy arc. There were three large trailers and two smaller ones. Parked near-by were two late model Buick Specials, a Cadillac Imperial, a Chrysler Town & Country station wagon, and a Jeep Wagoneer, all with trailer hitches. Folding chairs and camp tables were scattered among the trailers. A few had canvas awnings extended.

I supposed twenty people or so could travel in real comfort in such a caravan, go about anywhere they wanted, and pick up and move rapidly if they needed to.

How, though, could Arlo move that big a cavalcade halfway across the state under the nose of the State Police and go undetected?

While I was considering the problem, Arlo walked over, trailed by Thomas Lee. By the time I got out of the car, he was standing there.

"You're the friend of Will Owens," he said, extending his hand. Not a question. A statement to be confirmed and considered, a claim that required verification.

I nodded and reached for his hand.

His grip was strong, his skin smooth like leather. I had the impression he could drop me to my knees with a squeeze if he chose, but that he was a gentlemen and courteous.

Slowly he turned my hand over, looked into it, looked up into my face, then back down into my hand.

We stood that way for a moment; Arlo Lee looking into my hand; me standing uncertainly, not knowing what to do; Thomas Lee off to the side, watching. No one else was around, not even dogs.

It was an odd moment there in that clearing; patches of ground fog shifting and swirling, and everything quiet except for the sound of water rushing past.

Then Arlo let my hand go and stepped back.

"You can help us as Will Owens would have?"

I didn't carry Will's reputation or have his skill. My byline wouldn't possess the authority his did. I was fairly certain, though, that my story would be enough. No need to confuse things with caveats. Rule #7 from the Will Owens Playbook: " Reveal only what you have to reveal."

"Yes," I said.

While we were talking, a woman came up and stood by Arlo's side. I didn't see where she came from. The exchange with Arlo was so intense, I was focused on nothing else but his eyes.

Once again he reached for my hand. He took it, turned it palm up, looked into it, and then motioned for the woman to look. She took my hand in hers. Her touch was unlike anything I'd felt before—a feeling in my mind, not on my skin, relaxing and comforting. I couldn't tell whether she was young or old. The sun still hadn't pierced the overcast, and the light in the clearing was weak. Her face was hidden by a large, blue scarf. All I could make out were her eyes, which were dark. She looked at my hand, and then into my eyes. How long we stood like this I don't know. Not long. I lost track. In time, she gave me my hand back and turned to Arlo. If she said anything to him, I didn't hear it. Then she was gone, and it was just Arlo and me again.

I gathered myself and brought my attention back to Arlo.

He turned away, motioning to me to follow.

They were welcome at Golden Pond.

They repaired the moonshine stills and built new ones. No one else had the metalworking skills they had. No one else could be counted on to keep the location of the stills secret. So the locals protected them, looked forward to their fortune telling and their music. The occasional preacher might rail at their arrival, but it in general it was harmonious, friendly, and protected. They had no other haven like it. In most places they were the undesirables. The police hassled them. The Gadje thought them evil. A week in one spot was about all they could count on. If they stayed longer, the local law was ready to escort them to the county line. But not at Golden Pond. They stayed until all the stills had been attended to and longer if they liked, bothering no one and savoring the peace of it all.

Golden Pond was the western-most stop on their fall circuit. When they finished there, they turned and headed back south again, cutting down across Kentucky and Tennessee to spend the cold months around the beach towns on the South Carolina coast.

Arlo talked and I listened, determined not to interrupt, intent on letting him tell the story completely before I distracted him with questions.

He had just the slightest accent, not one I placed.

The clearing we were in was empty of people. Though the morning was nearly gone and the ground clear of fog and the sun shining nicely, everyone was somewhere else—the men in the woods, I supposed, working; the women, with children in tow, looking in on farm houses, telling fortunes, selling dolls and pottery. That, or everyone had been told to stay away while Arlo made his case to the Gadje.

We sat on the trunk of a fallen oak by the side of the creek; no one near us, watching the last of the autumn leaves spin down through the current.

After a while, Arlo stood and walked to the edge of the creek. He said nothing for a moment, then turned to me.

"We were on our way to Golden Pond. I had a message from Miss Adeline. That's the only reason I was there. The creek place isn't on our route this time of year. We come through there in the summer.

"We have ways of getting messages to each other while we're on the road. Sometimes we leave a note with one of the people we do business with along our routes. Sometimes we make messages out of stones placed by the roadside. Sometimes we use the sixth sense. You know what that is? This was a note, though, sent through a friend who knew our route. The message said 'Come see me. I need to talk with you.'"

Arlo told me he had known "Miss Adeline"—Adeline Hockensmith, now Purcell—all his life.

The kumpania had been using the site on the creek since before he was born. They were always welcome there. He didn't know why—some favor, some debt from sometime long ago being returned or paid.

Miss Adeline had taken a special interest in him. She taught him to read and write the Gadje tongue. Most Gypsies couldn't. They were never in one place long enough to enroll in the regular school and would not have done so anyway. They didn't trust the Gadje. So she taught him—a few weeks each summer from the time he was eight until he was almost eighteen—enough so that he could get by. Miss Adeline and her father, old Mr. Hockensmith, were good to him. She had wanted to see him. So he was there.

"I was the only one of us on the Hockensmith place that morning," he said quietly. "The others had already left. That's why the police didn't find us."

He eased back onto the log and sat with his arms on his knees, leaning forward.

Hard though it was, I waited.

After a time, Arlo got up again and walked to the creek's edge. Only the flow of water over stones and an occasional bird call from the trees intruded on the hush around us.

He stood watching then turned and walked back to me.

I tried to look reassuring, but I don't think he noticed. He was too far into his story to be sidetracked by my look or manner.

"I was with her in the kitchen of the big house that morning," he went on. "She told me I was to inherit a part of the farm, the section of land along the creek where we camped each year. Can you imagine that? Being told something like that? Coming out of nowhere?"

The look of bewilderment in his eyes was as clear as the tone of his voice was disbelieving. He shook his head slowly as if still trying to absorb the weight of it.

"She was dying. That's why it was so urgent she see me. She had a cancer. Of the brain. She was afraid that when she died our welcome to the farm would be revoked. She didn't want that. She wanted us always to have a home there on the creek. She was changing her will to provide for that. She showed me what she had written out in her own hand and was going to give it to her attorney that afternoon to be put into the proper form, " he said, looking back down at me.

I was as astonished by this news as Arlo. Adeline Hockensmith Purcell had a terminal illness the day she was murdered? She was willing a valuable parcel of prime Bluegrass land to a wandering Gypsy?

"Who else knew about this? Did she tell you?

"Her aunt knew."

"Her daughter didn't know; her brother didn't know?"

Ron Rhody

"Only her aunt knew her plan. She wanted her aunt to be a witness when she signed the will, so it couldn't be challenged."

Adeline Purcell feared that her daughter or her brother might challenge the will after she died? I supposed I could understand that. What rational person would will a part of one of the richest farms in the county to a nomadic outcast with no ties to the family, or the county, or even to the culture of the place? Of course it might be challenged. Except for the witnessed signature and the aunt's testimony to Adeline Hockensmith Purcell's sound mind.

"Did the others know about the cancer?"

"Only her aunt. She didn't want the others to know"

I studied Arlo carefully. He was agitated but not in a way that suggested the excitement of a man on whom a great deal of good fortune had fallen. He seemed almost regretful, as if he had been given a burden rather than a treasure.

"How much land is involved?"

"I'm not certain. Our kumpania is large. Our campsite stretches along the creek—a half mile or more.

I didn't know what Bluegrass land was going for per acre, but I knew it was among the dearest in the state.

"Why was she so concerned for the welfare of kumpania?"

"I don't know. I don't."

"Had she signed the will? Before she was killed? Do you know?"

"The lawyer was to come that afternoon."

Arlo turned away from me then and walked back to the edge of the creek. Through the trees I could hear the sound of people assembling and smell the wood smoke of campfires being lit. I stood up from the oak log on which I'd been sitting and walked over to stand beside him.

"You must write nothing of her sickness or of the will."

"Why?"

"Her sickness was a private matter for her. I won't dishonor that. And the will, well, the will, that was for her to say, not me."

I could see that. I wouldn't use it. Will would call me foolish. I'd argue I had no way to verify it.

"What are you going to do about the police?

"I will go to the nearest State Police office in the morning. They can ask me anything they like. Then I will go on to the Sheriff." Arlo paused, "I could not have had a hand in her death. I left the farm right after our talk. I was in Bardstown at the time the news report on the radio said she died."

"You can prove this?"

"I stopped at a restaurant in Bardstown around lunch time. Maybe someone will remember me."

"Why tell me about the cancer and the will if I can't use it?"

"So you will believe me. I have no way of knowing what tales her brother or the Gadje Sheriff will tell. I have been open with you. You will give me the benefit of the doubt if it comes to my word against theirs."

"Is that what you saw in my hand?"

He didn't answer.

THIRTEEN

The drive back was long and lonely. The night was clear but the moon was down.

The questions I should have asked but hadn't kept crowding my mind. Had he seen anyone that morning who seemed suspicious? Did Mrs. Purcell seem upset or apprehensive? How did he know that the police were searching for him? News on the radio? Or maybe the sixth sense thing really worked.

Did I let Arlo off too easily? Was I too gullible? What would Will have asked? I was uneasy that my inexperience had let something important go unexamined. Yet as I replayed the day in my mind, I felt good about the outcome. It had been one of the strangest experiences I had ever had. The campsite in the mist. My hand in the hand of the woman he called Galiene. Bewitching. Was I bewitched? Had they worked a form of magic on me?

The Courthouse clock was striking nine when I pulled into the little parking lot in the alley by the *Journal*. Dulin was at his desk.

"Dulin, I—" He stopped me.

"I know. Will told me where you were. What did you get?"

"I don't think the Gypsies were involved. Give me a little time and I'll knock it all out for you, but I need to talk with Will. Where he is?"

"Home."

That couldn't be. Will would never be home at this hour with the paper running up to deadline.

"What's wrong?"

Dulin didn't answer that. He didn't nod or shake his head or frown or pass it off. He just looked at me.

FOURTEEN

Will lived just a block from the *Journal*. He had the whole second storey of an old, red-brick mansion on the corner of Washington and St. Clair. It had high ceilings and hardwood floors, a chandelier in a formal dining room, and bay windows from which he could look out and see down St. Clair.

The house fronted on Washington Street, but had a private entrance to Will's rooms on the St. Clair Street side—a filigreed iron staircase leading up to a small railed landing. I knocked and waited. And knocked again. A car passed on Washington and further down the street on St Clair a few people were beginning to straggle out of the Presbyterian Church. It was Wednesday night. Choir practice night. Once more I knocked, and finally the door opened.

Will stood there, but I couldn't see him clearly. The room behind was dark and the streetlight on the corner put only a feeble glow on the landing. A long moment passed.

"Ah, Theo," he said at last "What momentous event brings you to my door?"

He leaned against the doorframe, his face still indistinct.

"I just got back, Will."

Silence, as if he was collecting his thoughts.

"Oh, the Gypsies. Yes, of course. The Gypsies. Come in. Close the door behind you."

He turned then and led the way inside.

I followed as he touched on a light and made his way across the room to drop into an overstuffed chair in the corner by a window.. Literally. Didn't sit. Dropped. Now that there was light and I could see him more clearly, he looked worn out. No. More than worn out. He looked drained. His shirt was open at the collar and his tie loosened. His sleeves were rolled up on his forearms. He lay back in the chair like a man who could barely hold himself upright.

"Are you okay?"

Dumb as it was, that was all I could think to say. Of course he wasn't. He must have been sitting in the dark, the window letting in an occasional wink of light from a passing car, but otherwise the room was full of shadows and cheerless. Next to him, on a side table by the chair, sat an empty crystal tumbler.

What I was trying to say was, "what's wrong, what can I do to help?" But you don't ask a man like Will Owens if he needs help. I knew the type. I'd been with them on the trail back down from Chosin. Bloodied men barely dragging along, waving off buddies trying to lend them an arm, telling the Corpsmen, "help the guys who need it." The Will Owenses of the world would make it on their own or not at all.

He looked at me through half-closed eyes and tried a smile.

"A momentary indisposition. Don't give it a thought."

"You look like hell."

"I'm fine."

"I don't think you are. I think—"

"Leave it alone."

"Will, I'm just—"

"Leave it alone, Theo. Leave! It! Alone!"

The anger in his voice was like a slap. He was sitting forward now, animated. My intrusion into whatever it was he was protecting, or trying to hide, had made him mad enough to energize him. His eyes were fully open, and he was starting to rise. He didn't though. He was too weak. Easing himself back into his chair, he gave me a long, hard look and shook his head. Then he laughed.

"You're a hardhead, Theo Clark. You can't let a thing go, can you? Forget about how pretty I look. Concentrate on doing your job. Sit down and tell me what you found."

There was nothing else to do. He wasn't going to talk.

"Fix me a drink first. The bourbon's on the sideboard. Should be some ice left in the bucket. Make one for yourself. You look like you need it."

He was right about that. I'd not slept for almost twenty-four hours, had driven over five hundred miles that day, had been through a strange experience in a Gypsy camp—I could use a drink.

We were in what I took to be Will's den. Two walls were lined with books. There was a desk in front of the bay window on the front wall with a typewriter centered on it. The sideboard and a large stereo were on the opposite wall, flanked by two ceiling-to-floor windows.

I'd never been to Will's place. So far as I knew, no one from the office had except Dulin. But I didn't know that. I'd never heard anyone talk about being there. Will was friendly, but not fraternal. He didn't permit intimacy, which was confusing because his nature was so open and cheerful.

The bourbon was in a crystal decanter. Sitting next to it were six crystal tumblers and a silver ice bucket. I dropped three ice cubes in each of our glasses, covered them with the golden brown liquid, brought Will his, carried mine to the chair across from him and sat down.

Will took a sip, leaned back, then raised the glass to the light.

"Bourbon is made only in Kentucky. Did you know that? It was born here. The only whiskey that can carry the name bourbon is sour mash whiskey made in Kentucky. Decreed by an Act of Congress. All the rest, the Jack Daniels and George Dickels, they're sour mash whiskies. Good enough, but not bourbon. And the best of all the bourbons is made right here in the Bluegrass. It's our limestone water and tender seasons. That's the reason."

He lowered the glass.

"That's why we drink it out of crystal and let only the smallest bit of water mingle. You don't drink much, do you?'

"Not much," I said.

Still, I was Kentucky bred and born and there are certain responsibilities that accrue to native sons. If you are a Kentuckian, you are expected to be chivalrous to women and to hold thoroughbreds in high regard. You are courteous to everyone. It is a given that you show respect to your elders, mind your manners, and are able to carry on an interesting conversation. And when you drink, you drink bourbon.

You drink only on special occasions.

Births, deaths, and marriages are special occasions. So are baptisms and graduations and college football games.

Late afternoons after dove hunts, standing around the truck at the edge of the cornfield with the sun going down and the smell of cordite on your hands, definitely qualify. You'd have a sip of bourbon then, passing the bottle around and chasing the rich taste of it with cold water from the creek.

Successes clearly are special occasions, and you toast those. And losses.

You'd have a drink around the campfire at night with the whippoorwills calling and the dew beginning to form to honor the dark.

You'd drink to seal an agreement. Or to savor a love.

And you sometimes have a nightcap, if the day has been particularly good or particularly bad.

But you seldom drink alone, unless there is no one else around, and you want one.

You never drink to excess and you always drink with discipline—one drink an hour—enough to spark and maintain a proper glow, but not enough to impair your senses.

"No, not much," I said, smiling myself.

Telling him the whole story, from Thomas Lee's appearance on my balcony to my presence at his door, with his questions interrupting me, took almost an hour. I was particularly conscious of the time because I still had a deadline to meet and not a word of copy in my head so far.

Will was singularly interested in the bequest to Arlo. It made no sense. Why would Adeline Hockensmith Purcell leave a valuable piece of one of the most envied farms in the county to an itinerant Gypsy?

"Arlo had no thoughts about what might have happened in the house after he left that morning?"

"No."

"The handwritten will he said she showed him—what happened to that?"

"He doesn't know."

"Had he seen anyone else around? Anything that looked suspicious?"

"He'd seen the same guy I'd run across, the one I told the Sheriff's people about. Arlo seemed to know him. But he didn't talk to him and he didn't know whether the tent was still there when he left or not."

"A suspect?"

"He didn't seem threatening. All he wanted was to be left alone."

"What did the Sheriff's people do about it?"

"It took them two days to get out there. By that time he was gone. So far as I know they did no follow up."

"Count on Woodrow Peavler," Will said.

"The weather is turning too bad for him to be camping anymore. I may be able to get a lead on him through the Veterans Administration."

There was nothing more to cover. Will seemed a little better than when I arrived. I think our talk helped recharge him. But he still looked drained. I couldn't imagine what physical load he could be carrying that would tire him so.

I stood to leave, but then I thought to ask, "How do you know Arlo Lee and the Gypsies?"

"They've camped at the spot on the creek every summer I've been here. The stretch they're on is good smallmouth water. I fished it a lot. I met Arlo there."

"Did you meet the lady that looked into my hand? Galiene is her name, Arlo said."

Will nodded his head, "Yes."

"Do you believe there is a Sixth Sense?"

"Go write your story," Will said.

Dulin was waiting for me. I know he saw the concern in my face and I know he saw how exhausted I was, but what he said was, "We'll talk about Will later. You've got an hour. I'll hold Page One."

I looked up to the clock. Eleven o'clock.

I handed Dulin my copy a little after midnight.

Dulin turned the story face down on his desk when he finished.

"Why didn't Mr. Lee come back when he learned the Sheriff wanted to question him?"

"You know why. He was afraid he'd be framed."

"And he thinks your story will prevent that."

"He hopes it will. At the very least it should make it difficult for him to be tossed in jail where bad things happen to people with no clout."

Dulin nodded.

"Okay. For now.

He picked the story up again and turned it over, looking at me as he did it.

"Can you make the byline 'Theo Clark and Will Owens,'" I said.

"You want Will on this one?"

"His name will give the piece more authority."

"For Mr. Lee's sake?"

"For mine, too."

He turned back to the copy, slugged a head on it, and sent it back to composing, then he stood up.

"Let's take a walk."

Downtown after midnight is fairly lonely. The streets are deserted. The restaurants and the stores are closed. The two movie theatres have let out. Only the bars at King's Hotel up Main Street and The Wheel down St. Clair are open. There is a White Castle hamburger joint further up Main at the foot of the New Bridge where you can get a hamburger and a cup of coffee all night long. The cab stand on the corner across from the New Capitol Hotel usually has someone awake. There are lights on at the Fire Station and the Police Station. But for the most part, the town is yours.

Dulin and I stepped out into that peaceful quiet and started up Main to the White Castle. All I wanted was coffee, and all Dulin would drink was the same. There was a little crescent moon hanging over Fort Hill, and the stars had the glint of silver in the cold morning sky

Neither of us said anything for a block or so, then Dulin broke the silence.

"Will Owens is a very private man. And a very proud one."

A long pause.

"And pretty much alone."

He was speaking slowly, considering his words carefully, as if he wasn't entirely certain he should be telling me this.

"The only family he has is in Virginia. A sister. Married. He has a wide circle of acquaintances but only a few close friends. Doc Rail is one and Gideon, the black bartender at King's."

"And you," I said.

We waited while the street light changed. No cars were on the street. Dulin was taking his time.

"And me," Dulin said.

The green light flashed on. We crossed the intersection and moved on up Main Street past dark stores toward the lights of the New Capitol Hotel, walking unhurriedly, Dulin considering and me keeping my silence. Finally it came.

"Will has a problem. It will get worse."

He let that sink in.

"It's up to him to tell you about it. I don't think he will. And you can't ask."

Our footsteps were the only sound on the street.

He kept walking as he told me this, looking straight ahead. I couldn't read his face, but the tone of his voice told me he was as angry as he was sad.

We were in front of the White Castle by then. The door opened and a cabbie came out, the smell of coffee and frying onions trailing behind.

"Coffee doesn't bother your sleep?"

"Never has."

"Well let's get a cup and then you get your ass home and into bed."

My phone rang long before I was ready to get up. I didn't recognize the voice, and then I did. Maise Jones. Sheriff Peavler's secretary.

"Maise, it's the middle of the night."

"It's after eight and the Sheriff wants to see you. He said you can hurry on down, or he'll send a squad car to get you."

"I'm still in bed."

"Too bad."

There was a no-nonsense tone in her voice.

Sheriff Woodrow Stanley Peavler must have read my story.

"Give me time to shower and get dressed. An hour. I can make it in an hour."

"You better," was all she said and hung up.

I sat on the side of the bed and tried to gather my thoughts. I didn't know what I was dealing with, but I didn't like the idea of being awakened at the break of day and ordered to the Sheriff's office. Was I over-reacting? No, dammit! He'd issued an order! No question about that. Which made me mad. Which in turn jolted me fully awake. Which finally started my mind to working. I didn't want to trip innocently into whatever Woodrow Stanley Peavler might have waiting for me.

Though it was early and he'd probably had no more sleep then I, I called Dulin.

"He what?" Dulin said. "Get dressed. I'll meet you there."

When I pushed through the frosted glass doors to the Sheriff's office, Will was there as well as Dulin. I hadn't expected Will.

"Damn," I said relieved. "The heavy artillery."

They both smiled. Dulin, with his red bowtie and tweed vest, looked almost professorial. And Will, Will looked fine. I could see the hint of tiredness in his eyes, but he was alert and energized and appeared eager for whatever was going to develop.

Maise watched us warily as she picked up her phone and dialed the Sheriff.

"He'll see you now," she said and pointed us down the hall.

As I passed her she whispered, "Behave yourself."

FIFTEEN

Woodrow Stanley Peavler wasn't alone. With him was Judge Ira Hockensmith. The Sheriff sat behind his desk, an imposing mahogany structure whose surface glistened in the morning sunlight filtering through the window at his back. The only object on it was a copy of the *Journal*.

The Judge, in a black suit and the personification of judicial authority, was perched in a large, red leather chair by a bookcase on the far wall facing us. Neither of them looked friendly.

"You brought company," the Sheriff said, "I should have had extra chairs brought in."

The only other chair in the room was a straight back wooden chair at the side of his desk. It was obvious that's where the malefactor sat while the Sheriff satisfied his curiosity.

"That's alright, Woodrow," Dulin said. "Now what's this all about?

Both he and Will were smiling. I seemed to be the only uncomfortable person in the room. Will walked over and took the seat by the Sheriff's desk.

" Haven't seen you around, Will," the Sheriff said as he sat down,

"I imagine you'll be seeing more of me as this Purcell story unfolds," Will said.

"That's the thing" the Sheriff said, "that's what I want to talk about."

"The Judge, too?" Dulin asked. "I thought he said he didn't want to talk about the case."

"Never mind the Judge," the Sheriff said. "What I want to know is did Theo withhold information about where the Gypsies could be found just so he could get a story? Everyone knew I wanted to question them."

He grabbed the paper and held it up to me. Dulin had run my story with an eight column banner. You could read it from across the room. "Elusive Gypsies Found. Will Talk With Police Today."

"You did, didn't you? You knew where they were, but you didn't tell me. That's obstructing justice. That's criminal!"

"You're not serious," Dulin almost laughed.

"You're damn right I'm serious!"

"Didn't you read the story? He didn't know where they were. The Gypsies contacted him. They had a guide take him to where they were. Theo had no idea of their location until he arrived at the spot yesterday."

"So he says!"

"Even if Theo had known where the Gypsies were, he was under no obligation to tell you. You hadn't, and haven't, named them as suspects. He didn't know where they were. I'll vouch for that. Do you have any suspects? This case is over two weeks old. What have you been doing?"

The Sheriff jumped up from his desk. "I'll tell you what I'm doing when I'm good and ready. And I'll not have you or Will or this boy interfere or second guess me! Understand! Don't interfere! That's obstruction."

Glaring at Dulin, he turned to the Judge. "Right, Judge? Tell him!"

Will laughed out loud. The Judge twisted uncomfortably in his chair and held out a placating hand.

"Gentlemen, let's keep our temper."

Will laughed again and stood up. He walked over beside me.

"Your idea was to get Theo in here and try to scare him? You wanted to intimidate him. You should have done better homework. This "boy" fought his way back from the Chosin Reservoir with the 1st Marines. You weren't going to scare him. Hell, you probably weren't even going to get his full attention."

"Nothing of the kind," the Judge said from his chair. "The Sheriff wanted to reassure himself that information important to the investigation hadn't been withheld. You've assured him of that."

He turned to the Sheriff. "That's all that's needed. You're satisfied aren't you, Sheriff?"

Before he could answer Dulin asked, "Why are you here, Judge?"

At this point the Judge stood up, too. We were all standing. Didn't need any extra chairs now. In fact, we had more chairs than were needed.

Judge Hockensmith took a depth breath. I wondered if someone had taught him that as a calming device. It bought time anyway.

"Sheriff Peavler wanted an objective witness to what was said. I'm satisfied. I'm sure the Sheriff is, too."

Woodrow Stanley Peavler wasn't going to disagree with the County Judge.

"But I'll tell you this," the Sheriff said glaring at me, "you better show some respect. And you better show some manners. And you, Dulin Monroe, you better keep a close watch on your people. I will absolutely not tolerate any interference with this investigation!"

Dulin smiled. "The election is two years off, Sheriff. No need to don the cloak of righteousness so soon."

As we left he said over his shoulder. "We'll be watching you."

The sun was shining brightly as we walked out the Courthouse door and down the stone steps. A salubrious morning. I almost skipped, but in deference to my mentors and defenders, I managed a more dignified descent. Damn I felt good. Dulin and Will did too. I could tell by the smiles on their faces. Woodrow Stanley Peavler had intended to have me for breakfast. Instead, the big bad bear had been bearded in his den, and the prey came away with the honey.

December descended on the valley. Morning fog wound round the town like a fine grey scarf. Frost sometimes coated the fields until noon. All the leaves were gone. The oaks and the maples and the sycamores by the water lifted bare branches to the sky. Most days were clear. December can be a jubilation in the Bluegrass if the rain holds off. We'd had no snow so far, but it was forecast for the weekend. Snow is fine. Snow is grand. The streets turn quiet, and the world looks clean.

Arlo Lee had his session with Sheriff Woodrow Stanley Peavler on Friday. That night he stopped by the *Journal* on his way out of town to thank me and Will. Dulin hadn't met him, so we introduced him. Dulin, on learning that Arlo had never been inside a newspaper office, gave him a tour of the operation. The Gypsy was fascinated by the teletypes—news from all over the state and all over the world appearing magically from little machines beside the editor's desk— and the linotypes casting perfect words from molten lead into silver slugs that would be assembled into page forms and make tomorrow morning's newspaper. Like most people, Arlo had given no thought to how a newspaper is made and seeing the thing actually taking shape—he counted it a form of wizardry. He told Dulin so and Dulin, a man who had never lost his wonder at how ideas could be given form and life in print, beamed.

We adjourned from the *Journal* down to Mucci's on the corner to escape the clatter and the noise in the newsroom and find a little quieter space where we could talk. The crowd was light. We'd hit the lull between the Friday night dinner crush and the after-game herd. Both local high schools had home basketball games that night, and soon all the tables would be full and the old soda-fountain style counter packed deep with fans and followers.

We found a quiet table in the far corner of the room with no one near. It was a chilly night, but the room was warm and cheerful with Christmas decorations already up around the big mirror on the far wall.

"The talk with the Sheriff went okay?" Will asked as we the waited for the coffee.

Arlo frowned.

"I suppose."

"Meaning?"

"Sheriff Peavler would find it more convenient if my story wasn't true."

"He said that?"

"He didn't need to."

"Did he charge you with anything—say you were a suspect?"

"No. Not yet, at least. He said he was going to check on whether I was actually at the places I said at the times I said and then decide. But he said not to go anywhere without letting him know."

"Is that a problem?"

"If we stay too long at Golden Pond, we'll wear out our welcome."

"Where would you go?

"South. Down to the Carolinas. Where it's warm."

"So tell the Sheriff."

"Where we go and when is our business."

"Don't give the Sheriff an excuse. If you wind up in his jail, he might give you a reason to change your story."

"I know," Arlo said.

"Did you tell him about the man you saw on the property?

"He already knew about that."

All this exchange was between Arlo and Will. I sat and listened. Through it all Arlo seemed resigned, seemed as if the suspicion was something usual, something expected, something to be accepted and lived through.

I remembered the title of a book I'd read doing my research on Gypsies— *Bury Me Standing, I've Been On My Knees All My Life.*

Few ethnic groups had been as maligned and mistreated. In World War II the European Gypsies suffered losses in the Nazi extermination camps that were proportionately greater than those suffered by the Jews. In this country they've faced discrimination every bit as bitter as that focused on blacks and native Americans. None of this generated much public attention. There weren't very many of them and their victimizations were small events, not worthy of major media attention.

It was thought the Gypsies came originally from India, becoming wanderers for reasons unknown, arriving in Europe in the fourteenth century. The story they told in the medieval cities to explain themselves was that they were persecuted Christians escaping from Muslim Egypt in search of religious sanctuary. For a while the fiction worked. They were welcomed into the cities, given food and shelter. People thought they were Egyptian and called them so. Over time "Egyptian" eased into "Gypsy".

The charade didn't last. They refused to integrate into the societies that hosted them or to accept the norms of the cultures they found themselves in. They refused to settle in any one place. They wandered freely from village to village, country to country, keeping their own strange ways.

They were accomplished metalsmiths and uncanny horse-traders. No one knew horses better. They worked when they had to. When work was scarce, they begged and stole and ran elaborate swindles on rich and poor alike. They came to like this lifestyle. It was easy and the Gadje were easily deceived.

This did nothing for their reputation.

And then there were the spells and the fortune telling and the music and the dancing—and the charges that they kidnapped Christian children and used them as slaves or sold them off to the heathen for who knew what purposes. Most damming of all, they would not go to church in a time and on a continent held hostage by the Church.

So Gypsies were met with suspicion and hostility everywhere. In many places they were routinely jailed or beaten and run out of town by angry mobs—and not infrequently hung in town squares.

The first of them began to arrive in the United States in the 1800s. They came from Serbia and Russia and Austro-Hungary, from southern and eastern Europe, from England and Ireland and Scotland. They called themselves the Rom, after Romany, the language they all spoke, but they belonged to highly distinct family groups: the Kalderash from Russia, the Machva from Serbia, the Ludar from Romania.

Arlo Lee was of the Romnichels, the English Gypsies. He wasn't a Tinker. Tinkers were Irish Gypsies.

I think neither he or his people expected they would get understanding or fairness from the Gadje and were not disappointed when their expectations were met.

Will was finishing a sentence, and Arlo was just beginning to rise as I tuned back into the conversation.

"What will you do about the inheritance," Will asked him.

"If there is one." Arlo said. "Perhaps she was killed before the new will was signed."

Arlo reached out his hand to shake both Will's and mine, thanked Dulin for the tour, shrugged on his coat and walked out the door into the night.

SIXTEEN

Snow came as promised. The first of the season. A languid, windless snowfall. Big flakes floating softly down. It began shortly before midnight as I was finishing my piece for the morning's paper. After I gave my copy to Dulin, I walked to the big front windows to watch it fall. The room was warm; the teletypes yattering. Dulin was there and the sports editor, who was wrapping up his piece on the UK basketball game, and there was the normal bustle in the backshop as the make-up men put type in the page forms getting them ready for the press. It was comfortable and reassuring and safe.

We had snowfalls like this on the way back from Chosin—beautiful, peaceful snowfalls, the flakes white against the black of the night, smoothing over the impact craters in the trail and hiding the frozen bodies under a spotless blanket of white—everything transformed, the landscape softened and the harsh sounds muffled. Could make you think of home—until the bugles, those damn bugles, started blaring and the Chinese started coming again.

Late June 1950. The Cold War turns suddenly hot.

Communist North Korea, backed by China and Russia, invades across the 38th parallel, the border with South Korea, convinced they can conquer the country before any outside force can interfere.

They almost do.

But South Korea is a U.S. ally and President Truman badgers the United Nations into forming an international peace keeping force with the U.S. as the principal supplier of men and materials. General Douglas MacAurther is named Supreme Commander. By the time the UN and the U.S. high command get organized, the Communist North has overrun the country and trapped what remains of the Republic of Korea's army and the few U.S. troops supporting them into a small defensive pocket at the port city of Pusan on the southern tip of the peninsula. It seems only a Dunkirk-like evacuation is all that remains before complete surrender.

We're able to get in a few reinforcements— elements of the Eighth Army from Japan and a hastily assembled brigade of the Fifth Marines from Camp Pendleton in California. They hold on long enough to give MacAurther time to plan and stage a surprise amphibious attack nearly one hundred fifty miles behind enemy lines, on the west coast near Inchon. Conventional wisdom says that the tides are too treacherous and the beaches too narrow to permit an assault from the sea there. But the First Marine Division, deployed directly from the U.S., manages it. Racing from the beach-head, our forces take back Seoul, the South's capital city, open up the airport and establish an anvil on which joint ROK and American forces, counterattacking from Pusan, can break out and roll-up the North Korean Army.

My reserve unit is activated in mid-September, just about the time of the Inchon landings. I'm just beginning my sophomore year at the University. We leave out of Lexington for the Marine Corps depot at San Diego, go through a hasty combat infantry refresher there and ship out for Korea, getting there too late to take part in the landing, but fed into the fighting as we push out of Inchon.

Most of the regiment are regulars—experienced men who fought at Peliliu and Tarawa and Iwo Jima. Most of the rest are like me, eighteen-year old reservists with no military experience and in the unit largely because we liked or needed the extra money. A few of the reservists, though, are the real thing— Marine veterans of World War II, which had ended barely five years earlier— young men working at building careers and families.

The fighting is bitter and bloody, and we take and give many casualties, but Inchon breaks the back of the North Korean army. We have them on the run and are pushing them steadily north toward the Manchurian border, the border with China.

China warns it will come into the war to assist its Korean allies. MacAurther doesn't believe it. He says the war, not quite six months old at this point, is practically won and that he'll "have the boys home by Christmas."

To clinch it, he sends the Eighth Army up the western side of the Korean peninsula and us, the First Marines, up the eastern side— a pincher movement to trap and destroy what remains of the North Korean army against the Yalu river and force a surrender.

MacAurther disregards advice that to launch a winter campaign in the rugged mountains south of Manchuria is suicidal and ignores intelligence that units of the Red Chinese army are already across the Yalu.

So we head north. A four-hundred-thirty-thousand man Red Chinese field army is waiting in ambush.

Almost immediately the Chinese maul the Eighth Army coming up the western side, sending it reeling back south. We're at Yudam-ni, a small village near the Chosin Reservoir, fighting our way north as part of the pincer. We've already defeated the Chinese in a three day battle at Sudong, about thirty miles south of the reservoir and are attacking to take the high ground at Yudam-ni when we're ordered to turn west and go to the rescue of the Eighth Army, which is now in full retreat.

Before we can move out, we're surrounded too.

The Army's Thirty-Second Regiment is hemmed in on the eastern side of Chosin Reservoir and slaughtered. A few survivors escape by fleeing across the frozen lake to our lines at Hagaru-ri.

By the evening of December fifth, we are completely cut off at all locations. In Washington, they believe our whole twenty thousand man division will be destroyed. There is no way to extricate us and no military force with sufficient skill and numbers to come save us.

The media, privy to situation reports being received in Washington, feed the story out internationally. The drama and suspense of the situation captures the world's attention. They call us "The Lost Division." They say it will be "The worst defeat in U.S. military history."

Except we're still fighting.

We're ordered to withdraw and on Wednesday, December sixth, a day too cold to snow with fog on the lake and a freezing mist hiding the ground, we begin our march back down out of the mountains to the Sea of Japan.

A correspondent asks General Oliver Smith, our commanding officer, if we're retreating. "Retreating? Hell no," says the General, "we're attacking in another direction."

The last of the rear-guard clears Koto-ri at midnight.

We attack down seventy-eight miles of narrow, twisting, icy road. Deep ravines fall off one side. Snow covered ridges teeming with Chinese rise on the other.

A subarctic cold front sits on the trail. Temperatures at night drop to twenty-below; climb slightly during the day.

Most of the fighting is done at night. The Chinese prefer to come in the dark with bugles blowing and mortar rounds falling. There are so many of them, they are numberless. They spend men like we spend ammunition, coming in waves.

Snow falls almost constantly and we attack around the clock. We have to take the high ground. We have to clear and command the ridges, so our column can creep slowly down the road.

We fight uphill, struggling to the top of the ridges through knee-deep snow, clawing at rock-hard ice, hands freezing, feet numb in the cold, but fighting. We fight with rifles and grenades and at the end, hand-to-hand with bayonets and knifes.

Almost half our force is suffering from frostbite. Almost that many are wounded. We climb and fight anyway.

Thirteen days.

It takes thirteen hellish days and nights.

Will asked me what it was like.

How can such a thing be described? How can the pain and the fear be conveyed? And the excitement and the awe? How can the exhilaration of having made it out and the misery at the death of friends who didn't be tolerated? How can the pride in having been part of it be borne with all that sorrow and guilt weighing you down?

I decided not to think about it.

I decided that Scarlet O'Hara was right. Think about it tomorrow.

For this midnight on Friday, the second day of December in the Year of Our Lord One Thousand Nine Hundred Fifty-Five, I'd watch the snow fall.

And think of Allie, of walking in the snow with Allie on a December night when we were still unmarked.

SEVENTEEN

Developments in the Purcell case didn't wait on my convenience.

That snowy Saturday morning, Major Tanner of the State Police announced that they had a suspect in hand.

Though I was there in the hastily called press conference in the Sheriff's office and heard it said, I have to admit I didn't expect it.

The suspect was Emma Purcell Kane, the victim's daughter.

Yes, Andy Thomas's story in The *Lexington Herald* earlier in the week had said Emma's recitation of her whereabouts the day of the murder didn't check out; but I assumed, as I think most of us assumed, that some explanation would be ginned up, some half-way reasonable excuse for her "mis-remembering" would be found, and the whole embarrassment of the thing pushed under one of the convenient rugs of the establishment and mentioned no more as was the usual practice.

In this instance, though, the finger was being pointed by the State Police. The information linking Emma Kane to the crime was developed by Major Tanner's criminal unit and not subject to Sheriff Woodrow Stanley Peavler's editing. The Sheriff let the Major break the news. He seemed to want to distance himself from it.

An incredulous question came from the back of the room.

"Adeline Hockensmith Purcell's one and only child beat her head in with a flatiron and stuffed ashes down her throat?"

Sheriff Peavler jumped up.

"Let's not get ahead of ourselves here," the Sheriff shot back, hands on hips, eyes glaring.

"We're talking about the daughter of one of the most respected women in the county and the niece of the County Judge. There's no conclusive evidence here. It's all circumstantial. "

"Will she be arrested? Jailed?" asked a man with a mike in his hand.

"Emma Kane is no flight risk. There is no reason to put her through the disgrace and discomfort of a jail cell. She's not going to run away anywhere."

The Sheriff looked to Major Tanner, an expression of both anger and defiance on his face.

'No. She's not going to jail!" he said.

"She'll be brought in for questioning?"

"Of course."

"When?

"When I'm ready," Sheriff Woodrow Stanley Peavler replied. "We're finished here."

I can't be sure, but I believe Major Tanner had a smile on his face as we filed out.

Before I did anything, I needed to talk with Will.

There was no need to rush to write the story. By the time tomorrow morning's *Journal* hit the streets, the news that Emma Purcell Kane was suspected of murdering her mother would be worn out. Radio would have it all over town by noon. The afternoon papers in Lexington and Louisville would elaborate with anything they could come up with. We'd be left holding an empty bag.

I found Will at the far end of the bar at King's Hotel. It was almost noon— too late for him to be still at home and too early to be in the newsroom yet. That left only the bar at King's. Elementary.

Outside, people were in a good mood, laughing and caught up in that child-like excitement the first snow always triggers. Inside it was warm and dark and empty except for Will and Gideon Elkins, an enormous black man, black as coal, with a wide smile and biceps like barrels—one of Will's fishing buddies. They were standing at the far end of the bar, talking quietly. The room was a long, high ceilinged, windowless rectangle entered from the hotel lobby. It was paneled in rich oak. Three walls were hung with a fortune in Paul Sawyier watercolors. A magnificent lion's head, taken by Mr. King on one of his African trips, was mounted above the mirror that ran the length of the room on the wall behind the bar. The bar itself was a gleaming expanse of mahogany stretching off into the shadows with a polished brass foot rail to rest against.

Will had a cup in front of him. I'd bet it was filled with hot coffee topped with a jigger of bourbon—no better way known to man to start a winter day.

"Can I have one of those," I said.

The light was behind me. They couldn't see me clearly. As I got closer, Gideon recognized me.

"You sure you're old enough, boy?" he said, grinning at me.

Will had me focused by then.

"Ah, here you are."

He studied me for a moment, took a sip from his cup, and smiled into the mirror.

"Interesting day."

"You heard?"

"I heard."

Gideon set a steaming cup in front of me.

"Bring it with you," Will said, moving away from the bar and across the room to a table on the far wall beneath a Sawyier that pictured a fisherman peeking around a big sycamore to a stretch of water on a creek we all knew.

Will took a chair with his back to the wall. He did that religiously, regardless of the room or the circumstance. I asked him once why he did that.

"Wild Bill Hickock," he said.

"What?"

"Wild Bill's rule was never to sit with his back to the door. The one time he didn't was in a poker game in a Deadwood saloon. It turned out to be his last one. Broken Nose Jack McCall slipped up behind him and put a bullet in his head."

"You're kidding me," I said.

He laughed. "You think so? Maybe. Take no unnecessary chances, kid."

I took the chair across from him, realizing a little uneasily that I couldn't see behind me, or for that matter much of the room, without turning.

"So what's your plan," he asked as I sipped on my coffee.

"You're my plan," I said.

He nodded.

"Tough situation. The story is old before we get a chance to do anything with it. What we have to do now is come up with something no one else has."

"How do we get that?"

Will smiled. "Let's go see Major Tanner."

Contacts.

Will made a phone call and an hour later we were in Major Tanner's office at the State Police barracks, snow and Saturday notwithstanding.

The Major was waiting for us. Freshly pressed shirt, creased trousers, tie neat and firm, hair in place, firm handshake, and friendly smile. His second floor office looked out on the New State Office Building. The site previously was occupied by the State Penitentiary, but that was torn down to make room for the 20-storey office building needed to house some of the workers who did The People's business. I don't think any irony was intended in the metamorphosis from a prison to a state office building. It just happened that way.

Tanner was one of those men who had command presence. He projected confidence and authority. When he walked into a room, you had the impression he knew what to do and how to do it and could do it himself if necessary. He had served with the 82nd Airborne, had a Master's in Criminal Justice from the University and had joined the Kentucky State Police as soon as he got his degree. He'd worked his way up from Trooper to Major and, at age thirty-five, Colonel was clearly in sight.

The contrast between the Major and Sheriff Woodrow Stanley Peavler was complete.

We spent the barest of time in the small talk expected in such circumstances before getting to the matter at hand. Neither we nor the Major had time to waste.

Will leveled with him; told him what our problem was and what we needed.

"I can't speak officially or for the record, Will, you know that."

"Of course," Will said. "Whatever you give us will be attributed to "informed sources" or "people with knowledge of the investigation," Will said. "No names named. No one put on the spot."

They'd played this game before. Both knew the hazards and the rules.

"None of this has been made public yet," the Major said.

"Where's the problem in making public the information you have?" Will asked.

"The Commonwealth's Attorney wants it that way.

"Work on her nerves?"

Major Tanner frowned, "Maybe. Or maybe he's being cautious. Sheriff Peavler was right in that the evidence is circumstantial."

He paused, "But some of it is damning."

"Specifically, Mrs. Kane cannot account for her whereabouts from ten a.m. the morning of the murder to three p.m. that afternoon. None of the places that she said she visited have any record or recollection of her being there.

"She's changed her story to account for this. She says she was confused and embarrassed at the time she gave her statement. She said she had a hurtful argument with her husband that morning and was so upset she just took to her car and started driving aimlessly.

"She says she has no real recollection of where she went or if she saw anyone. She tried to visit a close friend who lives out on the Owenton Road. The gate to the lane leading to the house was closed. She ruined her shoes walking in the muddy lane to open the gate. The friend wasn't home.

"We found the shoes in a trash can behind the horse barn. They were a mess all right— muddy and soaked through. We ran them through the crime lab. There was more than mud on them— there was blood on the left shoe ... blood of the same type as her mother's.

"There's more. Her fingerprints were on the flatiron.

"The capper is this. We found a trace of ash in the cuff of the slacks she wore that day, ash of the same composition as that found in her mother's throat."

"Sheriff Peavler knew all this?"

"Some of it. The blood and the ashes were found in our lab analysis. He didn't know about that until we told him."

"Yet he was still reluctant to name her as a suspect?"

"Sheriff Peavler has an aversion to upsetting his betters."

"Well, hell, Tanner," Will said laughing, "Woodrow Stanley Peavler has an aversion to anything that doesn't make him money or get him votes. All this may be circumstantial, but it seems more than enough to bring charges. What more does the Commonwealth's Attorney need?"

"Motive," the Major said. "We have no apparent motive for the crime."

So we had what no one else had. And we used almost all of it, withholding only one piece of information. We didn't report that blood and ashes had been found on the clothing Emma wore the day of the murder, only that tests were underway in the State Police Crime Lab. That's what Major Tanner wanted, and we were happy to oblige.

Our story, the lead story in the Sunday morning paper, ran under an eight column banner "Daughter Main Suspect In Ashes Murder." The deck read "Police Search For Blood & Ashes In Clothes Worn That Day." All facts were attributed to "informed sources" and "officials close to the investigation." Even so, I was sure Sheriff Woodrow Stanley Peavler would have a good idea of the source.

The gossip and speculation dominated the town's attention all the next week. Adeline Hockensmith Purcell was too prominent a woman and the Judge, her brother, too well known to escape it.

"Her own daughter? Scandalous!"

" I always thought that girl had a mean streak."

"Something's rotten in that family."

"You know that girl was pregnant when she got married, don't you? She and Adeline had an awful fight about it."

And so on and so forth.

As we moved closer to Christmas, the planning and anticipation for the holidays began to push the Ashes Murder into the background—not completely, the particulars of the crime were too sensational to fade. But interest was less feverish. Nothing new was being developed.

By the week before Christmas, no formal charge had yet been brought against Emma Kane. The matter was just there, lurking like a big black cloud on the horizon. Nothing was likely to happen during Christmas week. No one could imagine the authorities having such bad taste as to bring murder charges against a member of so prominent a family during Christmas week. Nor for that matter in the week between Christmas and New Year's. So the odds that nothing of consequence would happen in the Purcell case until after the first of the New Year were very, very strong.

I have to admit this prospect pleased me. My creativity was running thin, and my energy was wearing down. Trying to make something out of nothing is a monumentally wearing process.

"Hang in there, son." Will kept telling me, smiling as he said it, "You'll be a better man for it all."

Maybe. I do know that I was becoming adept at drawing people out, at mining the most ordinary of matters for readable material, at hanging on until I got what I wanted. I found I could dredge something interesting out of almost anything. Overweening curiosity will do that for you.

The most important finding, though, was that I could get people to trust me. Perhaps this spoke to my inexperience or even my naivety. Whatever the reason, people seemed to feel they could rely on me. I had to stay true to my word. I had to do what I said I would do. I had to do what I was expected to do. All that, yes. But what I got in return was trust—and with trust came confidences.

I learned that Emma Kane was in fact pregnant at the time of her marriage and that her mother had forced her into the match only after concluding that having Marko Kane's legs broken and dumping him somewhere on a deserted country road might be a less punishing fate than forcing him to live with Emma.

I learned that the Judge, Judge Ira Hockensmith, Emma's uncle and the victim's younger brother, lived above his means and had to entreat at his sister's knee for the funds to keep living in the style he thought his due—a necessity he found demeaning and unfair.

I didn't learn these things all at once. Or easily. And I didn't take them at face value. People always have agendas; even the most righteous of people. And people will use you—even the ones you think won't. Will's rule, Rule # 2 in the Will Owens' Playbook: "Never believe what you hear. And only half of what you see."

I wasn't quite that cynical, but I knew enough to verify a thing for myself before I bought it.

EIGHTEEN

Will went to his sister's place in Virginia for Christmas. I helped him onto the train at the station downtown with snow falling and The Salvation Army Band playing carols. He had several brightly wrapped packages in his arms and nostalgia on his face. His color was not good, and he looked weak but seemed happy, waving as the train moved away—a man going home to family for Christmas.

With Will away we were a man short, so I filled in to let others on the staff get a little extra time off.

I spent Christmas day sitting in the newsroom listening to the teletype chatter and ready to grab the phone if it rang with some bit of news.

We went to press early Christmas night. The paper had been locked up since eleven o'clock. There was no need to hold everybody longer.

I took my time getting home. The snow had stopped. Ice crystals sparkled in store windows. The streets were white and empty. Each lamp post was topped with green garlands and red ribbon. As I passed the corner of Wapping and St. Clair, the faithful were trooping into Good Shepherd for midnight mass, stomping their feet on the steps to knock the snow off their shoes. The opening and closing doors flashed warm yellow corridors of light on the street outside. I started to go in. But I didn't. I kept on straight to the bridge. The night was clear, the sky sparkling. Stars twinkled in an inverted obsidian bowl. A light fog lay over the river, tracing a grey-white path through the snow on the banks. Upriver, the Armory stood protectively on East Main Hill, bathed in light. Downriver you could tell where the bend began by the way the ribbon of fog curved, but otherwise it was dark except for a lone light at what must have been the end of Wapping.

As I turned to head home, I could hear the congregation at Good Shepherd. They were singing "Silent Night." I leaned on the railing—listening—looking at the night,

My apartment was dark when I opened the door, but the little Christmas tree I'd put up in the corner was blinking happily. I turned on the lights in the kitchen, made myself a drink, turned them off, and took the chair by the window to watch the empty street below while images of other Christmases played in my mind.

After a while the phone rang.

I had expected it might, hoped it would, and would have been disappointed if it hadn't.

"Merry Christmas," that soft voice said.

"Merry Christmas," I whispered back.

"Are you okay?"

"A little lonely," I said quietly. "A little sad. You?"

"A little lonely. A little sad."

"One of these days," I said.

"I know," Allie said. "One of these days."

There was a long silence.

"Good night, hero."

"Goodnight, lady."

Will came back on Monday, the day after New Year's. He looked rested and in a way rejuvenated. Whatever his sister and her family did with him, it put color back in his face and a bounce in his step. I couldn't quite picture Will sitting around a big family Christmas tree with a nephew on his knee singing carols. I almost could, but it was hazy. Some of the magic of the Christmases of his boyhood must have come back to him there—home ground—blood of his blood around him—the unconditional welcome of family. He seemed a little less combative, a little more forgiving. I imagined it was a temporary condition.

Michael left to fly back to California the same day. We hadn't spent much time together. Rhae Dannan had filled his social schedule too full, and I had so much going on at the *Journal*. Michael and I were an unlikely pair. He was the son of Bluegrass aristocracy, and I the son of the beer-still operator at the distillery. Oddly, or perhaps tellingly, that social disparity made absolutely no difference to either of us, and certainly not to Rhae Dannan. The thing about us is that we matched. We thought alike. We were interested in the same things.

And though it is immodest to say, we were very good at everything we tried: athletics, school work, winning friends.

We had New Year's Eve dinner together that year as we'd had every year since we'd entered high school. Rhae always organized it. Candlelight and crystal. Rhae regal in a gown of the latest design. Michael and I in our best blue blazers and newest ties; our grey flannels sharply creased and our loafers brightly shined. Just the three of us in the big dining room at the farm. Rhae's theory was that however the night might actually turn out for us, we should start it properly—civilized, disciplined, and cognizant of who we were and what we could be. Rhae thought we were destined for great things—both of us.

Rhae Dannan's confidence in us had its effect. We behaved ourselves. We were examples of how proper, young Kentucky gentlemen should conduct themselves. Well, Michael was. I'm Irish so a bit of latitude must be afforded me.

The next morning I drove him to the Lexington airport to catch his flight back to San Francisco. The pastures along the way that are so luxuriant in the spring were in the grip of winter, the trees stark and leafless, the fields icy and black. Even so, the rolling landscape, girded with its intersecting white fences and horse barns rising like little castles, was beautiful.

"You still have your heart set on New York?" Michael asked as I maneuvered through the turn at Versailles to make the final run into Bluegrass Airport.

"As fast as I can after I graduate. You still gonna be Lord of All You Survey?"

"As fast as I can after I graduate."

We both laughed.

Michael would get his MBA from Stanford this coming spring. He was already being courted by a big California conglomerate expanding rapidly abroad. He would likely make his goal.

So would I.

NINETEEN

Dulin's patience wore out on the fiftieth day. It was as if the Ashes Murder had vanished. The State Police were offering nothing on the results of the testing being done in their crime lab, although we knew the findings since Major Tanner had told us two weeks earlier, and our esteemed Sheriff seemed to be ignoring the matter completely in hopes it would go away.

"Dammit," Dulin said to me and Will, "we've got to make something happen. Keep the pressure on. Keep the interest high."

He assigned Will to do a major no-holds-barred feature, recapping the whole affair, starting with the prominence of the Hockensmith family, the importance of their farming and breeding operations and their distillery's role as one of the major employers in the county, then move on to the victim's role in local social and charitable affairs, replaying the murder, sparing no grisly details, and focusing on the failure of the investigators, particularly the Sheriff's office, in finding the murderer and bringing him (or her) to justice.

He wanted me to concentrate on Emma Purcell Kane. I was to produce a full-blown profile of the girl, a feature that would reveal the person.

"We'll devote Sunday's front page to the two stories ... all of it. If Sheriff Woodrow Stanley Peavler thinks this story is going away, he's in for a big jolt," Dulin said, smiling for the first time that day.

The assignment he had for me wasn't one I wanted. Good profiles draw conclusions.

I didn't want to draw conclusions about Emma Kane. I didn't want to knit together a story that would influence how others would judge her.

"Ah, Theo," Will sighed when I laid out my problem to him. "You've got to grow up. Of course you're going to judge. Spewing out facts is nothing. Facts are indifferent. They take on any meaning any fool cares to give them. What you're after is truth. Somewhere out there is the truth about the kind of person Emma Purcell Kane is. You're too find it and tell us."

Dulin was listening, tilted back in his desk chair, arms folded across his chest, an appraising look on his face.

I looked to the clock on the wall above the teletypes. Two p.m. Wednesday. I had a little over three days to understand a girl who might have murdered her mother and put my understanding into words.

I started with her teachers, worked through the friends who would talk, both past and present, interviewed her pastor and her Sunday School teacher, the owners and clerks of the places she shopped, and then tried the relatives who were still among us.

The Purcells, her father's kin, were few—two cousins in Lexington. Under no circumstances would the cousins "involve themselves in this matter," they told me.

On her mother's side there was only one living relative—her mother's aunt, the spinster sister of her grandfather Hockensmith.

And there was Allie.

It took me awhile to talk myself into calling her. I didn't know how well she knew Emma, but I knew they knew each other. I was reluctant to put Allie in a position of talking about Emma to please me, or to help me, but in the end I called her.

"I have to write a piece about Emma Kane—Emma Purcell—and I'm running up against stone walls. You knew her, didn't you?"

"What happened to 'Hello,' or 'How are you?'"

"What? Oh. I'm sorry, Allie. I'm a little embarrassed calling you about this."

"Why?"

"It might be something you don't feel comfortable talking about."

"But you think I would just because it's you?"

"Damn, Allie, I'm really sorry. I'm not doing this well."

I could hear the smile in her voice.

"That's okay, hero. I know you. What is it you're doing?"

"It's a profile. For Sunday's paper. On Emma Purcell Kane. What kind of person is she."

"Is she the kind who might kill her mother? Is that what you're getting at?"

"All I want to do is a straight job of reporting … a piece that describes, as well as I can, what kind of person Emma is, or that people think she is. They can draw their own conclusions."

"She was a sweet girl. I liked her. We were Kappa Delts together at UK until she left at the end of our sophomore year. We've kept in touch since then. You know her, too," Allie said.

"I know her? How?"

"You forget so easily, Theo. She was Dave Todd's date the night of the big spring dance our senior year. You danced with her. She sat next to you. All night. We made breakfast together at Nancy's that morning."

I remembered the night and the morning, but I had no recollection of Emma Purcell.

"I don't—"

"Never mind. Emma remembers you."

Silence. I had no idea what that meant or what she was thinking.

"Yes, I know Emma," she said after a while.

Now the silence was on my end. I'd touched all the bases there were to touch, and I still didn't have any real feel for Emma Purcell Kane.

Allie broke it.

"The person you should talk with is her Aunt Livia. Her great aunt, actually. She was close to Emma all her life from what Emma told me. I could call her for you. Livia Hockensmith, Miss Liv."

I didn't make the connection until Allie said that. Aunt Livia. Miss Livia Hockensmith. Emma's favorite aunt. Miss Liv had been our sixth grade teacher at Second Street. She was retired now, in her seventies and lived alone in a spacious apartment overlooking the Capitol. I'd been one of her favorites. I was her champion speller. I won the school spelling bee that year, the first time the sixth grade had ever won it. Surely she would remember, wouldn't she?

My question was answered the minute she opened her door. She threw her arms up to hug me, kissed me on the cheek and asked as she ushered Allie and me in, "What was your winning word? Do you remember?" I hadn't. But I'd looked it up beforehand. Smiling as wide as I could, I stood tall, looked straight ahead, and said, "Asceticism. A-S-C-E-T-I-C-I-S-M. Asceticism: the practice of self-discipline and abstention from all forms of indulgence, typically for religious reasons."

She laughed with delight and clapped her hands.

"Oh, Theo, Theo, Theo. It's so good to see you again. Come in. Sit down."

She beamed at us as Allie and I took seats on the sofa by the big front window looking out on the Capitol grounds.

Miss Liv was an institution. She'd taught at Second Street, the town's largest grade school, for over forty years, ever since her graduation from Sophie Newcomb College when she was twenty. She never married. Her students were her tribe. She was universally loved and respected. She liked boys particularly and was particularly insistent not only that our studies be rigorous, but that our manners and our appearance was consonant with the standards she thought properly brought up young men should adhere to. I know men even today who won't use cuss words in public because Miss Liv thought it a sign of low intelligence and ill manners.

I had on my best blue blazer, a new white button-down, an understated rep tie, sharply creased grey flannels, loafers polished to a high shine, with my hair combed and in place, and my nails trimmed and clean.

I wouldn't have thought to put myself in Miss Liv's presence in any other state.

She seated herself across from us in a big, blue wing-back chair, a wall of books behind her, a grand piano to her left.

"I was so worried about you during that awful time in Korea," she said, her hands clasped in her lap, "and so thankful when you returned safely. And all right. You are all right, aren't you, Theo?"

I was both surprised and touched that she had kept tabs on me.

"Yes, ma'am. I'm fine. Thank you for having me in your mind."

"I never let my boys get too far out of sight," she said, a tender smile again.

"And you were decorated."

"The Silver Star," Allie said. "For gallantry in action against enemies of the United States."

"It really wasn't much. It was mostly that I was there."

"Nonsense," Miss Liv said. "You were wounded."

"Not much more than a scratch," I said. "A bullet grazed me."

Allie leaned across and ran her finger along the faint diagonal line on the right side of my face just below the cheekbone.

"Showing off, were you," she said, keeping it light.

"Trying to hide," I said, laughing.

It took a bit of work to salvage the cheekbone but it all worked out. I didn't want to talk about it. Allie knew that.

"And now you're on your way to becoming a famous journalist," Miss Liv said, beaming again.

Ron Rhody

"I'll graduate this spring from UK. I hope to be good enough to make it in New York."

"You won't stay home? Surely there will be opportunities here."

"I love it here, Miss Liv, I honestly do. I'll never leave it, at least in my mind, but I have to find out how good I am. The only place I can find that out is New York."

She turned an inquiring look to Allie. I knew she was wondering about the relationship between us. Then she turned back to me.

"And your friend Michael Dannan. How is he?"

"Michael's finishing up his MBA at Stanford. He'll graduate this spring. He already has a couple of big corporations after him."

"So we'll lose both of you," she said.

"We'll just be out on loan, Miss Liv," I said, smiling.

"Well, at least you're here now," she said, and brightening, "Allie said you wanted to talk with me about Emma."

I explained my assignment. Assured her I'd be fair and write as balanced a piece as the facts allowed.

"What you really want to know is Emma the kind of person who could kill her mother, isn't it?"

I started to protest, but she stopped me.

"Oh, Theo, that's what everyone wants to know."

I had no alternative then but to ask the obvious.

"Is she?"

We talked for most of the afternoon. Miss Liv stopped once and made tea for us. Then we continued; Allie sitting on the couch beside me, her shoes off, her legs tucked up beneath her, listening, nodding occasionally; Miss Liv in her big wingback chair, remembering, laughing at some incident recalled, becoming somber at others, and tearing up once, but only once; me leaning forward, note pad on my knee.

The lights were coming on out on the Capitol grounds when Allie and I finally stepped out into the twilight. Miss Liv kissed me on the cheek when I left.

"The poor child. She tried so hard," was all she said.

Allie took my arm and we walked down the street to my car, stepping carefully over those few places where the roots of the big oaks had lifted the pavement and easing past houses where wives were starting dinner. She leaned in close to me all the way, neither of us talking.

At my car, as I opened the door for her, she said, "It's going to be hard, isn't it."

"It's going to be almost impossible, Allie."

I went home, turned on the lights, made myself a nice stiff bourbon, eased into the chair by the window. It was going to be almost impossible. Capture a person in two-thousand words? A person you know only through what others have told you—others whose memories have been edited by their own egos, who have agendas of their own? And which person do you portray? Emma the daughter? Emma the wife and mother? Emma the unloved little rich girl yearning to be liked and accepted? No person is one person. There are too many creatures lurking in each of us for anyone to ever really know us. And I'm to explain Emma— to us all.

These were the basic "facts" I had about Emma Purcell Kane:

She was twenty-two. Daughter of Adeline Hockensmith Purcell and Lawrence Purcell, both deceased – she murdered, he killed in an automobile accident when Emma was seven. No siblings. Married to Marko Kane, age thirty-one, a foreman at the horse farm owned by her mother. Some gossip that it was a marriage of necessity. One child, a three year old boy. She had him the year she married. She was eighteen.

No police record, not even a speeding ticket. No recorded drug or alcohol problems. A member of the First Baptist Church. Downtown. A long drive from the farm each Sunday morning, but the traditional church of the city's old-line Baptist families. Attends church spasmodically. Graduate of Elkhorn High School, one of the high schools out in the county much closer to the farm than Frankfort High. Not a standout in school. Average student. Not a class officer. Was a member of the Home Economics Club and the Math Club. Two years at University of Kentucky, majoring in mathematics. Withdrew at start of junior year to marry. Housewife. No indication of having made any waves anywhere or shaken any trees of any size.

It didn't read like the resume of a vicious killer.

My interviews fleshed out these basic facts; most important was my interview with Miss Liv.

Emma Purcell Kane was not a happy girl, Miss Livy told me.

She felt her mother didn't like her. Adeline Hockensmith Purcell probably didn't, Miss Liv said. Adeline had married late, in her thirties, and had Emma almost right away. Emma was a disappointment. She was a gnarly baby and cried too much. Adeline was at the time just coming into her own in Bluegrass society. She'd captured Larry Purcell, a guaranteed Bluegrass aristocrat— handsome, charming, of almost absolutely no use except on social occasions, although he thought himself an expert on horseflesh and used his marriage to Adeline, and her money, as a heaven-sent way to get himself into horse breeding.

To Adeline, the baby was an inconvenience and was Larry's idea anyway. The gnarly baby turned into a moody child of little personality and no endearing qualities. Adeline was embarrassed that Emma wasn't pretty and wasn't popular—that she wasn't class president or Homecoming Queen. Emma knew this. She cried about it. She tried to be popular, to be pretty. Trying made no difference.

Adeline, for her part, tried to buy popularity for Emma. Big parties at the farm, expensive birthday gifts for the popular girls Emma wanted to be friends with. It wasn't that Emma was disliked. It was that she just wasn't liked, and consequently was always on the outside. She had no close friends. No close female friends.

Boys were another matter. In her junior year in high school she discovered sex—and its uses. Emma matured early. Had a woman's breasts and hips by the time she was fifteen. Emma might not have been pretty, but she was available. That was enough for the boys. If Adeline was aware of what was going on, she ignored it. Emma had dates. She wasn't a wallflower. That was enough. If Larry Purcell had been alive at the time things would have probably been different. But he was killed in that car crash when Emma was seven.

Emma got safely through high-school, enrolled at UK, made a good sorority (the Purcell name and the Hockensmith money had appeal) and began to blossom a bit. She was very good at math and was excelling in class when Marko Kane arrived at the farm. He came in the spring with the Gypsies, stayed when they left. Some sort of falling out. The details were never clear. Adeline hired him for the horses. He was truly gifted with them; might one day have the capabilities to manage the breeding and sales operation. Marco was handsome. Had dark, curly hair, a friendly smile, an accommodating personality. Emma wanted to learn to ride. He gave her lessons. He was a man, not a boy, an authority figure. He paid attention to her. Before the summer was over, she was pregnant.

Adeline was apoplectic when she learned of it. She threatened to have Marko horsewhipped and ridden out of town on a rail, Miss Liv said. Of course, she wouldn't. There weren't those kind of rails around anymore, and besides, it would attract too much attention, create too much gossip.

Adeline insisted on an abortion. Emma, for the first time standing up to her mother, refused. Marko apparently had no say, or if he did, whatever he said didn't matter. The only alternative was marriage. "Serves you right," Adeline spat at Marko. "Having to live with Emma will be punishment enough." Miss Liv was there. She heard this. So Emma withdrew from university. She and Marko married in a small ceremony at the downtown church before she began to show, and ... .

I stopped. I realized I didn't know what followed the "and."

My drink was finished. The hour was late. Outside, the night seemed to be trying to work itself into a storm. I was going to have to start writing soon. Tomorrow. I'd start tomorrow.

But not now. Not tonight. I wasn't up to starting tonight. I put my notes away, carried my empty glass to the kitchen, turned out the lights, and let myself out. The wind was up, but no rain yet. I walked down Wapping Street toward the river, trying to think of nothing. Trying not to judge.

TWENTY

No muse came to me in the night. I awoke still as undecided about how to take the Emma story as I had been when I fell into bed just before dawn.

I had to talk to Allie. She would have already made her own judgment about the kind of person Emma Purcell was and what she might be capable of. I trusted Allie's judgment. I needed to know what she thought.

It was Saturday morning, early. She'd be home. I had until eleven tonight to turn in my copy.

"Any chance a guy could get a cup of coffee at this hour," I said when she answered her phone.

"Theo? What are you—?

"I didn't wake you, did I?"

"Of course not. I'm feeding the baby. Why are you calling at this hour?"

"I need to talk with you. I need help understanding the Emma thing."

I could hear Allie's little girl in the background.

"Allie?"

"I'm here. Be still."

It seemed forever before she spoke again.

"Have you had breakfast?"

"No."

"I'll see if I can scare something up."

Allie lived in a new subdivision east of town on the road to Georgetown. The developers had already filled in about a third of the best bluegill pond in the county and were steadily chewing up what had been prime corn and tobacco acreage. Her house was a small ranch style cottage with a big oak in the front yard and a pasture flanking the back. She'd taken it shortly after her divorce, financed largely by her mother. The divorce, not quite two years old now, had been contentious. She left it gladly, with a bit of child support for the baby but no alimony.

The coffee was hot and waiting and the baby fed when I got there.

"I thought you newspaper guys slept in in the mornings," she said as she led me into the kitchen.

"Thanks for seeing me, Allie. I know this isn't the way you planned to start your weekend."

"You're a bother, Theo Clark."

I took the coffee she slid across the table to me.

"Milk and two sugars?"

I nodded.

"You still take it the way your mother made it for you," she said, shaking her head and smiling.

"I'm just a poor country boy trying to do the best he can in a world he never made."

She laughed.

"O.K., country boy, for just a while pretend this is the two of us just having breakfast. Nothing important on our minds. Just us. Talking about old times. About friends. About UK basketball even. We'll just do this first," Allie said.

"Allie—"

"Remember the breakfasts after the dances?"

She was standing by the stove, sunlight from the window burnishing her hair.

The breakfasts after the dances, that year we almost had?

Allie looked as good now as she did then, alluring and mischievous and so innocently seductive I felt at once both helplessly aroused and consciously monkish, a disturbing urge on the one hand to possess and on the other to protect.

I smiled recalling what those summer dawns had been like—two or three couples, coming down from the excitement of a night of partying, high school behind us and taking the first eager, clumsy steps through the door to the rest of our lives—arriving at the truck stop before daylight, still in our tuxes, the girls in their party dresses, the restaurant nearly empty, a few drowsy truckers staring… or sometimes trying to whip up breakfast at one of the girls' homes without waking her parents, trying not to laugh too loudly. Yes, I remembered.

"The morning Bobby forgot to put the parking brake on in his Dad's car, and it rolled down the hill into the pond at Julie's place," I said laughing.

"Everyone at Caroline's, starving. And all there was in the pantry was peanut butter because her mother hadn't been to the grocery. We had peanut butter and jelly toast for breakfast," Allie laughed back.

"The walks we took around the Capitol with the full moon going down and the sun coming up, the town sleeping, nothing stirring, just you and me." I watched her eyes.

We both laughed.

Wherever that conversation was leading ended then. She stood up from the table and started clearing the dishes. "You dry," she said.

We talked of nothing of consequence while we worked. When we'd finished, she wiped her hands on the towel at the sink, pushed her hair up out of her eyes with the back of her hand, stood looking out the window, gathering herself.

"It's time for the baby's morning nap. I'll put her down then we can talk about what you came to talk about."

There was still hot coffee in the pot on the counter. I poured myself a cup and waited. She came back smiling. I looked at her questioningly. "Oh, nothing," she said. "Just the baby."

She stood a moment in the doorway looking at me, as if deciding something. She had on a UK sweat jersey and faded jeans. Her hair was back in a ponytail, and she was barefoot. No fair, Allie, I thought. No fair.

"Well, hero," she said, taking the chair across the table from me so that we were face to face.

I drew my mind back to where it ought to be. "What I want is for you to tell me anything you can that will help me understand Emma, anything that will help me write a story fair to her."

Allie looked away. The light coming in from the kitchen window had dimmed. She turned back, took a sip of coffee, then looked up at me. "Emma's a poor, sad, sweet girl," Allie said, " and I think it's awful this has happened."

I stayed quiet, waiting for her to tell me what she had to tell me in whatever way she wanted.

This is the gist of it:

Miss Liv was right. Emma felt unloved. She felt her mother didn't love her. She felt her husband, Marko Kane, didn't love her. She was too plain, too ordinary, too colorless to suit her mother's idea of what the daughter of Adeline Hockensmith and Larry Purcell should be.

Emma was a big girl, almost six feet tall, big hands, big feet, a body Rubens might have favored, but not to the mold of Southern belles. She wasn't unattractive, but neither was she attractive. It wasn't that she had a bad personality; she just seemed to have no personality. She was shy and achingly nervous in social encounters. Not a daughter that Adeline could be proud of or show off or bask in the light of.

Emma felt her husband, Marko Kane, was interested only in the one thing he got early and since then only in the thing he was enjoying now and hoped to enjoy even more in the future— her family's money. Marko didn't like her, she was sure of that, even though she tried to please him as she tried to please her mother. He was embarrassed by her. By her size, he barely came to her shoulders. And by her looks. They almost never went out. Marko was half Gypsy, maybe all Gypsy as far as she knew. He liked his women lean and sultry.

The only place Emma could turn for warmth and affection was her grandfather Hockensmith's sister, Miss Liv.

Emma was bright. Several of her teachers in high school suspected she might be very bright. Indeed, her grasp of mathematics, for example, was far beyond that of any of her classmates. She was too shy to let it show. At UK, Emma and Allie became friends. They were acquaintances before, both being from the same town and knowing each other from various high school events. They pledged the same sorority and Allie soon found herself the person Emma turned to when she was stressed or depressed. Emma's neediness appealed to something innate in Allie's character.

Allie liked Emma's determination to be accepted in the sorority, her discipline in her studies, her eagerness to help, whatever the need or the assignment. She had aspirations. She did well in school. Emma was going to get her degree in math, then go on for a Doctorate. But Marko Herring came along. Emma was devastated at having to leave school. Then she was mad, very, very mad. At Marko. At her mother. She could have had the baby and still have gone to school. It could have been arranged. She knew it could have. Her mother could have afforded it. But she wouldn't. Emma had to come home and be a proper wife and mother. Her anger turned to fury, and her fury burned down to resentful resignation. Emma went home a frustrated, insecure, bitter girl, simmering with the injustice handed her all her life.

Allie saw her from time to time. Their babies were about the same age. They sometimes ran into each other in shops. They had lunch now and then. Emma surely counted Allie a friend, certainly as much of a friend as she'd ever had. She continued to confide in Allie, to Allie's discomfort, but what could she do.

Emma reminded Allie of a picture she'd once seen of a cougar lying silently in wait above a water hole while a fawn approached. Focused. Patient. Innocently menacing. Emma would be rich one day—one day when her mother died. She could do what she wanted then. Maybe jettison Marko. Maybe keep him. Maybe sell the farm, move away. Her mother couldn't live forever. She could wait. Allie didn't want to know these things, but Emma confided.

Allie ended what she had to tell me with, "but I never, ever, saw her be mean or cruel."

TWENTY ONE

I'm afraid Dulin was disappointed with what I turned in. I made the deadline all right and I filled 2000 words, but I made no judgments. I presented in the story only what was verifiable fact, quoted only those people who agreed to be quoted, repeated no rumors, dignified no gossip. The result was, as you would imagine, bland and unexciting.

Most of what I got from Miss Liv and Allie I couldn't use. What they told me was opinion and impression, none of it verifiable objectively. Had they been willing to be quoted, I could have used it. But neither was willing.

The few people willing to be quoted were those with flattering things to say about Emma; most of it, I suspected, intended to curry favor with the Judge or with Emma herself. I used some of it.

The thought that here might be an angry, resentful, frustrated woman waiting for the door to open through which she could escape to a life she dreamed of couldn't be conveyed. I had no way to confirm it.

The story was informative and accurate. The whole county was interested in Emma. But as an exercise in exposing the character of the lady, it wasn't even a near miss.

Dulin didn't disagree with the way I handled it. I went through all my notes with him before I sat down to start writing. He agreed that we should go only with what we could verify. The usual tactic of getting confidential information into a story by attributing it to "informed sources" or a "person close to" was discarded. We were going to play it absolutely straight all the way.

I went over all this with Will too. I found him at what was becoming his usual stand. Gideon waved as I walked in, and Will looked up. "Theo. Come join me. The sun is over the yard-arm."

I pulled up a stool beside him.

"Can't. I'm running up against deadline."

"Then why are you here?"

I told him my problem. Went over my notes. Told him how I planned to handle the piece.

He listened, not looking at me, but watching both our reflections in the mirror behind the bar.

When I finished he said, "I'd find a way to use that material. You trust the sources, don't you? You believe them? That information is crucial to understanding the kind of person Emma is. It should be out there on the record."

That took me back a bit. I'd expected his support, his sympathy that I couldn't use the really good stuff, his applause at the decision to stay with only what I could verify. But I got no comfort from Will.

"What you've come up with speaks to motive. There's a plausible motive. Only you've no way to get it on the record. The only way to get it on the record is in your story."

"I can't quote the sources, and I can't independently confirm what they've told me. I can't use it."

He turned from the mirror to face me directly.

"Do you think Emma did it? Killed her mother," he asked quietly.

"I don't know."

"I didn't ask you what you know. I asked you what you think. Do you think she's capable of it? Crushing her mother's head and stuffing ashes down her throat?"

I stayed silent. I think anyone is capable of anything. Scare them enough, make them mad enough, play on their beliefs and prejudices enough, abuse and humiliate and exploit them enough, and anyone is capable of anything. I saw it in Korea. I know it to be true. But I didn't say so out loud.

"Would you let her walk just to keep your sources happy?"

"I'm not judging, Will."

"Ah, Theo" Will said. "Are you tough enough for this game?"

He gave me a sad smile then and said, "Well, it's your story," and raised his glass to me and drank it down. It ran, as planned, in Sunday morning's paper.

Early the next day, a cold, raw Monday morning, blustery and spitting snow, Emma, accompanied by her attorney, presented herself for arrest.

Waiting for her on the Courthouse steps were Sheriff Woodrow Oliver Peavler and her uncle, Judge Ira Hockensmith. She was told she was the principal suspect in the murder of Adeline Hockensmith and was released on her own recognizance. Whereupon they all returned to her home and had coffee and cinnamon rolls before most of the town was awake.

It was all very calm and dignified. No crowd, no photographs, no press. A non-event. I learned this from her attorney, James Hanratty. He got me out of bed to tell me. "You'd never forgive me, Theo Clark, if I let you sleep through the biggest story of the year," he laughed when I finally got the phone to my ear.

I didn't know Mr. Hanratty personally. I knew who he was. I knew his reputation. He was considered one of the best defense attorneys in the south, but I had never been in his august presence. I suppose I was supposed to feel both flattered and grateful that he had called me personally and got me on the story early. I suppose I was.

Hanratty was cheerful while we talked and offered to help me through the intricacies of a criminal trial since he knew I had no experience with them.

"We didn't offer a plea. The plea will come at the formal arraignment, which will probably be in late January. We will, of course, plead not guilty."

He paused. Then resumed."I expect that's it. If there is anything I can help you with, call me. I'll do what I can so long as it doesn't jeopardize the case."

I knew he was working me, yet he seemed to mean it.

"I don't want this to sound ungrateful," I said, "but why?"

He considered for a long moment. "My sister's son died at Chosin. Maybe you helped get his body back down that trail."

Despite the hour, I called Dulin. He was already awake. He'd been up since seven-thirty when the janitor at the Courthouse called him.

"The sight of Sheriff Peavler and Judge Hockensmith standing on the steps at daylight in the bitter cold struck the janitor as a little unusual," Dulin said. "So she's got Hanratty? That's about as much insurance as you can buy in a case like this."

James Hanratty had orchestrated successful defenses in four murders that had seemed open and shut cases—one a father accused of butchering his four children and long suffering wife and burning their house down around them, caught watching the fire with his shoes drenched in kerosene; one the rape and strangling of an eleven-year-old girl whose Girl Scout pin was found in the pocket of his client; one a straight away shooting with two eye witnesses; and one a cuckolded husband standing over the bed where his wife and her paramour of the week lay shredded by a twelve gauge shotgun still in his hands.

Hanratty had saved a governor from impeachment and a well known executive from a divorce settlement that would have bankrupted him.

Dulin went silent for a moment. I could picture him sitting at his kitchen table watching the blustery morning ease in, sipping his coffee and thinking.

I waited.

"You haven't talked with Will yet? Too early. Catch up with him sometime this afternoon and fill him in. I'll see the two of you at King's around six."

But Will Owens was nowhere to be found.

He hadn't been in King's. He hadn't been to the press room at the Capitol or to the *Journal*. He wasn't at home. No one had seen him or heard from him the live-long day.

I was alone when Dulin walked into King's that night.

"Gideon hasn't seen him?" Dulin asked.

"I can't find Gideon either," I said.

We were standing at the bar, two men I didn't know talking down at the far end and a couple of regulars, nodding to us.

"Find us a table," Dulin said.

I had my choice. The only people in the room were the four guys at the bar, the bartender, and us. A small table in the far corner, a decent remove from the others, looked like it would give us some privacy. I dropped a dime in the juke box to get a little life into the room, ordered a cup of coffee (black, no sugar, no milk, just hot caffeine—too much uncertainty all around to give away any edge to alcohol) and waited.

Dulin wasn't gone long. When he returned he sat down heavily. He still had on his topcoat, wet from the steady fall of sleet coming down outside. He sat there, shaking his head as a man does who doesn't believe what he's heard or doesn't want to believe it. He ran his hand over his eyes, glanced slowly around the room, settled finally on me.

"Are there any demons chasing you, boy? Any banshees wailing in your ear?"

The question surprised me. I know about demons—and banshees in the night. They congregated on the ridges above the road back from Chosin. In the beginning I thought it was the Chinese playing mind games—pale white figures slithering menacingly over the snow, ungodly moans pulsing through the frozen air. But now and again I saw blood-red eyes in alabaster faces, heard wailing that froze me in place. Oh, there are demons and banshees. I know it. Thank God they'd stayed behind—all that horror and suffering to delight them. But sometimes I think I see a shape slinking down an alley or catch a keen in the winds of a midnight storm. Not often, but often enough to make me shiver still.

I didn't tell Dulin any of this. What purpose could it serve? I just watched his eyes. He'd seemed angry when he sat down. Some other emotion was working him now— sadness, regret—something that softened him.

He sat staring at his hands. Then his mood changed again.

"Aw, dammit. Dammit to hell. Will's in Lexington. At St. Joseph's Hospital. Gideon is with him. You stay here. Gideon will bring him back when he's ready."

"A hospital? He's okay?"

Dulin didn't answer.

"What happened?"

Dulin stood up, looked down at me sitting there, shook his head again.

"Ask Doctor Rail."

TWENTY TWO

And that's how I found out about Will Owens—bane of the bad guys, champion of the little man, poet and scholar and bravest of the brave, true friend and seeker after truth.

But not about his demons. Doc Rail didn't know the demons.

The night had run up to midnight before I got to him. He was still in his office, the only lights on in that block of Second Street just across the New Bridge.

The sleet had stopped, but the streets were sloppy, and the puddles dotting the pavement were beginning to ice over.

I walked it.

A long walk, bordering on dumb in that kind of weather, all the way up Main to the New Bridge, across it, then two blocks down Second to his office on the corner of Shelby. My shoes were wet, and my feet were freezing. I had on my old Burberry, buttoned up and belted, with the collar up around my ears. This kept my body warm enough, but my ears were tingling and my nose running.

I think I wanted the discomfort. It helped focus me. I was on my way to find out about a man on a pedestal with demons on his back. I wanted to be clear-headed for that. I wanted any saccharine ideas about crusading journalists and God's righteous men to be stripped from my mind. I wanted to be able to listen dispassionately. But Lord, this was Will Owens we were talking about.

Doc Rail had left his office door open for me. He worked from an old one-storey house in what was still a residential area, though a new hotel had appeared a couple of blocks down, and one of the big-chain grocery stores was being built nearby.

The office looked like a house. A big front porch overlooked Second Street, and patients sometimes sat in rockers there when the weather was right, watching the passers-by and waiting for their appointed time—a friendly, comfortable place. Its interior had been converted into a large waiting room in front with examining rooms down both sides of the hallway that led to Doc Rail's office in the back, overlooking the river.

He was there waiting for me.

The room was warm and bright. There was a small fireplace on a side wall. As used to be the custom, he had a small iron grate in it and was burning coal which gave off a soft blue flame.

The Doc had on an old black cardigan against the drafts sneaking in from the windows in the back and a sad smile.

"Get out of that wet coat right away and get over there in front of the grate and get warm," he said.

I was happy to comply, shucked my coat and put myself in front of the fireplace, letting the warmth from the coal fire envelop me.

I didn't know how to begin, what questions to ask, what words to use.

Doc Rail understood and began for me.

"He's killing himself, Theo. It's as simple and as complicated as that. He knows it. There's a chance he can change the outcome. Not a big chance, but a chance. He knows that too, but he won't do it."

I shook my head, not comprehending.

"Sit down." He pointed to a chair by the side of his desk.

"He's okay for the moment. The police found him unconscious lying in the alley behind the *Journal* just after daylight this morning. They thought he was drunk and had passed out. No telling how long he'd been lying there. He probably was leaving after the paper had been put to bed. So it could have been hours. He was on the verge of hypothermia. The police took him to the emergency room at the hospital here. He was conscious by the time they got there. He insisted they call me."

I was still confused. "I don't understand," I said. 'He's killing himself by exposure to the cold?"

"No. No," Doc Rail said. "It's the drinking. It's killing him. His plumbing is shot. He can't get the poisons out of his body. That's why he's in Lexington. St. Joe's has a dialysis machine. If we hadn't gotten him to it when we did, he'd be dead now. He either gives up drinking or he dies. Soon. But he won't. He's determined that he's going to live his life the way he wants to live it, and if he wants to drink then by damn he'll drink and to hell with the consequences."

"That's crazy, Doc."

"Of course it is. He doesn't doubt what I'm telling him. It just doesn't matter."

"That's even crazier."

"We diagnosed this problem over a year ago. I told him what he needed to do. He gave me that big smile of his. 'Not to worry,' he said."

Doc Rail looked almost helpless. A small man in a drafty room in the middle of the night, lamenting for a friend.

"This is the second time we've had to rush him to Lexington this year. You've seen how weak he is. How tired he gets. And how angry. He's outraged that something like this is happening to him. It's not addiction. I don't think he has the physical need most alcoholics have. I think he could walk away from drink as easily as crossing the street. It's something else. Something almost like a compulsion."

"Demons," I said.

"What," he looked at me as if I'd startled him. "Demons?"

"I was just thinking of something Dulin said."

He kept his eyes fixed on me, questioning. "Demons?" A long, thinking pause.

"Demons?" Another long pause, "If we don't find out soon and do something about it, we'll lose him."

The walk back to my place was starless and grim. The night seemed colder, though it may not have been. My shoes were still wet, and my spirits much lower even than when I'd started. I didn't repeat my steps but stayed straight down Second to the Old Bridge. The river was black as I crossed, the sky a dirty blanket of roiling clouds. Even the lights of the Arsenal up on the hill seemed dimmed. I didn't pause. I didn't linger. There were demons abroad and banshees wailing. I wanted a warm bed and covers up over my head.

I tried to sleep and probably did a bit, but images kept filtering through my mind. The one that woke me was the road back from Chosin. It was night, too cold to be snowing, and still—so still the crunch of the snow could be heard when you sat a boot down. The four of us were climbing a ridge, the only sounds our labored breathing and the crackle of snow underfoot. There was a soft thud. I looked up and saw the grenade. It appeared from nowhere and slithered toward us. I saw it as clearly as I saw Sammy Hern's back ten paces ahead of me.

When I came to, Jimmy Jensen lay to my right, half his head blown away. Sammy and Mike Goins were flung down the hill below me, sprawled in a Rorschach of red on the glistening snow. I lay there dazed. There was no sound at all. And I was warm.

I didn't know whether I'd been hit or not. I didn't care. It was pleasant where I lay. I felt like I could go to sleep and sleep warm and snug. Then someone was kicking my boot and shouting.

"Get your ass up, Private."

I pulled myself back from the edge of unconsciousness. Sgt. Zelskey stood over me, darting glances around the landscape, M1 ready to be brought up to firing position instantly.

"Get up. You're not finished."

I wanted him to go away. I didn't want to think about where I was or what had happened or what was likely to happen. I just wanted to sleep. A kick again and the gruff voice again.

"Suck it up Marine. We've got things to do. On your feet."

The image of the boy on his knees with coach standing over him yelling filled my head. "You gotta suck it up and go! Suck it up!" Sgt. Zelskey stared down at me. Damn if I was going to lay there. Hell yes, I can suck it up. I struggled to my feet.

It was a little after four. The four a.m. willies often got me. I'd wake then, something pushing me awake—some worry, some apprehension. It was no good to try to go back to sleep. All that was to be done was to get up, make coffee, find a book and read until daylight came.

I stuffed Chosin back into that little room in my mind where I try to keep it under lock and key and opened another to hold Will.

Dulin and I didn't speak of it at first. He only nodded when I walked into the newsroom that day, and I said nothing. It was as if it might go away if we didn't talk about it. But of course it wouldn't and of course we did.

Dulin broke the spell. The paper had been put to bed, the press was running, and we were the only two left in the newsroom.

"Well," he said.

"Well," I repeated.

"He's not going to stop. He'll keep it up until he kills himself."

"It makes no sense, Dulin."

"You'll have to carry the load by yourself. He'll keep getting weaker. He'll want to be part of it, but he won't be able."

"Haven't you talked with him? Can't you make him see?"

"At the rate he's going, Doc says maybe the machine will help him one more time. If they get him to it fast enough. Or maybe it won't. Maybe he'll hold on long enough to finish out this story with you. Probably not."

"Can't anything be done? Isn't there some hospital he can go to, some special place?"

"He's not going to any hospital."

There was such finality in Dulin's voice, I knew it must be true.

"But why, for God's sake? Why?"

Dulin only shook his head and looked away.

I should have been shaken at the prospect of having to go the rest of the way on my own. So much was riding on how well I handled this. But I wasn't. The short time I'd had with Will guiding me and Dulin making adjustments had given me more confidence than I realized. No, what shook me was the difficulty of accepting that a man as smart and accomplished as Will Owens would knowingly, willingly, do to himself what he was doing. And that no pleas from his friends could deter him. Maybe there were demons abroad that would find me?

TWENTY THREE

Emma had turned herself in Monday morning. Earlier in the morning of that same day, Will had been found unconscious and subsequently rushed to Lexington for dialysis treatment. The next day, Tuesday, the fifty-sixth day since the murder of Adeline Hockensmith Purcell, Sheriff Woodrow Stanley Peale threw his monkey-wrench into the proceedings.

He'd found the man I'd encountered on the creek near the Hockensmith place the day of the murder. He now had, he said, new evidence that pointed to the Gypsy, Arlo Lee. Lee and his kumpania were thought to be in South Carolina. He'd alerted the South Carolina authorities and asked that they find, arrest, and return Arlo Lee. Extradition papers had already been filed.

It turned out they were unnecessary. Arlo Lee presented himself to Sheriff Peale on Thursday. He'd heard of the charge, made the long drive to the Capital City and put himself in the Sheriff's custody voluntarily. This presented an awkward situation for the Commonwealth's Attorney. As the prosecuting authority, his office had the responsibility for charging and prosecuting capital offenders. In the case of the murder of Adeline Hockensmith Purcell, he already had a suspect under arrest. Now he was faced with the prospect of adding another. Could two people be charged with the same murder?

Whatever Sheriff Woodrow Stanley Peale had in mind, he had not endeared himself to the Commonwealth's Attorney. I called Hanratty as soon as I heard about Arlo. Hanratty had offered to steer me through the legal mazes. This had to qualify as one hands down. Hanratty's answer was no. Unless the two suspects acted simultaneously—pulled the trigger at the same time, plunged the knife together – that sort of thing – two people can't be charged with the same murder.

"What's the Sheriff up to, then? Just grandstanding?" I asked.

Hanratty laughed. "Not likely. Woodrow's too smart for that."

"What then?"

"I have no idea, but however this plays out, having a second "suspect" in the case is a big advantage for Emma's defense. It raises a reasonable doubt. The prosecution has to prove guilt "beyond a reasonable doubt." With a second suspect on the books, I can make the reasonable doubt case much more effectively. Depending on what the Sheriff has, I might even be able to get the case against Emma dismissed."

"You didn't know anything about this?"

"Of course not."

"Why would the Sheriff keep his teeth in this? He's embarrassed the Commonwealth's Attorney. He's risking his connections with the county political crowd. What can there be in it for him?"

"Well," said Hanratty, "maybe Woodrow thinks Emma is innocent and can't bear to see an injustice done. Or maybe he's put together some sort of deal with Judge Hockensmith or Emma that's made running the risk of disjointing the Commonwealth's Attorney and looking like an idiot worthwhile. I don't know. But I do know that Woodrow Stanley Peale doesn't do something for nothing."

We left it at that.

I found Arlo in a cell in the County Jail behind the Courthouse. Unlike Emma Kane, even though he had voluntarily turned himself in, Arlo was a Gypsy and by definition, a flight risk. Only the hospitality of the County would do for him. He looked tired. He'd been on the road over twelve hours, was unwashed, unshaven, and hungry but somehow managed to project a composure I didn't expect. The cell was Spartan, but clean enough, and the food would be sufficient once supper time came. I wasn't concerned for his physical well-being. Given the attention his arrest would generate, Sheriff Woodrow Stanley Peale would see to it that Arlo was well taken care of. But I couldn't imagine why Arlo would voluntarily put himself in the lion's den again.

It turned out he didn't want the location of the kumpania revealed. A police search would have focused attention on them and in the end revealed the location of their camp. They were getting by without problems. He wanted that to continue.

"What does the Sheriff have that trumps your alibi?"

Arlo didn't answer.

"You told me everything? You didn't lie to me about anything?" He had a habit of looking off over your shoulder before answering questions he didn't like. I waited. He finally turned his head to look me straight in the eyes.

"Everything I told you was true."

"But did you tell me all of it?"

He hesitated, took his eyes off mine and looked off over my shoulder again.

"I told you I was in the house that morning. I didn't tell the Sheriff."

"Did he ask?"

"Yes."

"You lied to him?"

"He would have whipped me off to jail right then if I had told him I'd been inside the house, and that would have been the end of it."

"How did the Sheriff find out?"

"A witness. The young man who'd been camping on the creek saw me. He told the Sheriff."

"Is there more?"

"The Sheriff didn't find anyone to confirm I'd been in Bardstown at the time I said."

The bad weather was hanging on, the skies like slate; cold rain falling and producing that wet cold that penetrates to the bone. I was tired of it. I wanted sunshine and shirtsleeve days. I wanted star-lit nights and warm breezes blowing—and it wasn't even the middle of January! Suck it up, buddy!

Dulin was up front in the newsroom when I got back to the *Journal*. I shook off my dripping Burberry and hooked it on the coat tree by the front entrance.

He motioned to a chair by his desk.

"Arlo's got a problem. He lied to the Sheriff. "

"About?"

"About being at the scene of the murder. Arlo was in the house that morning."

"We knew that, didn't we?"

"Yes. That's where Mrs. Purcell told him about her decision to change her will. He told us about that."

"But when the Sheriff questioned him?"

"Arlo lied."

"He owned up to that?"

"No. The Sheriff finally came up with the Korean vet I ran into on the creek shortly after the murder. He's the eye witness."

"Damn," Dulin said, "The Gypsy should have been smarter."

"Worse, Arlo says the Sheriff didn't find anyone to corroborate his story about being in Bardstown at the time of the murder."

Dulin mulled over that a moment, then said, "I wonder how hard Woodrow Stanley Peavler tried? No matter at this point. Your Gypsy's in the soup. Can you find that young Marine again, find out exactly what he told the Sheriff?"

"I can try."

But first I had to check on Will. I'd been stopping by his apartment daily since he came home from the hospital, reassuring myself that he was recovering from the beating his body had taken. It was just a short walk down to his apartment, so I headed out the front entrance and made my way through a mist-like rain to his place on the corner. When I got there, the building was dark. I climbed the outside stairs to the landing and stood there hesitantly. I knew he needed sleep more than he needed to talk with me, but I knew I'd have no comfort until I'd seen him myself and knew he was okay. I knew it was selfish, but I haven't claimed to be saintly. As I debated whether to satisfy my wants or let Will get his rest, I realized how dark it was on the landing and how quiet. No light escaped from any of the windows or from around the doorframe. It was as if the place was deserted.

Then the realization struck me.

No one was there.

Will Owens, Pride of the West, was abroad in the night.

I knew this with sorrowful certainty. And I knew exactly where he would be.

And that's exactly where I found him. At his usual spot. A drink on the bar in front of him. Looking amused as he listened to something Gideon was saying.

I damn near exploded.

"What the hell are you doing," I yelled, launching myself at him. Gideon was quicker. He put himself between us and grabbed me.

Will looked around, surprised.

"Theo!"

Others were staring at me, too. It was still early. Not many people in the bar. Enough, though, that my outburst caught the attention of the six or eight who were there. Gideon, still holding me immobile, smiled at everyone. "Nothing to get excited about folks. Go back to your drinks."

The room was intentionally dark enough at all times that it was difficult to make out faces at any distance and since nothing seemed about to happen, the assemblage returned to their glasses after exchanging looks of curiosity but not of interest.

Gideon still held on to me, though, not sure I'd cooled down enough to be let go.

"Where's your head, boy," he growled.

I struggled against his hold.

"Let go of me, Gideon."

"Settle down, boy. Settle down."

He had me encircled, my arms pinned to my sides. I'd been in my share of bar fights in the Corps, and I'm not a small man, but I had no chance against his strength. Even my anger couldn't help.

"Look what he's doing! Stop him!"

Will was standing in front of me by then.

"Oh, Theo," Will said, a sad smile on his face. "You've come to save me, haven't you, boy." He turned to Gideon. "Let him go, Gideon. He'll behave himself."

The anger that had been coursing through me like a flood began to dissipate with that. Will looked genuinely pained that he had caused me so much distress that I'd rushed into a public bar and made a scene.

Gideon let go and stepped back. My anger faded into embarrassment. Will saw that. He turned to Gideon, "Let me talk to him privately for a few minutes."

We sat in the far corner of the room, our backs to the walls, at a small round table with a flickering candle casting unobtrusive light too faint to make us recognizable to anyone at a distance. Melancholy music drifted from the juke box. It seemed a little early in the night, but surely someone of the few in the almost empty bar felt it was needed.

It fit my mood well enough.

Will had brought his drink with him. He held it up to eye level for us both to see. The candle's pale light reflected off the amber liquid. He studied it a moment, then said in a soft voice, "I often wonder what the vintner buys one-half so precious as the stuff he sells." After a moment he set the glass down and turned to me. "Do you know the *Rubaiyat*?" My face must have told him I didn't. "You must read it. All seekers after truth should read it."

I studied him. He had not seemed infirm walking to the table. His hands didn't shake, and he sat straight in the chair. Though the light was dim, his eyes seemed clear and his person neat. If I hadn't known the hit he'd taken just four days ago, I would have given no thought at all to his physical condition. In fact I began to wonder if Doctor Rail was right in his assessment that Will was only several steps away from a self-inflicted death.

Will continued, "You need to know and accept something about me, Theo. I live my life the way I want to live it. I won't be intimidated by the doctors or the preachers. The risks I run are of my own choosing. I understand the risk Doctor Rail thinks I'm running. Father O'Reily thinks I'm running a few on his side of the fence too. They are probably right. There are consequences to every action. I understand that. I also understand that the cost of my indulgences may be severe. That makes me very angry and I think it's grossly unfair. My vices are innocent enough. But it makes no difference. I accept the consequences. So don't upset yourself. What I do is of my own choice. I call my own tune and march to my own drummer."

He said this last smiling kindly but with so much determination in his eyes that I knew without any question that what he said was true. He would call his own tune and to hell with the consequences.

There was nothing more to be said.

I stood. "I've got to get back to work." I started to leave, then turned back.

"Will?"

"Yes."

"Demons?"

"Demons?" he replied, puzzled.

"Are there demons in that parade?"

"Ah," he said, "demons." He raised his glass to me. "Here's to demons."

TWENTY FOUR

A week passed. Sheriff Peavler was silent, declining any comment on the case. The Commonwealth's Attorney was likewise circumspect. I visited Arlo in the County Jail a couple of times, principally to keep his morale up and to make sure he wasn't being mis-handled. Emma Purcell's attorney, James Hanratty, also checked in on Arlo. If he got anything to bolster his defense of Emma, he'd hold it until the trial. I met with Will a couple of times, ostensibly to bring him up to date on what I was doing, but really to check on how he was doing. He looked a little paler, a little thinner, but his energy level was high, and he seemed in good spirits.

I spent most of my time searching for my creek Marine. I assumed he'd be fairly easy to find through his connection to the Veteran's Hospital in Lexington and because of his dependence on it, would be somewhere close by. I was right about that but wrong about how easy he would be to find. I finally unearthed him purely by chance—hitchhiking on the Versailles road from Frankfort to Lexington. I was on my way there to make the late round of the likely bars in hopes he'd turn up in one of them when my headlights caught a slight figure limping up the side of the road with a thumb in the air and not looking back. He had on a fatigue cap, a worn field jacket and looked miserable. It was a clear night, but so frigid you feared the cold black sky might shatter.

My man was on a lonely stretch of road flanked by nothing but Bluegrass meadows for miles and miles. Why he was on this road was beyond me. Unless it was a UK game night, the traffic was usually sparse. But there he was, and I recognized him the moment my headlights found him. I pulled off on the shoulder and waited until he caught up.

When he got to the door, I rolled the window down. His face was partally lighted by the lights from the dashboard. He looked dazed, holding on tightly to the window frame and as I had thought, absolutely frozen. Only the residue of booze or drugs could have kept him upright on this hard a night.

"Need a ride, Gyrine," I said as I leaned across to open the door. His head came up at that. He tried to focus. He recognized the friendly tone in my voice, but more important the fraternal word. Only a Marine would call another Marine, "Gyrine." He gathered himself and managed to get his face into a grin. He didn't reply, just pulled the door open and collapsed onto the seat beside me, shivering.

"Bad night to be out," I said.

He just nodded his head and leaned closer to the heater vent. We rode for a while in silence. He sat slumped back in the seat, eyes half closed, while whatever he'd been on was working its way out of his body. As we neared the fork where the road splits to Versailles, he became more alert. He straightened up and turned to me.

"I'm headed to Lexington," I said, answering his unasked question. I could see relief in his face, then recognition. He hadn't really looked at me when he got in the car, just collapsed into that enveloping warmth. Now he did.

"I know you." He struggled with that a moment, then his face opened. "The creek! I know you from the creek!" he said, twisting in the seat to get a better look at me. "I'd been camping. Yes, I remember," he said, obviously pleased that his mind was managing to bring it back intact. "The 1st Marines. Chosin. You're the reporter."

I laughed and nodded. "You got it right. I thought I recognized you there on the side of the road. That's why I pulled over. What are you doing out on a night like this?"

He didn't answer that.

"I'm not being nosey," I said, "just curious. Just making conversation."

He eased up then, and we gradually fell into an easy exchange.

He told me he was staying with a nurse who worked at the Veteran's Administration Hospital where he was still being treated for the wounds taken during the Battle of the Hook. That was in October of 1953, over two years ago. I was on my way home by then. He was with the Seventh Marine Regiment, part of the 1st Marine Division, my division, but had joined too late to make the Chosin donnybrook. I figured him to be a couple of years younger than me, maybe twenty or twenty-one. He was a small kid. He'd probably just barely made the height and weight requirements. Watching him limp up the side of the road in the cold and the rain made me think of the boys like him I'd known that vile winter—small, but tough as hell.

The Hook was the last major battle of the Korean War. It was an awful fight, so much artillery laid on that the hills were almost leveled. He'd caught shrapnel from a mortar round. The blast knocked him unconscious briefly. When he came to, the Chinese were overrunning his squad's position. He struggled up to a knee, got off a round from his carbine, but not before taking a Chinese bayonet in his side. He fell to the ground and lay there bleeding while his squad rallied. A Corpsmen dragged him back to an aide station. The bayonet had caught a kidney; the shrapnel ruined his hip. Navy doctors in Japan put him back together fairly well, but he had a stabbing limp when he walked, and the pain in his gut was still considerable. He was floating in and out of the VA Hospital in Lexington trying to get clear of the drugs and the booze that made his days and nights bearable.

We'd covered all this that afternoon on the creek—my fun and games at Chosin, his on the hillsides above the Samichon Valley. While we drove we talked about our time in the Corps. Laughed at the good times. Let our pride at having been a part of it warm us and our anger at the senseless and waste of that war get voice.

I didn't bring up the murder or the Gypsies. Neither seemed to have any hold on his memory. So I let our conversation flow as it would and enjoyed it. When we got to the place he was staying, it was close to midnight. Lights were on in the second floor windows of a small apartment on Limestone not far from the University.

"Come on in," he urged, "have some coffee. You've got time, haven't you?" We'd been having a good time talking in the car, and he didn't seem to want to let it end.

"Your roommate?" I asked.

"She won't mind. She'll be up. She worries about me. Come on in."

Lucy Chesney didn't mind. Rather, she was relieved that he was back and seemed pleased that he'd found someone lucid and sober to bring him home. Lucy Chesney was about thirty, substantially built, dark hair to her shoulders, green eyes, large, strong hands, and a knowing smile. It seemed she had more or less taken him home with her and had set herself to keep him out of trouble and to administer what he needed, medically or physically. I imagined she was the kind of nurse you'd want on your side if demons were howling at your door.

Lucy made coffee; we talked a bit; she and Josh (Josh was his name—he wouldn't tell me it on the creek but had volunteered it tonight) sitting on her

Ron Rhody

small couch; she snuggled in closely to his side; all of us warm and cozy in the softly lighted room and then, facing an early shift at the hospital, she excused herself and left Josh and me to finish off the night.

I'd put off my agenda long enough.

"That day we met on the creek. You remember?"

"I remember," Josh said.

"It was a couple of days after the murder of Mrs. Purcell."

"She let me camp on the creek. She was a nice lady."

"I was working on a story about it. You told me you'd seen a man coming out of the front door of the Purcell house. You didn't remember exactly what he looked like, and you weren't exactly sure which day it was, but you thought it might have been the day she was killed."

"I did?"

"Sheriff Peavler asked you about that man recently, didn't he?"

"Yes."

"What did you tell him?"

Josh fidgeted, started to stand, then sat back down and regarded me with a look of embarrassment on this face.

"I must have been confused when we talked that day. I sometimes get confused, but I'm getting better. The man was the Gypsy. His name's Arlo. I know him. From camping on the creek near where they stay. I've had meals with them. Sat around the campfire with them. I know Arlo."

What he'd seen, he told me, was Arlo leaving the Purcell house, walking down the path to a car and then driving off. He was wearing a black raincoat and a beret. I knew Arlo sometimes wore berets because I'd seen one on him. Josh was fairly sure it was the day Mrs. Purcell had been murdered. He didn't know what time of day that was. He didn't wear a watch. But it was sometime around mid-morning. Josh himself was on his way back to his camp. Mrs. Purcell had seen him walking in the misty rain and called to him to come inside and have coffee with her. She sometimes did that, he said. She'd given him permission to camp on her property a year or so ago when her foreman discovered his camp on the creek and was set to run him off. She let him stay and on occasion, when out riding, would come upon him camping and stop to talk a bit. They had become friendly. Josh seemed to have a talent for awakening protective feelings in older women.

"You told all this to Sheriff Peavler?"

"Yes. Shouldn't I have?"

"It's alright, Josh. Did you see anyone else, notice anyone else that morning?"

Josh shook his head again. "I don't know. I was on my way back to my camp. It had begun to rain It was hard to see. There was another car. It came down the lane after the Gypsy's car left. I didn't see who was in it. I was cold."

Another car? A traffic cop must have been needed on the Hockensmith lane that morning. Daughter Emma dropped the baby off with the victim and then headed out. One car. Then Arlo arrived and left. Two cars. Then this third car.

"Did you tell the Sheriff about this car, too."

Josh looked confused. "I don't remember," he said.

If Arlo was to be believed, Adeline Purcell Hockensmith was alive when he left her around ten-thirty or eleven that morning. Another car had arrived after that. Was she alive then? Whose car was it?

Josh watched me anxiously as I ran all this through my mind. "Have I made a problem for you," he said. "Did I do something I shouldn't have?"

I managed to pull off a laugh. "No. No problem. You did exactly what you should have done." I glanced down at my watch. "One-thirty," I said, looking up at him, still smiling, "I better get on the road. Thanks for the coffee and the conversation."

"No. Thank you," Josh said. "Thanks for the ride. I'll see you again?"

"I imagine," I said at the door.

I had to unload all this on somebody. My first thought was Will, but I still hadn't come up with a way I could accept what he was doing to himself and felt uncomfortable trying to fake it. Dulin, I thought. He'd still be at the *Journal* waiting for the first copy of this morning's paper to come off the press. I pulled up to a pay phone at the first filling station I came to and called him. "Wait for me," I said, "I need to talk with you."

The newsroom was funereally still when I got there. The place was deserted except for Dulin. No phones were ringing; no typewriters clacking. The AP and UPI teletypes were still running though. Dulin wouldn't shut them down until he left. A major story might break. If one did, if the Second Coming occurred or World War III broke out, I had no doubt he'd stop the presses single handed, tear out the front page, write whatever needed to be written, and get a new edition on the street in time for everyone to have the big news before they knew they needed it, and he'd have one helluva grand time doing it.

"I hope you've got something more exciting for me than the garbage coming across the wires tonight."

"How about another car came to the house after Arlo left."

Dulin dropped the spooled wire copy in his hand, turned and eyed me with no expression on his face, then walked the few steps to his desk and sat down. He stretched his arms up to the ceiling, brought them down, put them behind his head, leaned back, and said, "Well, well, well—a complication," smiling as broad a smile as I've seen him mount.

He rubbed his hands together, motioned me to the chair beside his desk. "Tell me all of it."

He listened intently, asked only a few questions.

He was smiling, almost straining at the bit to get his arms around this when I finished.

"Find Will," he told me. "We're going to unravel this thing."

"It's almost four o'clock in the morning," I protested.

"Try his place. No, try King's first. Breakfast is on me if he isn't there."

King's bar at four o'clock on a Saturday morning still pours generous, and the place is still hospitable and agreeable, but no one's there except the few regulars who give it its character and the several drop-ins who need a shot before facing their daily chores.

But there he was, just as Dulin thought he would be, down near the end of the bar talking with Skeeter Mullins and Gideon. Skeeter was a stringer for a couple of Cincinnati papers, and he and Will were long time cronies.

Will saw me come in and waved me down.

"You know Skeeter?" he said. "Helluva reporter. We covered the Big Fish Binge together. He's the guy who figured out what was happening." They laughed at that, and Skeeter poked Will playfully. "You'd have thought of it," he said.

On the other side of the bar, Gideon was laughing too.

"You don't know the story, "Will said. "You may have been away when it happened. Anyway, one afternoon we start getting calls from people all up and down that river that the fish are acting strange … running in circles on the surface, jumping out on the bank. Like they're crazy. A few enterprising souls, seeing some nice size catfish and bass flopping around on the surface figure they can catch them in landing nets, so they jump in their boats and pretty soon are bringing in loads of fish. No one can figure out what's causing it until Skeeter walks down to the river's edge and cups up a handful of water. He drinks it, gives me a big grin and says, "They're drunk!"

"What," I said. "How can that be?"

Skeeter pointed to the river, cupped his hand again, drank it down, smiled and said, "Take a sip."

"I did and damned if it didn't go down like a stiff bourbon and water. The river was full of whiskey! The fish were drunk. Pretty soon we had more people chugging down dippers of river water than chasing fish with nets. It was a very happy afternoon." The three of them burst into laughter again.

The incredulous look on my face got him.

"I'm not making this up," he said. "What happened was that the big distillery just upstream near Lawrenceburg caught fire that morning. All the warehouses collapsed and barrels full of hundred-proof bourbon burst and flowed into the river. All the warehouses. All the bourbon. As that massive shot of whiskey worked its way down the river, it depleted the oxygen in the water. The fish couldn't breathe and they rushed to the surface where they were easy pickings. We called it 'The Big Fish Binge.' Skeeter and me were the only guys with the story. All the papers ate it up." He laughed again and slapped Skeeter on the shoulder. "Now that's reporting, Buddy."

"I'll drink to that," Skeeter said and hoisted his glass.

"Not alone," said Will and, still laughing, raised his too.

Gideon only shook his head at me with a warning smile.

The drummer was drumming, I guessed.

Finally Will turned to me. "What are you doing here at this hour? Shouldn't you be on your way home to bed?"

"Dulin wants us. New fodder for the mystery mill."

We met Dulin for breakfast at a back table at Red Yancey's place a couple of blocks down from the *Journal*; the sun still not up yet and the day ahead uncertain.

"Okay," Dulin said, "let's review the lineup." I nodded and started. "Emma. The daughter. She's the Commonwealth Attorney's choice. Arlo the Gypsy. He gets the Sheriff's vote. In third place is whoever was in the car driving down the lane to the house after Arlo left."

Dulin looked to Will. "The circumstantial evidence points to Emma," Will said. I can't see Arlo doing it. He had nothing to gain. Why would he kill her before the will was signed?"

"So?" Dulin said.

"Emma, probably. Arlo, no."

"The mystery car?"

"I'd like to know who was in it. And what its business at the house was."

"Find out."

The odds of that happening ranged from zero to almost none, I told Dulin. There were no houses along the lane leading to the Hockensmith place, so there were no watchers peering out windows. The rain had kept workers out of the fields that bordered the lane that day, so there were no people around to see anything if anything was to be seen. Only Josh, my wounded Marine, had seen something and whether he was seeing clearly or through a haze of alcohol or drugs wasn't known.

"I thought he hadn't seen who was in the mystery car," Will said.

"That's what he said."

"So?"

"So maybe he didn't want to talk about it. Maybe he didn't want to be involved. Or maybe his memory has improved and he might remember a little more clearly if asked again by the right person in the right way."

"He trusts you?"

"I think so."

"Can you find him again?"

"Can I finish my coffee first?" I said.

Dulin pulled out his wallet and paid for breakfast anyway. We stepped out into a morning clear and sparkling.

TWENTY FIVE

I wasn't sure I could find Josh, but I was sure I could find Lucy Chesney, the nurse. If the hospital wouldn't give me her number, Andy Thomas, my friend at the *Herald* had the kind of local contacts that would produce it. The hospital wouldn't. Andy did. He was curious about why I wanted it. I was vague with my answer. He wasn't happy, but accepted it. "You owe me," was all he said when he called back with the number late that afternoon.

I decided to wait until the next morning. Better odds of catching Josh on a Sunday morning than on a Saturday night. He lived there. Or he did the last time we talked. But with Josh nothing was certain.

The phone rang, and rang, and rang. Just as I started to hang up, the receiver was lifted and a sleepy male voice said "Yeah?"

"Josh?"

"Who is this?"

"Josh. It's me. Theo Clark."

There was a long pause. I could almost hear his mind clearing as he came awake.

"Theo of the 1st Marines?"

"The very same," I said, putting a laugh in my voice, wanting to get this started in a friendly way and not spook him.

"What time is it?

"Time you were up. It's a beautiful day."

"It's too early to be cheerful. What do you want?"

"To talk."

There was a long pause. I could hear shuffling in the background.

"What's going on?" I said into the silence.

After a moment Josh said, "I'm making coffee." There was more shuffling, then the sound of a chair being pulled out. I waited.

"You want to talk some more about that day at the farm, don't you? I thought you might. I don't want to talk about it."

" I need your help, Josh. You wouldn't leave a buddy hanging, would you? You wouldn't. I know you wouldn't. I have to get this right. You're the only one who can help me. I can count on you, can't I Josh? You wouldn't leave me hanging, Josh.

This was the worst kind of manipulation, playing on his loyalty and his pride, not knowing what state he was in, whether he was coming off a high or in the grip of the drugs he was taking for his pain. I should have been ashamed. In the silence I could hear him breathing, then moving and a radio click on. A DJ's voice I recognized came up in the background and then Rosemary Clooney started in on Mambo Italiano. "I like music in the morning," he said to me, coming back on the phone. "I don't like the silence." We listened for a bar or two, then he said, "Okay."

Josh Logan was a country boy, bred and born on a hill farm near Jamestown, just north of the Tennessee border and not far from Cumberland Gap. His folks came through it from western Virginia not long after Daniel Boone had opened the door to Kentucky during the Revolutionary War. They dropped off in Russell County and had been there ever since. He was, as most country boys are, polite, respectful of authority, modest and shy, and loyal to a fault—when he was sober. I'd never seen him drunk or mad, but I imagined he could be a terror. Country boys can be when they're in that state.

Josh was in Korea because that was what the men in his family did. When the war drums beat, they came. They had fought in every American from the War of 1812 forward. Josh volunteered for the Marines because he thought it was the elite of the American fighting forces. He'd gone in straight out of high school and was barely nineteen when he was wounded. Recovery had been slow and agonizing. The drugs that dulled the pain almost did what the bayonet and the mortar didn't. He became addicted. Now he was fighting to get rid of that demon. He was fragile and hurting and a long way from home and only had Lucy Chesney for support. He had drinking buddies and druggie buddies as long as the monthly government checks lasted, but no one he could count on except Lucy, and no one who understood. I think he had thought, I think he hoped, that I would be that friend he needed, like the kind of friends he'd had in the Corps, who'd risk their lives for you, who wouldn't leave you lying bleeding in the mud, who wouldn't leave you behind.

Which is why, though he didn't want to talk about it, he was going to.

We sat in Lucy Chesney's kitchen that sunny Sunday morning with the radio playing in the background and Lucy, still in her nurses uniform, leaning against the kitchen counter, drinking from the second pot of coffee Josh had made. She had been on the night shift at the VA hospital and arrived at about the same time I did.

Josh was in better shape than when I saw him last. He was focused. He was lucid and articulate. He seemed physically stronger and much more in charge of himself. I didn't know whether this was the result of Lucy's ministrations or the treatments he was getting at the VA, or both. Whatever the cause, the result was good, and I hoped he could find the discipline and the determination to stay with it.

I took real pains to put Josh fully in the picture. I explained everything we knew. I wanted him to understand the situation and why we needed to know all we could about the morning and the day of the murder. I was also very clear that I had a personal stake in the outcome, that handling the Ashes Murder story well could be my ticket to New York. That muffing it would, without doubt, be my ticket to nowhere.

"Why don't you let the Sheriff do all this? It's his job," Josh asked.

I hesitated in answering. I had to make my answer make sense to him.

"I think the Sheriff has already decided who's guility, or decided who he wants to be guilty and is trying to build a case to support his view."

"He wants the Gypsy to be guilty?"

"I think so."

But you don't think the Gypsy did it?"

"I can't figure out any reason why he would have."

Josh considered that, then said, "I can't figure out why anyone would have killed her in the first place."

"You saw another car come down the lane and stop in front of the house after the Gypsy left, but you said you didn't see who was in it, remember?"

Josh nodded.

"The killer could have been in that car."

Slowly Josh said, "I suppose."

"Try to picture that again, Josh. Think about it again. Look again with your mind's eye. Can you see the same picture now? You might not have been seeing things all that clearly that morning. Can you see it any more clearly?"

He stared at me. Then at Lucy. Then got up and walked to the window and looked out.

I looked to Lucy questioningly. She shook her head as if to say stay quiet. Let him think.

Finally Josh turned, walked back to the table and sat down. He picked up his cup, took a sip, then looked up at me.

"It's clearer. When I think about it now, I had seen the car before. I think it belongs to her brother, the Judge."

"The car you saw coming up the lane after Arlo's car had left belongs to Mrs. Purcell's brother, to Judge Hockensmith!"

"I think so."

"Could you see who was in it?"

"Not real clear. There was a misty rain and I was some ways away. The car came up the lane, pulled up in front of the house and parked."

He stood up again and walked to the counter to stand by Lucy.

"That's it, Theo. I hope I've helped you but I won't be part of any trial. I've told you what I've told you as a friend. I'm through with this."

Lucy put her arm around his shoulder and kissed him on the cheek. I almost did, too.

TWENTY SIX

Churches were just letting out when I made it back to town. Everyone was enjoying the sun and the warmth. This January had been as cold and dreary as any I could remember and the first good day in what seemed like ages had people who lived in walking distance of the churches leaving their cars at home. The Baptists of the First Baptist and the Catholics of Good Shepard, their churches almost across the street from each other, dispersed laughing and talking across the Old Bridge and along St. Clair. Two blocks down and around the corner, the bells of the Episcopal Church were pealing. I drove slowly, looking for faces I knew, catching splashes of color in the scarves of the women in the otherwise flow of somber winter coats. People seemed happy and relaxed. We all craved spring and gave even the slightest hint of it our fullest gratitude.

Allie would have been in the Baptist multitude if I had been by at the right moment. She was the one I was looking for. Allie and her mother seldom missed Sunday mornings at the church by the bridge. When I was a boy, my mother and I never missed. I was baptized there. I sang in the choir there. Lord, I thought, to sit in that big high-ceilinged room again surrounded by the men in their suits and the women in their Sunday best, with sun streaming through the stained glass windows and the preacher in the pulpit and the choir in its wine-colored robes with hymnals in their hands, leading us in the songs we all knew by heart—no demon could hang on there.

Dulin was already at his desk in the newsroom. We were to meet Will for lunch at Mucci's.

"Anything?" he asked me as I walked in.

I nodded.

"Hold it then. No need to tell it twice. Let's see if Will got us a table."

We stepped outside into the sunshine and walked the block up to Mucci's without conversation. At the corner, while we waited for the stoplight, Dulin looked up at the sky—that clear, cloudless indigo blue sky that only the Bluegrass can conjure in the winter and said, "My God, this is what winter is supposed to be like. You'll not find anything like this in New York, boy. You remember that."

Will had us a back table away from the door and the counter. The restaurant, an almost traditional destination for the after-church flock, was packed. Dulin shook hands and patted shoulders as we made our way back to Will.

"Our young paragon has news," Dulin said. We took our seats and opened our menus. Will smiled up at me. He nodded to the cup at his hand. "Coffee," he said. "Black. Nothing in it. Tastes awful." He grimaced. I couldn't help laughing.

We ordered, and I began to recount my sessions with Josh Logan— how I found him and what he told me.

Dulin was silent when I finished. Will looked at me quizzically. The drone of table talk hummed in the background punctuated by the clink of cutlery and the tinkle of tableware.

I waited. Finally Dulin spoke. "We've got everything and we've got nothing."

"What?" I said, surprised.

"We have someone who saw Judge Hockensmith's car approaching the Purcell place. It's practically certain the driver was the Judge. If there was a woman in the car with him, the odds are the woman was Emma. They would have been the last people at the house. They were there at a time consistent with the time the murder was committed. Which would lead to the reasonable assumption that one or both of them killed her. Pretty picture, isn't it? The victim's brother and the victim's daughter? Makes a very strong circumstantial case."

"Then why do you say we have nothing?"

"There is no way to get any of it in play. If Josh Logan refuses to talk, we don't have anything. No basis for questioning the Judge. No basis for investigating his movements that morning. All we have is a suspicion we can't back up."

"What about the Gypsy? Arlo must have passed the Judge's car coming in on his way out?"

"Probably. But what good is the word of someone himself accused of the crime? Who would believe him?

Will broke in. "Are you sure Josh won't tell what he knows? If he understands that his friend's killer might go free? If you play that loyalty card again?"

I looked at him in disbelief. Finally I said, "He wouldn't. And I won't"

"You won't what?"

"Play what you call 'the loyalty card' again."

Will shook his head, smiling dismissively. "Theo, you've got to toughen up."

I felt the anger rising. "Josh is done with it, Will. He's trying to make his way back, and he's hanging on by a thread. The pressure would push him back over the edge. No, I won't pressure him again."

"If the court knew he was a witness, it could force him to testify—or go to jail for contempt of court."

"He'd go to jail, Will. Now leave it alone."

Dulin broke in.

"Take it easy. Nothing's gained by fighting among ourselves. "

I didn't realize until then how close Will and I had been to the edge. We were both leaning across the table into each other's faces. Will looked at Dulin, then forced out a laugh. "You're right. Nothing to be gained." He sat back in his chair.

I let go of my anger and sat back, too, wondering if Will really would drive a contact over the edge to get the result he wanted. I wondered if Dulin would. I wondered if, in time, I would.

"So where do we go from here?" Dulin asked.

TWENTY SEVEN

Nowhere seemed to be the answer. We left that lunch frustrated, disappointed, and for Will and me at least, with a sense of a lingering anger.

Later that night, after I'd turned in my copy and the paper had gone to bed, I sat at my desk reading through the page proofs for the morning's edition. Rule # 1 in the Dulin Monroe Rule Book—it seemed everyone who was my senior in the game had a Rule Book—was "Read your own newspaper thoroughly ever day to determine what stories are to be followed up or investigated." I figured one day I'd write my own rule book but in the meantime, I'd follow the lead of my elders.

The jewel was hidden on the Communities Page— the page where we ran news from each of the little outlying communities in our circulation area— Bridgeport, Bald Knob, Peaks Mill, Forks of Elkhorn—church socials, bake sales, club meetings, crop conditions, that sort of thing.

The story that caught my attention was about two Forks of Elkhorn teen-agers who were being given a special "Good Samaritan" Award by their church. The boys had rescued a hunter who had slipped crossing Elkhorn Creek near the Hockensmith farm on the opening day of rabbit season. The hunter had fractured his head on a rock, broken an arm, and was lying half in the creek unconscious and in shock. The boys waded in and pulled him out. One built a fire to warm him, and the other ran for help. Their quick thinking and fast action saved the hunter's life.

The bit that sparked me, though, was the comment that the boys themselves had been hunting that day, hunting up the fence-line along the creek behind the Hockensmith farm. The opening day of rabbit season was November fifteenth.

November fifteenth! November fifteenth was the day of Adeline Hockensmith Purcell's murder.

As long shots go, this one would be monumental if it proved out.

I copied the boys' names, looked up their families' phone numbers, and tried to contain my impatience until the morning got old enough that I could call them.

J.B. Goins and Bobby Lee Johnson should not have been on the creek that day. They were supposed to be in school, but they cut class so as not to miss the opening day of rabbit season. They were fifteen, sophomores at Elkhorn High, average students, enthusiastic second-stringers on the basketball team, FFA members and faithful congregants of the Forks of Elkhorn Baptist Church. Both boys lived out in the country. Both their fathers grew up on farms too small to support the family of the second son and had been drawn to jobs in town. They both worked at the distillery now. Good jobs. Good pay. But they couldn't get farming out of their blood, so they had bought little places out in the county where they could still get their hands in the soil and make things grow in their spare time.

They put shotguns in the hands of their boys when they reached the age of ten and taught them how to hunt quail and dove and squirrel in the woods and fields around their places. And rabbit. Cottontail rabbit. Fried rabbit, milk gravy, mashed potatoes and peas, and baking powder biscuits. There ain't no finer eating.

Opening day of rabbit season was a special day in their families. The boys hadn't missed one since they got their first shotguns—little four-ten single shots that were light, safe, and demanded absolute accuracy. J. B. and Bobby Lee knew there'd be consequences for skipping school. They also knew they weren't going to miss opening day.

"Thank the Lord, they didn't," Mrs. Augustus Goins said, smiling proudly at J.B. as we sat talking in the principal's office at Elkhorn High, "else that poor man would have died."

"Not that it's okay to skip school," Gus Goins said, looking sternly at his son. " I don't want him to get the idea that he can ignore rules, but, yeah," he smiled, "I'm kinda proud of him. He knew he'd have to pay for missing class. We talked about it the day before. Used to be around here that opening day was an unofficial holiday. Everybody went hunting." Gus had nostalgia in his voice. "I gave him permission so long as he took the consequences."

And there were consequences. The boys got a week of after school detention-hall and no movie privileges for a month. And, oh yes, hero treatment for the rescue of the unlucky hunter. They thought it a fair trade.

I'd made my calls to both families as early that morning as I could to catch them before the Dads left for work and the boys for school. Neither of the families had made any connection with the boys' hunting trip and the Ashes Murder. No reason they should have. Both the men knew the Hockensmith name, of course. Hardly any farmer in the region would not have. And they had followed the news of the murder closely and recognized my name from the byline.

Then Gus Goins made a further connection. "Was your Dad Bernie Clark? Worked at the distillery? Was the beer-still operator?"

"He was," I said. "Thirty-five years. He was at work when the heart attack got him."

"I'll be damned. I knew him. Liked him. Jim Jammesson knew him, too. Well, I'll be damned," he said.

After that there was no question of whether or not we could talk; the only decision was when and where.

We decided to wait until after school, so the boys wouldn't miss more class time. Gus Goins would take the afternoon off from work. Bobby Lee's Dad couldn't but his mother, Nancy, would be there. So would J.B.'s Mom, Jenny. The Elkhorn High School principal volunteered his office, a large corner room on the first floor of the big brick school building looking out toward the intersection of the Georgetown and Lexington roads. The school was in farmland when it was built but was rapidly being surrounded by sub-divisions as Frankfort expanded.

Folding chairs had been brought in for our meeting and had been arranged around the big old oaken desk the principal ran the school from. I'd never conducted an interview with a batch of spectators looking on. I almost felt like I was on stage, should make opening remarks, tell a joke or two, get the audience relaxed.

The boys seemed nervous, too. They has just come from their final class, Algebra I think it was, had been perplexed enough by that and then had been funneled into the principal's office, a place students almost always entered with apprehension. They were seated side by side on folding chairs in front of the desk, their mothers beside them. They knew what I wanted to talk about. I'd been over all that with their parents. Still, they were nervous and I didn't blame them.

J.B. Goins' mother patted him on the hand, smiled at him, and said "Now don't you be skittish about this. Just answer Mr. Clark's questions as best you can. It'll all be alright."

J.B. looked over at Bobby Lee. They both seemed to relax a bit.

I came out from behind that big desk, walked around it and sat back on a corner, close to them, no big barrier between us.

"That's right, J. B, Bobby Lee. This isn't a test. No right or wrong answers. Just what you remember." I laughed. "I'm as nervous as you are. I've never done an interview before an audience before. Let's just forget they're here and talk."

Jenny Goins laughed too, and so did the others. Everyone's mood lightened.

"So tell me about it," I began. "How did you come to be hunting the Hockensmith place?"

"We've been hunting there for the past three years," J.B. said, looking at his father who nodded okay.

"Mrs. Purcell gave us permission. Bobby Lee and me have been working summers for her, doing odd jobs around the farm and helping get the hay ready for baling and hustling the bales up on the wagons. After the hay has been cut in the fall, that big field is the best rabbit hunting place in the county. It's a fairly level field with great cover for rabbits, but not so thick you can't get a good shot when you kick one up, and he starts for the corners. Bobby Lee and me asked Mrs. Purcell and she gave us permission— just us two. Nobody else. We had it all to ourselves."

"And that morning?"

J.B. looked questioningly to his Dad again.

"It's okay, son. Just tell Mr. Clark what you saw."

J.B. said, "That morning we were working up the fence-line at the edge of the field where it skirts the creek. We'd already kicked up a couple, missed 'em both."

"You could see the house clearly from where you were?"

"Sure. The front of the house looks out on the hay field and down to the creek."

"And you saw a car parked there?

"Yes sir. Judge Hockensmith's car. He'd just come up the driveway and parked in front of the house."

"How did you know it was the Judge's car?"

"We know the car. It's a black Buick. We've both seen it parked in front of the house lots of times."

" He's Mrs. Hockensmith's brother. He was there a lot in the summers," Bobby Lee broke in.

"Did you see the Judge that morning?"

"Sure. We saw him get out of the car and start up the steps to the house."

"That right, J.B.?" I asked.

"Yep. That's right."

"Anybody else?" I asked.

J.B. thought about it. "We didn't stay and watch. We were hunting."

I laughed. "Of course. And then what happened?"

"We kept on up the fence-line to the end of the field, then climbed over and started up the creek."

"That's when we saw Mr. Harper. Lying in the creek. Head bloody," Bobby Lee added.

"And that's when you rescued him and became heroes," I said smiling.

"Well," J.B. shifted in his seat, a little rush of modesty on him, " we did what we could to help him."

"And you did it like true Samaritans," I said. "Way to go, boys. Way to go."

And I had it! I had Judge Hockensmith at the scene of the murder at the time of the murder and two credible witnesses who could identify the car and him.

At that moment I was almost euphoric. I felt like jumping up and down and clapping my hands. Despite that, I managed to show a little control. I thanked the boys, shook hands solemnly with the men, kissed the women on the cheeks and told the principal the *Journal* was beholden to him for his hospitality. I made them all promise not to discuss what we'd talked about with anyone until tomorrow. By then, my story would be in print, and everyone would be talking about it anyway.

I had a clean beat. I can't explain how good a clean beat feels. How physically good it feels. Like being three-sheets in the wind, but not drunk. People don't understand the intense competition among newspapermen to beat the other guy to the news, the drive to show how good you are. Damn, we were good. Damn, I was good! New York would have to notice.

When I turned in my copy Dulin read it, smiled that big smile of his and said, "Go home." Will was reading over his shoulder. He clapped. I hadn't been to bed for almost forty hours. I did.

Will called Major Tanner of the State Police just before midnight and gave him the details of the story. "Take care of your contacts." The rule is somewhere in the Will Owens' Playbook, but I forget where it is on the list. The Major wouldn't be taken by surprise when he started getting questions in the morning.

But Sheriff Stanley Woodrow Peavler would. When Sheriff Stanley Woodrow Peavler opened his favorite newspaper that morning, the news that greeted him in a big black eight-column banner on the front page would be "Judge Placed At Victim's House At Time Of Murder: Surprise Development Adds Unlikely Suspect to Ashes Murder Case."

Maise Jones, the Sheriff's secretary, didn't wake me. The Sheriff did. "Damn you, Theo Clark," the high-pitched voice yelled in my ear when I finally picked up the phone. I searched through sleep-clogged eyelids in the still dark room for the luminous numerals on my bedside clock-radio that would show me the time. Seven o'clock! Seven-damn-o'clock!

The voice didn't let up. "Are you trying to make me look like an ignorant ass? My phone's going to start ringing off the hook. You should have talked with me before you wrote this! You're withholding important information needed in a criminal case!" His voice rose to almost a shout. "You're obstructing justice! You get your butt down here right away. You've got a lot of explaining to do!"

"Hold on, Sheriff," I tried to break in.

"Hold on hell," he practically shouted. "Get your ass down here right away, or I'm going to have a warrant issued for your arrest!"

I woke Dulin and he woke Will. None of us had any sleep to speak of and me even less than the others, but I was determined I wasn't going to walk into Sheriff Stanley Woodrow Peavler's office looking haggard and bedraggled. Coffee brewed while I took a fast shower and shaved. My blue blazer was fresh from the dry cleaners. I pressed a pair of grey flannels, unfolded a freshly laundered white button-down from the shirt drawer, slid a blue and red rep tie off the tie rack, pulled on a pair of navy blue socks, buffed my cordovan loafers, assembled all this on my still sleepy frame, drank down a cup of hot black coffee in two gulps, inspected myself in the mirror, found the image acceptable if not imposing and walked out the door.

The morning was cold and grey. Fog was rising from the river. I wished I'd grabbed my Burburry on the way out, but I hadn't. The chill was good for me. I came fully awake as I made the short walk to the Courthouse. Only a few cars were on the streets and no pedestrians. The Courthouse clock struck the half hour as I hurried up the outside steps to the big entrance door.

Inside it was warm. Maise was turning on the office lights in the Sheriff's office as I opened the door. She looked sleepy and cross. "What have you done now," she said, as I walked in.

Before I could answer, Dulin made his entrance. When he saw me he came over, put his hand on my shoulder, and shook his head disbelievingly. "Pathetic, our Sheriff."

The phone rang. Maise didn't touch it. She looked up from her desk. "It's been ringing constantly. Sheriff said not to answer."

The phone was still ringing when Will came through the door. The cold had put some color in his face. He looked tired but eager to confront the Sheriff.

"Well," Dulin said turning to Maise, "Mr. Clark is here as the Sheriff requested. Let him know that, please— and that he is accompanied by Mr. Will Owens and Mr. Dulin Monroe."

The tempest didn't last long, but it was vigorous.

Sheriff Woodrow Stanley Peavler shouted, pounded his desk, kicked the wall, and all but spit. The *State Journal* was running a personal vendetta against him to ruin his standing in the county and get him defeated in the next election! I had withheld important information in a murder case! This was not the first time I had done it."

We listened. There was little else we could do. The harangue was like a gale force wind.

We were standing in his office, the three of us, in a line in front of his desk, Will and Dulin on either side of me. The Sheriff hadn't bothered to offer us chairs. The minute Maise ushered us in, he jumped up. He was thrown off stride to see Dulin and Will there with me, but his anger was so hot he plunged right in.

"So you brought your gang again, did you Theo Clark? Well, I'm not impressed. You're messing with things you shouldn't be messing with. You hear that phone ringing! That's going to go on all day.

"Do you have any idea of what you've done! The Judge is one of the county's ... one of the most respected men in the county. It's his sister who was murdered! You're saying he was there! Maybe had a hand in it! The whole town is going to be horrified!"

He was talking non-stop. When he paused to take a breath, Dulin broke in. Calmly.

"You have a real problem, Woodrow, but it's not the *Journal* and it's not Theo."

"Yeah?" the Sheriff barked back. "Well if this hot-shot would quit interfering, we could put the guilt where it belongs and stop harassing and embarrassing decent people."

"The Gypsy?" Dulin asked quietly.

The room became very quiet.

The Sheriff stared at Dulin, clenched and unclenched his fists, started to speak and didn't, shook his shoulders like he was shrugging off a coat, knew he was challenged and knew he had to be careful.

"The Gypsy lied. He was there. The evidence against him is as good as it is against Emma Purcell."

"No it isn't, Woodrow"

"I say it is," the Sheriff hissed.

Dulin studied him coldly. The phone started ringing again. The Sheriff glanced toward it, then glared at me and Will.

Dulin grunted dismissively. "I'll tell you something, Woodrow. Theo has no obligation to share information with you before we print it. Whether he told you about the Judge's car late last night or you read it first thing this morning, the result is the same. If you're embarrassed that a reporter uncovered a very important fact concerning the Ashes Murder that you missed, or ignored, that's your problem. My problem is the way you're trying to strong-arm him. If it happens again, Sheriff, I guarantee you the paper will be on your case, and you will have more problems to deal with than you can possibly imagine. And I also guarantee you that we won't stand by and let you railroad the Gypsy. Will? You agree?"

Will grinned evilly at Sheriff Woodrow Stanly Peavler. "Absolutely and positively." Dulin looked to me. "Theo?" I straightened my tie, stood up straight, and said with real satisfaction, "I'm in all the way."

The phone was ringing as we left.

TWENTY EIGHT

As word spread that the County Judge might be connected with a murder, worse, with the murder of his own sister, the community was shocked. There was a collective intake of breath and a growing feeling of unease. The County Judge was the public personification of the establishment. Awarding favors to cronies was to be expected. A little graft was permissible. But murder?

The situation was one the "Massas" couldn't let stand. This was the name Dulin gave that loose coterie of bankers and merchants and lawyers who ran things, always had and always would. He took it from plantation days when the slaves called their masters, "Massa" ... "yes, Massa; no Massa, please Massa." Rules were fine and laws were to be obeyed, but when it came to the way things were actually done and who or what would be tolerated, punished, or rewarded, the Massas decided.

For the Massas to have one of their own implicated in the Ashes Murder was not to be permitted. The charge against the Judge's niece was bad enough.

All this meant that Sheriff Woodrow Stanley Peavler had a problem of real severity. If he didn't keep the Massas happy, he'd be gone. And if he didn't get the spotlight off Judge Hockensmith and find a credible way to erase the thought that the Judge might have been present at his sister's murder, there would be no joy in Mudville. For good measure, he'd better see to it that Emma was exonerated as well.

We'd expected the latter from the beginning. Almost everything the Sheriff had done since the beginning of the investigation seemed focused on getting Emma off. He hadn't really checked her whereabouts on the day of the murder. Andy Thomas' coverage in the *Lexington Herald* proved that. Nor had he questioned her in any depth. He'd taken the story he got from the Judge at face value and was incensed when the State Police, on the basis of forensic evidence, named her the principal suspect. From the moment he'd learned Gypsies were on the farm property, he'd concentrated on making the case that the Gypsy did it.

Sheriff Woodrow Stanley Peavler wasted no time. He could hardly afford to. Deluged by phone calls from the media and underscored by a few from men Woody could not afford to disappoint, he announced at mid-day that his office was conducting a full review of Judge Hockensmith's movements the day of the Ashes Murder—an action he felt unnecessary since it was plowing ground already plowed, but made obligatory in light of the confusion stirred up by the story in the morning paper.

Shortly thereafter word began to get around that the boys must have been mistaken. They're only youngsters, it went. They may have seen a car in front of the Purcell house, but they weren't focused on cars. They were hunting, for god's sake, walking slow, eyes scanning the stubble, murmuring, "jump up, little rabbit, jump up." You know what that's like. You know how the excitement gets you. They glanced up maybe and saw, way across that big meadow, a car in the driveway. The boys probably didn't even know what time it was. It might even have been the Judge's car at a later time when he'd come back to the house with Emma. Not that the boys would make anything up. They're good boys. They're just mistaken. They had their minds on rabbits.

The story was reassuring. It was plausible. It was easier to buy that than the county's highest elected official was party to the murder of his sister. It played, with minor variations, at the Rotary Club meeting and the Garden Club gathering, over drinks at the Country Club and in the bars downtown, and the reasonableness of it all made sense. The mayor thought so and said as much in response to an inquiry from the *Lexington Herald*. The manager of the downtown Sears store thought the entire hullabaloo was ridiculous. "Judge Hockensmith involved in the murder of his sister? That's absurd."

The Judge himself wouldn't take calls from the media, but his pastor, Pastor Abner Goodman of the downtown Baptist Church, the largest church in the county, said on-air in a response to a question from a reporter for the local radio station that Judge Hockensmith told him face-to-face that very day that his one and only trip to the Purcell home had been exactly as he had told of it to the Sheriff and that the personal distress being caused him and his family by this spurious accusation was very painful. "We should all erase this unfortunate incident from our minds and move on," the Pastor said. It looked like that was exactly what would happen.

Dulin was fairly certain where the story started. You don't keep getting elected as Woodrow Stanley Peaveler did without understanding how to float an idea that favors your position on the county gossip stream.

For appearances' sake, the Sheriff went through the motions. His deputies re-checked the in-and-out times at the parking garage at the Courthouse. There was no record for the Judge that day. He had walked to work from his home at the end of Wappping Street near the river. The Judge was questioned. His movements the day of the murder had been exactly as had earlier been reported. If this really happened, if the Sheriff really questioned the Judge it would have been the first time. None of us, neither Will, nor Dulin, nor I, could picture Woodrow Stanley Peavler interrogating the Judge, actually putting hard questions to him. Our esteemed Sheriff had been happy to take the Judge's word for his movements the day of the murder. There was no reason to think he wouldn't take the Judge's word about the car.

It was a different matter with the boys.

By the time Woodrow Stanley Peavler was through with them, their story had changed.

Being awakened at daylight by the flashing lights of a police cruiser sitting in your front yard waiting to transport you downtown had a tendency, if you were a fifteen year old and never been in the back seat of a police car or set foot in the county Courthouse, to make you a little apprehensive. Under the aggressive questioning of a skeptical authority figure in official uniform and with a gun on his hip, you had to begin to wonder if you really saw what you thought you saw. The boys were resolute that they saw a car, but they couldn't swear on the Bible—Woodrow brought one into the room with him and had it sitting in the center of his desk as he questioned them—that it was the Judge's car or exactly what time they had seen it.

The net of it all? If there was a car (our esteemed Sheriff stressed the if) it wasn't Judge Hockensmith's car. And if there was a car, it might or might not have a bearing on the murder. In any event, no one else had seen it; no one had any information on it; there was no adequate description to ask the State Police to undertake a state-wide search. The Gypsy's car was the only car at the scene of the murder. Conclusion? The Gypsy must have done it.

I felt liked punching somebody. There was no question in my mind that the Sheriff had thoroughly intimidated the boys. He'd tried it with me. I felt bad that I'd put the boys and their families in such a situation and outraged that the

Sheriff was going to get away with whitewashing the Judge and digging a bigger hole for the Gypsy.

Will and Dulin let me rant. When I finally ran down, Dulin said "See what Major Tanner has to say."

TWENTY NINE

The State Police had no jurisdiction. The Ashes Murder was a county matter. The only way the State Police could be involved was if Woodrow Stanley Peavler invited them in. Not only unlikely—unthinkable. Set aside the Sheriff's vexation at the gall of Major Tanner in naming Emma as a principal suspect on the basis of the circumstantial evidence the State Police crime lab had uncovered. Overlook his embarrassment over the Phantom Car episode that Tanner seemed to know all about when Woodrow didn't. Our esteemed Sheriff just plain didn't like Tanner. This is sometime the result when tall, good looking men and skinny, thin-faced men find themselves ragging at the same problem. But even though not officially on the case, we knew Major Tanner would be on its periphery. His role as the chief investigator for the Prosecuting Attorney would require it, and his personal distaste for Woodrow would inspire it.

We met late that night at a truck stop just outside town on the Louisville Road. The rains had returned, cold and doleful, puddling in the poorly lit gravel parking lot.

We were in a back booth, me working on a Weideman's and Will suffering through a cup of black coffee. He'd never been a beer man, could hardly stomach the stuff except on simmering hot summer afternoons, coming off the creek with an empty creel and a boiling thirst. Nothing better then. But only then.

Major Tanner came in shortly after midnight, shaking water from his Trooper's hat and shrugging off a black raincoat. He hung up his raincoat and slid in beside me, facing Will.

"You pick some lively joints," he said.

"Thought you could find the place," Will said.

Tanner nodded and smiled. "Jamsie Keanan shot his girlfriend here and beat the guy she was two-timing him with to death with a beer bottle. Took four troopers to get him cuffed."

"The beer bottle never broke," Will said.

"The night was sort of like tonight. Cold. Rainy. More people though."

"It was a Saturday," Will reminded him. "Saturday's the big night here."

The Major nodded.

"So?"

Will shifted in his seat, looked slowly around the room. A bartender, a cashier, and a tired looking trucker sitting at the bar. The cashier got off her stool and walked over and put a coin in the juke box. A moment later, Tennessee Ernie Ford's big, deep bass began filling the silence. Tanner caught her eye and nodded. She smiled and went back to her stool, studiously ignoring us.

"What's your take on The Phantom Car and the County Judge?"

Major Tanner grinned. "The Phantom Car. I like that."

"Sheriff Woodrow Stanley Peale thinks he's made it disappear and the idea that the Judge might be implicated in the Ashes Murder go away." Will said.

Still smiling, the Captian said, "The Judge left his office about ten the morning of the murder. He didn't return until shortly after noon. His secretary has no record of where he was. He was late to a luncheon meeting with the County Road Supervisor. He left his office again at about two-thirty. The next we hear of him he's at the Purcell house calling the Sheriff."

"You know this for sure?"

"We did some "unofficial" investigating. Gave the information to the Sheriff for follow-up."

"And?"

"Looks like he ignored it or satisfied himself that the Judge's unexplained absence during the hours the murder was likely committed isn't important."

I watched Will mull this over, swirling his cold coffee around in the cup and peering into it as if seeking divination. He looked back up at Tanner, "So what do you think? I'm not asking you what you know or what you can prove. I'm asking what you think?"

Tanner took his time answering. "I think those rabbit hunting boys saw what they said they saw."

"He says he wasn't there. The Sheriff says he wasn't there," I offered.

Will and Major Tanner glanced over at me, a momentary interruption.

Will turned back to Tanner, "So your boys couldn't find anyone to corroborate the Gypsy's story that he was in Bardstown at the time of the murder?"

"No one asked us to try. It's the Sheriff's investigation"

"He wants to pin it on the Gypsy."

Tanner nodded.

"So what's to be done?"

Tanner smiled again. "What's always done. Nothing. Short of being caught standing over the body with the pistol still smoking, or both hands full of money and the county till open, men like the Judge don't get brought up on charges You know that."

Exactly as Major Tanner predicted, nothing happened. There was a little talk of the Phantom Car for a day or two more. Then it faded. People were losing interest, even in the gossip. The murder was now over two months old. There was more conversation about the lousy season UK was having in basketball than about who killed Mrs. Adeleline Hockensmith Purcell and stuffed ashes down her throat.

Coach Rupp was calling the 1956 Wildcats the worst team he'd ever fielded. Not the sort of talk Kentuckians, used to the winningest collegiate basketball program in the nation, found reassuring. Emma Purcell was still the principal suspect in the Ashes Murder. Sheriff Woodrow Stanley Peavler was still insisting the Gypsy, Arlo Lee, should have that honor. The Commonwealth's Attorney, who would prosecute the case in Circuit Court, since capital crimes were beyond the purview of the County Court, still hadn't made his choice. All was in limbo.

The Circuit Court set February thirteen, a Monday, as Emma Purcell's arraignment date. At that time she, or the Gypsy, depending on who the Commonwealth's Attorney felt he had the best chance of convicting, would be formally charged and a trial date set. Most likely, the trial could get underway no earlier than the first week in April— another two months away—and there was no telling how long it might run once begun.

I was appalled at how slowly the justice system moved. Part of this was due to the attorneys. The defense wanted as much time as possible to prepare its case. So did the prosecution. Neither side was pushing for an early trial. The bigger consideration was the Kentucky court system. Our Circuit Court Judges preside over courts in a number of counties and move through them on a regular "circuit"—much like the circuit riding preachers of old who journeyed from church to church spreading the good word and admonishing sinners. Franklin County had to wait its turn.

Arlo Lee, the Gypsy, had by now been in the County Jail for almost three weeks. He was not formally charged with anything, but was being held as a "material witness" until the Sheriff could convince the Commonwealth's Attorney that he should be charged with the murder of Adeline Hockensmith Purcell.

The ruse was outrageous but legal. The prospect that Arlo might have to endure two more months in a jail cell bothered us all. There was nothing we could do about it. Bail wasn't an option. So there he sat, four whitewashed walls, a metal bed with a thin mattress, a sink, a seat less toilet, a single window looking out on the alley that ran behind the *Journal* and the Catholic school up on the next block, an hour's outdoor exercise twice a day in good weather, and three plain, hot meals a day. Emma Purcell, the prime suspect, enjoyed the comforts of her home and freedom of movement.

I visited as often as I could, bringing magazines and books, fruit sometimes, and copies of the *Journal. Tolkien's Fellowship of the Ring* had just been published. The story helped give him some of the escape he craved. He wanted a radio. We got him one. Still, confinement for someone as free as Arlo had always been was almost torture. He didn't complain. He had no regular visitors. From what I understood of the close family bonds of the members of the kumpania, I was surprised that none had come. When I asked about this, he said he'd told them to stay away. He feared they'd be questioned and harassed in an attempt to get information about himself. He preferred his loneliness to that possibility.

January segued in February. Cold rain and grey skies oppressed us all. Despite Dulin's doggedness to keep the story alive, there was nothing. I went back to covering city council meetings and high school basketball games. I even started making morning classes again at the University.

Will was spending most of his time at the Capitol. The Legislature was in session and Happy Chandler was back. Albert Benjamin "Happy" Chandler. Mesmerizer. Magician.

Serving his second term as Governor, a triumph never before achieved in Kentucky politics, Happy had wrestled the Democratic gubernatorial nomination out of the grasp of the Democratic Party machine controlled by U.S. Senator Earl Clements and outgoing Governor Lawrence Wetherby in a bare-knuckle campaign. Happy unleashed all the showmanship and charm that had won him his first gubernatorial chair.. His campaign slogan was "Be Like Your Pappy.

Vote For Happy" and his campaign song "Happy Days Are Here Again." The voters loved him.

In the general election, he swamped his Republican opponent, a U.S. attorney from Rockcastle County in the Cumberland foothills, by the largest margin ever recorded in a governor's election. He'd moved back into the Governor's Mansion only weeks before and was already creating a commotion—just the sort of excitement and confusion that could keep Will entertained while we waited.

But for me, there were no distractions. Arlo Lee in jail. A Phantom car somewhere waiting to be found. Josh fighting his demons. The boys getting made fun of at school. Adeline Hockensmith Purcell with her head bashed in, and her throat stuffed with ashes. Dulin's smoldering indignation at the arrogance and excesses of the establishment. I couldn't submerge all that.

The case meant more to me than it did to Will. I had developed a mania to find the killer. At the beginning I really didn't care. The murder was a challenge, a mystery, an opportunity— a game with a big prize at the end for me if I played my part well. I was on the sidelines. Not involved. Watching. Waiting. But Sheriff Peavler's attempts to lay the murder off on the Gypsy, the special treatment being given Emma Kane, the Massas' blanket of protection insulating the Judge—the unimpeded use of power and special privilege began to so outrage my sense of fairness that soon I cared very much.

I felt I had exhausted all avenues that might lead to the killer. All but the ashes. Their use was such a bizarre facet of the crime.

Will thought them a diversion, a puzzle intentionally planted to mislead investigators—at best a message from a sick mind, so we had spent no time trying to unravel the mystery.

Our esteemed Sheriff Woodrow Stanley Peavler didn't. His folks came down to the Bluegrass from the ridges and the hollows of the eastern mountains bringing their superstitions with them. Ghosts who come back to punish or warn. Strange apparitions who wait on lonely roads in the dead of night to waylay lonely travelers. There were women who cast spells and told the future; people who talked in tongues and handled deadly snakes—creatures of the new moon and the full moon and mid-summer's dusk. The line between the real and the supernatural was unstable—could be slipped across. Woodrow didn't admit to any such ideas, but he felt it in his blood. A lot of people did.

Woodrow Stanley Peavler suspected the ashes had something to do with a Gypsy ritual. This added fuel for his condemnation of Arlo Lee, the Gyspy.

Dulin? Dulin withheld judgment. He thought the use of them barbarous and wanted the person responsible named and prosecuted. Adele Hockensmith Purcell had been a friend. To so debase her person outraged him.

I leaned towards Will's thinking—but was perfectly prepared to agree that the line between the real and the unearthly was porous and shifting.

With nothing else of any real importance to pursue in front of me, I decided to focus on the ashes. Why would anyone do such a thing? Who would do such a thing? If I could find the answer to that, everything else might fall into place. "Try it," Dulin said.

Will thought it as good a use of time as anything else while we waited for the formal arraignment date, though when he gave me his blessing, he smiled a wry smile and said, "Demons."

THIRTY

My little excursion into the mystery of the ashes started, and ended, with Major Tanner. His crew had done the actual crime scene work and his laboratory, the analysis.

There wasn't much. The Major re-confirmed that Adeline Hockensmith Purcell was dead when the ashes were stuffed in her mouth and that doing it would not be an easy job.

"Someone had to lift her head, hold her mouth open, and cram an unstable substance down her throat," Tanner said.

"Someone?" I said. "You think two people might have been involved?"

"Hard to imagine just one person managing that and not making a mess, but I suppose it could be done. She was killed in the kitchen. Apparently she'd made a small fire in that old wood stove to take some of the morning chill off the room. That's where the ashes came from. Our analysis showed them to be a mixture of oak and paper—mostly paper. Whoever handled the ashes did a careful job. The was no mess in the kitchen—just a small smear near the stove. There was a trace of ash on two of the steps down to the cellar, then a scattering where her head lay on the cellar floor."

"The ashes were stuffed in her mouth in the cellar?"

"It seems so," said Tanner.

"She's killed in the kitchen, dragged or thrown down the cellar stairs, then the killer follows and stuffs her mouth with ashes?"

Major Tanner nodded, "Yes."

"The same ash? Ashes from the stove?'

"Yes, the same—paper ash with a small trace of oak."

"No way to connect them to any person?

"The only connection we have is the amount we found on the slacks Emma Kane was wearing that day."

"You don't think this is some magic ritual sort of thing, some Gypsy curse, some odd religious ceremonial?"

Ashes were a symbol of remorse and redemption for some religions, a marker of the release of the soul from its earthly body for others. They could be an element of ritual purification or a powerful ingredient for spells and curses.

Tanner laughed. "I think the only way we'll get an answer to the reason for the ashes is if the murderer tells us, and we'll be doing nothing but spinning wheels trying to figure it out with no more to go on than we have."

That made so much sense that, though disappointed that the ashes were a dead end, I thanked him and took my leave. Maybe I could talk Will into letting me bird-dog him as he made his rounds up at the Capitol.

We were still a little over two weeks away from Emma Purcell Kane's arraignment date. I assumed it would be Emma. The evidence against Arlo Lee, the Gypsy, was too weak, though the Sheriff kept up at his argument that Arlo was the killer.

I was at home when the call from Hanratty came. It had been a day of nothing of consequence. I'd done a City Council meeting story and a short piece on the Rotary Club's speaker. I'd left just after the paper was locked up, walked home through the silent streets to my apartment, shook the sleet off my raincoat, and made a night-cap.

"Theo, this is Pete Hanratty," the voice said.

Hanratty? Emma Kane's attorney. At this hour? I looked at my watch—two o'clock.

"You're working late, counselor," I said, hiding my surprise.

He ignored the comment.

"I didn't want to catch you at the paper. I figured you might be home by now."

I waited.

After a moment, he continued. "Emma wants to talk to you. I've advised against it, but she is insistent."

"An interview?" I couldn't believe that. An interview with the principal suspect in the Ashes Murder before her arraignment date! Impossible. I'd tried for an interview before and been turned down every time.

"She says she knows you. She thinks you'll be fair. She wants to tell you her story of what happened that day. Her way. In her own words. Not filtered through an attorney."

"You'd permit that?"

"I don't like it, but yes—with one condition."

"Which is?"

"You can't use any of it until the trial is under way."

"I don't understand," I said. "Why would I do that? Why would she want me to? Why are you willing to let it be done?"

"Emma knows that whatever story the jury hears will be shaped by the facts the attorneys present and the questions they ask her. If you know her story, what you write won't be confined to what's heard in court. You'll have the background to write a fuller account and a truer account. That's her reasoning."

"And she thinks I'll do that, expand on what's said in court with material I've gained from a talk with her? That I'll take what she tells me as being the truth and use it fairly?"

"Yes."

"Hell of a gamble," I said.

There was a long pause. Finally he said, "I'm assuming Dulin Monroe will assign you to cover the trial, not Will Owens. Will's tied up with Happy and the Legislature now. I know Will's condition. He can't be counted on. Dulin will give the assignment to you. What you write can't affect the course of the trial. The jurors will be sequestered. No newspapers, no radio, no TV. The effect of what you write will be felt by the community, by the people Emma has to live with. That's what's important to her in this. How they feel about her. What they think about her."

When he finished I said, "You're trusting me to keep what Emma tells me confidential until the trial starts and then to present it fairly in my stories?"

Another long pause, then, "I'm a gambler too."

THIRTY ONE

Emma set the interview for the Friday night before the Monday arraignment date—in the living room of the house where her mother was killed—ten o'clock sharp.

The agreement was that attorney Hanratty would not be present. No one would be present but Emma and me. Emma wanted no one whispering in her ear, no one hearing what she had to say but me. I was to bring no tape-recorder, to rely solely on my notes and to discuss with no one what I learned, including, and especially, Will and Dulin. I could ask any questions I liked except the key one —had she killed her mother.

Dulin wasn't happy with this, but was willing to let me accept the conditions in order to get inside the story in a way none of our competitors could.

Will was suspicious. To set the interview for ten o'clock at night in the home where her mother was killed, just the two of us alone! This had him running disaster scenarios through his mind. He didn't trust Hanratty. He didn't trust Emma Kane. He felt the set up was bizarre, unlike anything he'd ever heard of. In the end though, like Dulin, he couldn't resist the temptation. "Be careful," he told me. "If you're offered a nightcap, don't take it. If she wants to cry on your shoulder, don't let it happen. You're not her friend, and you're not her confessor. Remember that road out of Chosin with danger all around. Pay attention to small things. Stay focused. Get what you came for and then get the hell out of there!"

Will's attitude surprised me, but as I let what he told me sink in, I began to understand in a way I hadn't before the sorts of unsuspected landmines scattered around the landscape.

I remembered what Allie said when I talked with her about Emma Kane, about the Spring Dance when we were high school seniors, that "Emma remembers you." I wondered at the time what she meant. With Will's admonitions in my ear, I decided I better know for sure before my date with Emma.

I remembered the night well enough. And the dance. And the morning after. But not Emma-Purcell-now-Kane.

We were all graduating that summer. Emma, though, went to Elkhorn, a county school, and Frankfort High boys, as a rule, didn't date county girls. I'm not sure why this was. There were some awfully pretty ones.

I guess it was mostly a matter of proximity. They weren't around. They weren't at our hang-outs after school or after games. They weren't at our dances and didn't go to our churches. We didn't see them, so we didn't know them. And there was the matter of distance. Getting access to a car wasn't automatic, and you didn't walk a county girl home after a movie or a dance. Maybe we were just lazy.

Anyway, I didn't know Emma-Purcell-now-Kane. Allie did. The girls seemed to know each other better. Maybe they were in the same clubs or had activities they did together. Or maybe it was a matter of sociability. The girls were more open.

The boys, consciously or unconsciously, were always in competition—among ourselves, of course, but that was routine; that was within the tribe. With the county boys, it was different and it revolved mostly around sports. None of the county schools played football. We did, and we felt a little superior about it. They all played basketball, though, and some of them beat us fairly regularly. They were rivals. There wasn't a lot of fraternization among the boys.

I hadn't thought much about any of this until the prospect of the interview with Emma-Purcell-now-Kane, came up. In fact, I hadn't thought about the matter at all.

Allie was my date that night. We doubled with Dave Todd who had his father's car. I think Allie engineered the match between Dave and Emma. Dave was a little shy, sometimes went without a date just because he was embarrassed to ask. Dave played tackle on our team, was a champion debater and President of the Key Club. Everybody liked him. Allie wasn't going to let him swing in the wind trying to get a date to the Senior Prom. I'm sure she arranged it.

"You really don't remember," she said when I asked her to explain.

"I remember you," I said, "and making breakfast at Barb's. I remember the night and the morning. I don't remember Emma Kane."

Her eyes searched my face, looking for some sign. Whether she saw it or not I don't know, but after a moment she said, "She kissed you. Or you kissed her. I'm not sure which. You were gone for awhile. I walked out on the porch that overlooks the garden, you remember it? You were there. In the shadows."

She waited and watched me.

"Allie, I didn't even know the girl!"

Her look softened.

"You were a little drunk. Emma had a way of coming on to boys she liked. You were always horny. Add a little bourbon and a strange girl out to hook you … your discipline gave way."

"Allie—"

"It's alright, hero. I was mad and hurt, but I was mostly mad at Emma. You were too big a temptation. You and Michael were the big catches that year. Football heroes, popular, and so straight-arrow that we sometimes made fun of you behind your backs. All our mothers loved you. Most of us did too. But I had you. Emma knew that. She just couldn't resist. You all didn't see me. I walked back inside, and you two came in shortly afterwards. I guess your discipline finally kicked in."

"Allie—"

"Don't say anything." She leaned in and kissed me on the cheek. "We had a fine night and a fine morning. A special night. A special morning. Remember?"

Remember? A full moon shining on the river. The sand cold but the blanket warm. The taste and the touch of her. I remembered.

"Allie—"

"Oh, be quiet." She smiled then. "So Emma's spinning you into her web again? Be careful, hero. You seduce so easily."

I truly did not remember that thing with Emma. Do not remember it now. Allie accuses me of having the gift of selective denial. If I don't want to remember a thing, it didn't happen. Some things I don't want to remember, I can't control though. They come to me in the dark—with the demons.

THIRTY TWO

The night came.

I prepared as thoroughly as I could. Put on my this-is-serious-business uniform of blue blazer, grey slacks, Bass loafers, white button-down and rep tie. Shaved again at six, so no beard showed. Trimmed and cleaned my nails. Brushed my hair. Got a fresh note pad and sharpened three copy pencils. Went over my list of questions again with Dulin. And sat impatiently in the newsroom waiting for the clock above the AP ticker to arrive at nine-thirty.

I figured about twenty-five minutes out to the farm. I wanted to get there right at ten o'clock, as agreed. There should be no traffic. It was a clear night. I knew the way. Should be no problem.

Will was at the Capitol sitting in on a night session of the Legislature. We'd talked earlier in the day, and he'd admonished me again to be careful. As I stood to leave, Dulin motioned me over to his desk. He fixed me with that look of his that never reveals anything. Eventually he said, "Just do what you know how to do."

A more experienced man going into a situation like this might be a little excited at the promise the evening held, but he'd be too seasoned to be nervous. I was nervous. Everyone I'd talked with—Will, Dulin, Allie—all made it clear that here might be dragons. On top of this was my own clear understanding that how well I handled this could be the deciding factor in whether or not I earned that ticket to Manhattan.

I was also nervous about how to manage Emma. Allie's warning was in my mind. And the fact that Emma had asked for this interview and made the offer specifically and exclusively to me must mean that she thought she had some connection with me that could work in her favor. Yes, I was nervous. And apprehensive.

There was no moon. I could see a few stars poking through the scudding clouds, but the lane back to the house from the highway was a shadowy tunnel through an uninhabited land. All the fields were dark. There were no houses. No light. Isolated. Lonely.

It seemed to take forever in the dark to make it through that stand of woods, then on the far side of an open gate, I could make out the outlines of the meadow where the house stood, the porch light shining like a beacon in the night.

Emma met me at the open door. That door had been open on my first visit to the Purcell house. Then it had been left open accidentally. This time it was intentional. Emma saw my car lights coming down the lane and opened it to stand there waiting for me. Our first meeting should have been awkward, but it wasn't. Emma smiled, took my hand, and led me inside.

Through all the events leading up to tonight, I had never really had a chance to see her. The Judge kept her isolated after the murder. She turned herself into the police in what amounted to a private rite in the early morning dark. She'd not been in public since. All I'd seen of Emma-Purcell-now-Kane had been in pictures—none of them recent, few of them good.

I studied her now as she stood smiling at me beside the fireplace in the big living room. As everyone had said, she was a big girl, almost as tall as me, broad shouldered, wide-hipped. When I'd taken the hand she offered me, it was strong and firm. She had a full, buxom figure, a plain but not unpleasant face, and long black hair that hung to her shoulders and glistened in the firelight. Her eyes were gray, her smile even and pleasant, her voice soft, and if she sang, I imagined she would be a contralto. She wore a plaid skirt of circumspect length, a white cowl-neck sweater I supposed to be cashmere, and brown penny-loafers. In the soft glow of the firelight she looked like a young girl, which she was; unsullied, which she was not, and though there was certainly nothing magnetic about her, she looked promisingly seductive.

I didn't remember her.

But Emma-Purcell-now-Kane acted as if we were long-lost friends and our last meeting only yesterday. She led me into the living room to a big leather chair facing the fireplace and stood behind its twin on the other side of a large cherry coffee table between them.

"What can I get you to drink," she asked brightly.

"Thanks. Nothing," I said, taking out my note pad.

"A cold night. A nightcap. Warm you up," she coaxed.

"No. Really. Thanks."

"Oh well," she said, moving around the chair and taking her seat. She leaned far forward toward me, smiling. "Do you remember the kiss?"

I must have sat back, surprise showing in my face.

"You do, don't you?" she said laughing.

While I imagined my face coloring in embarrassment she said, " Never mind. I made up with Allie. She was boiling mad at me. But she finally came around. She knows my weaknesses. I expect it turned out pretty good for you, though. Allie wouldn't let a challenge like that go unanswered." She laughed. "I think you owe me."

She'd put me completely off balance. I didn't know what to say or how to react. I felt like I'd taken a couple of fast jabs to the gut, a little breathless, a little disoriented.

I tried to gather myself. "You asked me here to hear your story about your mother's murder."

Still smiling she said, "Yes. That too. I just couldn't resist a visit to old times. Time to get serious. You agree to the rules? Nothing I say can be used until the trial, if there is a trial."

"If there is a trial?" I said, surprised.

"There may not be one. They still have to decide if they want to try me or the Gypsy. It could be the Gypsy. Or the Judge at the arraignment may decide there's not enough evidence to bring a charge against me. And you can't discuss what I tell you with anyone … absolutely no one. And you can't ask me if I did it."

I focused on her eyes for any sign of apprehension or nervousness. I saw none. She was completely at ease.

"Deal?" she said.

"I don't have an option. We do it your way or not at all."

"That's right," she said, still smiling that assured smile.

I nodded then.

"No," she said. "Say it. I want to hear it out loud."

I let a couple of beats go by, then said "Deal."

She crossed her legs demurely and folded her hands in her lap and sat there Sphinx-like. She had taken command of the proceedings and knew it. I felt like a canary with the cat slinking up.

"Do you have enough light?" she said.

"What?

"For your notes. Do you have enough light for your notes?"

The light in the room was muted, a single standing lamp in the corner and the glow from the fireplace. I pulled my note pad out of my jacket pocket, balanced it on my knee, and looked around uncertainly.

"Of course you don't," she said, rising and walking behind me to turn on a standing light to the side of my chair.

"There," she said with satisfaction. "Now we can begin." She took her seat again, settled back in a totally relaxed way. I'm not quite sure what I expected— that she would be nervous, defensive, apologetic, emotional, anything but the Emma she presented to me— composed, expressive, confident.

In a calm voice that broke only when she described finding her mother, this is the story she told me—looking directly into my eyes and without artifice.

She had gotten up that morning looking forward eagerly to the day. Her mother was taking the baby, and she was to have the day to herself, lounging through the shops in Lexington, a visit to one or two of the art galleries, a leisurely lunch at a spot that would pamper her. She rose early, got the baby fed and dressed, pulled on a robe over her gown and took the baby up to the main house where her mother was waiting. They had toast and coffee together, then she returned to her house, dressed, and was just leaving through the kitchen door when Marko (her husband) wobbled unsteadily in. He'd fallen into bed at some hour in the early morning, stinking of cigarettes and booze. Now he was up, hung-over and mean.

"Where you going?" he demanded.

"Out."

"Make my breakfast."

"Make it yourself."

She started for the door. He grabbed her arm.

"I need a check," he said, hunched in his wrinkled pajamas, unshaven and bleary-eyed.

"You lost? Your promised not to play again."

"I need a check," still holding her arm.

"No. I told you. No more. Not ever again. No!"

He slapped her. "Bitch," he said, holding fast to her arm. "I need money!"

He'd never hit her before. The slap stung, but did no damage, except that he would presume that hitting her would outrage her. Emma is a big girl, taller than Marko, and strong. Incensed, she grabbed the metal coffee pot sitting on the kitchen counter with her free hand and with one long, sweeping blow, mashed the pot into his face and knocked him to the floor. She stood over him, blood trickling from his nose and mouth. "Don't you ever … ever … lift your hand to me," she told him. Then she dropped the coffee pot in his lap and slammed out through the kitchen door.

That melee changed everything for her, she told me. She knew Marco didn't love her, had never loved her, wanted her body for a while, but grew tired of that soon enough—but not her money. He would never grow tired of the money. She knew all this but refused to accept it. Until that morning. That morning she knew Marko would have to go. She had hoped to hold the marriage together for the sake of the baby. That morning she knew it was too big a price to pay.

The fight and the prospect of the future she faced upset her so that she drove aimlessly through the countryside, crying and thinking. She didn't remember where she went, which is why she was confused when the police asked where she'd been that day. She did remember driving to a friend's house who lived on a small estate outside town. The friend wasn't there, though, and she ruined her shoes walking in the mud to open the gate across the lane that led to the house. She thought about going to Allie, but she knew Allie was working. So she just drove, anywhere, trying to get the hurt out of her head.

Finally, emotionally spent, she returned home to pick up the baby and get ready for the confrontation she knew she had to have with Marco that evening.

Nothing appeared wrong when she pulled up in front of her mother's house. She left the car idling in the driveway, rushed up the porch stairs and through the front door. It was then that a feeling of unease began to rise. The house was dark. It was a rainy, dreary day. There should have been lights on. She called for her mother but got no response. Again, and still no response. Worried then, she rushed down the hallway toward the kitchen. It was dark too. But the door to the cellar was open. As she started across the room, she heard the baby's cries. Upstairs. Then she knew something was wrong. She ran up the hall, took the stairs two at a time, following the baby's cry to her mother's bedroom. There she found the baby, sobbing in his playpen. She grabbed him up and kissed him and began to sooth him, all the time calling for her mother. When the baby calmed, Emma began her search. She was frightened and apprehensive and reluctant to leave the safety of the upstairs room, but she did. Back down the stairs. Calling. No answer. And then she was in the kitchen again, facing the open cellar door. Though she didn't want to, she forced herself to it and to the top of the stairs leading down to the cellar. There she saw, at the foot of the stairs, her mother lying facing down on the cellar floor. She called to her. No answer. Again. Still no answer. Reluctantly, clutching the baby tightly to her breast, she inched down the cellar steps, calling "Momma, Momma," each step of the way. At the bottom, she saw the blood pooling at her mother's head. Panic overwhelmed her. She didn't remember how she made it back up the cellar steps or down the hall and up the stairs to her mother's room. But she knew she did, and she knew she locked it and put a chair underneath the knob so it couldn't be forced open and then called her Uncle, the Judge to, "come fast because Momma's hurt."

She was terrified while she waited, shaking and sobbing and scaring the baby, but she couldn't help it. When the knock finally came and she heard her Uncle's voice, she pulled in enough courage to open the door and to tell him, between sobs, what she'd found. Doctor Rail came in shortly afterwards with his nurse. The nurse took the baby. Doctor Rail gave her a shot. She went to sleep and didn't wake up until the next day.

And that was the story.

When she finished, she searched my face for some sign of what I was feeling. Then she rose, walked to my chair and knelt in front of me. She took the pencil from my hand, removed the note pad and took both my hands in hers. On her knees, in a voice of utter sincerity, she said, "I did not kill her, Theo. I did not."

I looked at her in astonishment.

"I know. I said you couldn't ask me that, but I didn't say that I couldn't tell you. I loved my mother, Theo. Whatever you may have heard from whoever you've talked with, I loved her. No one else could know how I felt. She was so good to me. She wanted only good things for me and gave me so much. I loved her and wanted to please her. Anyone who says that's not so doesn't know or is lying. I couldn't kill her. My own mother? Why would I? What possible reason could I have for wanting her dead? It's absolutely insane to think I might have done it."

Kneeling, holding my hands in hers, the room quiet, her eyes begging for understanding, I felt myself surrendering. Could this girl, this unassuming, unappreciated girl, kill her own mother? Beat her to death with a flatiron? Stuff ashes in her mouth? I sat there mesmerized, gazing into her imploring eyes. Then I remembered Allie's words, "be careful, you seduce so easily."

THIRTY THREE

There are questions I could have asked. Should have asked. They crowded my mind—after. Then, though, all I wanted to do was leave that house. It was a disturbing encounter—not an interview, a performance—a performance in which I was both a spectator and a player. Not at my behest. At hers. It unsettled me. Later, cynically, I wondered if she had rehearsed it all. If she knew she could play on my emotions. Could manipulate my thinking. Was she manipulating me? Was Hanratty? Had he orchestrated all this? To what end? My coverage of the trial, as Hanratty acknowledged, couldn't affect the jury. They'd see none of it. Was the actual objective to get a sympathetic hearing for Emma in the community, to protect her "good name" with her neighbors and friends, as Hanratty had told me? That would be moot if she were convicted. Good name gone. But if she was acquitted, or if the case were dismissed as Emma seemed to hope it might be, then what I wrote could be important to Emma-Purcell-now-Kane but maybe not to be Kane soon.

I didn't discuss this with Dulin or Will. I was too mortified to expose any part of my bumbling performance. When I got back to the newsroom about midnight, they were both there.

"So?" said Dulin, a big quizzical look on his face.

"It was strange," I said. "Not like an interview, more like an act in a play … dramatic lighting, a sympathetic heroine with a touching story, lines well delivered."

"But did you get anything useful," Will cut in.

"You know the deal. I can't discuss what she told me, but there were no noticeable changes in her story. I'll give her this, though. She tells it very well.

If it goes to trial, and she gets to tell her story in her own way, the jury doesn't stand a chance.

"If it goes to trial?" Dulin said.

"Emma thinks it might not. Maybe the Prosecuting Attorney will decide to go after the Gypsy rather than her, or that Hanratty can get the charge dismissed for lack of substantive evidence."

Will looked to Dulin, "The Massas working their will?"

Dulin stood up and walked to the AP ticker and fixed us with a glare. "You can bet your last dollar they're trying."

Emma's little scenario about an aborted trial didn't play out. The Prosecuting Attorney chose her for the honor, not the Gypsy, and the Court found the evidence sufficient to sustain a charge of murder. She pleaded not guilty. The trial was set to begin the ninth day of April, a Monday, in the Franklin Circuit Court, Judge Warren Watson presiding.

As before, and in this the Massas did have their way, Emma was not jailed or unnecessarily embarrassed. She was placed under house arrest, had freedom of movement on her own property and was not required to post a bail. It was not seen as necessary or civilized to subject her to a jail cell for the almost eight weeks until the start of the trial and for whatever time might ensue thereafter.

Arlo Lee, the Gypsy, got no such consideration. The Sheriff continued to insist that he was a material witness, might run if set free, and should remain a guest in the County Jail until the question of who killed Adeline Hockensmith Purcell was decided.

I dutifully wrote the story for the next day's paper. Summarized all the coverage up to that point and put in the new pertinent facts, but, as agreed, used nothing from my evening with Emma. Dulin played it on Page One.

Eight dragging weeks to the trial! We'd be out of winter and opening up to spring by then. I'd be pushing up on graduation day by then. Arlo would probably be out of his mind by then, held in that jail cell all that time. Eight weeks! My god, how would I navigate the wait? Will had Happy Chandler and the Legislature to distract him. Dulin had a newspaper to get out every day. All I had was this story. Or that's the way it felt to me. I'd become hooked on the excitement and the suspense and the mystery. Eight weeks in limbo. Lord.

I couldn't sit on my hands all that time. What other avenues could I pursue, should I pursue? Emma's performance that night at her mother's place stayed in my mind. Though in part it seemed artificial and rehearsed, it was nevertheless a moving experience. I half-way believed her. Maybe more than half-way. Should I look for markers that supported her story? Or for particulars that eroded it? Hadn't I already covered all that ground?

Motive. Motive seemed to be the pivot. So far, the Prosecuting Attorney had given no indication that his investigation had isolated a plausible motive. Emma, herself, on her knees, had beseeched me to explain to her what possible reason she could have that would cause her to murder her mother—her own mother. I had no answer.

If Arlo was to be believed, Adeline Hockensmith Purcell's intent to change her will and leave a sizeable portion of the farm on Elkhorn to him could have been a spur. If that was true, it would erode Emma's inheritance. If it was true, it could also affect Judge Hockensmith, since a sizable portion of the estate would flow to him, her brother.

Mrs. Purcell's aunt, Miss Livia Hockensmith, Miss Liv, my old teacher, knew of Adeline's intent to change her will. She was to witness its signing. Adeline's attorney also knew of the intent, but not the specifics. He was to get that information when he came see to her at her home the afternoon of her death.

None of this would make any difference at the trial. It was all hearsay. There was no proof.

What happened to the handwritten copy Mrs. Purcell had shown Arlo? And why would she leave anything, much less a piece of her valuable farm, to a Gypsy?

The only person I could imagine who might have an idea as to the reason for Adeline Hockensmith's mystifying generosity to a wandering Gypsy was Miss Liv.

To cross check my thinking, I went over all this with Dulin. There could be a story here. At the very least, chasing the leads would give me something worth doing while we waited for the trial to begin.

I would have gone over all this with Will, but Will was more and more marching to his own drummer. He was turning out his columns regularly and they were good, but he was doing little else. If he wasn't at the press room up in the Capitol, or rattling around through the offices of the department heads and functionaries that filled that august building, he was at the bar at King's, telling stories and singing songs. I knew I could find him there, regularly, from one-thirty or so in the morning 'til dawn—any morning.

His physical condition was deteriorating while I watched. Dulin would only shake his head. "Nothing to be done," he'd say. "He's meeting his deadlines. Turning in good copy. You're not his mother." Doc Rail said, "It's only a matter of time." The thing is Will realized this. In a way it seemed to release him. He was cheerful and relaxed. He had crossed a line of some kind and was glad of it. He was moving on and not looking back.

This made me monumentally sad, though in a way I admired him more. He made me think of the man in Invictus—the night dark as the pit, lightening flashing and rain slashing, massive waves rolling and wind howling, staring straight and unafraid into the eye of the terrible storm—holding to his own course—the master of his fate, the Captain of his soul.

But my God, what a waste.

I said as much to Gideon. I was standing at Will's side, my hand on his shoulder, while he lay with his hands on his arms on the bar at King's. Passed out? Asleep? Maybe the same thing. I don't know. Morning was just beginning to sneak a little light in through the open door from the hotel lobby.

"Why does he do this?"

Gideon eyed me for a long time. "Not many people know much about Will."

"Dulin?" I said.

"A little. Not much. He guesses at most of it."

"And you," I said softly, "you know."

Another long wait and a low sigh. "Yes, I know."

"Tell me," I said.

He studied Will still asleep on the bar. Then me, standing there hurting. He motioned to a table in the corner. "Sit down. I'll get us some coffee."

Once upon a time, in a land of gentility and tradition, the story began, an heir was born to a family whose holdings had been a fiefdom since good King James granted the second charter to Jamestown in 1642. The family prospered. They became successful tobacco planters, successful exporters back to England. When the Revolution came, they risked it all and stood with George Washington. When the Civil War came, they stood with their friends. That war almost ruined them, but they persevered. As the years passed, they turned from planting to commerce. And prospered again. Much of their land was converted into capital, which in turn was invested in manufacturing, which in turn grew into more capital. There were setbacks, of course, but by the time the new prince arrived on the scene, the family name was known and respected and the family's fortune considerable.

Like most of the young men of his generation and class, the young prince was well educated, well mannered, well dressed, charming, arrogant and privileged. No one thought much of it. It was his due.

In his freshman year at Washington and Lee, this would have been around 1940, with World War II just around the corner, he was pledged to Kappa Alpha fraternity and finishing the initiation ritual. The final hurdle was Swill Night. The idea was to test how well a prospective member could hold his liquor. The pledge took a two-ounce shot of bourbon every half hour, beginning right after dinner, and downed a bottle of beer in the intervals. If he could still stand up and was able to recite the Greek alphabet backwards at midnight, he was deemed worthy of the brotherhood. Seven of the ten who started were still standing when midnight came. Four managed the alphabet backwards. He was one of them.

It was a grand night. They were gloriously drunk. They'd passed. They were rulers of the Earth. They laughed and sang rowdy songs and howled at the moon. Oh yes, gloriously drunk.

On the way back to the fraternity house, stuffed in a red Ford convertible, top open to the autumn night, still laughing and singing, weaving down a little two-lane road that snaked across the Virginia countryside from the Old Plantation House restaurant out in the country to town, they rounded a corner and came upon a pack of cars on the side of the road. The cars were parked in a circle, their headlights burning. In the center of that circle of light were five white men and a lone black man dressed in bib overalls. Drunk as he was, our young prince recognized the county sheriff. The sheriff was holding the black man's arms behind his back and a man he knew to be the owner of the local Five and Dime was swinging something. In the flash of light he saw blood on the black man's face and in the Five And Dime owner's hands, a club.

They zoomed past, not stopping. The singing and the laughing stopped. They sobered immediately.

"What was that," he yelled to the others.

The wind whipped in their faces "We don't want to know," the driver said, hunching low and kicking up the speed..

"That was the sheriff. I know it was the sheriff. And the Five and Dime man. I know it. I recognized them."

"Forget it," the other said, and they sped on through the dark.

The next morning the talk of the campus was of the lynching. A black man had been found hanging from the bridge over Chalk Mine Run. There hadn't been a lynching in Rockbridge County since Klan days.

The young prince heard it at breakfast with his brothers in his well appointed fraternity house.

He looked up the boys he'd been with. "You heard?" he asked. They'd heard. "We could have stopped that," he said. The others looked at him with wonder. "We could have gotten killed," one said. "Forget it," said another.

"We can't let this go. We have to tell someone. They can't get away with this."

"Shut up," the others said. "Forget it," they said. "They'll kick your ass out of school if you make a fuss about this. You want nobody to trust you, talk to you? You want to wind up beaten in a ditch? Forget it."

He agonized over it. In the end, he gave in to his peers' demands.

That's why he is the way he is. That's why he has to slay dragons and take on kings. He's proving to himself he's not a coward. That's why he's drinking himself to death. He's got a demon on his back.

"How do you know this," I asked. We sat in the far corner of the bar in the shadows sipping black coffee.

Gideon looked past me to the bar, watching to see if Will stirred. "One night when it was just the two of us here he told me. He was pretty far along … not all the way … but almost. Not slurring words or nothing like that. He never does that. But he had that glazed look in his eye and that whispery voice he gets when he's close to sinking under. He was sad. He was so sad. Never seen him so down. I guess it had been eating at him so much that he finally had to tell someone. I think he thought he was safe with me. Well, he never told on that sheriff, but he quit that school and left that place—got himself accepted in another school … up north somewhere. New York, I think. From that day on he set himself against the high and the mighty … and started trying to wash the memory of that night from his mind." Gideon paused and looked back at me. "A lesser man would have let it pass. All his buddies did. The whole town did. Not Will Owens. Nothing cowardly about that man. No finer man. Nowhere."

We sat silently looking for whatever we could find in each other's faces.

"No finer," I finally said. "Nowhere."

THIRTY FOUR

Anyway, I didn't go over my plans with Will. Dulin was okay with it, so I descended on Miss Liv.

"Come for tea," she told me when I called her to ask if she'd see me. "Bring Allie with you if you like. She brightens the room. Wednesday? At four? I'll so look forward to seeing you."

Allie was less gracious.

"What are you up to?"

"I'm following up on an idea."

"About Emma? About the murder?"

The way she said it made me feel a little guilty.

"Does Miss Liv know that?"

"She didn't ask, and I didn't say exactly."

"You haven't seen Miss Liv in years and now you come calling twice in a month? She knows."

"I'm going to lay it all out for her when I see her."

"You better. What are you going to lay out for me?"

I hadn't told Allie about my evening with Emma. I'm not sure why. All I said was, "Will you come with me?"

She finally gave me that little laugh of hers. "Oh, hero, you know I will. Mom keeps the baby while I work. She won't mind. Pick me up at the office about three-thirty. We don't want to be late for Miss Livvie."

After her divorce, Allie had gone to work. She was uneasy about being away from the baby so young, but she had no choice. She had to work. She'd finished two years at UK with no major selected. Her only asset for a possible secretarial job was her skill as a typist, which she'd picked up in Ms. Luktemeir's class at

Frankfort High. That and her personality and her determination. The combination was good enough to get her hired by a small local law firm with big aspirations. She fit right in and was now the assistant to the managing partner.

Wednesday came. Snow came with it. A clinging snow, coating the trees and blanketing the roofs with a soft white shawl. The day was immaculately clear, but cold, so cold nothing was melting. The streets and sidewalks lay beneath an inch or so of powder, showing footprints and tire-tracks in busy patterns but cushioning all sound and softening all edges. I walked that morning—the full circle—up the north side of the river to the New Bridge then back down the south side to the Old Bridge and across it to Main and the left turn to the *Journal*—just for the pure pleasure of it.

Miss Liv's living room was warm and welcoming when we got there. A coal-fire was burning in the fireplace, and Miss Liv's silver tea service was glistening in the afternoon light streaming in through the window.

"What a beautiful day," she said as she took our coats and ushered us in. "What a beautiful, beautiful day. Perfect for a visit. Perfect for a good hot tea." Smiling, she pointed us to the couch, then took her usual seat in the big armchair facing the fire.

There are some women, a few women, not many, who have a way about them; their smile, the way they talk to you, understandingly, encouragingly, the warmth they surround you in—that makes you wish all women were so, but since they are not, makes you feel doubly glad that one is and that she's paying attention to you. Miss Livia Hockensmith was one of them.

She sat there beaming at us for a moment. "You make such a nice looking couple," she said. "Are you?"

I'm sure the surprise on my face registered immediately. I didn't see Allie's reaction, but I'm sure she blushed.

Before either of us could manage a reply, Miss Liv said, "Oh well. If you are not, you should be. Now, Theo Clark, I imagine you have more on your mind than just the pleasure of my company. What is it?"

It took me more than a moment to pull my mind back from the answer to Miss Liv's question that I was struggling to find and get focused again on what I'd come for.

She waited, watching my confusion with an understanding twinkle. Allie, too, was watching expectantly.

So I started with my evening with Emma—how it had come about—what it was all about. I didn't break my deal with Emma, but I did tell Miss Liv how it seemed that Emma was staging a little show for me, a scene from a play, how she had even knelt before me to protest her innocence, but that in honesty, I halfway believed her. Miss Liv listened quietly through all this. Didn't interrupt. Asked no questions. Allie was silent as well. I could feel her body shifting on the couch beside me but had no idea how she was taking what I had to tell.

As I talked the afternoon faded.

Miss Liv sensed I had finished what I wanted to say about my meeting with Emma and began to rise from her chair. "Time for tea," she said. "Theo, put a few more chunks of coal on the fire and poke it up. Allie, come help me with the service."

I did as she asked and then followed them into a little sunroom beyond the living room to a circular table covered with a white cloth, a vase of blood red roses in its center. Three places were set and a slew of cookies on a silver platter was waiting. A bay window looked out on the park-like grounds that led up to the Capitol. The pink light of the setting sun reflected off the snow, and the few cars that were beginning to make their way up the avenue to the Capitol had on their headlights.

We sipped our tea and worked at small talk, distancing ourselves for a moment from Emma's plight and the murder.

"There's still more," I finally said.

Miss Liv nodded. "I was sure of it."

We left the table and returned to our seats by the fire.

That is when I told Miss Liv about Arlo Lee, the Gypsy, and what he had said about the bequest from Adeline—and about a new will.

The room was almost dark and the silence almost complete when I finished. The only light was the soft glow thrown off from the glow of the coal in the fireplace. We could hear the grandfather clock ticking in the hallway and occasionally the muted sound of a car passing by. In the room there was only the sound of quiet breathing.

I couldn't read Miss Liv's reaction. Nor Allie's. It seemed as if neither had moved as I told them about Thomas Lee rap, tap, tapping on my balcony window, of our drive to Golden Pond, my meeting Arlo Lee in that strange setting by the little creek and how he was counting on me to help establish his innocence in the murder of Adeline Hockensmith Purcell.

Miss Liv seemed not to be focused on me but on what she was seeing in her mind. Allie had moved closer to me and had put her hand on my shoulder.

"Arlo Lee said the only reason he was at the farm is that Mrs. Purcell had sent a message asking him to come. She had something important to tell him," I said.

Miss Liv turned her gaze back to me then. "And that was?" she asked softly.

I paused. I felt as if I was trespassing. But it wasn't enough to keep me from going on.

"A strange story. Hard to believe because it makes absolutely no sense."

"Do you think that only the things that make sense are believable, Theo?"

I considered that for a moment. I knew of a lot of things that didn't make sense but happened anyway. "No ma'am," I said, "but it takes a real stretch to believe this one."

"Well, tell me."

I took a deep breath and plunged ahead with it. "Arlo said that Mrs. Purcell was going to leave a large portion of the farm to him. She was going to change her will, cutting into Emma's and Judge Hockensmith's bequests. She didn't explain to him why she was doing this, only that it would happen. She wanted him to know because she was dying from a cancer of the brain and she had little time left to live."

Miss Liv sighed. "Poor Adeline. Poor, poor Adeline."

"Mrs. Purcell told him her lawyer was coming that afternoon to hear her changes and draw up the new will. She said no one knew about the cancer but you, Miss Liv, and that no one knew about the new will but you. Your signature on the finished document was to attest to her sound mind and real intent, so that it could not be challenged by her daughter or her brother after her death."

I stopped and waited, expecting some sort of reaction from Miss Liv. When none came, I went on, "Was she dying? Was she going to change her will? Was she going to leave a sizeable portion of her farm to a Gypsy—at the expense of her daughter and her brother? It doesn't make sense."

Allie squeezed my shoulder and whispered, "gently, gently."

Miss Liv found my eyes in the darkened room.

"Why is it important now?"

"If she was going to change her will and make a sizeable cut in Emma's inheritance and the money to be left to the Judge, that could provide a strong motive. On the other side of it, if she was going to leave a sizeable inheritance to Arlo Lee, it's not likely he'd get mad about it and murder her. It is very important, Miss Liv."

A sad little smile formed, and she shook her head gently at me. "You have to do this, don't you, Theo Clark? Of all of them, you were always the one who had to know why. Even when it got you in trouble. Sometimes it's best not to know. Sometimes it's best just to let things be." She turned to Allie. "He can be a vexation, girl. Be careful of him."

She fixed me with that frowning, brown-eyed stare that used to make us all feel like deer caught in the headlights and took her time, deciding.

Then she began, softly, talking to Allie, not to me.

"They came every summer, the Gypsies. They used to camp on the edge of town close to the river out beyond the distillery, but some of the town bluebloods got together and had the police tear up the their camp, arrest a few of them, and run the rest off.

"My brother was friends with their head-man, a man the towns-folk called Gypsy Nick. His real name was Nicolae, but in that insulting way people have of calling people they think they're better than almost anything they please, Gypsy Nick is how he was called.

"Ezra and he had done business together. Something with horses, I think. The Gypsy was beaten badly in that raid and taken to jail. The only person his family could think of who might help was Ezra. They sent one of their young men out to the farm. Ezra went back to town, bailed his friend out of jail and had a local doctor treat him.

"Ezra was so angry at what he called, 'the better-than-thous' that he vowed the Gypsies weren't going to be treated that way again in this county so long as he could do anything about it. What he did was offer Nicolae Lee and his tribe a sanctuary on the farm … a place they'd be welcome and safe, anytime their travels brought them this way.

"A lot of the local folk didn't like this at all. The sheriff warned Ezra that there better be no trouble stemming from 'that gang,' and even his preacher got on him. But Ezra didn't care. The Gypsies were welcome. I was proud of him for standing up like that."

Miss Liv smiled at me then. "Ezra had his faults, but kowtowing to the "better-than-thous" wasn't one of them."

I said, "Mrs. Purcell's father made a promise to Nicolae Lee? Arlo is Nicolae's son? Mrs. Purcell felt she should honor that promise?"

"It's more than that."

"More?"

"Nicolae is Arlo Lee's grandfather. Arlo's father is Ezra Hockensmith, my brother."

THIRTY FIVE

The Gypsies all gathered at their campsite on the creek that night, the night Ezra Hockensmith rescued Nicolae Lee from the tender mercies of the sheriff and delivered him, delivered all of them, to the safety of the farm. What a celebration they had. What a sense of relief they felt. It was late June, a soft summer night with a gibbous moon. There was laughter and music and dancing and song. Delight was in the air. It was a night to honor heroes, and Ezra Hockensmith had the spotlight.

She wasn't there, but this is the way Miss Liv imagined it as Ezra tried to explain. "He wouldn't use those sorts of words, of course, he was far too plain a man," she said, "but that's the picture I see."

"Ezra didn't drink much. He was a hard-shell Baptist, but he had his passions. He was a vigorous man, a very physical man. He had been alone for a long time, two years or more since his wife died. I can understand how the singing and the dancing and the moonlight and the liquor went to his head. And the attention. All that attention. That, by itself, would have been enough to befuddle him. The girl certainly did. He'd never seen anyone so exotic and tempting. Whether she actually had feelings for him or was simply reflecting the gratitude of her father and her clan made no difference.

"When the Gypsies returned to the camp on the creek the following year, the girl had a baby in her arms."

"Arlo," I said.

Miss Liv paused a moment, then continued.

"Adeline must have been about ten that year, trying to be the woman of the house with her mother gone, and Ira about four. Ezra had a women in to do the cooking and the cleaning and another to take care of Ira during the day, but it was hard on Adeline—and hard on Ezra.

"One morning that summer, Adeline and I were in the kitchen, cleaning up after breakfast. I was just back from finishing up my schooling at Sophie Newcomb in New Orleans, lazing away the summer waiting for fall to come and the teaching job I was going to at the girl's college over in Midway. There was a knock on the kitchen door. We thought it must be one of the field hands come to ask a question of Ezra, but when I opened it, there stood the most striking creature I had ever seen. She had flashing emerald eyes that were almost hypnotic and flawless skin that looked golden in the morning sun. Sleek black hair hung to a tiny waist. She wore large gold earrings in perfectly formed ears, and when she smiled, the force of it seemed to wrap around you like a friendly hug. The girl, because she was a girl, she couldn't have been much older than eighteen, had on a full black skirt that hung to her ankles and a brightly colored blouse cinched at the waist with a belt made of gold coins. The long skirt and the loose blouse accentuated her figure rather than hiding it. She was barefoot, her nails painted a bright red. She had tiny feet—and a baby on her hip.

"Adeline and I stared open-mouthed. 'My name is Keira,' she said as I opened the kitchen door to her. 'My father is Nicolae Lee. We arrived last night.'

"Adeline and I still stood speechless.

"'I would like to see Mr. Hockensmith,' she said, 'My father has a message for him.'

"'My gracious,' I finally managed to say. 'Forgive me keeping you standing here. Do please come in. Yes, come in. What a handsome baby. Adeline, can you find your father? Would you like some coffee? Please sit down,' I said, ushering her in and to the big table in the center of the room. 'Keira? You said Keira? What an unusual name.'

"'It is from the Irish, I think. It means dark princess. I don't know what my father was thinking,'

"Adeline reappeared almost immediately. 'He's coming,' she said, then moving closer to the table and Keira and the baby. 'What's his name? Can I hold him?'

"Kiera stroked the baby's head then held him out at arm's length, smiling and the baby smiling back. 'Yes,' she said, 'but hold him tight. He wiggles. His name is Arlo.'

"Adeline took the baby eagerly and started cooing to him. At that point Ezra walked in. He saw Keira first and was smiling at her as he moved across the room when his eye caught Adeline and the baby. He stopped in surprise, then looked questioningly at Keira. 'Good morning, Mr. Hockensmith.' Keira said. 'I have a message from my father.'

"Ezra looked around the room to me and then to Adeline who was holding the baby. I could see the confusion in his face. 'The baby will be all right with your daughter while we talk,' she said. 'Can I, Daddy,' Adeline pleaded. 'Can I?'

"This was all such a strange thing happening on a sunny summer morning in a room where almost nothing out of the ordinary ever happened.

"Ezra looked around again, eyes dazed, then nodded to Adeline and led Keira out of the room, I presumed to his study at the far corner of the house.

"They were away about half-an-hour. When they came back, Keira looked relieved, and Ezra looked somber. She collected the baby, said her goodbyes to Adeline and me, nodded to Ezra, opened the kitchen door, and was gone."

Miss Liv stopped then. Allie moved closer to me. I sat entranced, lost in the story. I had long ago stopped taking notes.

We sat that way until Miss Liv said, "We've let the room go cold. Theo, put more coal on the fire. Let's get some light in here. There is no need to sit in the cold and the dark."

That broke the spell. I got up to attend to the fire while Allie started toward the lamp on the table behind the couch.

Miss Liv stopped her. "Allie, don't turn on the lamps just yet. My mood isn't right for too bright a light. Do you need more light, Theo? No? Good. Now isn't this better? A nice glow from the fire, the room getting warm, shadows to hide in." She was smiling bravely but both Allie and I caught the ache in her voice.

Allie was standing behind me. Her hand found my shoulder, then she walked over, leaned down and kissed Miss Liv tenderly on her cheek. She came back, sat down beside me and whispered in my ear, "She's crying. Don't appear to notice."

Then I truly felt like the intruder—embarrassed to be putting Miss Liv through enough travail to make her cry—ashamed at taking advantage of her liking of me. Maybe Will was right. Maybe I wasn't tough enough for this game.

There was a flash of white as Miss Liv lifted a handkerchief to her eye.

"It would have been an awful scandal, you know," she continued in a very soft voice. "Ezra Hockensmith the father of a Gypsy child! That was worse than if he had congress with a black. People were awfully prejudiced back then, not much better now, but then—well, the scandal would have been dreadful. Ezra was an elder in the church, he was chairman of the Farm Board. Can you imagine?" She stopped then, shaking her head again at the prospect of it all, "Can you imagine?"

She wiped a tear and then looked up to Allie. "I'm dreadfully dry, my dear. There is a nice little sherry on the sideboard. Will you pour me some? Will you join me? Theo, you as well? A touch of sherry would do us all good."

We sat in silence while Allie filled the little crystal glasses and brought them to us. I could think of nothing to say. The glow from the fireplace gave just enough light to let us make out each other's forms, but not the expressions on our faces. Through the window I could see that night had come outside.

The feeling of guilt that I'd been fighting since we arrived kept rising. I knew Allie sensed it since she moved closer and took my hand.

"Miss Liv," I said into the quiet, "I didn't mean to cause you distress. I had no idea. Allie and I should go now. We can talk another time."

"You sit still, Theo Clark," Miss Liv shot back with a tone in her voice I remembered from days in her classroom. "You opened this door and I stepped through it. You sit still. I'll finish what I have to say."

It didn't take long. My attempt at apology shook her out of the tearful mood her remembering had triggered and back into the no-nonsense lady who had made such an impression on all of us who knew her.

There was only the firelight when she finished. Allie had moved close to me on the couch and was sitting with her legs tucked up beneath her. Miss Liv was a dim figure in the chair across. I was leaning forward, arms on my knees, caught up in her story.

She wouldn't, she told us make apologies for Ezra Hockensmith. He was a good man. He was hard in some matters. And opinionated and sometimes overbearing. But he was fair to everyone and honest in his dealings. He was very loving with his family and tender in that hesitant, embarrassed way strong men have about them. No, she'd make no apologies for Ezra Hockensmith, "she said.

About Arlo, neither she nor Adeline knew that Arlo Lee was Ezra Hockensmith's son until the day Ezra died. He kept it secret all that time.

THIRTY SIX

"The Gypsies came every summer and camped on the creek, and Ezra visited them and spent time there, but Adeline and I didn't see the baby again;the baby that the Gypsy girl, Keira, brought to the house that summer morning, until years later," Miss Liv told us.

"He showed up at the horse barn one morning with Ezra who had brought him up from the camp to teach him to ride properly, not like the Gypsies did, but like Kentucky boys did. Ezra introduced him to us. We had lemonade and lunch. His English was understandable, but halting. Among themselves the Gypsies speak their own tongue, Romany. They learn English to be able to get along with us.

"Adeline took to him immediately, as she had when she first took him in her arms that day Keira brought him as a baby. He was a handsome child, around eight or nine years old, well formed, with black curly hair spilling down around his ears and smiling green eyes like his mother. And outgoing. Not shy at all. And he seemed to take to her.

"In no time, Adeline was tutoring him in English. He even stayed one full summer with Adeline and Ezra. He must have been about fourteen or fifteen then, remaining after the Gypsies left that summer. He lived in the big house with them; worked around the farm tagging after Ezra, letting Adeline polish his reading and writing.

"Ezra was very good with him. He and the boy, Arlo, made a connection I never understood until that day, the day Ezra died. Holding Adeline's hand, he told us of the Gypsy girl and Arlo. Ezra asked us not to think badly of him. He was weak, and Keira was beautiful. There was no question that the boy would be raised a Gypsy. Keira and Nicolae both wanted it that way. So Ezra saw Arlo in the summers, spent time with him in the summers, but did not acknowledge him. Arlo never knew. From what you told me, he still doesn't know.

"When Adeline learned she had incurable cancer, she came to me. She told me what she had in mind. She wanted to be sure Arlo and his family had land of their own, a place where they could be safe. She had arranged for her attorney to come to the farm, so she could tell him exactly what she wanted done.

"Adeline wanted me to witness the signing of the new will because she felt sure that Ira would challenge it. Ira was jealous and resentful of Adeline, even as a child. Big sister lording it over little brother. He never outgrew it. When their father died and Adeline got control of most of the money and all of the power, it infuriated him. Though Ira was well provided for, he had expensive habits and grand plans. He was often overextended and had to come hat-in-hand to Adeline to bail him out. They had some awful arguments. Adeline knew any attempt to give a portion of the estate, a portion that might cut into Ira's possible inheritance, and to give it to a Gypsy, would guarantee a fight. Emma? Sharing wasn't one of Emma's strong suits. Adeline felt certain Emma could be influenced by her uncle Ira to fight about it, too. My witnessing the will would attest to Adeline's sound mind and to her exact instruction and would blunt any challenge that Ira or Emma, or the both of them together might raise, she felt. But I never got to attest a new will, did I? Adeline died before there was one."

Miss Liv paused then, looking to me in the dim light. "What happened to the handwritten copy of the will the Gypsy said Adeline showed him?"

"I don't know, Miss Liv. Arlo doesn't have it."

Another pause, reflecting.

"A pity. Ah, well, I think that's all of it. Does what she was trying to do make more sense to you now? I don't know if Emma or Ira knew about her plan. Adeline might have told them, but I don't think so. She might have told her attorney, and he might have told Ira, but I don't think so. Adeline said the attorney was to get the information that afternoon—the afternoon of the morning she died, so I don't believe he knew. You said Arlo Lee didn't know himself until that morning.

"If Emma and Ira didn't know, where is the motive? And isn't what I've told you and what the Gypsy told you just hearsay, something with no actual proof behind it ... just a 'he said, she said' thing that can't be verified? What has all this gotten you?"

I shook my head in frustration. " Nowhere, I guess, Miss Liv."

I could see her lean forward in her chair.

"Now you listen to me Theo Clark. I never expected that this story would be told. I don't want it told now. You have a rule at your newspaper, don't you, something about 'off the record?' If a journalist is told something 'off the record,' it can't be used? I had no idea what I was going to tell you when we began talking, but now that I know, everything I've told you is 'off the record.'"

"But Miss Liv," I said, "if you want something off the record, you have to say so before you begin spilling the story."

"Don't you argue with me, Theo Clark!"

A thundering silence.

And then into it a little laugh that couldn't be contained. Allie, sitting beside me; she tried to muffle it but with no success.

The command in Mis Liv's voice was a tone I'd heard a hundred times before in her classes, a tone I was never brave enough or foolish enough to disregard. It was that "if-you-know-what's-good-for-you" voice. There was no mistaking it. Even Allie heard it.

I hoped that in the darkness Miss Liv couldn't make out the grin that spread on my face, too, but when I responded, "Yes, ma'am," my voice must have betrayed me.

"Are you laughing, Theo Clark?" she said.

"No, ma'am?"

"Is there something funny here?"

"No ma'am."

"Then it's all off-the-record? I have your word?"

"It's all off-the-record. You have my word."

"Good then. Allie, light the lamps, please. Theo, poke the fire back up. I'll pour the sherry myself."

Afterwards, after the fire was blazing and the room bright and the sherry warming our insides, Miss Liv turned to me and said, "I'm not mad at you, Theo. Ezra's secret is safe with you." Looking across to Allie, she said, "And with you, Allie."

At that she paused, seeming to confirm a judgment in her mind, then said, "I imagine you keep secrets very well." Then she turned back to me. "Don't ask me if I think Emma killed her mother. Emma could be a sweet child. She could be mean and vindictive, too. We all can be, can't we?"

"Now," she said, beginning to rise from her chair, "no more talk. All this remembering and confessing has tired me out. Go home."

THIRTY SEVEN

Allie hurried to unlock the door and get some lights on while I carried the baby in. Her mother had fed her, put her in her nightclothes, and had her sleeping soundly. She stayed asleep, bundled up against the cold and cradled tightly in Allie's arms while we made the short drive over the icy roads from her mother's place to hers.

"Stay," she said as she took the baby from me and started to her little room. "I'll make us some supper. Bacon and eggs? Coffee?"

The baby started to stir. Allie kissed her on the forehead and smiled. "She'll go right down. Won't wake up until morning. You're in no hurry. Stay." And disappeared down the hallway.

I stood staring after her, suddenly aware of the possibilities the evening held and realizing the danger.

After a few minutes she returned. I was still standing there, still in my coat, struggling with my yearning and my damnable compunction not to do dumb things.

Seeing me so, she stopped, puzzled, put her hands on her hips, cocked her head to the side and said, "What's wrong? You're not hungry? I'll even throw in a bourbon on ice;" and in a laughing mimic of Miss Liv, "Don't you argue with me, Theo Clark."

An hour or so later we were sitting on the couch side by side, our legs stretched out to the coffee table in front of the fire, watching the blue flames flicker in the darkened room. Outside, snow was falling again—gently—wide flakes floating softly down. I sipped contentedly on a drink Allie made for after supper— hot milk, black coffee, and bottled-in-bond bourbon in equal measure with two spoons of sugar stirred in. The sugar has to be stirred in after the milk and coffee but before the bourbon or it doesn't work, Allie said.

A snowy night, a sheltering room lighted by fire-glow, soft music playing and Allie beside me. I couldn't remember when I'd felt so safe and favored. Or so tempted.

I walked away that June—that June of Korea—a beautiful June, a perfect June, mellow days, soft nights, the full moon never bigger, the scent of honeysuckle never sweeter.

Though we were best friends, Michael Dannan and I both vied for Allie from the time we first saw her. We were standing on the corner after church, watching the girls go by. A group we'd known most of our lives came toward us. In their midst was a golden blonde in a wide brimmed hat with a trailing red ribbon. She paid no attention to us, not even a smile, as she sauntered by.

We were captured.

She was new in town. She got there in time for the last semester of our senior year in high school. Michael and I dated her through that spring and summer and through our first year at UK.

I can't be certain which of the two of us she favored most. I think it was me, which may be only my ego showing, but I never found out for sure. I withdrew from the contest—out of pride—a conceit that afflicts me grievously.

None of this has anything to do with Mis Liv's story or Adeline Purcell's will, or any of the other things that had been occupying my mind. It has to do only with Allie, who is always somewhere in there.

"Remember walking around the Capitol that night in the snowfall?" Allie whispered.

"After the Christmas dance? You in a green gown," I said, "and those flimsy little shoes. My coat around you to keep you warm."

"There was a full moon," she said.

"And snow was falling."

"You carried me from the car to the promenade to keep my feet from getting wet."

"I sat you on the wall above the steps."

"We were all alone. No other cars, no other people. So quiet. Remember?"

I remembered—the two of us at the top of the Capitol steps looking down that grand, wide avenue, with the streetlights glowing through the falling snow. I remembered how still the air was and how hushed the town. And I remembered Allie at the center of it.

"There were snowflakes in your hair." I said.

"You were beginning to shiver. I kissed you to warm you up."

"But you didn't give me back my coat."

I felt her hand take mine, her head lift, her lips on mine.

"For old times' sake," she said.

THIRTY EIGHT

February gave way to March. Snow to rain. Clouds to spells of clear. There was just enough hint of warmth in the air to make you know spring was nearby.

Dulin kept me busy with the routine of a small town daily newspaper—bread and butter stuff loaded with local names.

As often as I could, I trailed after Will as he covered the Legislature and fashioned his column. I wanted to learn how he did it. Watching him at work drove home that who you know is often more important than what you know, and that often the most important "who's" aren't the rich and powerful, but the men and women in the trenches—the people doing the everyday jobs. They are the ones who know what's going on and how it's being done.

Will even took me in to meet Happy once. Rising from his big leather chair there in his office in the Capitol Building, the Governor was all smiles and handshakes and personality. Seeing Happy's blue eyes sparkling, still radiating charisma at fifty-eight, I knew at once why voters kept returning him to office, whether he kept his promises or not. As we were leaving, he took my hand again and winking to Will said, "Remember son, the secret to getting elected is to tell them what they want to hear. The trick is to know what that is."

The Ashes Murder drifted along submerged—there but not in sight. I stayed as close as was possible, but Dulin assured me that nothing was likely to happen except by accident. So I waited and fumed, checking regularly on Arlo to make sure he was holding up okay in the confines of the County Jail, which he wasn't. The imprisonment was eroding him physically and mentally.

The information I had from Mis Liv might have sprung him, but there was no verification of any kind and my hands were tied by my promise to her anyway.

It occurred to me I'd been handing out promises freely and not getting anything in return except crucial information I couldn't use. What would Will say about that?

I assumed that Emma's attorney would seek a change of venue. That would at least be a story. The speculation around the county was that he would. There had been so much attention to the murder and so much gossip that it seemed likely that everyone in the county had heard of it, and most of them had an opinion. Which would argue that an unbiased jury couldn't be seated and that Emma couldn't get a fair trial.

When I asked him, Attorney Hanratty wanted none of that. He wanted the trial right here, heard by people who knew the Hockensmith name, people that Emma had grown up among. The idea that Emma would kill her own mother, smash her head in with a flatiron, cram ashes down her throat, a well bred, church going young woman—the idea that a loving daughter would do something like that, well, you'd have to prove it; you'd have to come up with a mighty strong reason why a loving daughter would do that to her mother. The prosecution hadn't come up with one yet. Emma and her mother were on good terms, he'd argue. Mrs. Purcell was baby-sitting Emma's child, for Chrissake! The whole idea was ridiculous!

All the nasty gossip and smarmy joking that entertained the community notwithstanding, Hanratty believed that at the end of the day he would find someone on the jury who would give a hometown girl the benefit of the doubt.

THIRTY NINE

The case of the Commonwealth of Kentucky vs. Emma Purcell Kane began on the ninth day of April in the courtroom on the second floor of the Franklin County Courthouse, Judge Augustus Maxwell presiding.

It was a Monday.

Spring was inching in. Trees were beginning to leaf and jonquils were already blooming. The morning was soft and bright—too fine a morning to be sitting in a courtroom.

Jury selection was underway when I entered. Emma sat at the defense table looking innocent and confused. She was dressed in muted colors and plain fashion—a simple white blouse, an ankle length black skirt. Her hair was put up in an unadorned bun. Very little make-up—a bit of rouge on her cheeks, a little shade on her eyebrows and lashes, a light pale red on her lips and her nails—schoolmarmish. She glanced behind her at the packed courtroom and to the jury pool to her right with a look that asked "Why am I here?" Attorney Hanratty sat next to her, patting her hand to reassure her and leaning in to whisper in her ear.

I spent the first several hours watching as the attorneys questioned prospective jurors. The jury pool took up almost half the courtroom. They were the normal mix of types you'd see in the crowds downtown on a busy Saturday afternoon. Housewives, farmers, state workers, shopkeepers. I recognized Winston Thomas who managed the local Sears Roebuck store. One of the women looked familiar—youngish, a pretty face. I think she was a waitress at Yancey's. There were only two blacks in the jury pool; both were middle-aged men.

From this assemblage, the attorneys would eventually agree on twelve plus two more for alternates—if not today, then tomorrow, and if not tomorrow, then the next day. No hurry. Take your time. Enjoy the show. And clearly it was going to be a show—the best entertainment since Happy Chandler beat the machine and staged his big parade through town and up to the Capitol.

If the Circuit Court could have sold tickets, a guaranteed seat in the upstairs courtroom would have gone for as much as a courtside ticket at a UK sell-out. As it was, and even though jury selection was the only thing going on, it was standing room only.

Betting men around town would give no odds on the outcome of the trial. The feeling around the county, as best I could determine, was that Emma did it, that the spoiled little rich girl got mad about something and did her mother in. That's the way the gossip and the chatter ran.

But no one was willing to bet that Hanratty couldn't get her off, especially when you noticed that there seemed to be a considerable lack of enthusiasm on the part of the Commonwealth's Attorney for the case.

Dan Lindsey, who held that post, was a fire-eating, ambitious man with eyes on the Governor's chair. With all the visibility the Ashes Murder offered, nailing the villain who crushed Adeline Hockensmith's head and stuffed ashes down her throat would seem a valuable advertisement for a motivated politician. But putting Emma Purcell Kane behind bars didn't seem to be high on his list. He'd held no press conferences and given no interviews. He wasn't even conducting the questioning of the prospective jurors. Admittedly, the Commonwealth's Attorney is a busy man with many responsibilities. Still, it seemed strange that Dan Lindsey wasn't in the middle of this.

Hanratty was on his feet in front of the jury box, finishing up his examination of a young lady who worked on the bottling-line at the distillery—Mrs. Purcell's distillery. Late twenties, I'd say. She lived out of town with her husband near Jett in one of the new houses being put up on the way to Lexington. He also worked at the distillery. She was pretty in a plain sort of way, dressed in her Sunday best and her hair nicely done, obviously nervous, sitting in the jury box all alone and with all eyes on her as Hanratty asked his questions. Never had she had this much attention.

"You've read or heard about this case?"

A shy, "Yes, sir."

"Have you formed an opinion? Be careful how you answer."

She glanced at the Judge, then back to Hanratty.

A hesitant, "No, sir."

"You have an open mind about all this, despite what you've heard and read?"

She looked again to the Judge, hunched her shoulders, raised a hand to push back a wisp of hair, then straight at Hanratty. "I don't know what to believe, sir, I've heard so much. All I know is that whoever killed poor Mrs. Purcell and put those ashes in her mouth must be a monster."

Pointing his finger at Emma, Hanratty said, "Does Mrs. Kane, sitting there, does she look like a monster to you?" The woman followed Hanratty's gesture to Emma. Emma didn't flinch. She sat up straighter and faced the woman. They held each other's gaze for a long moment, then the woman turned back to Hanratty and said, "No, sir, she doesn't."

A small smile crossed Hanratty's lips. "If the prosecution could prove her to be a monster, would you vote for her conviction?"

The woman hesitated, glancing to Emma, then to the Judge, then back to Hanratty. "Yes, sir."

"Even if it meant she would go to the electric chair?"

The woman slowly bowed her head, breaking her eye contact with Hanratty. When she raised it again it was to look at the judge. "Yes, sir," she said evenly. "Yes, I could."

The questioning went like that most of the morning. Every single soul knew of the murder, had either read about or heard about it on radio or TV. All but three said they had discussed the particulars. But not a soul, not a single soul, admitted to having formed an opinion. Four asked to be relieved on religious grounds. They objected to the death penalty. And two were dismissed for hardship causes. But all the rest, they were all open minded, they swore. They could be objective.

Both the prosecution and the defense exercised their pre-emptive challenges—not for any reason more substantive than could be laid to any of the seated jurors, just to be doing it.

The Commonwealth's Attorney's team seemed satisfied. Hanratty certainly was. Dan Lindsey's people apparently got what they felt was a set of jurors inclined to be "objective" in favor of the prosecution. Hanratty got a cadre he seemed comfortable would be "objective" in favor of the defense. Fair trial coming up.

This was all accomplished in record time. The jury was selected and sworn in by late afternoon. The formal trial would begin at nine the next morning.

Arlo Lee, the Gypsy, walked out of jail that night.

Nothing spectacular. No alarms blaring or spotlights flashing. He simply walked out.

You have to understand that the County Jail is not a high-security establishment. It's in an annex to the backside of the Courthouse on the alley that runs from Main to Wapping—the one with the paperboys' entrance to the *Journal*—a two-storey white concrete block building with an office, a guard's room, three cells on the first floor and four cells on the second. Its clientele is usually drunks, combatants in bar fights, and the occasional bad check passer. You could call the atmosphere "relaxed."

Arlo got along with the guards. He was quiet. He caused no problems. Fairly quickly he dropped from their list of concerns and became just someone who was there, not to be worried about.

After lights out that night and after bed check at midnight, Arlo rose from his bunk, quietly opened the door to his cell with the key he'd pick-pocketed, walked past the sleeping guard and out into the night.

Later, the guard would say he was drugged. A Gypsy potion was slipped into his coffee. That was why he was unconscious when Arlo escaped. However, no compounds were detected in his coffee on later inspection though no one expected a Gypsy potion to leave a trace, and Arlo had no visitors that day.

That was the explanation Sheriff Woodrow Stanley Peavler gave us. Privately, the guard believed he'd been hexed.

I found out about the escape long before the Sheriff did. Thomas Lee called on me again, catching up with me as I walked home after the paper was put to bed that morning. I didn't hear him approach, didn't see him until all at once he appeared at my side as I made the turn onto Wapping Street.

"Damn, Thomas," I said, startled. "Where did you come from?"

He fell into stride with me. "Arlo escaped."

I stopped dead. "What?"

"He sent me to tell you."

"How? When?"

A car passed, its headlights flashing briefly on us.

"We should keep walking," he said.

I was so surprised I felt like sitting down.

"We're close to my apartment. Come on."

"No," Thomas Lee said. "I don't have time. Arlo said to tell you he'd had all he could take. He won't be any place they can find him."

"Wait," I said as Thomas Lee turned away from me and started toward the river. "Wait, dammit," I yelled after him as he disappeared into the fog.

No one at the County Jail knew about Arlo's departure until breakfast. His cell was empty when they came with his tray.

There was hell to pay when the Sheriff showed up. That was six-thirty. Arlo Lee, the Gypsy, had been gone by then for almost six hours.

In six hours you could be across the border into Tennessee, or well up into Ohio, or into West Virginia if you headed east, or across the Mississippi and entering Missouri going west. Yes, Sheriff Woodrow Stanley Peavler was apoplectic.

I saw some of it. I walked into the jail while Woody was berating his deputies. The guard who'd been on duty was standing rigidly in the center of the room, red-eyed, unshaven, and sweating through his uniform shirt. The rest of the deputy force was squeezed in around him. It looked as if the Sheriff had called them all in, rousted them all out of bed and commanded them to the scene of the embarrassment. Woody was fully turned out in a pressed uniform and cleanly shaven. He knew the cameras would be showing up soon.

He broke off his tirade when he saw me.

"Were you in on this?" he yelled.

"What's happened, Sheriff?" I asked, trying to sound as surprised as I could.

"Don't give me that." He turned away from the guard and toward me. "Get out of here!"

When Thomas Lee disappeared into the fog, I stood staring after him with absolutely no idea what to do. It must have been four-thirty or so in the morning, still dark, daylight not coming for another couple of hours. No point in getting Will or Dulin up. Nothing they could do. In fact, there was nothing I could do. I considered calling the Sheriff's office and reporting Arlo Lee's departure, but they'd find out soon enough. Why spoil the surprise?

I decided instead to go home, make myself some coffee, maybe cook a big breakfast, and wait for the sun to come up. Which put me at the jail in time for the Sheriff's little performance, and then back across the alley to the *Journal* to call Dulin.

By the time the case of the Commonwealth of Kentucky vs. Emma Purcell Kane convened at nine that morning, our good Sheriff had a salvage plan underway. He had a deputy waiting upstairs to collar the reporters as they walked into the courtroom and send them down to his office. At that point the Gypsy's escape wasn't known outside the Courthouse complex. If the news had to get out, Woodrow Stanley Peavler wanted to tell it his way, and the surest way to guarantee that was to tell it first and tell it himself.

Fuming, he flung at those of us assembled in his office, "The Gypsy's gone! He broke out this morning. The guard on duty was drugged." He fixed us with a righteous glare. "This proves what I've been saying all along. The Gypsy is involved. Innocent men don't run."

He stared directly at me, daring to be challenged.

I waited a moment, feeling the tension rise. "Are you saying the Gypsy is a suspect now? Weren't you holding him as a material witness, not as someone suspected of the murder?"

"You're damn right he's a suspect now. Always has been in my mind," Woodrow Stanley Peavler shot back. "Yes, I was holding him as a witness. I wanted him in hand if the jury acquits Emma Kane. I'm not going to let the killer of Adeline Purcell get away. We'll find him. Bring him back. Put his Gypsy ass on trial!"

I waited a beat, then said, smiling the most guileless smile I could manage, "Can I quote you on that, Sheriff?"

A wave of light chuckles ran around the room.

Woody looked startled. His anger had been so focused on me he'd forgotten the room full of reporters. He realized he'd let his indignation take him further than he wanted. He took a step back, looked slowly around the room, then nodded and found a sheepish grin somewhere.

"Sorry, boys," he said. " I got a little carried away; this thing frustrates me so much. Maybe my language was a little too colorful for a family newspaper. I know you'll use the right words. But you get the drift. We'll find him. We'll bring him back. Then it's up to the Prosecuting Attorney."

Woodrow Stanley Peavler looked around the room again, determination on his face. "That's it. No time for questions. Check later today. That's all."

A few hustled out to find telephones —the wire service reporters, the radio guys, the afternoon papers; this was breaking news for them. For the rest of us, it would be old by the time we could get it in print, so we started back up the stairs to the second floor courtroom. I wondered, as I climbed those marble steps, where Arlo Lee, the Gypsy, might be. Somewhere they'd never find him, Thomas Lee had said.

FORTY

The courtroom was packed when I got there—all seats taken and a line of eager citizens ringing the back and side walls.

I managed to push my way thorough to the press table and squeezed in beside Andy Thomas of the *Lexington Herald*. An attorney I didn't recognize was rising to speak. I nudged Andy, "Who's he?"

Andy whispered, "One of Dan Lindsey's boys. Seems the Prosecuting Attorney has a conflict this morning. This is his number two, Hud Exeter."

"Dan Lindsey's passing this up? Isn't the opening statement one of the big moments of a trial?"

"Yep," Andy grinned.

"Strange."

"Strange trial."

I looked around the courtroom. People were crammed in the seats so tightly it seemed there was no room to move. They were shoulder to shoulder where there was space to stand, all leaning forward expectantly, waiting for the story to unfold.

They were mostly women. You could tell the church ladies and the Garden Club set by their dress, proper and dignified, and the Country Club duchesses, outfitted for afternoon tea or a day of bridge. Not many working women. It was a work day at the distillery and the shoe factory and the garment factory, and few were willing to lose a day's pay this early in the proceedings.

Only a smattering of men had shown up. The farmers were easy to recognize by their sunburned faces and the band of white around their foreheads from where their hats shielded them in the fields. The suits identified the businessmen.

Emma Purcell sat next to Jim Hanratty at the defense table facing the judge, eyes fixed on Hud Exeter as he began to lay out the case against her.

She seemed very vulnerable sitting there with only her attorney beside her and all those people staring at her back. As on the jury selection day, she was dressed modestly—a long-sleeved white blouse again, today, with a ruffled collar and ruffles at the cuffs; a simple black skirt, today to just below the knees; hair in a plain bun again; no make-up. The absence of make-up made her look wan and in need of protection. She'd worn no jewelry the first day. Today she had a gold chain with a Celtic cross at her neck.

Hud Exeter was standing in front of the jury, arms at his sides, beginning to tell the jury what the prosecution would prove and why it would lead them to judge Emma Purcell Kane guilty of the savage murder of her mother.

I looked back at my notes to re-familiarize myself with this collection of "twelve good men and true," this "jury of her peers" who would absorb what the attorneys had to say, observe Emma Kane as she endured the testimony, marinate it all in the juices of their own prejudices and suppositions, and judge her.

The jury was comprised of a woman who taught the sixth grade at Peaks Mill; a mechanic who repaired cars at Thompson's Auto Shop on River Road; the manager of Woolworth's Five and Dime; the chairwoman of the Frankfort Garden Club; a secretary who worked for the State Highway Department; a grandmother whose husband had the farm on the eastern side of the Hockensmith place; the manager of the local Allstate Insurance agency; a Sunday School teacher at First Baptist; the young woman who worked on the bottling-line at the distillery; a tobacco farmer from the Bridgeport community; a clerk at Hudson's Ladies Fashions; and a housewife with two children of high school age who lived in Thorn Hill. The bottling-line woman had a large three-ring notebook on her lap. The grandmother had brought her knitting. Four men. Eight women. They ranged in age from twenty-seven to sixty-three. No blacks.

Hud Exeter had their undivided attention. I gave him mine too.

"The prosecution will prove," he was telling them, "that beyond any doubt, Emma Purcell Kane did, with malice aforethought, bludgeon Adeline Hockensmith Purcell, her mother, to death. She did it by crushing her mother's skull with four vicious blows from a flatiron. Not one. Not two. Four!

"She then drug her mother to the stairs leading from the kitchen of her house to the cellar and flung her body down those steps.

"Then in an act hard to imagine, she followed and stuffed ashes down her mother's throat, the mother she had just killed—ashes down her murdered mother's throat.

"The flatiron used to bludgeon Mrs. Purcell to death has Emma Purcell Kane's fingerprints all over it.

"Her mother's blood was found on the sole of one of her shoes, a shoe she claimed to have lost but which our investigators found hidden in a trash bin outside a farm building near the murder house.

"Damningly, ashes identical to those stuffed in her mother's mouth were found in the cuff of the slacks Emma Purcell Kane wore the day of the murder.

"Mrs. Kane can't account for her whereabouts at the time of the murder and has no valid alibi.

"As we present this evidence—in detail—it will prove conclusively that Emma Purcell Kane did, in fact, and with malice, murder her mother, Adeline Hockensmith Purcell."

Exeter paused to let his statement sink in.

"I know you will find this hard to accept," he resumed, "hard for you to imagine a person doing such things—a daughter killing her own mother. And doing it in such a monstrous way. And I apologize in advance for having to put you through the details of this awful crime. I ask you not to let your emotions overcome you. I ask you to consider the facts dispassionately. And I ask you to do the duty you've sworn before God and your neighbors to do. If you do, you will return a finding of guilty in the case of The Commonwealth of Kentucky vs. Emma Purcell Kane."

He scanned the jury again then turned and made his way back to the prosecution table.

Hud Exeter was a redhead. We don't have many of those around here. He was tall, but not so tall as to be intimidating, and had a boyish look, though I'm sure he was well into his thirties. He used his voice well, sometimes speaking so softly you almost had to strain to hear it, or putting timbre in it when he wanted to make sure you didn't miss his point. A pleasant voice. Very believable.

Emma's attorney sat motionless while Exeter took his seat between the two other attorneys who made up the prosecution team. One was a prim young woman in glasses and the other a heavy-set man shifting through a manila folder. Bookends, I thought.

Hanratty waited until the prosecutor was settled and the courtroom quiet. Then he stood, turned square to Exeter and clapped. Slowly. Four times. The sound was like rifle shots in the quiet chamber. Anyone inattentive was not now.

Immediately, from the bench, the Judge slammed his gavel down and shot at Hanratty, "None of that, sir! I'll have none of that!"

"My apologies, Your Honor. I get carried away when I see a great performance." He turned to Exeter, made a slight bow and smiled.

The exchange stilled the courtroom. No one was shifting about or whispering or fiddling with a purse. All eyes were on Hanratty. Even the woman in the jury box with the knitting put it down and was staring expectantly.

Hanratty turned back to the table where Emma sat, smiled reassuringly, then walked slowly to stand in front of the jury.

He stood close enough to reach out and shake hands if he wanted, and it looked like he might. You could read the uncertainty and suspense on several of their faces because they knew he shouldn't, but if he did, how were they supposed to react?

"Mr. Hanratty," came the caution from the bench as if the Judge himself was uncertain.

Hanratty let the tension play a moment longer, then said. "Yes, Your Honor. I'm ready."

And so Jim Hanratty launched the defense of Emma Purcell Kane.

He began wordlessly, standing with his hands clasped together in front of him and engaging each juror, one by one. He caught their eyes and held them—as if he could see into their hearts and as if he was letting them see into his. Each juror. Singly. In turn. It took a while. The silence became uncomfortable.

Again from the bench came, "Mr. Hanratty… ."

Stepping back, Hanratty turned from the jury to the defense table where Emma sat. His gaze drew everyone else's there to the young woman all alone, looking lost and frightened and vulnerable.

He straightened his shoulders and looked back at the jury.

"Ladies and gentlemen, you've witnessed a fine performance this morning, a very fine performance. The prosecutor is a fine young man, an accomplished young man. The story he told you, and he told it well, was the shocking story of an awful act."

A long pause; a slow look along the rows of jurors.

"That's all it was. A story. As in make-believe. As in wishful thinking. As in fiction."

Again he paused and turned to Emma at the table. Then back to the jury.

"Emma Purcell Kane did not kill her mother. She loved her mother and her mother loved her. Emma Purcell Kane was an adoring daughter, a fine young wife and herself a mother, a dedicated member of the church she and her mother attended. She did not murder her mother. The accusation that she did is make-believe. It is wishful thinking. The accusation is a fiction!"

Here he slammed his right hand down on the railing of the jury box so hard the crack of it made the Sunday School teacher jump.

"All of the evidence Mr. Exeter so dramatically cited is circumstantial. Easily explained, which I will do. The prosecution has nothing to offer as real proof. It can't even produce a motive—a reason so compelling that it would spur a loving daughter to brutally murder the woman who had birthed her and cared for her and nurtured her through her whole life long. No proof! No motive! All the prosecution has is a story—something they've made up to fit the circumstances—a piece of fiction!"

Hanratty placed both his hands on the jury box rail and again scanned the jurors one-by-one.

"Ladies and gentlemen, Mr. Exeter apologized for having to put you through the details of this awful crime. I do as well. He asked you not to let your emotions overcome your fair judgment. I do as well. He asked that you consider the facts dispassionately. I do as well, with the admonition that you consider just the facts ... and ignore the suppositions! If you do, then I have every confidence that you will fulfill the duty you've sworn before God and your neighbors ... and that, contrary to Mr. Exeter's conclusion, you will return a finding of not guilty in the case of the Commonwealth of Kentucky vs. Emma Purcell Kane."

He paused again, letting his gaze run slowly over the jurors in their seats, stopping to linger for just a second on the face of the young woman who thought the murderer must be a monster. Softly he repeated, "Not guilty."

Then he turned and strode back to take his place beside Emma.

Everyone expected a long trial.

It lasted six days.

That included the day given to jury selection and the day-and-a-half the jury took in deciding Emma's fate.

Monday to Saturday night. Unheard of for a capital case.

Much to the disappointment of the gossips, the prosecution seemed to have no interest in dirty linen or scandalizing reputations. Hud Exeter made no attack on Emma's character; ignored the rumors of her teenage promiscuity. He didn't exploit the matter of her shotgun marriage to Marko Kane or her anger at having been forced by her mother to leave school to accommodate it. He left the door closed on testimony that might have shown Emma to be rebellious or resentful or prone to rash acts.

I couldn't fathom the strategy. The circumstantial evidence against Emma was thunderous. But where was the motive? Anger, resentment, rebellion—all these could be reasons. Exeter let them pass. Ignored them. He, or more likely his boss, the Commonwealth's Attorney, seemed determined to make the case on the circumstantial evidence alone.

"He can't wash her dirty linen in public," Dulin said when I asked him what he thought. "The Country Club set would never excuse him, win or lose. Bad form. Just isn't done. I'd bet our favorite Commonwealth's Attorney wishes he'd never heard of this case"

My routine those trial days was unchanging.

Up at five-thirty, a rundown Wilkinson to the Railroad Bridge at the foot of Broadway, a left turn and across the river there, then down the short hill to the little iron bridge over Benson Creek and into Bellepoint and up to the Frankfort High football field. Two laps around the goal-posts, fifty push-ups, then back to my place. Shower, shave, dress and make breakfast. Two cups of coffee minimum, with milk and two spoons of sugar in each—I'd have to drink it black the rest of the day.

I was in the newsroom by seven each morning. No one else got in before nine—except sometimes Dulin when he wanted a head-start on the day.

I liked that. I liked being there early with the teletypes chattering and bright lights shining. There was always a muted sense of excitement in the air, a feeling of expectancy—like something important was about to happen, and I'd be there as the curtain went up.

I'd scan the *Herald* and the *Courier-Journal* to see what our competition was up to, re-read my story in the morning's paper, make notes on what to follow-up or pay particular attention to, and be in my seat in the jury room well before nine.

The days were long but never boring. Although I probably knew more about what happened in the murder of Adeline Hockensmith Purcell than anyone in the courtroom except Emma, I'd never seen a trial. Watching Hud Exeter perform and then, when it came his turn, Jim Hanratty, was like watching a play unfold, a play with masterful actors whose ending you couldn't imagine.

No, there was no boredom—either for me or for the jury or the audience that was packed shoulder to shoulder in every seat in the courtroom through all those days.

The Judge let the proceedings run until around five or five-thirty. The women in the audience, who made up most of the crowd, needed to be able to get home to make supper. The Judge understood that.

I'd hang around a bit as the courtroom cleared, sometimes trading impressions with Andy Thomas of the *Herald*—we sat next to each other and were becoming closer friends as the trial progressed—or waiting to put a question to Hanratty or Exeter.

"Are you going to put Emma on the stand," I asked Hanratty the second day. He looked around to see that no one was nearby. "Why would I?" he said smiling. "There's no need."

That made the headline for my story the next morning. "Emma Won't Take Stand." Dulin slugged it for the top of Page One. It turned out to be an exclusive. No one else had thought to ask Hanratty his plan, or if they had, he'd no-commented it. I didn't share the word with Andy. We covered for each other, but sharing headline-making information wasn't part of the canon.

"What do you have going with Hanratty?" Dulin asked as he read my lede. I thought of Hanratty's comment about the road back from Chosin. I didn't tell Dulin about that. "He likes me," I said.

For every day of the trial, I was back in the newsroom by six. I did whatever follow-up and fact checking that was necessary, re-read my notes carefully and thoroughly, then sat down behind my typewriter to see what would come.

I'd usually finish by eight. Then I'd place my copy on Dulin's desk and take the chair beside the slot while he read it. I watched anxiously as his copy pencil moved—changing a word of mine to a more accurate one, striking a clause he thought confusing or too pretentious. I have to admit to sometimes getting carried away and forgetting I was writing news, not deathless prose.

Though I no longer felt like the rookie I was when I began the exercise, I knew I was not in the league of the Dulin Monroes and the Will Owenses. I had, and have, a large ego, but I never made an argument when one of them corrected me.

I didn't see much of Will during this time. He was busy with the Legislature and his column, and I was too busy with the trial to trail around after him. I'm embarrassed to admit that my coverage of the trial so dominated my mind that it crowded out everything else. Even Allie. All I could see were the lights of New York beckoning, my byline in the Times, and fame and fortune and the grand days ahead for me if I did this well.

But then I'd remember that I wouldn't have even a remote shot at it but for the help of Will Owens, and I'd feel guilty. God, I hate the feeling guilt gives me.

The night after the second day of the trial was one of those moments. I turned my story into Dulin, waited for his judgment, then headed out the door and up the street to King's Bar. I didn't expect Will to be there. It was too early. But Gideon would be, and he'd know what I wanted to know.

The day had been pleasantly warm and, with the sun down now, a soft night was rising. I was stopped twice by people to tell me they liked my stories. That felt good. They all felt the jury would find Emma guilty. Most of the courtroom crowd did too—or seemed to want it. You could almost feel the pleasure being taken in that prospect. This could have had less to do with whether Emma was actually guilty than with the smoldering resentment ordinary folk have for the rich and powerful. Anyway, the feeling was in the air. Bring 'em down off their high horses. Make 'em eat dirt!

"Whacha doing here so early," Gideon called when I walked into the bar. He glanced up at the clock and then back at me. "Nine o'clock? Ain't even supper time yet."

"I came to see you. Couldn't wait," I laughed back.

"Oh, that sounds serious," he said. "What's on your mind, boy?"

He reached across the bar and shook my hand as I took a seat near the end. We had the place to ourselves.

"Will's on my mind," I said without preamble. "I haven't seen him in a couple of days. Just checking to make sure he's doing okay."

Gideon closed his eyes and shook his head. "Oh, I don't know, Theo. I just don't see how he can be. He's in here every night, stays til almost daylight. He's laughing and joking with the guys when they're here or sometimes just sitting quiet by himself at a table in the corner. He doesn't seem sad. In fact he seems to be having a good time. Like he's working at having a good time. But, Lord, Theo, he's got a glass in front of him all the time, and you know what the Doc said about that."

"He's holding up okay?"

"That man holds liquor better than any man I ever saw. But his hands are trembling some, and he has trouble standing, like his legs ain't strong enough to push him up. He's lost weight too. I don't think he's eating much."

"Damn, Gideon, what are we going to do?"

Gideon held the shot glass he'd been polishing up to the light. Inspected it slowly. When he was satisfied, he sat it down and filled it with Ancient Age, one hundred proof, then pushed the glass across the bar to me.

"We ain't gonna do nothing, Theo. We gonna let the man do what he wants to do. Give him what help he wants. Respect his decision. And stay out of his face. We ain't got no business getting in his way. Now drink your drink and think of happy times."

Hud Exeter laid out the bulk of the prosecution's case the next day, Wednesday, the third day of the trial. He'd begun it the afternoon of the day before, the day both sides presented their opening arguments.

Exeter had his tightly packaged.

He told the Judge he believed the State could complete its case against Emma before the day was over. A gasp of surprise came from the spectators, and even Hanratty seemed caught off guard.

"Today?" the Judge repeated. "I want this case heard with all due speed, but there is no need to rush."

"I'm not rushing, Your Honor," Exeter replied. "The evidence the State has is incontrovertible and uncomplicated. It requires no lengthy elaboration. It speaks for itself and," he said, turning to the jury, "it will prove Emma Purcell Kane guilty of the murder of Adeline Hockensmith Purcell, her mother."

The Judge banged his gavel down to quiet the buzz that began to rise.

"Can you be ready to begin presenting the case for the defense on such short notice, Mr. Hanratty?"

Emma's attorney stood, adjusted his jacket, and turned slightly to face Hud Exeter. He let a small, knowing smile form for just a moment. Then turning back to the Judge, "Yes, Your Honor, I can."

"Very well," said the Judge. "We'll take a short recess. I imagine you have a few steps to put in motion, Mr. Hanratty. We'll reconvene in half an hour."

People started standing up and stretching and forming little groups of whispered conversation. I felt a tap on my shoulder. Will was standing there. "Move over," he said and slid in beside me.

"What are you doing here?" I looked at my watch. 'You ought to be in bed."

"Dulin got a tip. He thought something interesting might happen."

"Exeter's move?"

"Right."

"I don't get it."

"His boss is up to something. The fast wrap-up could put Hanratty in a bind. Hanratty won't have time to fashion a specific rebuttal to the exact points the prosecution draws from the evidence. Or it could be a move to get this over as fast as possible and escape with only minimal damage to our beloved Commonwealth's Attorney's political career."

"You better unravel that for me."

"If Emma's acquitted, Hud Exeter takes one for the team and Dan Lindsey doesn't have to send Judge Hockensmith's niece to jail. If she's convicted, Hud Exeter gets tagged as the man who sent her to jail, not Lindsey, but Lindsey gets to share the honors as the guy behind the scenes managing the strategy. Machiavelli would love it."

Will seemed fully energized. He gazed around the courtroom, feeding on the excitement. Gideon was right that he looked frail, but there was no indication he was unsteady. His eyes were clear, his grip firm as he used my shoulder to lower himself into the seat, and he was turned out in his usual neat attire, tweed sport jacket, freshly laundered shirt, carefully knotted tie, sharply pleated slacks. It wasn't what I expected. The image I had in my mind was of bloodshot eyes and unshaven features and a frame so fragile it surely must break.

"You're looking pretty good this morning," I said.

"Don't I, though," he said grinning.

Which made me think that Will Owens might pay with his life for whatever peace of mind the bourbon gave him, but not with his dignity.

FORTY ONE

When court reconvened, Hud Exeter opened with the County Coroner.

He had started with the Sheriff immediately after the opening arguments the day before.

Woodrow Stanley Peavler told how he had been called by County Judge Ira Hockensmith, the deceased's brother, to the Hockensmith Farm. How he found Adeline Purcell at the bottom of the cellar stairs with her head crushed and her mouth stuffed with ashes. How he and his men had made a thorough search of the vicinity and questioned everyone in the area, including a Gypsy who admitted to being in the house the morning of the murder and a young Marine veteran of the Korean War who had been camping on the property.

Neither the Gypsy nor the young Marine could be directly connected to the murder, though the Gypsy, who was being held as a material witness, broke out of jail the day the trial began and that might indicate something, but so far he had not been found.

Emma Purcell Kane also admitted to being in the house on the morning of the murder. She had taken her baby there to her mother, who was baby-sitting for her, before leaving for a day of shopping.

The Sheriff said robbery was not a motive. The house had not been broken into, and nothing of value was missing.

There was a smudge of ashes on the kitchen floor. One of the victim's shoes was found there.

Emma Purcell Kane was arrested and charged when it was found that the story she told of her whereabouts the morning of the murder couldn't be corroborated and after tests conducted by the State Police Crime laboratory produced evidence supporting the accusation that Mrs. Kane was the murderer.

I had already reported all this. Nothing was new. Woody, though, took the afternoon to get it told.

The County Coroner repeated, when Exeter put him on the stand, that death was due to blows to the head from a blunt instrument—in this case an old flatiron. This one was an heirloom. Brought by Colonel Hockensmith's people when they emigrated from Ulster. It crushed her skull and drove bone into the brain

"Is this the murder weapon?" Exeter asked, lifting a flatiron and holding it high so everyone could see.

At one time every house in the county had one. In the days before electricity, it was the only appliance the women had to do the ironing. Now they were used as door-stops or sometimes as a decoration if the lady of the house was going for the rustic look or the antique. In those settings they were innocent enough, but held high above Exeter's head in the context of the picture he was painting, this one loomed menacingly deadly. It was big and black and heavy—a single piece of thick cast-iron, square at the back, wide in the middle, curving to a point at its tip, suspended from a large wooden grip.

Exeter walked forward and handed it to the Coroner, making a show of its heft.

"A blow from this killed Mrs. Purcell?"

"Yes."

"A single blow?"

"There were four. The first blow was the fatal one. It crushed the back of her head and drove bone into her brain. She was hit three times more."

"Three more times?" Exeter said. "Why?"

The Coroner shook his head. "There's no way I can know that. Rage. Revenge. Hate. You'll have to ask the murderer."

Exeter glanced at Hanratty, "If the defense attorney will put his client on the stand, I will."

"Objection," Hanratty said, rising.

"Sustained," the Judge said. "You know better, Mr. Exeter. Sit down, Mr. Hanratty."

Exeter turned back to the Coroner.

"What did you establish as the time of death?"

"Around noon. I can't be more accurate than that."

"Was death instantaneous?"

"It's impossible to tell, but I would say yes."

"How about the ashes? She didn't suffocate?"

"The ashes had nothing to do with her death. They were stuffed into Mrs. Purcell's mouth after she expired."

"Have you ever seen anything like that before?

"No. Never."

"What do you make of it?"

The Coroner turned slowly to look at Emma. "I make it a mighty nasty thing," he said.

Exeter glanced at Hanratty again. Emma's attorney shrugged.

Between taking notes on the testimony, I watched Hanratty, wanting to see how he played it. He hardly looked at the witness or at Exeter. His focus was on the jurors—watching their expressions, studying the way they clasped their hands or leaned forward or back when a particular thing was said. Occasionally he made a note. Occasionally he reached over and gave Emma a reassuring touch. You'd be wrong to think he wasn't listening intently. I'd see him frown now and then at an offered fact and smile a faint smile at something only he knew how he was going to refute.

I know the jurors felt his eyes on them. You'd see some of them glance at him now and then to see how he was reacting to something said, to wonder what he thought of them? I couldn't tell. But I know they felt his presence. I'd find it irritating, even intimidating. Others, though, might find it reassuring, empathetic. Well, Hanratty knew his business. I was just watching.

Hanratty looked like a man you'd want as an uncle. He seemed the kind who knew how to do all sorts of useful things, important things, things you might want to know how to do or ought to know how to do. The kind of man who would understand you and stand up for you and cut you a little slack if you needed it, but not put up with any foolishness. He was obviously very smart, maybe brilliant, but not a show-off, and good looking in a plain sort of way. He was about my height, graying hair, a portly build, fiftyish or so, a self-confident way about him. I liked him. I made a mental note to make sure that didn't influence my coverage.

"I have just one more person to call, Your Honor," Exeter was saying, "then the prosecution will rest."

The door at the back of the courtroom opened and Major Tanner of the State Police walked in.

Well, here it comes I thought. Major Tanner has the real evidence. For all his posturing, Sheriff Woodrow Stanley Peavler had come up with nothing. Everything that tied Emma to the murder of Adeline Hockensmith Purcell had been developed by Major Tanner and his people.

Tanner's was the evidence that resulted in Emma being charged. Whether he had anything new to add to what was already known, we'd find out as Exeter rolled out his questions. We still didn't know if the prosecution had come up with a motive. Convicting Emma of the murder of her mother without a witness and without a motive—on circumstantial evidence alone? Well, we'd see.

If presence could carry the day, Major Tanner brought it. Impressive carriage, honest face, radiating authority.

He was sworn, took his seat, and nodded solemnly to the jury whose members all seemed to sit up a little straighter in his presence.

"Major Tanner," Exeter began.

"Yes, sir," a rich baritone voice.

"Your organization conducted the principal investigation in this case?"

"Yes, sir."

"This is a county matter. The State Police have no jurisdiction in the county. Why are the State Police involved?"

"We were invited in by the County Sheriff. The Sheriff doesn't have the forensic capabilities we have, specifically, a fully modern crime laboratory. Also, the Sheriff's office has limited experience in conducting a murder investigation. We can bring a level of experience and expertise they don't have."

"Your team has extensive experience in homicide matters?"

"Yes, sir."

"Tell us then, please Major, what your investigation found."

The Major turned to the jury and addressed his remarks to them.

"First, we found that Mrs. Kane's alibi for her whereabouts at the time of the murder didn't check out."

"She lied?" Exeter broke in.

"She wasn't were she said she was."

"She lied," Exeter repeated.

"She changed her story," the Major said.

"Please explain."

"She said she was upset the morning of the murder and didn't clearly remember her movements. She'd had a fight with her husband, had rushed out, gotten in her car and had driven around aimlessly for a while. She tried to visit a friend who wasn't home, drove some more, then finally calmed down and came back to her mother's house. Her mother was baby-sitting for her. That's when she reported finding the body."

"Could you corroborate any of this?"

"No sir."

"Two stories. One an outright lie. The other unverifiable."

"Yes, sir."

"So she could have been at the place of the murder at the time of the murder as the evidence says she was?"

"Yes," the Major said.

"Go on, Major. I'll try not to interrupt again."

Tanner unbuttoned the flap on his shirt pocket and took out a small black note-book. He opened it, glanced up at the jury, then back down to his notes and began laying out the case the State Police had constructed.

He and his crew—the sergeant in charge of the crime lab and a trooper experienced in murder investigations—arrived at the crime scene at twenty-six minutes past twelve in the afternoon, shortly after receiving the call from Sheriff Peavler. The Sheriff and his team of two deputies were already there.

"It was an overcast afternoon," the Major said. "A light rain was falling. This is important because it meant no workers were in the fields, and consequently, the likelihood that someone might have seen an intruder entering or leaving the house was very small.

"The body was, as already reported, lying at the bottom of the cellar stairs. The murder weapon, an old cast-iron flatiron was lying on the floor about twenty inches from the body, tilted over and outside the pool of blood around the head.

"We secured the crime scene, and Sergeant Fain, the crime lab manager, and Trooper Benjamin began our investigation.

"The first blow was struck in the kitchen. The final blows were delivered to the body as it lay on the cellar floor."

Exeter jumped to his feet. "After she was dead? While the body lay on the floor?"

He let that picture sink in. "My God, how monstrous!"

"Counselor," the Judge warned from the bench.

"My apologies, Your Honor," Exeter said. He walked back to his seat shaking his head. "Go ahead, Major Tanner."

I leaned over to Will. "Did they rehearse this?"

"Of course," Will said.

Tanner waited another minute to let the moment marinate, then resumed.

"We found ashes on the kitchen floor around the stove. And on the cellar stairs and on the floor near the victim. The victim's mouth and throat were full of them.

"All of the ashes were of a kind—that is, they all came from the same place—the old wood stove that Mrs. Purcell kept in the kitchen. She must have made a small fire that morning. She probably wanted to take some of the chill off the room. The ashes in her throat matched the ashes in the stove."

You could sense the people in the courtroom, jurors and spectators alike, picturing all this in their minds, horrified by it, titillated by it. The woman with the knitting had stopped and was staring straight at the wall, seeing something that greatly disturbed her.. The girl with the notebook sat open-mouthed, shock on her face.

"There was a splatter of the victim's blood by the table in the kitchen and a few drops on the stairs."

Major Tanner flipped a page of his notebook, looked down to check something, then looked up with his eyes lighting on Exeter.

"Emma Kane's fingerprints were on the murder weapon—the flatiron.

"The victim's blood was on the sole of a shoe Mrs. Kane was wearing the day of the murder and which she discarded in a trash bin behind a shed on the farm.

"Most conclusively, though," and here the Major paused again and waited to be sure he had the jurors' attention, "most conclusively, ashes that matched those found in the victim's mouth were found in the cuff of the slacks Emma Kane wore that day."

At this Hud Exeter rose and all eyes swung from Major Tanner to him.

He lifted a single shoe from the evidence table, a muddy blue leather pump, its heel broken off, and a pair of trim grey-cuffed slacks.

Taking them to Major Tanner, Exeter asked what we all knew he would.

"Are these the slacks? Is this the shoe?"

Tanner examined them silently, then handed them back.

"Yes, sir. This is the shoe You can still see the blood stain on the sole. And these are the slacks that had ash in the cuff."

"And they belong to Emma Kane?"

"They belong to Emma Kane."

Exeter seemed to consider that, then said, "Don't tell me, Major, please. Tell the jury. This shoe with the blood of Adeline Purcell on it, these slacks with a trace of the ashes found in the throat of Adeline Purcell, they belong to Emma Kane and are what she was wearing the day of the murder?"

The Major turned slowly to be full face to the jury. "The shoes and the slacks are Emma Kane's. She wore them the day of the murder."

The courtroom had become so quiet I could hear Will breathing beside me.

"Emma Kane's fingerprints were on the murder weapon?" he asked.

"Yes, sir."

"Her mother's blood was on this shoe?"

"Yes, sir."

"The ashes that were found on Emma Kane's slacks...the slacks she wore the day of the murder...those ashes were the same as the ashes that were stuffed down the victim's throat?"

"Yes, sir."

"No doubt about any of this? No chance the findings could be wrong?"

"No, sir. No chance."

"What is to be drawn from all this, Major Tanner?"

"That is for the jury to say, sir."

Exeter stood looking at him thoughtfully for a moment, then turned to the Judge sitting elevated above them on the dais.

"Your Honor," he said. "I have a concluding statement to make, then the prosecution will rest its case against Emma Purcell Kane."

"You're positive, Counselor?"

Exeter didn't hesitate. "Yes, Your Honor. The prosecution is positive."

Turning away from the Judge, he strode down along the rail of the jury box to its center. There he stopped and faced the jurors, hands resting on the railing.

"Emma Purcell Kane murdered her mother."

He said it in a voice that was devoid of doubt.

"She did it in an act more brutal and demeaning than any of us have ever seen"

He stood there, staring at Emma.

Emma had been as engrossed in Exeter's litany as the jury, straining forward to hear. Now when he turned to her, she shrank back. Hanratty reached for her hand and whispered something none of us could hear, but which seemed to soothe her. She sat up straight then and returned Exeter's stare, shaking her head angrily.

Exeter ignored it and turned back to the jury.

"Let me reconstruct the morning for you, as the evidence shows it unfolded.

"Mrs. Purcell, the victim, was baby-sitting Emma's baby boy so that Emma could have a day of shopping in Lexington.

"Emma dropped the baby off that morning with Mrs. Purcell, then left. An hour or so later she returned, unexpectedly. We don't know why she returned, and it doesn't make any difference. Emma came back for reasons of her own.

"There was an argument. We don't know what the argument was about, but that makes no difference either.

"In the course of the argument, which took place in the kitchen—we know it was the kitchen because that's where we first find the victim's blood—Emma grabbed a flatiron, a family heirloom that her mother kept sitting on an old wood-stove there. The stove was used only rarely when the victim liked to make a small fire to take the chill off the room. Mrs. Purcell had made a fire that morning. The ashes in Mrs. Purcell's throat came from that fire.

"At some point in the argument, Emma grabbed that flatiron and smashed it into her mother's head. Emma's fingerprints are on that flatiron. Then Emma dragged her mother's body across the kitchen floor, opened the door to the cellar—her fingerprints are on the doorknob—and either shoved or threw the body down the cellar stairs.

"She followed, and as her mother's body lay there on the cellar floor, Emma Kane delivered three more blows. By the time she finished, her mother's skull had been crushed like an eggshell.

"Then, in an act that defies understanding, Emma Kane knelt by her mother's body and stuffed ashes down her throat. Picture that. Emma Kane on her knees beside her mother's body … stuffing ashes down her throat!"

He stopped then. He seemed to be seeing it himself, and a look of utter disgust came over his face. If he was acting, he was superb.

"Afterwards," he said, "she left, drove around the back roads of the county to consume enough time to make it appear she had been on a shopping trip to Lexington.

"She then returned to the murder house, called her uncle, the County Judge, and reported that she had just discovered her mother's beaten body dead at the foot of her cellar stairs."

Exeter stopped again, letting the silence sharpen the picture all of us were imaging. "I do apologize to you for being so repetitive with these awful facts, but it is crucial that you have them and the order of them firmly in your minds.

"Emma Kane lied about where she was at the time of her mother's murder.

"Her mother's blood is on her shoe.

"Her fingerprints are on the murder weapon.

"Ashes identical to those found crammed in her mother's mouth were found on the slacks Emma Kane wore the day of the murder."

Exeter rested his hands on the railing and leaned intimately in toward the jurors.

"The evidence is incontrovertible. Emma Kane is guilty of the murder of her mother, Adeline Hockensmith Purcell."

He straightened up then, studying them, trying to judge whether he had reached them. When he was satisfied, he left the railing and walked to stand before the Judge. "The prosecution rests, your Honor."

FORTY TWO

No one was leaving. The Judge had banged his gavel, the jury had departed, the deputy accompanying Emma had escorted her out, yet there were still knots of people standing around in agitated conversation.

Exeter found himself in the middle of an impromptu press conference as soon as the Judge left the courtroom. The AP grabbed him at the corner of the prosecution table as he was shoving files into his briefcase, and we all rushed down.

Sam Stivers of the Associated Press, "Why close it so fast?"

"The evidence is clear. It's incontrovertible. It doesn't require elaboration. We saw no advantage in belaboring the points. They speak for themselves."

Ed Hutchinson of the *Kentucky Post*, "This must be a record for speed."

"Maybe. That's not the point. The point is to bring a criminal to justice. It takes whatever time it takes."

Jack O'Conner of the Louisville *Courier-Journal*, "Why hasn't your Boss made an appearance? He seems to be either disinterested in this case or wanting to put distance between it and himself?"

The political question had to come. Everyone knew Commonweath's Attorney Dan Lindsey's ambitions. I was beginning to like Hud Exeter. I hoped he had an answer that wouldn't get him in trouble.

We were huddled in a little semi-circle around the edge of the prosecution table, probably eight to a dozen of us, notebooks in hand, jockeying for position, edging in to make sure we didn't miss anything, trying to nudge close enough to get in a question. Exeter was in the center with the table serving as a buffer.

"Is that you, Jack?" Exeter replied with a long-suffering smile. "This is a murder trial. That sounds like a political question."

He got the round of laughter he expected. Even O'Conner laughed.

"Come on, Hud. This is the kind of exposure ambitious politicians lust for. Why isn't Dan Lindsey anywhere in evidence? Does he think you all are going to lose it, and he's going to let you take the fall? Or does he think you all are going to win it, and he's not sure how being known as the man who sent a daughter of the landed gentry to the penitentiary will go over with the people who pony up the money for successful political campaigns?"

Exeter shook his head as if at a man deserving enlightenment.

"The Commonwealth's Attorney is a very busy man, managing a number of important cases. This one doesn't require his personal attendance. Are you unhappy with the way I'm handling this, Jack?"

"Can you convict her?"

"I don't do that, the jury does."

"Will they?"

"We'll have to wait and see. That's all, fellas. I've had a long day, and I've earned a stiff drink and a good night's sleep. See you tomorrow."

He closed his brief case, smiled again, and waded out through the crowd to the street.

I made my way up to the press section where Will was watching the scrimmage, seeming relaxed and amused.

"Could you hear him?" I asked.

"Just barely, but well enough."

"What do you think?

"Dan Lindsey's got a star on his hands. I don't think he realized that when he threw the redhead in. Win or lose, this boy's going to get a lot of very useful notice, and I don't think Lindsey's going to like that."

Dulin was waiting for us when we walked back into the newsroom.

"Well," he said.

"It was about what you thought it would be," Will replied. "They wrapped it up in record time. They didn't touch her reputation. They're hanging it all on circumstantial evidence. They have no motive. And Dan Lindsey was nowhere in sight."

Dulin turned to me.

"Knock out a couple of grafs for the wire, then come join Will and me for dinner. We'll talk there. Serafini's when you finish."

I headed for my typewriter. They walked out the door.

April evenings in the Bluegrass are soft; the dark is gentle.

There is a silky feeling to the night and a hint of promise in the air. I pulled it around me with pure pleasure as I walked down the street to the corner where Serafini's sits.

Streetlights were coming on and storefronts lighting up. It was still fairly early—just before sunset. This time next year I'd be crossing Forty-Second Street, heading to my desk at the Times. Or maybe on down the few blocks to the *Herald-Trib* on Forty-First. The park-like expanse of the Old Capitol was just in front of me. In the beginning it had been the town's public square. After Frankfort was picked to be the seat of government for the grand and glorious Commonwealth of Kentucky, there was no finer place to site the Capitol building than in its center. The first two burned down, then, in 1830, this one was built out of Kentucky River marble and fashioned after the Temple of Minerva in the holy city of Priene. For eighty years, until government outgrew it and the Capitol moved across the river to bigger quarters, the business of the people was done here.

As I got closer, the elegant Ionic columns and proud green cupola of the old building glowed in the light of the spots placed around it to showcase it at night. Large oaks and maples all around were in full leaf. Half close your eyes, and you'd think you'd time-traveled back to a forest meadow in ancient Greece.

I knew New York was full of wonders. Could it offer scenes as magical as this or evenings half as mellow?

Over dinner, our talk turned to Arlo Lee. He'd disappeared as easily as he had walked out of jail. No one seemed to be as excited by his absence as Sheriff Woodrow Stanley Peavler, but the State Police issued a be-on-the-lookout-for bulletin to all their offices and sent alerts to their counterpart in the neighboring states—not a high priority alert, but one that would get a serious response all the same.

"I wish the Gypsy hadn't done that," Dulin said. We had a table at the window looking out on Broadway and the Old Capitol ground, almost dark now as we finished our dinners. "Where do you suppose he's run to?"

Will looked at me as if he thought I might have an answer.

I shrugged. "Far enough to be out of the reach of the Sheriff."

Will frowned. "No. I think he's hiding in plain sight. He knows our favorite Sheriff will think he's trying to get as far away from this place as he can. He'll figure the State Police are thinking that, too. So he'll fool them."

"Which would put him where?"

"The creek. He could get there fast. Traveling in the dark, he could get there without attracting attention. He knows the ground. He could hide a small tent easily along the creek bank. No one is likely to surprise him, not any of the fieldhands; there's no work down there. Maybe a fisherman, but it's awfully early in the year. And Woodrow Stanley Peavler and the State Police aren't likely to look for him there. It's too close."

It made sense.

"But why would he want to stay around here?"

Dulin picked it up. "There's too much we don't understand about Arlo Lee and the Hockensmiths. He's Ezra Hockensmith's son. Adeline's brother. But he doesn't know it. Or so far as we know he doesn't know it. Or didn't know it. Maybe he knows now."

"Slow down," I said. "Where are you going with this?"

"Here's the nub of it," Dulin said. " I don't think Arlo Lee walked out of jail because he couldn't stand the lock-up any longer. I think he has an agenda, and he needs to be free to pursue it."

"Amen," Will said. "Amen."

FORTY THREE

Strange thing that next morning—the morning Jim Hanratty was to put on his show.

I had just about finished my run and was on that short incline that feeds down to the narrow little bridge that crosses Benson Creek. It was a foggy morning. A cold fog. Gun-metal gray. Thick and shifting. Viscous in some spots, transparent in others. Snaking through town and piling up where Benson fed into the river.

As I started onto the bridge, a figure materialized coming toward me. I could only make out a form in the mist. A woman, I thought. One of the faithful on her way home from early Mass. In a long dark coat with a heavy shawl swaddling her head. As we passed I heard, like a whisper in my ear, "She killed her mother" and was four strides beyond before the words registered. I stopped and turned. No one was there, no one I could see in the shifting fog. I stood— wondering, confused. I couldn't remember what I had been thinking about. The trial? Surely. I must have been thinking about the trial. That's where the words must have come from. I was imagining things. Still, it was odd, and the memory of it stayed with me as I got ready for the day.

By the time I got to the Courthouse, whispers in my ear out of thick fog were forgotten. I was eager to watch Jim Hanratty work his spell. That's what I'd been told to expect. That's exactly what I expected to see.

Dulin called him the best in the state. Will said he was a wizard.

That he often got people off they thought were guilty wasn't held against him by them. It was by others, but not by Dulin and Will. They believed in Benjamin Franklin's old saw that it's better a hundred guilty men go free than a single innocent man be convicted.

While Hanratty might get more than his share of guilty men off, it was unlikely that any innocent man he represented would be convicted.

For Hanratty, the issue wasn't guilt or innocence. It was the fundamental protections guaranteed all Americans. If a person was to be deprived of life or liberty for an alleged crime, the accuser had better be able to prove, beyond a shadow of a doubt, her guilt. And the accused, regardless of the horror of the crime, had the right to a competent defense.

I never determined where Hanratty came down on the matter of guilt and innocence. We became fast friends during the years after the trial. I admired his abilities, and I admired him as a person. He was as principled a man as I knew. But he never seemed to care whether the person he represented had done the deed or not. It seemed to be enough for him that the accused had the right to the best defense he could afford. And Hanratty was pleased to provide it.

He bored easily, and I think, at its core, all this was a game with him, a contest of wits, matching his mind and skills against the other guy's in a matter of life and death—and winning. The high of that must have been exhilarating.

He paid for it. A thirty-eight caliber slug just above the right eye, delivered by the father of a raped and mutilated twelve-year old girl as he walked out of the courtroom where his wiles had just set her accused attacker free.

That was later, though, much later.

I had just made it to my seat when the deputy brought in Emma. The courtroom was already full. Hanratty was at the defense table looking through a file. He rose and walked to meet her, a reassuring smile on his face.

Emma seemed relaxed and fresh. She'd chosen, or someone had chosen for her, a black knit sheath dress. She wore no jewelry other than the small gold chain with a cross suspended from it, the Celtic cross that we'd seen before, and very little make-up, a touch of color on her checks and lips, eye-shadow lightly applied. Hanratty pulled her chair out for her, and she took her place. He whispered something, then turned to survey the courtroom.

As it had been every day, the room was packed. The ones with seats had gotten to the Courthouse before daylight. Later arrivals were standing along the walls at the back of the room. Hanratty's gaze swept past me, and he nodded in recognition. Andy Thomas of the *Herald* sat to my right. "Just barely made it," he said. "Fog had traffic crawling. Then, dammit, all the parking spots were filled. This town needs more parking."

"I walk," I said.

"Nice, and you can get to your desk about an hour before I can. Not fair," he said. He frowned at me, then grinned. "You think Hanratty can shake all that circumstantial evidence?"

There was a little commotion at the door in the wall beside the jury box. It opened and the jury began to file in. Nothing could be told from their faces. They were solemn and reserved, taking their seats rapidly and arranging themselves as comfortably as possible on the hard-back, wooden chairs.

When they were settled, a male voice cried, "All rise."

The room quieted. The Judge swept in. He stood on the raised dais, his eyes ranging wall to wall and then to the jury. He nodded sternly at them, then back to the hushed courtroom. "Be seated," he said and banged his gavel down.

Hanratty remained standing, waiting for the shuffling and the settling to stop.

"Is the defense ready?" the Judge asked.

"Yes, Your Honor."

Hanratty was dressed that morning in a dark-blue double-breasted suit; a blue so deep it seemed almost black. It was perfectly tailored and made of silk, so Andy whispered, impressed. His shirt was white, with crisply starched collar and cuffs and set off by a rich wine-colored four-in-hand knotted in a wide Windsor. He wore a red boutonnière in his lapel. It seemed a bit grand for a foggy morning on St. Clair, but it was producing the effect I came to understand Hanratty always sought. This is a man of authority and dignity, his appearance said, a man to be listened to, a man to be believed. Take notice.

Hanratty left his position at the defense table and walked forward to stand in front of the jury. He had no notes or files in his hands, none of the props used to buy time while the speaker tries to collect his thoughts or to stage little dramatic pauses.

I felt I already knew the strategy he planned to use. He'd told me as much in the early hours of the morning after my story had been filed. I was on my way up to King's Bar thinking Will might be there when I noticed the light was on in his office in the McClure Building as I crossed the intersection of Main and St. Clair.

He was sitting at his desk, shirt sleeves rolled up, tie loosened, pouring through a file of newspaper clippings when I walked in.

"Mr. Hanratty."

He looked up in surprise. It took a moment for my face to register with him. "Ah," he said when it did, "Mr. Clark."

He looked at his watch, then back at me.

"I'm sorry," I said. "I saw your lights on and thought I'd take the chance you might be up here."

Hanratty pushed back from his desk.

"Want some coffee?"

There was a pot on a hot-plate in the corner of the room. He poured us cups and motioned me to a chair by the side of his desk. The coffee was black and strong and bitter, like it had been sitting in that pot over low heat for hours.

"Good, yes?" he said chuckling. "Keep you awake."

He walked to the window looking down on the corner. The only action was the street-light flashing.

"Anybody out there," he said to me, still looking out the window.
"Not that I saw."

"You like rattling around these dark and empty streets all alone, don't you?"
I did.

"Do you know why?"

I'd never thought about it. I liked the town. It felt good. I felt it knew me and I belonged.

"Are you a loner, Theo Clark?"

I'd never thought about that either. I was happy enough in my own company.

"You're a puzzling young man." He studied me silently for a moment, drank down the rest of his coffee and took his seat behind the desk.

Leaning back and folding his arms behind his head in a relaxed fashion, he said, "Do you think Emma did it?"

That took me off guard. While I searched for a reply, he said, "Don't answer. The jury will decide."

"Can you get her off?"

"You know that I don't have to prove Emma is innocent," Hanratty said. "You know that. I'd like to do that, but I don't have to. What I have to do is convince one person that the prosecution hasn't proven that she's guilty—beyond the shadow of a doubt—one person with the courage to stand up to the rest of them."

He began in a routine way, working first to establish Emma's good character.

He called the Pastor of the First Baptist Church. There was no man more respected anywhere in town. He put her Sunday School teacher on the stand, her faculty advisor at UK, her high school principal, the cook and the cleaning lady who worked for her mother and who had known her most of her life, two girls she'd known in high school and who were now proper young matrons. He called the farm manager, and he called the Chairwoman of the local chapter of the Daughters of the American Revolution into whose enviable ranks Emma ascended by virtue of the blood of the Purcells.

Hanratty did not call her great aunt, Ms. Livia Hockensmith, Miss Liv. And he did not call Allie. I may be the only person who noticed this.

All of the aforementioned attested to Emma's good character, even temper, and loving nature. Hanratty wouldn't have called on them if he thought they might do otherwise.

The entire morning went into this validation of Emma Purcell Kane as an exemplary citizen and dutiful daughter. It was fun to watch, but hard to swallow. By the time the Judge adjourned us for the lunch break, the mood in the courtroom had shifted from mildly tolerant to yawning boredom to undisguised irritation. Hanratty didn't care. He was playing to the jury, not the audience.

It wasn't until after lunch that he launched his real defense.

"Your Honor," he said opening the afternoon session," the defense has no further witnesses to call or evidence to present."

The Judge, who had been organizing a few papers, snapped upright. "What?" he said in surprise. "That's all for the defense?"

Hud Exeter, at the prosecution table, seemed just as startled. Emma looked skyward and closed her eyes.

Hanratty smiled. "Not quite, Your Honor. The defense has a few points to make."

Turning as he had done in the morning session, he walked to the railing in front of the jury box. As he had done in the morning session, he looked into each juror's face. They leaned toward him. What the jurors saw in his eyes I couldn't tell. One, the Sears store manager, frowned as if challenged. The waitress at Yancy's smiled, then lowered her eyes. The bottling-line woman seemed transfixed.

Whatever Hanratty saw, it seemed to satisfy him. He nodded his head approvingly then moved back to the defense table to stand near Emma.

Hanratty looked as fresh and as confident as he had when the morning began. The room wasn't hot, but it wasn't cool, and with all those bodies jammed into that confined space, it had gotten warmer as each hour passed. Everyone looked a bit wilted. Except Hanratty. His shirt was still immaculately smooth and white, his tie precisely knotted and firmly in place, no wrinkles in his suit.

I rubbed my hand across my chin and felt the stubble beginning to grow there. Hanratty looked freshly shaven. How had he done that? Had he somehow managed to shave, to change into an identical outfit when we broke at noon?

Taken the time to do that? For effect? There were things to be learned from Hanratty.

"I won't keep you long," he began.

A pause.

"Emma Purcell Kane," a longer pause, "is innocent." Each word said slowly and distinctly.

"Establishing that fact will require only that you listen carefully to what I'm going to tell you and apply the common sense you use every day in your own affairs."

As he stressed the words "common sense," he looked to the bottling-line woman, talking directly to her.

"You've already heard from people who know Emma Kane well. They are friends and neighbors of yours. Respected and honorable people. People you know you can believe. To a person, they have said that Emma Purcell Kane is a loving and dutiful daughter, a person of high character and firm morals, gentle and kind, a fine mother in her own right, a credit to our community, and a person incapable of committing the awful act the prosecution wants to lay at her feet.

"All that's left now is to understand how ridiculous the prosecution's case is."

With that, he got right to the point.

"The prosecution has presented no evidence that ties Emma to the murder of Adeline Hockensmith Purcell. They've presented supposition and floated inventive interpretations of questionable facts. But no real evidence. No proof! Their entire case is based on circumstantial evidence! Let me refresh your memory as to what the term 'circumstantial' means."

Here he lifted a large book with a blue cover.

"The Oxford Dictionary of the English Language," he said, holding it up for the jury to see. He opened it to a page already tabbed and then read to them these words. "In Law, evidence not bearing directly on the fact in dispute but on various attendant circumstances from which a jury might infer the occurrence of the fact of the dispute."

Placing the dictionary back on the table, straightening up slowly, voice rising in disbelief, he repeated, "Evidence not bearing directly on the fact in dispute? From which the jury might infer the occurrence of the fact in dispute?"

Spinning around to face Emma, "The prosecution wants you to infer," he paused again, anger beginning to show on his face, "infer from evidence not directly bearing on the fact in dispute that this woman," pointing to Emma, "brutally murdered her mother. They want you to find her guilty and send her to prison. Possibly to the electric chair! They want you to infer"—the way he spit out "infer" made it sound like a dirty word—"infer, from the flimsy evidence they've presented, with no proof of any kind, that she, and no one else, is guilty. That is outrageous!" he thundered.

The outburst took us all by surprise. My head was bent down taking notes, and his tone jerked me up. The Judge, too. Even Emma, stared wide-eyed. I took a fast glance at the jury. They were riveted.

Hanratty's approach so far had been very controlled. He had kept his voice low. That forced the jury to strain a bit to hear him—a tactic to make sure they paid attention. His presentation was restrained and dignified—the look and sound of reason.

He let the moment build; then, leaving the defense table, he took up his spot again in front of the jury box.

His manner now was back to that of a man of genuine reason, the Hanratty that started the day—dignified, controlled.

"Let's examine briefly the evidence presented by the prosecution," he said when he resumed, "the circumstantial evidence. Remember, they've offered no proof. No proof at all."

He pointed to the Evidence table. "Much has been made of Emma Kane's fingerprints being found on the flatiron that the prosecution says is the murder weapon. Of course her fingerprints are on the flatiron. She was in that kitchen almost every day. She must have lifted that iron or moved it a dozen times. Of course her fingerprints are there. So are the cook's and the housekeeper's. So are Judge Hockensmith's, Mrs. Purcell's brother. He was in that kitchen often. And so are Mrs. Purcell's herself.

"Were Emma Kane's fingerprints put on that flatiron the day of the murder? The prosecution doesn't contend that. They only say that her fingerprints are there. Those fingerprints could have been put on that iron anytime during the last month.

"And the blood, the blood on her shoe? Of course there is blood. When Emma Kane saw her mother lying unconscious on the cellar floor, she rushed to her. There was blood on the floor by the body. She stepped in it. What does blood on the sole of her shoe prove? It proves only that she was there, close to the body—a natural response of a concerned daughter.

"The contention that Emma tried to hide that shoe is absurd. She had to get out of her car to open a gate on a country lane leading to the house of a friend she was on her way to visit. There had been rain. The lane was muddy and full of puddles. Her shoes were ruined. She didn't try to hide those shoes. She threw them away. Both of them. Shoes too ruined to be worn again. And if she was trying to hide them, surely she could have found a better hiding place than a trash barrel by a barn."

Hanratty turned and looked over his shoulder to Emma. She nodded in agreement.

"Now, " he said, focusing again on the jury, "the confusion about where Emma was at the time of the murder—yes, that's worrisome."

Emma sat back in her chair, folded her hands in front of her on the table, and lowered her eyes.

"It was a very bad morning for Emma Kane. Major Tanner of the State Police covered this in his testimony. Emma was upset and highly emotional that morning. The cause of her distress was a violent argument she'd had with her husband, the worst they'd ever had. He hit her. That hadn't happened before. Shocked, she ran to her car and began driving. She was so distraught, she hardly knew what she was doing. She drove aimlessly around the county that morning and into the early afternoon, trying to come to grips with her situation. When she finally calmed, she returned to her mother's house and that is when she found the body.

"Sheriff Peavler was told that Emma had been shopping in Lexington at the time of the murder. Emma didn't tell the Sheriff that. Her uncle, Judge Hockensmith, did. Later, when the misimpression could have been corrected, Emma was too embarrassed to admit that her marriage was failing. She let it stand. This was a wrong decision, but understandable for a proud girl. Emma, you should know, has started divorce proceedings against Marko Kane. Their relationship had been deteriorating for over a year. When he hit her, that decided it. She filed the formal papers just before the trial began."

A gasp of surprise ran through the packed audience; women turning to each other with raised eyebrows and whispering.

"Order," the Judge said, banging down his gavel.

Emma had already told me most of this in our secret interview at the farm— the fight with Marko, her anger and confusion, but nothing suggesting she was considering a divorce. From her tone of voice and her attitude at the time, it was clear that her relationship with Marko Kane was perilous. I had the impression she barely tolerated him. But I wondered if the decision to jettison him was hers or Hanratty's. "If it is going to happen anyway, do it now and use it to add credibility to your story." I could see Hanratty making that suggestion. A chess move.

Emma sat stiffly in her chair, her head bowed. She raised her eyes briefly to the jury, then lowered them again.

Hanratty had covered everything the prosecution had presented as evidence, everything but the ashes—the ashes Major Tanner of the State Police considered the most damning. I waited to see how he would bat this away, if he could.

"Now," he said, "we come to the matter of a trace of ash found in the cuff of the slacks Emma Kane wore the day of the murder."

He shook his head and spread his arms like a man asking for forgiveness.

"I must admit I have no explanation for that. A trace of ash in the cuff of a pant leg. What should you infer from that? And you must infer because that trace of ash isn't proof of anything other than that Emma Kane was in the vicinity of the woodstove in her mother's kitchen the day of the murder. But we already know that. We know she had coffee with her mother in that kitchen that morning. We admit Emma Kane was in that kitchen and in the vicinity of the wood stove that morning. The question is, so what? Does that trace of ash prove Emma Kane was there at the time of the murder? No! Does that trace of ash prove that Emma Kane killed her mother? Absolutely not!

"I can't explain how that small bit of ash came to be on Emma's slacks. Perhaps she brushed against the stove when she was searching for her mother. I don't know. But I know this—to infer from that insubstantial piece of evidence that Emma Kane murdered her mother is a stretch of the imagination so wild as to be grossly irresponsible."

This drew a frown from the Judge.

"I'm about finished, Your Honor," Hanratty said before the Judge could scold him.

"I ask the jury to remember that there were at least three other possible culprits at the Hockensmith farm on the morning of the murder. One was the Gypsy, Arlo Lee, who escaped from the County Jail the day this trial began. He was being held as a material witness, not as a murder suspect, but his breakout raises questions. He is now being sought by the State Police. Arlo Lee was in the kitchen that morning.

"Another who could have had the opportunity to commit the crime is a young Marine Corps veteran who had been camping on the property. He has drug and alcohol problems and is being treated at the VA Hospital in Lexington. The Marine was in Mrs. Purcell's kitchen that morning.

"The occupants of a mysterious car that was seen parked in front of Mrs. Purcell's home the morning of the murder is a third possibility. Those people haven't been identified nor has the car been found. Whether the occupants of that car entered the house isn't known.

"My point here is that you," and he looked directly at the bottling-line woman, "are being asked to convict Emma Purcell Kane of murder in the first degree based entirely on circumstantial evidence."

He let his eyes encompass the whole jury.

"There is no proof anywhere in the prosecution's case. And very tellingly, the prosecution has offered no motive—no reason why a loving daughter would savagely murder her mother. A murder without a motive? Surely not.

"Ladies and gentlemen, you must have in your minds the certainty, the absolute certainty … beyond a shadow of a doubt … that Emma Purcell Kane killed her mother. From this evidence, you cannot arrive at that conclusion!"

Hanratty stepped back from the jury box, let his gaze swing to Emma sitting alone at the defense table, then to the Judge.

"The defense rests."

The time was five-thirty-two in the afternoon. The day was Thursday, the fourth day of the trial. Tomorrow would be Friday, the thirteenth day of the month.

FORTY FOUR

There was no fog. No indistinct forms were rising from the mist and no whispers were in the air. It was as perfect a morning as could be conjured— a tender breeze and a cloudless sky.

As I understood the drill, when court reconvened at nine a.m., Hanratty would present the closing argument for the defense. Hud Exeter would do similarly for the prosecution. Then the Judge would give the jury its charge; the jurors would vacate the courtroom, file through that little door in the wall behind them and across the hall to the jury room and there decide the fate of Emma Purcell Kane.

In an hour? A day? A week? No one knew. Most certainly not them.

I finished my run and completed my get-ready-for-the-day routine. Both Dulin and Will were in the newsroom when I got there, sitting at Dulin's desk, talking over coffee. I wasn't particularly surprised to find Dulin in early, but to see Will in at that hour?

"I don't believe I'm seeing this," I said as I pushed through the door.

It turned out that Dulin had gotten up early. Will hadn't been to bed yet.

"I wanted to see you before you left for the courtroom," Dulin said.

"I just wanted to see your pretty face," Will smiled.

Dulin ignored that. "Neither of us remember a murder trial getting to a jury so fast. What's it been, four days counting the day for jury selection? I can't imagine what the jury thinks of it. They must have come in expecting a long trial. To get to the deliberation stage in just three days of testimony?"

"They have to think both sides believe it's an open and shut case," Will said.

"No other reason to race through the testimony," said Dulin.

"Make the win points, don't bore or confuse them, make the sale and get out," Will finished.

I felt like I was playing dodge-ball as they threw these ideas at me.

"So?"

"We expect a quick decision from the jury. I want to be the first in print with it," Dulin said. "I'll hold up tonight's edition until they put the jurors to bed. If they've not reached a verdict by them, I'll have a full crew in tomorrow morning standing by. As soon a verdict is reached, we'll rush out an extra. Tomorrow, the next day, whenever!"

Their excitement was catching. An Extra!

Nothing unexpected or dramatic occurred during the closing arguments by the prosecution and the defense.

Hanratty said nothing new and said it no better than he had the previous day, though that was quite good. No proof. No motive. No case.

Hud Exeter, too, had nothing new—the lie, no alibi for the time of the murder, fingerprints on the murder weapon, the blood on the shoe, the ashes on the slacks. Guilty as charged. He said it well and convincingly.

Judge Watson gave the case to the jury at a little before two p.m. and sent them off to begin their deliberations.

The place where they were to work was a large room looking out on Workhouse Alley and the Catholic school playground. The room was plain and unadorned. Twelve hard-back chairs sat along a big mahogany conference table. A couple of upholstered, casual chairs were along the walls. They'd have blank walls or each other to look at, and if the day was mild and windows were open, the sound of children playing in the school ground for background music.

As the jury filed out I tried to read which way they were leaning, but their expressions and their body language told me nothing. The almost unanimous opinion among my seasoned colleagues was that, circumstantial or not, the evidence the prosecution produced would get a conviction.

If that didn't do it, Emma herself would tip the scales, they said. She came across as too aloof and too arrogant to be likeable.

Hanratty's attempts to portray her as a sympathetic figure by the way he dressed her and the little looks of reassurance and courage he shot her during the trial didn't come off. Nor did his effort to picture her as an all-around fine young woman through the testimony of the character witnesses he put on the stand.

Emma was thought to be spoiled and quick tempered. The gossip and conversation of shop girls who waited on her in the stores and waitresses who served her in the restaurants spread that impression. Consciously or unconsciously, that would be in the jurors' minds and would have its effect, so my workmates said.

For the jurors, as it was for me, this was a new experience. None had served on a jury before. In a way, it was almost an outing. Being sequestered meant they were staying in a hotel, insulated from contact with their families and the public, and dining in the hotel's private dining room. Most of them didn't regularly stay in hotels or eat in restaurants, much less enjoy the luxury of room service. This was an event, a not unpleasant event with no real incentive to rush it to its close. Being able to have breakfast in bed wasn't something to be passed up lightly.

The last of them disappeared through the doorway; the waitress from Yancey's hurrying not to be left behind.

The courtroom emptied rapidly. In twos and threes the spectators piled out the doors and down the stairs, talking and gesturing. The wire service and broadcast reporters and the fellows covering for the afternoon papers headed to telephones to get their stories moving. Those of us who worked for morning papers took our time. We had until ten or eleven o'clock to get our stories written.

I walked the half block up the street to the corner by the post office with a batch of the reporters who were going to catch the bus back up to their newsrooms at the Capitol. We were still adrenalized from the excitement in the courtroom and caught up in predicting what would happen next.

"The jury won't come back with a verdict today. Too fast. Tomorrow? Maybe. Still awfully fast but who's going to want to spend an April Sunday sitting in a jury room arguing over Emma Purcell? They'll get it done tomorrow." That was the AP's view.

"But run it through Sunday, and you get another day of room service," cracked the *Times* guy.

"No. Monday's the day. The earliest day. Count on Monday," said the *Post*.

"What if this isn't as obvious as we think it is? What if someone gets stubborn? Could go all next week," Andy Thomas of the *Lexington Herald* offered.

"Smack that guy," someone yelled.

Still laughing and arguing, they boarded the little green bus when it came, and I turned around and started back down the street toward the *Journal*.

I had no real plan. There was no urgency to get back to the office. The afternoon was still young. I didn't have a deadline until almost midnight. The mellow sun and the mild breeze made me think of other bright afternoons,

afternoons before my little war. Allie's office was close by. I slipped into the payphone in the Courthouse corridor and called her.

"How long has it been since you've had an ice-cream soda?"

"A what? Theo, have you been drinking this early in the day?" she said.

"Can you get away for a bit? Meet me at LeCompte's? It's a beautiful afternoon. It deserves an ice-cream soda. Strawberry," I tempted.

She laughed. "Grown men don't do ice-cream sodas." A pause. " Give me ten minutes."

That first spring, the spring we met, our first date was a Sunday night movie at the Capitol Theatre. Walking. I had no car then. Barely money for the movie and popcorn. And an ice-cream soda after. At LeCompte's. Just across the Old Bridge. Walking her home.

I couldn't remember when I'd had an ice-cream soda last, but for some reason that afternoon I had an insatiable thirst for one—a strawberry ice-cream soda. And for Allie.

I got there first. The place had changed some, but not too much. The soda fountain at LeCompte's was only several blocks from Frankfort High and just a short stroll across the river from Good Shepherd. It still had a marble counter top, a long mirror on the back wall flanked by stained-glass panels, and round wooden stools that let you perch up to the bar. I hoped it still had the best ice-cream sodas in the county.

Allie walked in looking just as satisfying as I thought she would. I've searched for other adjectives for her but none are as right. To satisfy is to meet the expectations, the needs, the desires of someone. She satisfied me.

I don't remember what we talked about or what we laughed about. It was an interlude outside time. I think we were the only people at the soda fountain. Others may have come in. I didn't notice.

At some point, she looked at her watch then up to me. "I have to go, hero."

We walked back together, across the bridge and into town. The river was running clear. Fluffy white clouds floated overhead. We stood for a minute on the bridge and watched them as they scooted by, forming images of creatures and castles in the sky.

"The trial is almost over," I said.

"I know."

"If I've handled it well, I'll be going to New York."

"The prize."

"I'll miss you."

"You've missed me before."

"I don't know what to do."

"About?"

"I don't know what to do about you."

We'd both been looking upriver, not looking at each other but at the bend of the river.

She turned me to her and took my face in her hands. "No, poor hero. What you don't know is what to do about you."

FORTY FIVE

Dulin took the call from the Courthouse.

I was at my desk in the newsroom. Will was at the Capitol.

"They're coming in," he yelled to me. "Get going!"

Seven-thirty. Saturday night. The sixth day of the trial. The jury had had the case not quite a day-and-a-half.

I tore out the side entrance of the *Journal*, across Workhouse Alley and up the backstairs to the second-floor Courtroom.

I was the first there. The others were scattered around town, killing time and waiting. Most were lounging in the pressroom up at the Capitol. Andy's paper, The *Lexington Herald-Lea*der had a small office in the McClure Building in the center of town that also handled circulation and advertising. Andy was right after me. The others came rushing in like a cavalry charge.

The word was also getting around town because the courtroom was filling with spectators eager to be in on the finish.

Hanratty came in, alone, as he had been throughout the trial, looking tailored and unruffled and took his place at the defense table. Exeter and his team followed. Emma was brought in last, uncuffed, walking confidently. She was dressed in black. Black blouse with long sleeves to her wrists, slim black skirt. Almost regal. What image was Hanratty trying to project now? It was all over.

The door at the side of the courtroom opened, and the jurors filed in. They looked haggard, frayed, and anxious to get it over with. I searched for the bottling-line woman. Her expression was grim. She seemed to be avoiding contact with the other jurors.

Outside the sun had just set. A balmy breeze held the valley. The sky was turning an agreeable salmon-pink. The first of the night's stars was beginning to show.

The Courtroom bailiff had opened the big windows in the far wall and turned on the ceiling fans. The muffled sounds of the evening filtering in were overwhelmed by the hum of spectators jostling for places to sit.

That all stopped when the Judge entered. Even the outside sounds seemed to cease.

All rose.

He banged his gavel.

All sat.

And the Courtroom went still.

The Judge folded his hands in front of him, looking in turn to Exeter, then Hanratty, and finally to Emma. He studied them, unfolded his hands and placed them on the arms of his chair as if to rise, but didn't. Turning to the jurors looking expectantly to him, he said in a stern voice, "Has the Jury reached a verdict."

A small man, thin, balding, rose. I recognized him as one of the state workers, but couldn't remember in what department he worked.

"Will the foreman please read the verdict," the Judge said.

Clearly nervous, the foreman said, "Your Honor, the Jury is deadlocked. We can't reach a unanimous decision."

There was a stunned silence in the Courtroom, then an eruption of disbelieving voices.

"Order," the Judge shouted, banging the gavel. "Order."

When the room settled, he turned back to the foreman, still standing and looking more nervous by the minute.

"You've exhausted the issue?"

"We've taken eight separate votes since last night, Your Honor. The vote has always been the same … eleven guilty, one not guilty."

"If I return you to the jury room and instruct you to reach a decision, can you?"

Almost wilting under the stern gaze of the judge, the foreman replied, "No, sir. The person voting not guilty swears that her vote won't change. She believes there is a reasonable doubt. She won't change her vote. All the rest of us are convinced of that."

"And none of you are inclined to join her in that belief and change your votes?"

"No, sir. Not a one of us."

Hanratty was attentive. Exeter was frowning.

The Judge shuffled a few papers in front of him, ran his hand over his forehead, stroking his brow. Gathering himself, he addressed the jury. "Then I have no alternative but to declare a mistrial. Mr. Exeter, the Commonwealth may file for a retrial anytime within the next month."

He was about to declare the trial ended and dismiss the jury when Exeter rose rapidly to his feet.

"Your Honor, The Commonwealth will not seek a retrial!"

A jolt of shock reverberated through the courtroom.

The Judge studied Exeter carefully, trying to understand the move.

Finally he said, "The Commonwealth isn't required to explain its reasons, is it Mr. Hanratty? Well, if the Commonwealth finds no cause to pursue this matter further, I declare this a mistrial and declare the case against Emma Purcell Kane dismissed."

Pandemonium broke out. People rushed to the doors, yelled and pushed, some shouting "No, no!"

Exeter quietly gathered his papers and his crew and made his way out through the Judge's chambers, unaccented by either press or spectators.

Hanratty sat for a moment at the defense table, staring straight ahead. Then he rose and with great formality shook Emma's hand, turning just in time to greet the press rushing down on him.

There was no need for an Extra. Our regular edition would be out almost as rapidly as we could print an Extra. I don't know who was more disappointed. Me or Dulin.

Not until the paper was off the press with the banner headline "Emma Set Free" did we have a chance to post-mortem the event.

Sitting around Dulin's desk in the empty newsroom, we went event by event over the whole affair, trying to decipher what had happened, trying to anticipate what would come next.

The hung jury didn't attest to Emma's innocence, only to the Commonwealth's inability to prove—beyond a reasonable doubt to a single member of the jury—her guilt. Emma was free.

The prosecution had said she wouldn't be re-tried. Why?

Arlo Lee, the Gypsy, was still at large. Would an intensified effort be made to try to find him and attempts made to build a case against him? Or against my young Marine friend?

What about the mystery car, the one the boys saw at the house the morning of the murder, the one they thought was driven by Judge Hockensmith with Emma as a passenger? What about that? The car had never been found. It's occupants never officially identified.

Were there other possible suspects that the investigations hadn't uncovered? Marko Kane, Emma's husband? How carefully had his alibi been checked?

Or would the case be allowed to simply fade away and be added to the long list of unsolved murders that littered the county's history? The Commonwealth Attorney's office had washed its hands of it. If the matter was to be pursued, the responsibility now lay back in the office of the Sheriff.

What would Emma do? The mood around town seemed to suggest that in most people's eyes she was guilty. Of murder. Of the monstrous murder of her mother. How would she handle that? Cash in her inheritance and start a new life somewhere else? Ignore people's opinion and ride it out?

We had no answers.

Outside, Sunday morning was coming on. There would be people on the streets soon.

"I'm going home," Dulin said.

I tipped back the last sip of cold coffee, tossed the paper cup in the trash basket, stretched and yawned.

Will stood up, straightened his tie, took his jacket off the back of his chair and slid into it. "Somebody's got to still be at King's. I think I'll see if I can round up a few of the faithful and find breakfast somewhere. Want to come, Theo?"

I thought about it, tempted, then decided, "Thanks, no. I'm going fishing."

They both looked at me with puzzled expressions.

"You think Arlo's hiding out on the creek. The best way to find out without attracting attention is to walk that stretch with a fly rod in my hand."

Will nodded appreciatively.

"You know how to use one?"

FORTY SIX

I'd had no sleep but I felt fine—plenty of energy and wide-awake.

The section of the Elkhorn where the Gypsy's camped was one of the prettiest stretches of water on one of the prettiest creeks in the Southeast—long stretches of quiet water flowing with enough current to keep them fresh, interspersed with fast-running riffles, and pools twisting gracefully though meadows that are among the most fertile farmland in the Bluegrass. One stretch had a high limestone cliff where hawks nested. The banks were grass or small polished pebbles shaded by oaks and sycamores.

There was no better smallmouth water in the state. If you used a fly rod, you fished it wading.

I came in from the backside. There was no way I could escape notice if I came down the lane to the Hockensmith place. I knew a track off the Georgetown Road that would dead-end in a field where I could park, climb an old barbed-wire fence, and be in sight of the creek.

I hadn't had a fly rod in my hand since I returned from Korea. My Dad taught me. I was barely big enough to swing the rod when we started. We began with bluegill in the farm ponds around the county, then as I grew and could handle the water, graduated to bass—largemouth in the river, smallmouth in Elkhorn.

We fished almost every Saturday morning he had off when I was a young boy, Dad and his cousin, who I called Uncle but wasn't, and his two sons, both older than me.

My Dad and my uncle are gone now. The boys too. One lost at the Battle of Midway in World War II. The other to cancer.

My uncle and the boys were bait fishermen. We left them sitting on the bank, nice and dry and talking. My Dad and I took off upstream, wading, casting, tempting the smallmouth to come out and take our fly.

All that had slipped out of my mind until the cold waters of Elkhorn brought it back. And I'd forgotten the pleasure that being on a stream with a fly rod in your hand and fast water against your legs can give you.

What else had I let get crowded out of my mind? Too much of some things, not enough of others. Well, I thought, unlimbering the rod and making a false cast to get my line straightened out, I won't let this slip away again.

I splashed across the creek, climbed out on the far bank and began walking, rod in hand, looking for Arlo Lee.

I found his campsite about half an hour later, tucked almost invisibly in among some bushes near the tip of a small, grassy island in the center of the creek. It was Spartan, but sufficient. A small green tent, a mummy sleeping bag, a little propane cook stove.

He was nowhere around. I didn't expect him to be. Whatever he was hanging around for, sitting huddled in a cramped campsite on the banks of Elkhorn wasn't it. I now knew he was here. I knew I could find this spot again. That was enough for the moment. The questions I had for Arlo didn't require an immediate answer.

My immediate concern was Josh Logan, the creek Marine. As fragile as I assumed Josh's emotional state to be, I was concerned that if Sheriff Peavler felt a need to find a new culprit for the Purcell murder, and he couldn't drape it around Arlo Lee's neck, Josh would be it.

Josh had been on the place the morning of the murder. He had been in the kitchen with Mrs. Purcell. There was nothing to link Josh to the murder. But with enough pressure, Woodrow Stanley Peavler might be able to push him into admitting to something he didn't do.

I'd let Josh slip out of my mind, too. I'd not kept tabs on him since our last meeting, since he helped me. Was that what I was turning into—someone who forgot people who helped him? Damn.

I needed to find Josh. Talk with him. Make sure he understood the situation and didn't do anything dumb. My best bet for finding him was Lucy Chesney, the nurse.

It was almost dark before I reached her. I had called from my apartment as soon as I got back to town. No answer. I kept calling at one-hour intervals until I finally got a voice.

"Lucy, this is Theo Clark. The friend of Josh's, the reporter, the Marine. Do you remember me? Is Josh there?

He wasn't, she told me. He was at his family's place at Jamestown near Lake Cumberland. He had been there for several weeks.

"He's okay?"

"He's doing fine. He stopped drinking. He has the drugs under control. There's still pain, but he's handling it. I think he's going to make it," she said.

"Ah, that's great news. Listen, Emma Kane's trial got settled yesterday."

"I heard."

"The Sheriff may decide to re-open the investigation. He may want to question Josh again. Tell Josh to stay where he is and to stay low. Will you get that word to him?"

She understood. "As fast as I can," Lucy said.

Emma Kane had been missing that whole day, and we didn't know anything about it.

She had been driven to her cottage down the lane from the main house immediately after her release the previous night. There had been celebratory cocktails with attorney Hanratty and Judge Hockensmith. She'd had a light dinner alone, looked in on the sleeping baby in his upstairs bedroom, turned on the television and was watching the Jackie Gleason show when the cook left.

When Emma didn't come down to breakfast at the usual time the next morning, the cook thought she must be sleeping in after the exhaustion of the trial. Mid-morning came. The live-in baby-sitter that had been on hand since Emma was first charged had the baby up and fed and was playing with him in the den. Emma still hadn't appeared. The cook tapped on her bedroom door, then entered. The room was empty. The bed hadn't been slept in. The Judge was called. By nightfall, there was still no sign of Emma or word from her.

We didn't learn of it until the following day, Monday, when a contact of Dulin's called from the Courthouse to say that Sheriff Peavler was on his way to the Hockensmith place. Emma Kane was missing.

I got there almost as fast as the Sheriff. Judge Hockensmith's car was parked in front of the house, the Sheriff's just behind it.

The housekeeper opened the door at my knock. My favorite Sheriff, standing in the hallway talking to the Judge, turned to see what was happening.

"Theo Clark! Damn! What are you doing here?"

"We got a report that Mrs. Kane is missing."

"Oh, hell! That's all I need." He spun around angrily. "Close the door and come on in here."

"Good morning, Judge," I said pleasantly as I eased my way past him.

The Sheriff kept me standing in the hallway just inside the door. "Where Mrs. Kane might or might not be is her business," he said.

"Is she missing?"

The Sheriff gave a side glance to the Judge. "She's not here at the moment."

"There was a lot of anger after the trial Saturday. Do you think something might have happened to her?"

"We don't have a missing person report and Mrs. Kane's whereabouts is her business. Period. Now get out of here."

"So this is just a social visit?"

"I said get out!"

I made it a point to check on Arlo's hidden camp on my way back to town. It was gone.

Emma Kane reappeared two days later. Just after daybreak. Walking barefoot. Along the side of a gravel road near an abandoned distillery in a remote part of Fayette County.

A fork-lift operator on his way to work in Lexington saw her and stopped. She seemed dazed but physically okay. We found this out because the driver reported his find to the Fayette County Sheriff who made an entry in the Missing Persons log which is routinely checked by reporters for the *Lexington Herald-Leader*, who immediately ran out a short piece on the Associated Press state wire.

An unidentified and disoriented young woman wandering barefoot at dawn down a lonely country road was worth a paragraph.

When it became known that the unidentified young woman was Emma Purcell Kane, recently freed in the Ashes Murder case, the paragraph blossomed into a Page One story.

Emma came out of her dazed state about an hour after she was found. She knew who she was but said she had no memory of what had occurred during the days she was missing.

There was much speculation but no facts.

Sheriff Woodrow Stanley Peavler defended his stonewalling me with the excuse that the family—the family now consisting exclusively of Judge Hockensmith—had asked for the protection of privacy while the mystery of her disappearance was being unraveled. I told him we would have respected that. He said, "Ha!"

Emma was essentially unreachable. A wooden livestock gate had been hastily built across the lane to the farm. It needed paint. When I tried it, it was locked.

She wouldn't take calls from the press.

I called Hanratty to see if he could arrange an interview for me.

"No point in trying," he said. "She won't. She says she doesn't remember what happened during the time she was gone. I believe that. But there's something somewhere in her mind that's working on her."

"Remorse? Guilt?" I offered.

He snorted disgustedly. "Don't do amateur psychiatry, Theo. Emma didn't show me any signs of any of that during the trial. If she has a guilty conscience, it never showed."

He was right. I never saw any signs of it either. I thought to sign off, but then remembered. "I didn't get a chance to say it earlier, Mr. Hanratty. Congratulations. It was a real education watching you work. I learned a lot."

"Any one thing in particular?"

"Yes. One thing very much in particular. Facts never speak for themselves. They're neutral. They mean whatever a smart, articulate, credible man can convince you they mean."

That pleased him. "Drop in before you leave for New York," he said.

"No luck?" Dulin said as I hung up the phone.

"Dead end."

Dulin got up from his chair and walked slowly the length of the newsroom to the big front windows looking out on Main Street. He stood there for a moment, watching the traffic go by and the streetlights come on. Turning back to me he said, "Nice night."

Then he returned to his desk and leaned back in his chair.

"What do you suppose happened to Emma Kane those two days?"

"Damned if I can imagine," I said. "It's like she was spirited away to some deep dark, dungeon."

FORTY SEVEN

Rhae Dannan wanted to see me.

The note on my desk said so when I checked in at the newsroom Thursday morning.

If I wasn't already committed, could I please join her for dinner at the Country Club? Seven-thirty?

"Take the night off," Dulin said.

Though Rhae, as owner and publisher of the *Journal* was my boss and Dulin's boss, and everyone's boss, she was much more than that to me. I'd spent almost as much time in her house as in mine growing up. Michael and I played together almost every day, and that bond became even closer as Michael struggled to come to terms with his father's death.

We were nine when it happened. Mr. Dannan, Benjamin Dannan, was found dead on the side of a mountain road in the coal mining area of East Kentucky. He was over one hundred miles from home. There had been a big snowstorm that night. He was on foot, without a hat or coat. No one knew why he was there or how he got there. His car was never found. Benjamin Dannan was one of the most powerful and respected newspapermen in the state. He used the *Journal* as a cudgel against graft and corruption and made formidable enemies. Foul play was not ruled out. What really happened was never known. His death was, and still is, a mystery.

I helped Michael make it through all that as only a kid could, I suppose, understanding what he was feeling, pushing him, shaming him, laughing him into staying a part of what we were doing, not letting him withdraw, not letting him give in to his anger and his hurt.

Through the rest of grade school and high school, and into college, we were almost inseparable. Rhae Dannan appreciated that. She looked over both of us.

Michael hadn't done Korea. I might not have either, except that the Marine Corps Reserve unit I'd joined in Lexington my senior year in high school to earn a little extra cash for college got called up. Michael didn't need the money.

Rhae was standing near the piano in the bar area just outside the dining room when I arrived, talking with two men. She saw me and motioned me over.

"Senator Jenkins, this is Theo Clark. He's one of our star reporters," she said, taking my hand and smiling fondly. "You'll be hearing a lot from him."

The Senator, a tall, balding man who looked like he might have been an athlete once but was slowing down gracefully, extended his hand. "I've seen the byline. The Ashes Murder. I'm impressed."

Turning to the other, a man of medium height with a mischievous smile, Rhae said, "Ken Hart, Theo Clark. Ken is the manager of the local radio station, Theo."

"A pleasure to meet you, sir," I said.

"You must know our Don Wheeler. He covered the trial, too."

"I know him. He's first-rate."

"I think WLEX has its eyes on him. Are you still on the Emma Kane story?"

Rhae smiled. "If you will excuse us, gentlemen." She took my arm. "Dinner."

Our table looked out on the 18th fairway. Dusk was laying long purple shadows on the manicured grass. A few bats were darting over the green, picking night-flying insects out of the air.

Well-dressed women and successful-looking men filled the dining room. A buzz of subdued conversation and occasional laughter floated in the air. People seemed pleased with themselves and their station. Several dropped by the table to say hello to Rhae. She introduced me to each, and I was pleased at how many recognized my name from my stories in the *Journal*.

Rhae patted my hand. "Most of them have never come in contact with a reporter. They're suspicious of the breed. They think it's made up of wild-eyed liberals out to trash the things they hold dear. You don't look the part." She smiled at that and looked pleased.

When coffee came, she said, "I invited you for more than just the pleasure of your company. Two things. Michael's planning to come back for Derby weekend and wants you to join our party. Second thing," she said, reaching into her purse and pulling out an envelope, "this letter."

She didn't open it. She laid it on the table in front of me.

"I'm proud of you, Theo."

It was a plain white envelope with a red logo in the upper left hand corner that I couldn't make out.

"It's from Mike Daniels, the Executive Editor of the *Trib*. He's asking my okay to talk with you about coming to work for them."

The *Trib*? The *New York Herald-Tribune*!

Rhae smiled, "Ken Wynne, your advisor at the University—he's been sending copies of your stories and reports on how you've been handling the coverage of the Ashes case to Daniels. He and Dulin and Daniels all worked together on the old *Kentucky Post* in the Newport gambling-den days. Dulin has been sending along letters too, telling him you're the most promising young reporter he's seen. I have to admit I've written one or two myself.

All I could do was shake my head in euphoric disbelief.

"There is a gentleman's agreement, Theo. One newspaper doesn't try to lure away another newspaper's talent without asking permission first. That's why the letter came to me. The *Trib* seems to have decided you're a talent they'd like to have. What shall I tell them?"

"Rhae!" I said.

She laughed out loud," I think you'll eat up New York."

Dulin was beaming when I walked back into the newsroom.

I was beaming myself.

"The *Trib*, Dulin, the *Trib*!"

I grabbed his hand and shook it with so much enthusiasm he had to stop me. If I could have picked a New York paper, it would have been the *Trib*. It was known as a newspaperman's newspaper. They had the best writers in town and a style and flair to their coverage that nobody else came close to. It wasn't as big or as prestigious as the *New York Times*, but it was alive—it was eager and audacious and unpretentious. Oh, Lord, I was gonna love that.

"When do you graduate?

"The last Saturday in May. May 26th, I think."

"They'll probably want you as soon as you can get there."

"The next day," I said. Then again, "Damn, Dulin, thanks."

Will wasn't there. I wanted to tell him, wanted to share that feeling of pure excitement, pure delight—better than a bourbon high, better than, well, no need to overplay it, but awfully good that feeling, awfully good. I wanted Will to know that I knew I would have never made the cut without his help. But he wasn't there.

Allie. I had to tell Allie.

I looked at my watch. Almost midnight. She'd be home. But then I realized how arrogant, how self-centered it was for me to expect she'd be happy to see me in the middle of the night with news I wasn't sure she'd welcome.

So I let myself out the side door of the *Journal* onto the cobblestones of Workhouse Alley and started my long circuit home. Mist was rising from the river. The night was clear but there was no moon.

New York! Ah, the thought of it felt so good.

Sheriff Woodrow Stanley Peavler was having no luck in unraveling the mystery of Emma's disappearance. She still said she had no recollection of what had happened. He had no clues.

The hastily erected gate at the entrance to the lane leading back to the Hockensmith farm was replaced by a large steel affair that swung open from the middle with struts capped with spikes. It was kept locked. Big signs on either side warned against trespassing. Emma seemed to be pulling the farm in around her and was hunkering down.

We'd had a trial, gotten a hung jury and now the agencies of the Commonwealth responsible for finding and punishing the murderer seemed of the notion that one trial was enough.

Dulin kept pushing the Commonwealth's Attorney, insisting in editorials that a reason be given as to why no retrial was being sought. And if there was to be no retrial, what was being done to find the killer. He demanded an answer.

We got one. In writing. Not even attributed to Commonwealth's Attorney Dan Lindsey. Hud Exeter read it to the small group of us who had assembled in his office. Dan Lindsey was staying as far away from this case as he could.

The statement said "The Commonwealth has decided not to pursue the case against Emma Purcell Kane because it does not expect to be successful with a retrial. There is no new evidence. The existing evidence, while compelling, is circumstantial and apparently not convincing beyond a shadow of a doubt. Rather than waste taxpayer money and the valuable time and resources of the Court, the charge against Emma Purcell Kane is dismissed. The murder case itself remains open but not under active investigation by the Commonwealth Attorney's office."

"What does that mean?" I asked.

"It means that if someone walks in and gives himself up, we'll get a trial started. Otherwise, any further investigation is up to the office of the Sheriff of the county in which the crime occurred."

"Peavler!"

"Exactly," the redhead said.

"He knows that?" I said, trying not to grimace.

"It's his ballgame."

Dulin's reaction bordered on the apoplectic.

"Nothing's going to happen if Woodrow has the charge," he said, slamming his fist down on his desk. "You know how many of these unsolved cases we've had! It's outrageous. It's ridiculous. It's shameful!"

He jumped up and started pacing.

"The Jellison case! He had the gun in his hand! That was a hung jury, too. But no retrial. The Blasingame case. She was found frozen to death in a home freezer in her garage—a freezer that locked from the outside! They ruled it suicide. Glenn Newland, drowned in his own bathtub in less than two inches of water, fully clothed, smelling of alcohol. A big bruise on the side of his head. Nobody home but him and his wife. Her gown is drenched when the Sheriff arrives. Got it wet trying to get him out of the water, she said. The bruise? Must have got it when he fell in the tub.

"My God! Want to kill somebody, bring them here! At least no one tried to claim that Adeline Purcell's death was a suicide!"

As he cooled down, I began to understand why he had been so adamant that we keep attention focused on the Purcell murder and that the State Police stay involved.

Will came in through the back shop then, and I started to explain, but he said, "I heard. Be careful of Sheriff Woodrow Stanley Peavler going off on a 'serious' investigation. He might come up with results none of us like."

Dulin stopped his pacing and was watching Will, a questioning expression on his face.

"Major Tanner says the Commonwealth's Attorney's decision not to retry the case is the right one. He thinks the ash in the cuff is damning, but it's not enough. A motive's needed and they don't have one."

"We do," I said. "The will, the change in the will."

"That's only hearsay. The will disappeared. Arlo didn't have it and didn't know where it might be."

"Does Tanner still think Emma did it?"

"Without a doubt."

"But Tanner doesn't think the Sheriff will go down that road?"

"Not in this life."

"He thinks the Sheriff will just let it lie then?" Dulin said.

"He's not sure. Emma's mysterious disappearance is bothering the Sheriff. Woodrow can't figure what to make of it. He's worried that it might involve something that could put Emma back in the spotlight. Tanner thinks Woodrow might try to ring in another suspect—a suspect a case can be built against. The best prospect is your friend, the young Marine. He was there. He's unstable. He is, or was, on drugs and booze. He could have gone momentarily off his head and done the awful deed. Woodrow might be able to make that stick.

"What about Marko Kane, the husband?

"Possible, but not as easy a target as the Marine. Marko's alibi checked out on first inspection. Not sure how it would hold up if aggressively gone after. The guys who vouched for him could be lying—probably not."

"The occupants of the mystery car?"

"Not a chance. The strong possibility is that it was the Judge's car, just as the boys said. The Sheriff isn't going to go there, either."

"The Gypsy?"

"The Marine is easier. Drugs and booze. Out of his head. Easier."

"What are you telling me?" I said.

"If you know where that boy is, you better find him and get his story together."

It didn't matter.

When I reached Lucy Chesney to get directions to Josh down in Jamestown, she was crying.

"His sister called," she choked out. "They don't know whether it was accidental or intentional."

"Lucy, what are you talking about? What happened?"

"He overdosed. He overdosed! He was doing fine and then the pain came back worse than ever. It wore him out. It just wore him out." She began sobbing uncontrollably.

"My god, Lucy," was all I could say.

"I think it was accidental," she said. "He wouldn't do it on purpose."

The distress in her voice was painful.

Poor Josh. Did it make a difference whether he did it on purpose or not? I suppose it did—to his family, to Lucy. It would mean he hadn't give up; he hadn't quit fighting.

"No, Lucy. He wouldn't do that. He was a warrior."

"Yes," she said. "Yes, he was."

The funeral would be down there in the Cumberland foothills where he grew up. She'd let me know. Would I come?

Private Joshua Shelby Logan, USMC. Age twenty and a few months. Wounded at The Battle of the Hook, Republic of South Korea, October, 1953. Died Jamestown, Kentucky, April 1956.

Almost three years in the dying. Pain all the way.

Yes, I'd be there.

Saturday came.

The tingle of the news about the Trib was still running through me, but I was feeling the disappointment that came with the nagging certainty that the killer of Adeline Hockensmith Purcell would never be brought to justice. I began to understand the anger and frustration that Dulin felt.

Dulin looked up from the piece of copy on his desk, frowning, then to the clock on the wall.

"You're in early."

"Is it just going to go away?"

He laid his pencil down and leaned back. "You sound mad."

I slid into the chair beside his desk. "I guess I am."

"You don't like it that one person can hang a jury and let a likely killer go free?"

"What I hate is that someone's going to get away with it."

"You have any ideas on what to do about that?"

I had to admit I didn't.

Dulin nodded. He picked his pencil back up and started in on the copy again. "Well, then," he said, "get back to work."

What was there to work on? Frustrated that there seemed nothing but closed doors, angry with myself that I couldn't figure a way to get behind any of them, I let myself out of the newsroom and started up Main looking for Will. I don't know what I expected from him but damn it, he was Will Owens.

He was there at King's Bar where I thought he would be, talking with Gideon and cradling a bourbon.

"Why so glum, young master?" he said when he saw me. "You look like you don't know it's Saturday and the party's just begun."

I gave him a half-hearted grin. "I'm just coming to grips with the idea that Adeline Purcell's killer is going to get off scot-free."

"Emma?"

"Emma? Someone else? I don't know. Whoever it is is going to get away with it. That's awful."

He signaled to Gideon. "Bring this boy a drink, Gideon, please. I think he's on the verge of losing his virginity."

"Don't kid with me, Will, I'm not in the mood."

He looked at me more closely. "So I see," he said. "Let's find a table."

Gideon followed us and set my drink down in front of me. He looked to Will who signaled for another.

Will said, "You've talked with Dulin."

"I asked him if it was all over."

"What did he say?"

"He asked me if I had any ideas. I told him no. He said, 'well then, get back to work.'"

Will nodded his head, "What did you take that to mean?"

"I didn't know how to take it. That's why I'm here."

He paused and took a slow sip of his drink, watching me.

"The only thing that can get the trial re-opened is new information. Arlo Lee's escape from jail, then Emma Kane's disappearance and reappearance are connected in some way. I think you need to find our friend Arlo Lee."

Find a Gypsy in hiding? Look in the shadows. Find the secret places no one knows.

I tried.

There were no clues at Arlo's hidden campsite on the creek. The Gypsies had no friends among the Gadje in the county, so there were no leads to be uncovered there. The few who did business with them had had no contact since the previous summer and even that was of the most cursory type. One man, an Armenian scrap dealer in Lexington where messages were sometimes left and received by the traveling groups, wanted to help. He had seen my stories and believed that Arlo trusted me. But he had no information.

I even made the long run down to Golden Pond, leaving after the paper had been put to bed and making the town limits at about the same time the sun did.

I found the campsite by the little creek where I had first met Arlo, but it was just an untrammeled meadow full of wildflowers now. I checked out in the county, asked around in town. No one had seen Gypsies. Gypsies come in the fall, they all said.

Find a Gypsy who doesn't want to be found? Give him land to disappear into and night to mask his moves?

A Gypsy?

A lone Gypsy?

Might as well try to catch a phantom in the fog.

FORTY EIGHT

By the time dark came, I was convinced Arlo Lee wasn't hiding where I was looking and started the drive back home. A gibbous moon would rise later. By that time I'd be to the edge of the Bluegrass, and I'd have a long run across rolling meadows that would look like silver in the moonlight.

I decided to stop for coffee and a little nourishment at the truck stop Thomas Lee and I had stopped at on our way down that first time —in Beaver Dam— Abby's Diner.

The place was fairly empty. There were two truckers at the counter drinking coffee and eating pie and a man at a table in the corner of the room by himself. I didn't pay much attention, just stretched and started toward the counter when I realized there was something familiar about the figure at the table.

The shoulder-length black hair had been trimmed into a neat crew cut. The earring was gone. Rather than the black leather jacket and the black jeans, he had on a collarless white tee-shirt and khakis, but there was no mistaking him.

I must have stopped dead and stared. Of all the unexpected things, running up on Thomas Lee in this far corner of the Commonwealth at the end of a day of searching for Arlo was the most unexpected. It was too coincidental to be a coincidence. But how could it have been otherwise? No one knew where I was except Dulin, and even I didn't know I'd be stopping at this truck stop until an hour or so ago.

When I recovered from my shock, I nodded in recognition. He did the same.

"I've been waiting for you," he said as I sat down across from him.

"Waiting for me?"

"Arlo sent a message. We're finished with this country. The kumpania is already on the move. We won't be back."

"How did you know I'd be here?"

"Galiene knew."

"Galiene?"

"You met her at the camp outside Golden Pond."

Galiene. The lady with the magic hands. I remembered.

"Where is Arlo?" I said.

"Arlo said to tell you to stop looking for him. He has the answers you want. He will arrange to get them to you or to Mr. Will Owens."

"When? Where?"

"I wasn't told." He stood then. "Goodbye," he said. A moment later the sound of a motorcycle growled in the lot.

I didn't know where Arlo, the Gypsy, was. I had no idea what the enigmatic "Arlo has answers" meant. I knew not what to think of Galiene's ability to foresee what I was going to do before I did.

Of all this, I found that the most perplexing.

I had a long drive still ahead, down empty roads past lonely fields in shadowy moonlight. I decided not to think about that. I decided to think of New York.

Josh Logan's funeral was at the Pentecostal Church of Jesus the Redeemer on Spanner's Ridge outside of town.

The church was on the road that led down to the town boat dock. Michael and I had fished out of Jamestown, but I'd never noticed the church. Most of the time we were on the water before daylight and not off until after dark. I guess that's why I missed it.

Cars were parked along the road and on the grass. I found a spot behind a freshly washed black Ford pickup and walked back up to the church in the wake of a young couple who had a little girl in a pink dress by the hand between them.

Through the pines I could see Lake Cumberland shimmering in the afternoon sun. The Stars and Stripes flew at half-mast. Flanking it was the deep blue flag of the Commonwealth and on the other side, the scarlet and gold United States Marine Corps banner. An honor guard in dress blues stood at parade rest.

I couldn't help but think of Chad.

I tell people that I joined the Marine reserve unit to earn extra money to help pay my way through school. It wasn't only that. I could have earned more at other things. It was Chad. I joined because Chad was a Marine, and he thought there was nothing better a man could be. I felt I should try it.

You've known the kind of boy. Something so magnetic about them you are drawn into their orbit. He was several years ahead of me. I didn't know him as well as I wanted. The difference in our class years determined that. Sophomores didn't move in the same circles as seniors, but he was on the football team, as was I. We became friends.

Chad was in that first wave of Marines that were rushed to the rescue of the Korean and American troops trapped and fighting at Pusan. The war had just started. North Korean troops had overrun the peninsula and were about to push the few last defenders into the sea. The battle of Hill Chindong-Ni saved them. Chad died there.

There was no one gentler or kinder. Maybe it's the gentle ones who make the best fighters. He was a fun-loving, handsome, friendly boy who everyone liked. His loss seemed so grossly unfair.

Chad Burns. Chadwick Otis Burns.

Private First Class, Company E, 2nd Battalion, 5th Marines,

Killed in action while taking Hill Chindong-Ni, South Korea, August 8, 1950.

By enemy shrapnel.

Bled to death.

Purple Heart. Combat Action Ribbon. Korean Service Medal. United Nations Service Medal. The National Defense Medal. Korean Presidential Unit Citation. Republic of Korea War Service Medal.

Buried on a battlefield in South Korea.

Age twenty.

The first Franfort boy to die in that war.

Lord, what a waste.

And Josh.

Add Josh.

Afterwards, after taps had been played, and the Honor Guard had fired its salute and the folded flag had been placed in Josh's mother's hands, and the casket lowered into the waiting ground, Lucy Chesney came to stand beside me. People were making their way respectfully through the cemetery to their cars.

"You'll come back to the house? The family would like that."

"No, I have to get back."

"If I had been here, it wouldn't have happened," she said.

"Lucy, don't—"

"No. It wouldn't have. His mother said his pain was so bad that he took all he had. If I had been here, that wouldn't have happened."

"You weren't supposed to be here, Lucy. You couldn't be with him all the time.

"He was just trying to stop the pain, that's all, just stop the pain." She leaned against me and began to cry.

Presently one of Josh's brothers came. "Lucy, we're ready to go," he said, taking her arm gently.

I watched them walk to his waiting car, picking their way carefully past the gravestones.

I looked at my watch. Five-fifteen on an April afternoon, full of sun and tranquility.

We lost over one hundred-twenty thousand men and boys in Chad and Josh's war. Three years of it.

Hardly anyone takes notice now.

Semper Fi.

FORTY NINE

I felt like I was treading water, waiting for help to arrive.

As far as everyone but me and Dulin were concerned, and Will to a lesser degree, the Ashes Murder case was over.

It had been the focus of my attention and efforts for almost half the year. It had been a very good half year for me. I'd won my way to New York. I was on my way. And I'd had the time with Allie.

Yet the frustration of knowing that Adeline Hockensmith Purcell's killer was free, that efforts hadn't resulted in bringing the guilty person to justice—that rankled. That was a frustration that no distraction could mask.

I didn't know whether Emma had done it or not. Most of the town seemed to think she had. The jury judged her neither guilty nor innocent. The motions had been gone through and the protocols respected. If no killer was brought to the bar, so be it. There was no outcry for justice. The attitude was "We know who did it. Move on."

It rankled.

I actually cared. I hadn't particularly when the whole thing started. It was a great game for me. Exciting. Ego building. It was fun to play.

Now, though, now that we were finished, having won the prize I wanted was not enough for me. Dulin was pleased at that. He thought it said something about my character. Will was as well.

But I felt I was in a morass. Only the Gypsy's promise, delivered to me by Thomas Lee at the diner in Beaver Creek that strange night; only that promise held any hope of a satisfactory closure.

And when that promise might be fulfilled and what answers it might offer were as much a mystery as the ashes in Adeline Purcell's throat.

The carillon was playing as I walked across the campus to Professor Wynne's office. Classes were over and students were hurrying along to the dorms or the frat houses or to the cold beers waiting in the bars down Limestone. I hadn't been on campus since January. This was to be my last session with the Professor.

He had the windows in his office wide open, taking in the mild afternoon breeze and the mellow sound of ringing bells.

Before he could speak I said, 'I want to thank you again, Professor Wynne. It's like winning the Derby."

"The *Trib*?" He smiled. "Don't screw it up."

We talked about the last batch of my stories. I heard his critique of both my writing and my reportage. He was pleased with both. "The editors at the *Trib* are too. That's why they want you."

He told me I could spend the rest of the semester wrapping up at the *Journal* and getting ready to move. No need to take the final, but he'd expect me to be at graduation, properly gowned and crowned. Otherwise, he'd be looking to see my byline soon on Page One of the *Herald-Tribune*.

"A caution, Theo. New York can eat you up and spit you out before you know it. You're a country boy. There's nothing wrong with that. Country boys run the world. But to play the game you're fixing to enter, you've got to be smarter and tougher than you've ever been. Pay attention. Be respectful. But don't ever be deferential, no matter how rich or powerful or famous the person you're dealing with. They'll take it as a sign of weakness, and the weak don't count in the games they play."

He fixed me with a hard glare. "You got that?" Then he grinned, "and stay with bourbon. That other stuff will kill you."

I took the long way back, driving down Limestone to town then turning onto the Old Frankfort Pike to make the run west to the Capital City.

The road traversed some of the most graceful land in the Bluegrass, past rich horse farms with their barns as grand as castles and down an old two-lane road not much wider than a wagon track that was over-arched by ancient oaks. Fences of fieldstone hand-laid by craftsmen long dead lined the pastures.

The stones were selected and chipped to conform. They were laid dry without mortar. Many think these stone fences were built by slaves. They weren't. They were laid by Irish and Welsh craftsmen imported by the landed aristocracy for that purpose and for the mansions they wished to erect.

It was that soft time of evening when long shadows stretch across the fields and the lowering sun puts little flecks of silver on the edges of the leaves.

I pulled over beneath a great oak to admire it all for a while.

Derby weekend is like Maris Gras—a round of partying and feasting that begins with the Oaks on the Friday before the first Saturday in May, the traditional day for the Derby, and ends with Sunday morning brunches at homes and farms scattered throughout the Bluegrass.

Invitations to Rhae Dannan's Derby weekend parties were coveted. The partying began with dinner following the running of the Kentucky Oaks, the nation's premiere race for fillies on the Friday before the Derby, then moved on to breakfast at the farm on Derby Day morning and the first of the day's mint juleps, then the Derby itself, followed by dinner on the veranda of the Boone Club overlooking the Ohio River on the outskirts of Louisville, and finished off with gin fizzes Sunday morning at the farm. Whatever you fancied to drink was on hand and almost anything you cared to eat, with burgoo and country ham and beaten biscuits the highlight of the feast.

These frolics had built over the years. They were begun by Benjamin Dannan when he was publisher of the *Journal*, continued by Rhae after his mysterious death and then later expanded when she became president of Elkhorn Farms after her father, the late U.S. Senator Thomas Hopkins, passed.

She had just one box at Churchill Downs, so her immediate entourage for the Derby was small. Most of her guests, though, had boxes as well, and the atmosphere under the Twin Spires was like a giant fraternity party with gorgeous women in outrageous hats squired by successful-looking men sipping juleps and rooting their horses home.

We were twelve at the country club that night after the Oaks. Michael knew them all. I knew none of them, but Rhae was careful to introduce me and to point out, with a note of pride in her voice, that I would soon be leaving for New York to take a position with the *Herald Tribune*.

I was invited to join the group for the Derby, but it being Saturday, I had to work. Dulin would have given me the day off. It would probably be the last Derby I'd have a chance to make for a while, but I didn't want to ask.

Michael got a bet down for me. Eddie Arcaro was riding Head Man. He ran eighth. Michael didn't have the winner either. He had Terrang with Willie Shoemaker up. We'd bet the jockeys rather than on the horses. Needles won going away, coming from twenty-four lengths behind. Dulin played the story on Page One rather than on the Sports Page; it was that slow a news night. The biggest local story was a by-liner by one of our correspondents on plans of the state Fish and Wildlife Department to close the fish hatchery at Forks of Elkhorn.

I had no incentive to linger after the paper went to press. I took my regular stroll through town and was in bed at a reasonable enough hour to have no problem getting up and out to the farm for the Sunday morning Derby brunch.

A number of cars were already parked in the meadow beside the house when I got there and more were arriving. Long wooden picnic tables covered in white tablecloths were arranged beneath the trees along the fence line bordering the creek. There were two bars set up with white-jacketed bartenders mixing julips and making fizzes. Cooks were tending to three big black iron barbecues back up the lawn.

I guess the crowd was twenty or so when I got there. It would probably grow to seventy or eighty. The Sunday morning fete was a big social event, looked forward to by the regulars and those who hoped to make it onto the invitation list.

Dulin and his wife would be there. Will wasn't invited. He had never been, as I understood it. It wasn't that his coverage had embarrassed some of the guests or that his presence might make others uneasy. Rhae Dannon didn't care about that. In fact she enjoyed it. The reason was a sort of class distinction I would never have expected in Rhae and which I can't explain.

Dulin, as managing editor, was, well, I'm not sure exactly how to categorize the class he fit in for her: executive, patrician, peer? He was the only one of the *Journal's* staff ever invited, I was told.

I finally concluded, after wrestling with it, that Rhae was an elitist. She treated every one fairly and with respect, was generous, never discriminated, but she had certain standards which only a select few met. Those who did were her class.

I didn't flatter myself by thinking I fit that mold. I was Michael's friend. That was my pass.

As I looked around at this group, I could find nothing they seemed on the surface to hold in common. All were well dressed, some less formally than others but none sloppy or unkempt. The women ranged from the strikingly beautiful to the surprisingly plain, the men from fit to fat, some with the natural carriage of command, some so unprepossessing they faded into the background. None so young as Michael and me, none so old as to seem ancient. All were friends of Rhae Dannan. If these were the elite, it was comfortable to be among them.

I stayed in Michael's wake as we circulated. I'm not good at small talk. Michael is a master. I laughed when it seemed appropriate and otherwise kept my mouth shut and listened. I am a very good listener. Will tells me this is a talent.

After a while Michael and I drifted away and made our way down to the creek. We found a fallen tree that made a perfect bench. It looked out over a riffle that fed into a stretch of water bordered by swaying weeds on the far bank.

"So you're really going to the Big Apple?" Michael said.

"The day after graduation."

"I have a bid from a conglomerate" Michael said, "based in California. Marketing. They're all over the world. The job will probably be down south, L.A., to start. After that, anywhere. I think I'll take it."

"Rhae's okay with that?"

Michael shrugged a smile. "She'd prefer I come home and join the company, but yes, she's alright with it." He stood up and found a pebble and skipped it across the pool.

"Think you can beat that?"

"Left handed," I said and started to stand.

"Have you really thought through this New York thing?" he said.

I looked up at him in surprise.

"What do you mean?"

"Oh, I'm not talking about the job. You'll ace that. I'm talking about you leaving here. You don't realize how tied you are to this place. It's a part of you. You pull it around you and nestle down in it like it's a comforter. Have you thought how hard it will be to leave it?"

Yes, I thought about it. Sort of. Unintentionally. Every time I leaned on the railing at the bridge and saw the Arsenal spotlighted on East Main Hill; every time I walked down Wapping Street in the fog and thought I heard courtly music coming from Liberty Hall; every time I sat on the overlook above town in the moonlight and heard the Courthouse clock chime the morning hours.

I'd left before. Not voluntarily. The Marine Corps had taken care of that. But that time I expected to come back. This time I didn't. Coming back would mean I'd failed.

"You?" I said. "Will it be hard for you?"

"Not like for you, Theo. You're bound to this place."

FIFTY

I put Michael back on his flight to San Francisco the next morning. We'd had an early breakfast at the farm; he'd kissed Rhae good-by, and we made Bluegrass Field a good hour before his flight time. Michael wasn't one of the run-for-the-gate-get-me-on-just-before-the-doors-close types. He planned for the unplanned-for. Heavy traffic, blown tires, accidents, and wrong turns, he allowed the possibilities and left himself enough time to get to his seat on time. Missing flights was not in his playbook.

We talked of little things. He didn't mention or ask about Allie, and I didn't bring her up.

I walked with him to the gate. The next time we saw each other we'd be somewhere down the road to where our careers were taking us. It wouldn't be the same road. That was a strange feeling. Though school and war had taken us on different paths, we always assumed the road would eventually bring us back here—to little-Frankfort-nestled-among-the-hills.

Not anymore.

"Keep the faith," he said, smiling as we shook hands.

"Write if you get work," I replied.

We both laughed at the good-bye ritual we'd used since high school. He turned and headed through the gate for the flight back to The City By The Bay. I turned and headed for the parking lot and the road to Garden Spot of the World.

That evening, sitting at my typewriter trying to pick something interesting to write about from the School Board meeting a few hours ago, Dulin's phone rang, and I watched idly as he put it to his ear and listened. He looked at me, frowned, listened some more, said "okay" and hung up.

"Will's at his place," he said. "He wants us to come there."

Will at home at seven-thirty on a Monday evening?

"I know," Dulin said. "Don't ask questions I don't know the answer to. Just get your coat and let's go."

Will was standing on the little landing at the top of the outside staircase leading to his apartment, arms folded, watching in the dark as we walked up. The air was still warm. The sound of talking as the door opened and closed at the Presbyterian Church down the block floated toward us.

Will led us in and motioned to chairs.

"Drink?"

We both declined. He went to the little bar on the sideboard where the crystal decanter sat. Two ice cubes in a silver cup. Ancient Age to cover.

He poured and walked back and took a seat at his desk. There were papers scattered across his desk, a large book open on the shelf behind him.

He raised his cup. "To all the things we don't believe in."

He tipped the cup back, drank it all down, then leaned toward us and said, "I know why Emma Kane disappeared … and about the ashes."

The story Will unfolded for us is as strange as any I'd ever heard. I lay it out here in the way he told it, admitting that I may have missed a fact or two but guaranteeing that the gist is accurate. Even after having heard it spoken and after having reviewed and written it for this purpose, there are parts of it I find difficult to accept.

Will had been at the Capitol that afternoon. He'd stopped by to change into a fresh shirt before joining us at the *Journal*. When he let himself into his apartment, it was masked in that shadowy light that shows the shape of things but not the particulars. He shut the door and started through when a man's voice said, "Mr. Owens."

He turned in the direction of the sound. Standing at the side of his desk was an indistinct form. Another form, seated, materialized in the chair by the window.

"Don't be concerned," the voice said.

Will started to turn on a light.

"No. Leave it dark, please," a woman's voice said.

There was a long silence. The voice was familiar, but Will couldn't place it.

"Did you know that Miss Adeline was my sister? Did you know we were blood kin?"

Then Will recognized the voice. "Arlo? Arlo Lee?"

"I didn't know. I wasn't told until after I'd rejoined the kumpania at Golden Pond and was explaining to Galiene about the will and the land to be given us."

"Galiene?"

"My grandfather's sister."

"That's Galiene there in the shadows?"

"Yes, she's here. We have something to tell to you, then we're leaving. I've moved the kumpania. We won't travel this way again. Miss Adeline's death, though, you deserve to know about that before we go—and about what has been done."

Galiene's voice rose quietly in the darkness, taking over the story.

"We are a very old culture, Mr. Owens, older than you can imagine. To survive over all these centuries, we have developed laws to insure that we live and work together as a family—laws that all the Rom obey at penalty of banishment. At the core of these laws is the rule that no Rom may harm another—may not lie to another, or steal, or cheat, or commit adultery or rape.

"We also have laws that govern our relationships with the Gadje. One is the Law of Consort. We do not want to be part of the Gadje society. We believe the Gadje culture to be inferior to the Rom. Only in the rarest of cases is an intermingling permitted. Arlo is the product of such an intermingling. That fact has been kept secret from him until now and made known to him now only because of a responsibility that fell to him because of another law—the Law of Retribution. It is intended to help hold the Gadje at bay.

"Our people may be misused and mistreated by the Gadje, but the Gadje are fearful of doing us deadly harm. They know that if blood harm is done to one of ours, they will pay in ways unimaginable. This law is always honored. It may take years for the harm to be avenged, but it is always avenged. Adeline Hockensmith was one of ours. Blood harm was done her."

Galiene stopped here, and Arlo's voice slid back into the story. "Her death could not go unpunished. You understand? We waited to see what your Gadje system would do. When it did nothing, the duty became ours."

Arlo Lee had walked out of jail about as easily as I had imagined. He'd slipped past the drugged guard and out the door to no notice. Thomas Lee was waiting with a car at the far end of the alley. They drove to the creek on about the same route I'd followed, then down the gravel road with the car lights off. Arlo left Thomas Lee there, climbed the fence, waited for his eyes to adjust to the dark, then hiked across the field to the creek and waded to the campsite Thomas Lee had already prepared.

Then he waited.

The night the jury returned its verdict and Emma went free, Arlo slipped into her cottage, slid a handkerchief doused in a potion they make over her face, put her unconscious body over his shoulder and walked out—unseen and unheard.

There is an abandoned stone carriage house in a grove of English elms off a narrow dirt lane that cuts through the pastures along McConnell Run north of Switzer. Nothing is nearby, only cornfields. The house itself is barely visible from the lane, which itself can't be seen from the county blacktop because of the rise and fall of the land.

They took Emma there.

The carriage house was a harbor Galiene sometimes used for purposes that were hers. These purposes were not shared with Arlo or with any of the male members of the kumpania. Arlo had never been in it.

They were five: Galiene, Arlo, Thomas Lee, and two women of Galiene's order but not of her powers.

The word the Romani use for women of Galiene's gifts is Rhiannon. The Romani believe these women can tell the future, that they have the power to cast spells and lay curses that only their touch can heal. Rhiannon occur in every kumpania, but not in every generation. They are honored and feared.

Emma was still unconscious when they brought her to the carriage house. Galiene and the other women were waiting in a large dark room lighted only by candles. In the center was a chair and beside it a single candle on a tall black stand. The women were dressed in white robes with hoods that hid all but their eyes. In the shadows they seemed like wraiths.

Arlo and Thomas Lee were told to place Emma in the chair. Then the women put her in a black robe much like the robes they wore.

Their first act was to bring Emma back to consciousness so that she could take in her surroundings and be frightened. Then they gave her a potion much like the truth serum law enforcement agencies sometimes use. The potion put her in a trance-like state and while in it, Emma was made to live again the day of the killing.

She began with her awakening that day and ended with the sedating shot given her by the nurse, eyes staring into nothingness, arms stiffly at her sides, voice a low monotone.

The surprise in her story was that Adeline's decision to change her will is what triggered all that followed. Had Adeline not told Emma of her plan when she brought the baby that morning, that day would have unfolded just as any other day.

But Adeline did.

She told Emma that she was changing her will to include Arlo Lee, the Gypsy, who camped by the creek each summer. He was to inherit a large part of the farm. She showed Emma the handwritten copy she intended to give to her attorney that afternoon so that the new will could be formalized and signed. Emma was shocked at first, then hurt, then enraged.

They argued furiously but fruitlessly for Emma.

Emma left in a state of anger so intense her hands were shaking. When she calmed, she turned to the only ally she knew—her uncle, Judge Ira Hockensmith, whose future fortune would also be affected by Adeline's plan. Together, they drove back to the farm and confronted Adeline.

They cajoled, they reasoned, they shouted. Adeline would give no reason for her decision to enrich the Gypsy and ignored their appeals that she come to her senses.

Just the idea of including a Gypsy in the family treasures enraged the Judge. Finally, at the height of a shouting match between the Judge and Adeline, Emma snapped. Grabbing an old flatiron that sat nearby and running at Adeline yelling "shut up, shut up," she smashed it into the side of Adeline's head. The blow knocked Adeline to the floor. Without thinking, the infuriated Emma sprang over the prostrate body, pushed open the cellar door, grabbed Adeline by the neck of her sweater and dragged her down.

The Judge stood at the top of the stairs, frozen in shock, blood splatters on his shirt.

Emma gathered herself, rushed up past him, grabbed the handwritten will Adeline had left there, thrust it into the wood stove and yelled to the Judge to burn it.

The flatiron lay on the kitchen floor where she'd dropped it. Emma picked it up, ran down the cellar stairs again and, kneeling by her mother's body, she hit her three more times.

She was sobbing then, near hysteria, but she caught herself. After a moment she stood, brushed the knees of her slacks where she had been kneeling on the cellar floor and slowly climbed the stairs back to the kitchen. There she opened a cabinet drawer and found a large serving spoon. Then she swung open a cabinet door, took out a metal dishpan and crossed to the stove where she scooped the still warm ash into it. "Clean up this mess," she told the Judge as she passed him.

In the cellar, Emma knelt and quite deliberately began spooning the ashes down her mother's throat. "You liked this piece of paper so much you can damn well eat it!" she said as she crammed the ashes in.

At the top of the stairs the Judge stood horrified. "Stop it," he cried, "that's crazy."

Emma stopped and looked up at him. "It is isn't it," she called back. "Crazy! That's what the police will think when they find her. They'll think that some crazy person did this. Poor Mrs. Purcell was in her kitchen and some evil person slipped in and did this awful thing. Poor Mrs. Purcell."

Emma slid one last spoonful of ash into her mother's mouth, stopped to inspect her handiwork, then stood and started up the stairs. She left the iron sitting beside the body.

They cleaned the stairs and the kitchen and through the front room. Emma inspected the floors, the rugs, the furniture and utensils they might have touched. She left the loafer that had fallen from Adeline's foot in the kitchen where it lay.

Then they, she and her uncle, her murdered mother's brother, left together— Emma on her fake shopping trip around the county, the Judge to his home to change out of his blood splattered shirt, then on to the lunch he would be late for.

"And that," Will had said, "is why the ashes. They were the handwritten draft of the will."

Galiene and her coven had what they wanted—Emma's confession given unforced in her own way in her own words.

They put her back into an unconscious trance and let twelve hours pass. When they revived her, deep shadows clung to the corners of the room, but the center where Emma sat was bright with candlelight. A crystal chandelier sparkled from above and six large candles on tall black stands ringed about her.

Emma was no longer robed. She was dressed as she had been dressed when she was abducted. She was fully conscious, but unable to move—the effect of the potion that brought her back to awareness. She could see. She could hear. But her hands wouldn't clasp, and her limbs wouldn't move. Her feet were cold. She looked down and saw that they were encased in what appeared to be dirt— were sunk in rich black dirt in a small wooden barrel.

At this point Will stopped his narrative and looked pointedly at us.

"A curse was being conjured and placed on Emma," he said.

"Galiene would not describe how it was done. Only that it was done. And that Emma was conscious through it all. That was key. Emma had to know what was happening to her; she had to have the ritual sunk deep into her mind, had to know its finality and its terror, had to know she was cursed and could not escape.

"Isn't this great," he said, rubbing his hands together and smiling broadly. "It's like a scene from an old horror movie."

"Will! Please!" Dulin cut in. "A curse! Retribution! Magic potions and Gypsy spells! Please!"

"Wait," Will said. "You need to hear the curse.

"Emma is chained to the land. She will never be able to leave the farm. She had wanted it bad enough to kill for it. She would have it, then, and it would have her. If she ventures beyond its boundaries, she will die. She will feel as if her throat is full of ashes. She won't be able to breathe. She will die. If she crosses the boundaries of the farm, she will die.

"That's the curse. It will last until she falls to natural causes, kills herself, or goes mad.

"For good measure," Will said, "Galiene threw in nightmares—terrors that will come in the night and make Emma dread the dark."

He seemed delighted.

"Remarkable story, isn't it? I can almost get carried away by it."

"You want us to take this seriously?" Dulin said.

"Do we have anything better?" Will said.

"Let me be sure I have this straight," I said. "We're to know that Emma Kane killed Adeline Purcell because she confessed to a coven of Gypsy witches while she was drugged? The only piece of evidence that might have convicted her was stuffed down her mother's throat in the form of ashes? She was set free by a jury of her peers, but found guilty by the same Gypsies who put a curse on her and who demand retribution under a centuries-old law?"

"That's it," Will said.

"Justice is going to be achieved through a curse? Will, you can't believe that."

"It doesn't matter what I or you or Dulin believe. All that matters is what Emma believes."

"You mean if Emma believes she's cursed, she is? But if she thinks it's only nonsense and defies it, she might go happily on her way?'

Will nodded, still smiling. "I'm not sure I'd flout a Gypsy curse. But maybe."

There was nothing we could do with Arlo Lee's information. It was a fantasy without facts to support it. Take it to the Prosecuting Attorney as the basis for a new trial? He'd laugh us out of his office. Confront Emma and hope she'd confess? Ridiculous.

I couldn't let it go entirely, though. I had to make two last tries.

Emma's attorney, Jim Hanratty, was happy to make time for me. He'd heard about my good luck with the *Trib* and seemed to have a real interest in my doing well in New York. We sat in his office and talked about that. New York was his favorite city. There were a few haunts he wanted me to check out and a small but very special military museum in Brooklyn I mustn't miss. When I brought the conversation around to Emma and my frustration at the ambiguous resolution to Adeline Purcell's murder, I told him the Gypsy's story. He listened thoughtfully and without comment.

"Let go of it," he said after I'd finished. "There are going to be incidents in your career in which you want so badly to know the truth that you can taste it; incidents that demand justice so strongly you feel it in your blood—but you're going to get neither. You won't get the undeniable truth you want or see the justice done that the act cries out for. When that happens close the door. Close the door and leave it."

Then there was Allie.

I told her, too.

She looked away from me for a long while. We were sitting on the grass in the yard behind her house after dinner while night was rising. She'd just put the baby to bed. I'd poured the cold chardonnay.

"Do you want to believe it?" she said.

"I want to know the truth."

"You always do."

"Have you talked with Emma since the trial?"

"I called her once. To see if she wanted someone to talk to. She didn't answer."

"What am I missing, Allie?'

"Are you trying to find something that will let you believe Emma is innocent?"

"Why would I do that?"

"Guilty then?

"Just the truth."

"Most of the town thinks she's guilty. Most of the people on the jury thought she was guilty. The Gypsies say she confessed to them. The town, the jury, the Gypsies, how many more opinions do you need?"

"Just yours."

She looked at me searchingly, then reached out and stroked my cheek. "Ah, hero, you'll have to decide what you believe all by yourself."

FIFTY ONE

Will died that night.

In his usual spot.

Gideon was cleaning up the far end of the bar. The jukebox was playing softly, and the room was filled with music; just the two of them there at King's, moving into that time of the morning Will's Celtic forbearers called the time between times—night not quite over, daylight not yet come—when all rules are suspended, and the gateway opens to other worlds.

Will seemed far away. He was sitting quietly, slowly sipping his bourbon and looking into the mirror behind the bar in the way he had of disappearing into whatever he was seeing. Gideon heard a glass fall. Out of the corner of his eye, he saw Will slump forward. In the time it took to make the few steps to reach him, Will was dead.

A massive heart attack.

No one expected it.

We knew he would die soon. Doc Rail had said so. Will's drinking would kill him. His kidneys would fail. His system would shut down. It would be slow and painful.

But his heart went first. Fast and with finality.

Score one for Will.

Not that it didn't give those who admired him pain, but that the gods let him make his escape fast and clean—we felt good about that.

His younger sister, his only living family, wanted him brought home to Virginia.

Dulin took him, riding with the coffin east across the Alleghenies into the Shenandoah Valley. He was to be buried in the family plot in the cemetery in the churchyard in Staunton.

Those of us who worked with Will and drank with him gathered downtown to see him off on the afternoon train. An even larger group none of us knew gathered there, too. Word of mouth must have drawn them. There was no public announcement.

The mood on the platform as we waited for the train was like a good Irish wake—laughter, but with the sense of loss bittersweet in the air.

We watched while the coffin was loaded on to the train, then I walked with Dulin to his coach. We didn't say anything. What was there to say? We shook hands in a strangely formal way.

Will Owens, Bane of the Bad Guys, Champion of the Little Man, Poet and Scholar and Bravest of the Brave, was going home. I kept the train in sight until it disappeared through the tunnel at the end of the street.

King's would be filling. They'd be laughing and telling stories and offering toasts; they'd be remembering and embellishing and in their private way beginning the requiem for the passing of a prince of their own.

I wasn't up to that. The newsroom would be empty. I headed there. It would be a better place than any to do my mourning.

FIFTY TWO

Dulin didn't stay for the funeral. He made sure Will got safely to his family, then boarded the next train back. I was in the press room going over an early copy of the morning's paper when he came in.

"Everything okay here?" he asked, reaching out for the paper.

I had never seen him look so drained.

"You need some sleep," I said.

He set his bag down and scanned the front page.

"Slow news night?"

"Yesterday was better. How was it?"

In a tired voice and with no elaboration he told me all he thought worth telling. "He's home," he said.

Nothing else seemed necessary to say.

When I went back up front, Gideon was standing by the big window watching daylight come on Main Street.

"Gideon?" I said, surprised. "You closed the bar?"

Not in living memory had the doors to King's Bar been closed.

"For a bit. Still a little early for the early birds. You haven't been around, Theo. You okay?"

"Yeah, I'm okay."

"You missed a great party," he said. "Everybody was there. Will would have loved it."

"I'm sorry, Gideon, I just wasn't up to it."

"I know. Me neither, almost. Mr. Monroe back?"

There was no one in town closer to Will than Gideon; probably no one in town who would miss him more.

"The funeral will be day after tomorrow in the family plot in the cemetery behind the church he went to as a boy. His sister and her family will be there—and friends, some he grew up with, some from his fraternity. It won't go unnoticed. He'll be remembered."

Gideon nodded, satisfied.

"I brought you something, he said. "After that night—you remember, that night you came to the bar to talk Will into stopping his drinking?" He grinned. "He said when he was gone, I was to give you this and tell you he said pay attention."

Gideon had a book in his hand. He reached out and handed it to me. It was a copy of the *Rubaiyat*, St. Martin's Press edition. On the inside cover was the inscription "Will Owens, Pike House, Washington & Lee University. Lexington, Va. 1935. My personal copy. If found by you, read it then return to me post-haste."

I took it from him, trying to hide my reaction. After a moment I said, "Do you know this book?'

Gideon's grin widened. "You pay attention."

Not knowing for certain about Emma's guilt still hounded me.

My only possible in was through her attorney, Jim Hanratty. I called him and asked if he would see if she would talk with me. I was leaving for New York. I wouldn't be back. I wanted to do one final story on her case. Here was an opportunity for her to tell her story to the community in the way she wanted to tell it. I'd promise to write it exactly the way she told it to me, without editorial comment or gratuitous analysis. Would she see me? Would she see me before the week was out?

Hanratty was curious about my motive, but seemed satisfied that I had a terminal case of curiosity that presented no threat to Emma.

"I think she would be foolish to agree to this and will tell her so, but yes, I'll make the overture for you."

Emma's response was "Tell him to leave me alone. Tell everyone to leave me alone."

I wrote the story anyway.

A long wrap-up piece on the Ashes Murder Case for the Sunday morning paper. It was my swan song.

I told it all, or at least as much of it as I could tell. Nothing about Emma confessing to a coven of Gypsy witches, nothing about her condemnation by their curse to a life of imprisonment on the farm. I didn't write that Judge Ira

Hockensmith was with Emma when she returned to the farm and the murder occurred. The *Journal* didn't need a libel suit. I offered no explanation for the ashes.

I wrote it as catharsis.

I had to get Emma out of my mind. I suppose I should be grateful to her. If she hadn't stuffed those ashes down her dead mother's throat the case would have in no way attracted the notoriety it did. I wouldn't have had the big a story I had. And I probably wouldn't be on my way to New York.

In an almost obscene way, I owed Emma Kane. I supposed she'd always be somewhere in my memory. But there are still empty rooms in my mind where I can put her.

As I worked through all this, I came to understand that there would be many times ahead, too many important times, when my insistence on knowing a thing with certainty would be only an excuse to avoid a decision—even a form of cowardice, an unwillingness to take responsibility.

So I made the decision. Emma was guilty.

I couldn't write that of course.

What I could write, and did, was that the Ashes Murder Case had joined the long list of unsolved mysteries that weighed on the county's conscience and that its debt to Lady Justice had now grown monumental.

Dulin liked it. He ran it as the lead feature in the second section. It was my last by-line for the *Journal*.

As my time in town wound down, stories were circulating about strange happenings on the Hockensmith farm—of people seeing Emma standing for hours at the big new gate at the entrance to the farm, but not venturing out. Neighbors near enough to be in sight of her house reported the lights never being turned off at night. Sometimes she'd be seen on horseback at the edges of the property, looking tempted to jump the fence but never doing so. Her cook was heard whispering to her hairdresser about how haggard Emma looked. The baby-sitter and the housekeeper quit. They weren't gossips but they had to give some explanations to their families and their friends, which they did, and which rapidly became part of the whispers, "She washes her feet constantly. Her hair looks like snakes. She cries out at night and won't sleep in the dark." Emma still hadn't been seen in town. Emma hadn't been seen anywhere outside the farm. This curious behavior was being linked to what had happened to her during the time she'd been missing.

Listening and remembering what Will had said about the curse, I wondered if Emma was a gambler—whether she'd risk challenging the curse or wait for madness to come upon her by the creek.

Dulin staged a little going away-party for me in the newsroom the Monday before graduation—my last night on the payroll. At midnight. After the paper had been put to bed. The whole crew was there, even the society editor and the farm editor, who were never around at night. Rhea Dannan, too. Champagne in paper cups and small slices of white cake. Toasts and stories. I felt awfully good about that—and scared. They all seemed to have so much confidence in me that I couldn't tolerate the thought I might disappoint them. I knew I was getting by on luck and the coaching of men like Will and Dulin. Alone and on my own in the midst of the best in the business, I didn't know how long my masquerade could last.

Dulin walked out with me when it was over, through the back shop, past the pressroom, to the carrier's door on the alley—my usual way in and out.

There we stopped to say goodbye. The alley was dark, lighted only by the single street lamp that marked the rear entrance to the Courthouse. Dulin's face was in shadows, but I could see that he was studying me thoughtfully. There was just the slightest nod of his head.

"You can do this," he said.

I didn't need to say thank you for all he'd done for me. I didn't need to say I'll do my very best.

We shook hands and walked away.

The afternoon of graduation had been warm, but it was cool inside Memorial Coliseum where the class of 1956 marched proudly one by one to the stage and received their diplomas. And threw caps in the air and yelled hurrah when it was over. And hugged and kissed family and friends and in general filled the air with laughter and relief.

I stood aside and watched—happily. Happy to have been a part of it at last, happy to have it behind me, happy to be able to get out and get on to whatever there was out there for me.

After a while I made my way through the crowd, shaking hands with classmates, being introduced to families, finally finding my way to my car. The day was so pleasant I was in no hurry to end it, so I sauntered my way back, taking the road out of Lexington north to Georgetown, turning west there for a peaceful run along a stretch of Elkhorn framed by sycamores, past tobacco fields and rolling pastures where cattle were grazing to the Forks Of Elkhorn, then into town, down East Main Hill, past the *Journal* to my apartment.

The rest of the afternoon I spent packing. My wardrobe was simple. Along with my Royal portable and the few books I'd decided to take with me, it would fit easily in the back of my VW for the drive to New York.

For my last night in town, I'd asked Allie to dinner. I was almost as apprehensive about that as I was about my new job.

Allie had been right that afternoon on the bridge. It wasn't so much that I didn't know what to do about her. The thing I didn't know was what to do about me.

No one fit me better than Allie. I sometimes ached for her. She was always somewhere in my mind. What was I to do about that?

I'd picked a restaurant on the river that sat on a high limestone cliff. It had a flagstone patio, and we had a table where we could hear the flow of the current against the rocks and watch the play of the lights on the water. We ordered and talked of nothing that was on our minds; neither mine nor hers, I think, but found it comfortable. It was almost as if we were on a first date.

Before the waiter could come to ask about dessert, Allie said, "Let's have coffee at my place. The baby's at mother's. We'll have it to ourselves."

I paid. We left.

A full moon was inching up the tree line when we turned into her driveway.

"Pull a couple of chairs out onto the grass. We can watch the moon rise," she said.

"Allie—" I said, when she brought the coffee.

"I know," she said, sitting down beside me in the grass.

"You know what."

"I know you still don't know what to do about you."

"Allie—"

"Be quiet, hero," she said. "Watch the moon rise."

FIFTY THREE

The town lay sleeping on the valley floor, the river a ribbon of moonlight running through it. The Capitol dome and the Catholic Church spire gleamed alabaster white. Though dawn was coming, the moon was still high and would be in the sky long after daylight.

I sat on the overlook and saw it all spread out before me—felt the magic and pulled the memories around me.

Home.

I'd take it with me.

By the time daylight came I was almost to Grayson.

Will is dead.

The Ashes Murder is yesterday's story.

I'm on my way alone to the Capital of the World.

THE END

Acknowledgements

This is a work of imagination. With the exception of Don Wheeler, a long time friend who is mentioned briefly and who really is first rate, and even more briefly Ken Hart, a Kentucky broadcast executive and magazine editor for whom we both worked ages ago, and Chad Burns, the characters are fictional

Some who read this will remember Chad Burns. He was the first Frankfort boy to be lost in the Korean War. They'll take pleasure in the memory and feel the lingering sorrow of the loss.

Many of the other names in the text are names common in Franklin County. They refer to no one living or dead.

This was longer and harder in the writing than I expected it to be. Most of this is due to its nature as a prequel and the necessity to keep the story of Theo, Michael, Allie, and Rhae consistent with what will happen to them in the future when they take up their roles in the novel, Theo's Story.

My considerable thanks and appreciation goes to Rose Tomlinson for her invaluable help in making sure the grammar, punctuation, and spelling in this manuscript are correct and proper. If any errors exist, they are the result of my failure to make the corrections I was told to make.

My considerable thanks and appreciation also goes to my sister, Ann Hatterick, for her confidence in the story and my ability to tell it and for her contributions to its shaping and presentation; my brother, Don Rhody (this is beginning to read like a family project) for his early review of the manuscript and his valuable suggestions; and to Darden Chambliss, who had a big hand in Theo's Story, for his edits and always constructive critique.

Finally, as with Theo's Story, Linda Hobson's editing of the manuscript made it a much better story than it would have been without her.

To all of you, my thanks.

www.ingramcontent.com/pod-product-compliance
Lightning Source LLC
Chambersburg PA
CBHW050018180626
46810CB00002B/469